WITCHES of ASH & RUIN

WITCHES *of* ASH & RUIN

E. LATIMER

LITTLE, BROWN AND COMPANY

New York   Boston

Little, Brown and Company
Hachette Book Group
1290 Avenue of the Americas, New York, NY 10104
Visit us at LBYR.com

Originally published in hardcover and ebook by Freeform, an imprint of
Disney Book Group, in March 2020
First Trade Paperback Edition: February 2021

Little, Brown and Company is a division of Hachette Book Group, Inc.
The Little, Brown name and logo are trademarks of Hachette Book Group, Inc.

The publisher is not responsible for websites (or their content)
that are not owned by the publisher.

The Library of Congress has cataloged the hardcover edition as follows:
Names: Latimer, E. (Erin), 1987– author.
Title: Witches of ash & ruin / E Latimer.
Other titles: Witches of ash and ruin
Description: First edition. | New York : Freeform Books, 2020. | Audience: Ages 14–18. |
Audience: Grades 10–12. | Summary: Told in multiple voices, seventeen-year-olds
Dayna Walsh and Meiner King, witches from rival covens, team up in a small Irish town
to seek a serial killer with motives enmeshed in a web of magic and gods.
Identifiers: LCCN 2019049234 | ISBN 9781368052252 (hardback) |
ISBN 9781368054317 (ebook)
Subjects: CYAC: Serial murders—Fiction. | Murder—Fiction. | Witchcraft—Fiction. |
Magic—Fiction. | Bisexuality—Fiction. | Gods—Fiction. | Ireland—Fiction.
Classification: LCC PZ7.1.L3775 Wit 2020 | DDC [Fic]—dc23
LC record available at https://lccn.loc.gov/2019049234

ISBNs: 978-0-7595-5543-3 (pbk.), 978-1-368-05431-7 (ebook)

Printed in the United States of America

LSC-C

Printing 1, 2020

TO THE WITCHES: REBECCA, KAYLA, AND TIFFANY.
I LOVE YOU GUYS.

AND TO ALL THE WOMEN OUT THERE WHO HAVE A LITTLE
WITCH IN THEM. DON'T EVER FORGET YOU'RE MAGIC.

Chapter One

DUBH

The best way to hunt a witch was to look for patterns of three. Three stones set into a wild, overgrown path. Three chimneys sending twisting ribbons of smoke into a clear sky. Three gates before the inner sanctuary—each more heavily spelled than the last. Find the house of threes, and you'd find the coven.

Dubh had traveled for days. In fact, he'd almost driven past the place. His tourist map was filled with colorful pins at every stopover—*Kiss the Blarney Stone! Visit the Irish National Heritage Park!*—but this miserable little village didn't warrant a mention. He'd blown past the welcome sign without a glance, almost continuing into County Wexford. Almost. Something had pulled at his insides as he'd reached the village limits, tugging painfully at his guts. He'd turned the rental car around and followed the sensation down a rambling back road that twisted endlessly through green fields, leading him to this driveway in the woods. And there it was. A farmhouse with three crooked chimneys, windows shuttered against the dark forest.

The witch hunter watched the house. There was something unnatural about how still he was, the type of stillness reserved for death, or very deep water. He set his back to one of the oak trees lining the driveway, an ashy cigarette hanging between two fingers. The ember burned orange in the darkness, sending a thin spiral of smoke trickling up. At his feet, spent filters scattered the ground.

He knew why he'd been called. There were too many witches here for one small town. They were gathering.

In his pocket his cell phone buzzed violently, and Dubh shut his eyes. He raised the cigarette to his lips and took a drag. *In,* burning his lungs, filling his insides with fire. *Out,* tipping his head back, blowing smoke onto the breeze. He knew who was on the phone.

It rang again.

His brothers were in town. Soon they'd be reunited. After years of faded recollections and fuzzy, half-dreamed memories, he hadn't been sure they were real. And yet he did not wish to speak with them before it was time.

Eventually the phone went silent.

Dubh watched the house. Minutes passed. Flies buzzed around his head with the smoke, and his left arm ached. When he glanced down, four long scratches trailed along his forearm.

The women had all felt the same until now, a fleeting enjoyment. They'd stirred feelings in him, fire and righteousness. The way they stared at him, dark eyes, pale faces. Their hair caught in his fingers, their screams in his ears.

This morning had been enough to sate him temporarily, but he was never fully satisfied. He hadn't known what he was looking for. Hadn't remembered.

Until now.

There was a little witch in every woman, but not every woman was a witch.

This would be different. The power rolled off this house in waves. It raised the hairs on the back of his neck and sent goose bumps up both arms.

These witches would give him the first real fight in years.

He ran his tongue along the inside of his teeth, feeling the jagged edge of his right canine.

Not yet. He'd attend to the others first. His sword was ready; Witchkiller would taste blood again.

In a few weeks he'd return. Push his way through the middle gate, the one with the black iron that curved into sharp fangs at the top. Something to look forward to, to make the days go by faster.

He always saved the best for last.

Chapter Two

DAYNA

It was two o'clock in the afternoon, in the middle of a particularly monotonous lecture on particle physics, and Dayna Walsh was about to have a panic attack.

It started the same way it always did. Some small shift in the air around her. Subtle, but enough to make her breath catch. Suddenly it was all she could think about.

Her chest tightened, and Dayna curled her fingers around the edge of the desk, leaning forward, concentrating furiously on the front of the room. A muscle twitched in her jaw, and she scowled at the whiteboard. Of *course* it would happen in the middle of class.

The OCD could get especially bad at school. With nothing to draw her out of her own head, it was easy to get caught in the obsessive spiral. To zero in on her breath, how it entered and left her body.

Mr. McCabe's voice droned on, the marker squeaking across the surface of the whiteboard. Morgan Brennan's acrylic nails clicked sharply on her phone as she shot off text after text. Dayna's ex, Samuel, leaned over his desk beside her, dark hair falling over his eyes.

One breath in. Two. Three. Shit. Stop counting.

Dayna wrapped her fingers around the pendant on her necklace, letting the points of St. Brigid's cross dig into her palm. The conversation with her father this morning had kicked it off, so if she ended up having a massive **panic attack** in the middle of the classroom, she had the reverend to thank for it.

Not here. Not here. Not here.

Her mind kept swinging wildly from what he'd said earlier—*Your mother's back in town, she's finally coming home from camp*—to her breathing. If she could just fixate on something else, like the second hand inching across the white clock face, or the cringe-inducing marker shriek on the board. . . .

It was no good; her mind kept looping back.

Now she was forcing each breath, drawing it in, pushing it out. It felt unnatural. Wrong. Her chest ached, and the low buzz of panic surged, twisting her stomach.

Fiona Walsh had been at church camp for years; Dayna didn't even remember what she looked like.

Even the mere thought of Camp Blood of the Lamb made her pulse stutter, and she shifted in her chair, trying to force herself to think of something, anything else.

In front of her, Mia Blake brushed dark hair over her shoulder, and Dayna made herself focus on the way her hair fell in waves halfway down her back. Her own hair was only the tiniest bit wavy. Maybe she should curl it. . . .

God, this was stupid. And it wasn't working.

She smoothed a hand over the base of her throat, breaths coming short and fast.

There was a soft hiss from beside her, and she glanced over. Sam was leaning sideways in his desk, a scrap of paper in one hand. She could make out his blocky writing from there.

Someone forget to tell Mr. M it's the last day?

She grimaced at him, nodding. Every other teacher played games or watched movies the last day before summer, but Mr. McCabe decided on a lecture.

Sam tucked the note into his desk and glanced over at her again, brow furrowed. "You look pale," he whispered. "You all right?"

Most definitely not *all right.* "I'm fine."

The classroom dimmed suddenly, as if the sun had moved behind the clouds. But darker.

Dayna frowned, turning for the window. Beyond the green stretch of schoolyard the sky was speckled with black. It blotted out half the sun, a cloud of... what were they, bugs?

Murmurs started up around the classroom. Everyone was staring now.

"What is that?" Morgan Brennan shot out of her seat, her phone hitting the desktop with a *thud.* A second later someone cried, "Birds. They're birds!"

As if the revelation had cleared her vision, she saw them. *Flock* was the wrong word for this, there were too many. It was an approaching storm cloud, casting the school into shadow.

Nobody moved as the birds drew nearer.

She could make out more every second. A blur of coal-black feathers and wickedly sharp talons.

They were impossibly close.

The muffled screams of the birds reached through the windows the second before it happened, and someone had the sense to yell, "Get down!"

There was a rapid *thud, thud, thud* as feathery bodies hit the windows.

Shock rooted Dayna to the spot. She felt each impact through the soles of her feet.

The sound of shattering glass jerked her awake, and she dove for the desk as a blur of smoke-colored feathers hurtled toward her. She scraped the heels of her hands on the carpet, hardly registering the pain. From there she could see Morgan's legs, hear her screams. Students were falling, birds clawing their faces, wicked talons tangled in hair extensions, tearing at designer T-shirts and hoodies, bloodying faces.

Something hit her desk with a *thud,* and Dayna scrambled back. Her elbow smashed into the chair leg with a bone-jarring crack, and she gasped, blinking tears away as a bird glanced off the desktop beside her.

This was a nightmare, some bizarre dream. She'd wake up any second now.

Samuel was there suddenly, his arm warm against Dayna's skin, his back to the chaos as he tried to shield her. His eyes were wide, one hand clutched over his mouth. He gripped her arm, and she didn't pull away.

Something crashed to the floor behind Dayna, and she jerked back, nearly knocking Samuel over.

A crow lay on the carpet.

Although . . . not a crow, she realized. It was too big.

A raven.

The bird struggled, wings flapping, beak open in distress. A jagged piece of glass was embedded in its chest, glittering under the fluorescent lights. One shiny black eye blinked at Dayna. It seemed impossible the bird should focus on her, but it locked on her face and stayed there, shining with a kind of intelligence that made her stomach squirm. Its chest heaved once and then fell still.

A second later the classroom went abruptly silent. Some of the students had fled, others stayed huddled under their desks. Most of the ravens seemed to be dead or dying.

Dayna edged her way out to stare at the bird, her heart drumming hard against her rib cage.

The raven's eye had never moved from her face. Like it had been fixated on her right up until the moment of its death. Her hand shook as she let it drift toward the raven's chest, over the glass embedded there.

It looked peaceful in death, and strangely elegant. Long and sleek with coal-black feathers. The way it had looked at her . . . as if it meant to say something but hadn't had the chance.

Tears prickled the backs of her eyes. She knew Sam was watching, but she clasped her hands in the air over the bird anyway. Pulling them back, spreading them in a T-shape before her heart. The sign of the battle sword.

Ravens belonged to the Morrigan, and a witch could not allow their souls to pass this way, panicked and alone.

Dayna stayed beside the raven, curling her knees to her chest, blinking back tears. Her throat felt tight, and she wasn't sure if the tears choking her were over the shock of what had happened, or the sight of the dead bird at her feet.

At least she hadn't thought of her breathing this entire time.

She had to force down the hysterical laugh that threatened to bubble up.

The classroom was growing steadily colder now; the wind rushed in past the broken windows, and the teacher was rounding up the remaining students, ushering them out into the hall.

A thought kept coming back to her, and as strange as it was, she couldn't shake it.

What did the ravens want?

Chapter Three

DAYNA

"**S**o the sergeant is there now? Or did they send animal control?" Reagan Etomi's voice came from the passenger seat, a little fuzzy through the speakerphone, but Dayna could still hear the amusement in her best friend's voice.

"Or what passes for animal control in this town," she replied, easing up on the gas as she turned the corner.

"So . . . two guys and a butterfly net?"

Dayna snorted. "Hey, by the way, you know Morgan Brennan?"

"Like, Bible-study Morgan?" Reagan's voice was scornful. "The one who read your journal and spread your sexuality all over the school Morgan?"

"That's the one." Dayna grinned. "Is it awful to enjoy the fact that she got her face all slashed up?"

"Hell no, that's just karma. You're allowed to enjoy that."

Dayna smiled. Even though her hands were still shaking on the wheel, and she kept seeing flashes of black feathers every time she blinked, she could feel her shoulders relaxing.

"But you know what the others will say, right?" Reagan's voice grew serious. "It's definitely an omen. You're a witch. There's no way they crash into *your* classroom and it's a coincidence."

She sighed. Another uncanny habit of Reagan's: saying exactly what Dayna was thinking. "I know."

"We can do a reading. But you'll have to stop by Sage Widow; the aunties are out of tea. Bronagh says you should pick some up."

Dayna groaned. "Fine. I'll grab it on my way."

It wasn't that she minded the errand. It was that she'd have to go by the church on the way there.

The Church of the Blood of the Lamb was her father's territory, and it wasn't just because he was the reverend there, but because he seemed present in the very structure of the building. It was constructed of blocky gray stone and loomed above every building in the village. Its lines were perfectly straight, and the stained-glass windows of the tower were done in muted purples and blues.

This was a no-nonsense building. It did not tolerate revelry or foolishness.

It made her wonder what camp was like, if it had the same somber, prisonlike feeling.

The idea made her feel slightly nauseous.

There was a billboard at the bottom of the church lawn. Every week someone arranged the letters on it to spell a different message. Today it said, *Try Jesus. If you don't like him, the devil will take you back.*

It wasn't the billboard that made her nervous, though; it was the crowd gathering around it. The people at the bottom of the slope held an assortment of cardboard signs. One woman in a long flower-patterned dress held a sign that proclaimed, *Repent, Pagans!* Another wore a makeshift sandwich board with red marker across the front: *Thou Shalt Not Suffer a Witch to Live, Exodus 22:18.*

"Um, listen, I gotta go." Dayna jammed her foot down on the gas, alarm prickling through her.

There was a pause on the other end, and then Reagan said slowly, "You're sure you're fine? You're not driving like a maniac, right?"

"I'm fine. Listen, I'll see you soon, okay? Bye." She waited for Reagan's grumble of affirmation and then hung up before easing off the gas pedal. It should have been disturbing that Reagan knew her that well, but she was used to it.

Anyway, the sign was probably nothing to worry about. Even though it shook her, she knew it had nothing to do with her coven. Judging by the slogans, they were going after Metaphysical Gifts, the store on Main Street that touted itself as a "Pagan gift shop."

Over the years, her father's church had begun to stray into strange territory. Likely they no longer qualified as Catholic. As far as she could see, they did what the reverend told them to. Picketing, protesting, ruining people's lives and businesses...

They couldn't be going after Sage Widow.

The very idea made her tighten her grip on the wheel, anger sparking in her chest. They couldn't. She wouldn't let them.

Thankfully there was no one there when she pulled into the parking lot, no mad-eyed worshippers with angry cardboard signs.

Sage Widow was her second favorite place in town. It had started out as a tea shop and slowly, over the years, morphed into something more. Something exciting.

Of course, there was no *Witches Only* sign, and it was visited by a fair number of patchouli-burning hippies and vegan football moms from the next town, but this was the only place with the ingredients for most everyday potions, so Dayna knew a good number of the clientele at least had witchy tendencies. It was a small, dimly lit shop that often smelled strongly of basil, and the sign over the door hung slightly crooked, but there was a special sort of magic to it despite this. Or perhaps because of it.

The bell jangled as Dayna pushed her way into the low-light interior. Instantly she was hit by a wall of fragrance, a mixture of herbs and incense so strong it made her eyes water. Margery, the woman behind the desk, eyes fixed on the TV, gave her a cursory wave as she came in.

Dayna moved farther into the shop, past shelves of talismans and teas, wooden symbols and stacks of pewter bowls. As she made her way under the wooden sign hanging above the aisle—*Herbs & Oils to Bewitch the Senses!*—her cell phone chimed.

She grimaced down at the screen. It was Samuel.

Hey, I'm still shaken up about that weird crow thing. Are you okay? We should get a coffee. Tomorrow?

She sighed and shoved the phone back into her pocket. That was all she needed right now, on top of everything.

It had been three months since they'd broken up. Since she'd insisted she needed her space because of the rumors flying around the school. She didn't know how to talk to him now, how to deal with the shame that flared up and made her stumble over her words.

One day no one knew a thing, and the next, the entire school was whispering: *Dayna Walsh is a lesbian. Dayna Walsh is bisexual.*

No one seemed to know or care which one it was, just that she was hiding a secret that must be discussed, picked apart, delivered to anyone who didn't know.

Now every day at school was pure misery. It was walking down the hallway trying not to make eye contact or accidentally brush past someone. Every second was spent overanalyzing everything.

All of that was precisely why Sage Widow was one of her favorite places. Here, there was no way she would see anyone from school. And the church didn't seem to know about it. No one knew she was a witch, outside her coven, and she intended to keep it that way. Her father could continue believing her overnight stays with Reagan had been full of rom-coms and popcorn instead of spell books and cauldrons, that the summers had been beaches and barbecues, not nights of memorizing protection prayers and learning counterhexes. When she was very small she'd begged her father to let her be homeschooled with Reagan. She could think of nothing better than to quit private school and learn magic with her best friend. Of course, since Reagan and her mother weren't Christian—Yemi went to the mosque in Waterford once a week—the reverend had shot *that* down fast.

She moved through the aisle, looking over boxes of crystals and jars of clover and cardamom. It was tempting to buy something for her stash beneath the bed....

But she was here for Bronagh's tea.

She reached for the tea chest, directly beneath the black-and-white television on the top shelf, currently playing some kind of catchy jingle. She was mostly ignoring the commercial, but the words *Struggling to catch a breath?* jerked her upright. The woman on TV smiled wide, saying something about medication. Dayna staggered back, already fighting the first wave of panic, struggling to remember the cognitive behavior therapy she was supposed to be using.

One. The tea chest in front of her.

Two. The pink-jeweled mirror on the wall beside the shelves.

Three. Someone's hand. Slender fingers, short nails. Black polish—

Dayna's head snapped up as the owner of the hand came into view. The girl reaching past her was tall, nearly six feet. She was sharp-featured and pale, with dark brows and eyes. The black lines of a tattoo snaked up from the collar of her jacket and onto her throat. The girl's hair, wavy and just past her shoulders, was so pale blond it was nearly white, and one side was shorn just above the ear. The effect was striking, and for a moment Dayna only stared, which gave the other girl enough time to turn away, and Dayna realized she'd taken the last satchel of Ceylon black tea.

"Um," she stammered, caught between feeling foolish and indignant. "I was reaching for that."

The girl turned, and her dark eyes flicked over Dayna from her shoes to the top of her head. The light caught the ring in the center of the girl's lower lip, automatically drawing Dayna's eye. When she looked up, she felt herself blush nearly to the tips of her ears.

"Were you, now? Seems to me you were staring at the TV with your mouth hanging open." The girl's voice was low and a bit husky. She looked amused, which sent a flare of irritation through Dayna.

"I was distracted for a moment." It came out more defensively than she meant it to.

The other girl shrugged, hands tugging at the edges of her leather jacket in a way that was somehow dismissive. She turned on her heel. "You were too slow."

For half a second Dayna only stood there, stunned. *Are you kidding me?* And then as the girl began to walk away, she shook herself and followed. "Uh, no. That's my tea."

She didn't even turn around. "Doesn't look like it."

"Are you *serious*?" Dayna doubled her pace to catch up to the girl.

It wasn't like she was looking for a fight, but she wasn't going back without that tea.

She rounded the shelves, and there were suddenly three women staring at her. Dayna blinked, feeling ambushed.

"Made a friend in the tea section, have you, Meiner?" The girl on the far left crossed her arms over her chest. She was short, with straight blond hair and glasses, her skin tanning-booth bronzed. Her tone was inquisitorial, almost demanding, and the way she looked at her friend made Dayna wonder if they were an item.

"Not exactly." The other girl—Meiner—gave Dayna a wry look over her shoulder. "She's accusing me of tea theft."

"I'm sorry, but I was reaching for that." Normally she would have backed down. Been too shy to face off with a stranger as intimidating as this white-haired giant. But this was important.

Bronagh was waiting for this tea, and she'd be damned if she let some creepy frost giant–looking girl take it from her.

Okay, maybe she *was* looking for a fight. Just a little one.

The girl's other companion, an elderly white woman with steel-gray hair, seemed to be muttering to herself. "Should have known not to trust her with anything." She didn't look at Meiner or Dayna, glaring at the shelves around them. "What the hell is this place?"

As Dayna watched, the old woman fished into her pocket and pulled out a thin silver case.

Meiner looked irritated. "Gran, you can't smoke in here." She turned back to Dayna. "Listen, we should check with the store. Maybe they have more tea in the back room."

Dayna frowned, still a little indignant. "I suppose——"

"Here." Meiner started forward, suddenly so close that Dayna jumped. She was tall enough that Dayna had to tip her head back to meet her eyes. She froze as Meiner seized her wrist, pressing the tea into her hand.

"Go on, then, it's yours."

For a second, the taller girl held on, fingers loosely wrapped around Dayna's wrist, and Dayna blinked up at her, startled. Then the girl let go, stepping back with a smirk.

"Uh, thanks." Dayna held on to the tea a little tighter than necessary. She hadn't expected Meiner to give in so suddenly, and now she felt a bit silly. She'd really been ready to fight with a stranger just now. Over tea. *What the hell is wrong with me?*

Her face felt hot, and she opened her mouth—she wasn't sure what she planned to say—but Meiner was already turning away. The others followed without a backward look.

The awkwardness wasn't over, though, because she realized a moment later she couldn't just walk out. She had to pay, and she could already hear them at the counter.

Their voices drifted down the aisle, first the low, raspy tones of Meiner and then the higher, sweeter voice of Margery.

"I believe I've got overstock in the back. I'll check for you, love."

Dayna snorted. The idea of calling that girl *love* . . .

Her phone chimed, and she winced. She hadn't meant to stand in the aisle waffling, but now it was going to be obvious she hadn't moved from the spot.

She glanced down at Reagan's message, irritated.

Get your ass over here, the coven is waiting. Interesting developments.

Dayna frowned, typing back a quick *OMW* before turning for the counter and nearly running into Meiner again, who smirked and brushed white hair off her shoulder. She held up her own satchel. "Guess they had some. Day saved."

"Well, great," Dayna said automatically. Her phone pinged again.

Bronagh is freaking out. Def something she's not saying.

"Uh, see you around." Dayna left the frowning Meiner standing in her wake as she hurried to the counter.

She was so preoccupied that she bumped into a muscular blond boy on the way out. He caught her arm, steadying her, and she got a strong whiff of cigarette smoke. The scent made her inhale sharply, and she forced herself to concentrate on the moment, instead of the thought of the smoke entering her lungs.

The boy grinned, a toothpaste-commercial smile, and Dayna mumbled an apology before hurrying to her car.

Even completely preoccupied with forcing her thoughts into line, she couldn't help thinking about Meiner. She was effortlessly confident. Down to the way she held herself, like she couldn't care less if you disapproved.

It was a trait Dayna found particularly annoying.

Chapter Four

MEINER

The last thing Meiner King wanted was to return to Carman, to this goddamn backwoods village in the middle of nowhere. So, of course, that was exactly what her coven asked her to do.

They'd driven four hours to get here, and it was just beginning to get dark. They'd gone from the moss-draped forests and white-capped rivers of Limerick County to long stretches of flat countryside broken only by scrubby, uneven walls of shrubs and punctuated by cattle and clumps of dopey sheep. As they drew closer to town, houses cropped up here and there, tiny and picturesque, peak-roofed bungalows with old-fashioned stone siding.

Meiner had driven on, silently hating every one of them.

Finally they'd passed the *Welcome to Carman* sign, the streetlights illuminating a green-and-white-trimmed board surrounded by wilted geraniums. Seeing it brought back a flood of unwelcome memories.

That, together with thoughts of the girl from the store, distracted her enough for the car to drift toward the other lane. She jerked it back just as Cora said from the passenger seat, "God, Meiner. Do you mind not trying to kill us?"

This was followed by the pop and snap of gum, and Meiner tightened her grip on the wheel, her entire being pulsing with annoyance. "Shut the fuck up, Cora."

Cora snapped her gum defiantly. "Sure and I will, if you'll stop being a miserable bitch."

Meiner clamped her mouth shut, nostrils flaring. She was at the very end of her thin rope of patience. Stomping down on the gas made the car rattle beneath her, and the engine gave a satisfying roar. In the passenger seat Cora stiffened. "You're going too—"

A thunderous snore from the backseat interrupted her. Since the car was crammed with luggage, Grandma King was wedged against the door, but it didn't seem to bother the old woman. She'd fallen asleep the second they'd left the shop, face pressed against the window, gray curls falling in her eyes. Her mouth was open, quivering wider with each uproarious snore.

In waking life, Grandma King was a refined elder, one of the most powerful witches in Ireland. A woman who ruled her coven with iron-fisted dignity.

In sleep she was a sloppy mess.

Meiner snorted in disgust, refocusing on the road. Well, she had been a powerful witch. The truth was, Meiner wasn't sure *what* her grandmother was now. A doddering senior, maybe, if appearances were to be believed.

She glanced at the woman in the rearview mirror, eyes narrow. Grandma King's face was peaceful in sleep, an unusual expression for someone normally in the middle of saying something biting.

"This is a terrible idea." It had to be the tenth time Meiner said it, and it didn't get any less true. She hated this hick town, with its dirt roads and empty fields and the church that overshadowed everything. Places like this weren't just boring, they were poisonous. Dangerous to people like her, both as a witch and a queer girl. Neither part of her was welcome.

Cora leaned forward, peering at clusters of idyllic, thatched-roofed houses. The homes were surrounded by neat garden beds and carefully cultivated trees. "Maybe, but at least it's something to do. This is the town you lived in before your gran left her old coven, isn't it?"

This was delivered in the sly, underhanded way Cora had when she knew she was poking a sore spot. Meiner's temper was never far beneath the surface, and Cora seemed to pride herself on pushing her

Even knowing Cora was deliberately trying to aggravate her was enough to start her blood rushing in her ears. Meiner didn't answer, only clenched her teeth and stared at the road. She wished she were back home where she could retreat to the basement and batter herself senseless against the punching bag. Expend some of this restless, buzzing energy.

"So why'd she get kicked out?" Cora snapped her gum again, and Meiner glanced over, annoyed.

"She didn't say she got kicked out, just that she left."

Cora snorted. "Right. That's why you guys up and skipped town."

She didn't answer. Didn't want to admit she'd guessed the same thing a long time ago. Gran didn't talk about Carman or her last coven, and Meiner had never dared ask.

Cora didn't jump when Meiner slammed her fist into the steering wheel. "Gran has one vague premonition and we go running back to this place to join a bunch of strangers."

A wheezing groan from the back made Meiner stiffen, knuckles white on the wheel. She turned, dismayed to see her grandmother blinking around the inside of the car. "Where the bloody hell are we?"

Meiner hesitated, glancing out at the village, at the cabins and cottages as they drove past, the winding dirt driveways with the handcrafted mailboxes. Did Grandma King mean *Where the bloody hell are we?* as in when would they arrive at the coven house?

Probably she didn't remember insisting they stop at Sage Widow.

Maybe she didn't even remember they were in Carman.

It was hard to figure out what she was thinking these days, and asking could get you screamed at, possibly cursed if you were unlucky.

"We're in Carman, Gran," she said shortly, and was rewarded with a confused scowl. The irritation bubbled up, quickly turning to anger. Grandma King didn't remember why they'd come. "Remember your premonition?" She did her best not to sound irritated. "You said we had to go to Carman. Something's going to happen here."

"Apparently," Cora muttered, and Meiner shot her a warning look. Cora shook blond hair out of her face and rolled her eyes.

"Murder," Gran muttered from the back, and her eyes slid shut again.

There was silence in the car as Meiner breathed deeply and tried to wrestle her temper down.

Yes, murder, death, dismemberment. Lately it was one dire prediction after another with the old woman, but this was the first time she'd insisted on uprooting them all and traveling three hundred miles cross-country.

Following the GPS description, she turned onto a smaller road. It took all of ten minutes to drive across Carman, and they were approaching the other end, hedged in by tall oak trees, when the GPS went quiet and the radio kicked in.

"Construction on the North Ireland Pass has begun, as workers begin to bridge the gap between Scotland and Ireland. This move has long been supported by members of the Northern Irish Assembly, but it was not until late last year that funding was received for what some are now calling the Celtic Crossing—"

"Boring." Cora reached forward, about to change the station as a commercial for McLoughlin's Winery came on—*"Finest wines for finest occasions!"*—and then jerked in surprise when Grandma King said loudly, "Wine!"

Meiner clenched her teeth, taking a deep breath before answering.

"We haven't got any wine." She forced her voice to sound patient, though all she wanted to do was roll down the window, hang her head out and scream. "We're going to meet your old coven, remember?"

Thankfully Gran was already distracted. "What the devil is that?"

Meiner turned, irritated to see flashing blue lights just beyond the bend.

"Shit."

"Will you relax?" Cora tipped her head back, rolling her eyes. "It's Friday night. It's just a roadblock for drunks."

"There." Grandma King twitched the collar of her sweater up, pulling it over the thick, mottled scar on the left side of her neck. The habit—and the scar—had existed as far back as Meiner could remember. "That's it."

Cora smirked. "Is this about your vision?"

Her smugness grated on Meiner. Whatever wild claim Grandma King was making now, it was clear from Cora's mocking tone she didn't believe her.

"What is it, Gran?" More as a fuck-you to Cora than anything else, Meiner made sure her voice was grave.

Her feelings about her grandmother were complicated, but Cora had no right to take that tone.

Grandma King ignored Meiner, leaning forward to smack the back of Cora's headrest. "A witch died. Show some damn respect."

"It's probably just a roadblock, Gran." Meiner stepped on the brake as they approached the squad car, rubbing a hand over her mouth. She hated to see the woman who'd raised her lose herself bit by bit as much as she hated the mixed feelings that came with it, the relief she sometimes felt as Gran softened, and the resulting guilt.

And the more the woman's sense of self dwindled, the less likely she was to finish Meiner's training. All Meiner wanted to do was ascend, to become a full witch and get the hell out. Here was yet another thing the old woman was taking from her.

She slowed down as they approached the squad car angled across the road, squinting against the flashing lights. Several were parked along the side, and a cluster of uniformed officers stood in the field just beyond. There were lamps illuminating the area, set up in a circle, and a moment later she realized they were around the stone circles, which appeared to have been roped off entirely.

Cora was already hanging halfway out her window. "Is that yellow tape? Oh my god."

Meiner glanced in the rearview mirror, stomach plummeting. Grandma King was staring straight at her. She caught Meiner's gaze and arched a brow. Meiner jumped when a voice beside her said, "Excuse me, miss, you can't be here."

She turned to find a garda frowning at her through the open window. He was tall and lanky, with square, Dudley-Do-Right-ish features and very blue eyes. He looked like someone about to thoroughly disapprove of them.

"You'll have to detour."

"Is this a crime scene?" Meiner leaned over the wheel, glancing past Cora. One of the officers was circling the group now, taking pictures. It had begun to rain and Meiner wondered briefly if that would wash away evidence.

"I'm afraid we can't share details." His frown deepened. "I'm going to have to ask you to turn around."

Meiner scowled back at him, slamming the car into reverse. She was about to back up, when Gran croaked from the backseat, "What happened?"

The officer leaned forward, putting large, square-nailed hands on Meiner's window frame. "I'm sorry, but I can't give out that informat—" He cut himself off abruptly.

Meiner had been glaring down at his hands. When she looked up, she was surprised to see the officer's face had gone slack. "It's Judge O'Toole. God, she was friends with me mam. I don't know what to tell her." He paused and then plunged on, his face eerily blank. "We found her in the ditch. She's slashed up pretty bad. It's hard to know anything yet, but it looks like she was killed a few miles yonder and then dumped. I think it's the Butcher because of the marks he's left, and the fact he took her tongue, but there's this weird tree thing on her cheek and he's never done that before. I don't have a lot of faith the department will figure it out. Sergeant's about as smart as a sack o' rocks."

He'd said this all in a rush and then paused, sucking in a sharp breath, his expression caught between confusion and horror. Meiner blinked at him, stunned. She felt a little sick.

"I—uh . . . you'll have to detour, ma'am."

"Right," she said slowly, and eased her foot onto the gas, turning the car around.

They were silent as she drove down the side road, the only sound was the wet smack of droplets hitting the windshield. A moment later she realized her hands were shaking and tightened her grip on the wheel. Cora was staring in the side mirror, back at the officer, her mouth open. Meiner glanced in the rearview mirror.

Grandma King's eyes were shut. She was smiling, humming softly to herself, fingers drumming on the silver cigarette case on her lap.

Meiner shivered, forcing her gaze back to the road. She hadn't been expecting that. Hadn't seen Gran do anything like that in a very long time. She'd thought that part of her grandmother was gone.

Had hoped it was gone.

Just one more reason to ascend and get the hell out as soon as possible.

Finally Cora let out a breath. "That thing on her cheek . . . it's the tree of life. She's right."

"Aye, of course I am." Grandma King's eyes snapped open. "The woman's had her ascension."

"And then been murdered." Meiner pressed her lips together. Her throat felt tight.

The mark was something you got the day of your ceremony, the one supposed to connect you to the god of your choosing. To give you a direct line to their power and make you a full witch. The same ceremony she'd been waiting to do since she'd hit sixteen and become eligible.

She swallowed, mouth tasting bitter.

Cora was still staring in the side mirror. "Root ink only lasts a few days," she said shortly.

Meiner nodded. "Someone offed her three days ago at most."

"So she was a witch. Now what?"

They both looked back at Grandma King. The old woman was leaning against the window, her cheek mashed against the glass. She'd already begun snoring gently.

It appeared for now, she and Cora were on their own.

Chapter Five

SAMUEL

Wₕen he first heard the call it was choppy, half-lost in a burst of static.

"...code one-eight-six...circle..." The voice dissolved again, and Sam shot forward, nearly strangling himself with his headphones. The cracker box he'd been reaching for thumped to the floor, crumbs spraying across the carpet.

He twisted the knob frantically, until the channel was clear. "...on my way." The answering voice was deep and gravelly, immediately identifiable as his father's.

They'd been let out early after the bird incident, and he'd spent the rest of the day listening to chatter, hoping to hear something about it. His hand kept drifting to his face, fingers smoothing over the scratch on his cheek. He remembered feeling the carpet burn his palms, the screams and the thunder of wings, the way Dayna had curled up in the shelter of his arms. And her face...the way she'd looked at the dead bird...

He turned his attention back to the scanner on his dresser. He'd borrowed it from the back room of the station a couple of years ago. It was old and had been in need of repair, and his father had never noticed it was gone.

He glanced at the door, next to where his phone was balanced on his dresser blaring praise music. The guilt had faded over the years, because he wasn't *really* hurting anyone with his obsession. If his mother happened to think he was in here reading the Bible, he wasn't about to disabuse her of the notion.

He squinted at the radio.

One-eight-six didn't make sense. One-eight-six wasn't animal control, it was... He wracked his brain, frowning, fingers drumming on the top of the desk. Was it a B and E?

Wait, 186 was *homicide.*

That couldn't be right. He'd been listening to the channel for nearly a year now. Carman was not a murder town. It was a cat-up-a-tree town. It was illegal parking. Or, if he got really lucky, he might hear a call about the organist locking herself out of the church, or a family feud that had got out of hand. Before the last remaining pub had been shut down, sometimes he'd hear them respond to a drunk and disorderly, but even those had all but disappeared.

No, Carman did not have murderers.

Still, he shifted in his chair, glancing over at the door. Circle... that had to mean the stone circles just outside town. It was a ten-minute bike ride, tops.

The code probably meant something different. That someone had... stolen a sheep or something.

It was dark and wet outside, and he tugged his hood farther down over his eyes before biking out into the storm, squinting against the downpour, his binoculars knocking against his chest. The rain pelted his face, stinging the cut on his cheek, reminding him that he'd nearly called Dayna three or four times that evening. The urge hit him once again, and he blew out a miserable breath.

He just wanted to hear her voice. As weird and terrifying as this morning had been, feeling her in his arms again had been good.

Of course, whenever he thought about Dayna the guilt returned, flaring up in the pit of his stomach. Their breakup had been confusing and emotional, and there was a kind of awkwardness between them now. They were still friends, though. There was a still a chance.

He pushed the thought aside, concentrating on making it up the hill. His legs burned, and he lowered his head as the wind lashed sheets of rain at him. This was probably completely insane, biking out in the pouring rain to spy on a small-town misdemeanor.

Once he came over the hill, he pulled his bike to the side, rocks popping under the tires. There was an outcrop of scruffy bushes around the field that held the stone circles, where he intended to do his spying. Halfway there he halted, gaze caught by flashes of blue and white. Two police cars blocked off the road, and a third was parked in front of the stone circles.

The area around the stones had been roped off with yellow tape, black letters spelling out *Police Line, Do Not Cross.* Inside the tape a half dozen men worked, some taking notes and pictures, others helping to erect a wide canvas tent over a tarp on the ground. Lamps had been set up around the perimeter, painting everything in stark yellow light.

Sam stayed frozen where he was, fingers biting into the rubber grips of his handles. He'd been right. One-eight-six *was* a homicide.

This was almost too good to be true.

Breathing hard, he fished into the pocket of his rain jacket, yanking out his binoculars.

The scene was blurry at first; he had to adjust for the rain. When it finally cleared he could make out gardai crowding around the tarp, one snapping pictures as another lifted it off the ground. There was someone on the grass in the middle of the stones, arms and legs splayed. It was too far to see their face, but they weren't moving. *A body.* The thought made his stomach lurch.

On the other side of the stone circles stood his father. Sam watched the sergeant shift onto his heels, smoothing a hand over his face. Even at this distance he could tell his father was agitated, and he kept looking at the farthest stone circle.

Sam shifted the binoculars slightly, trying to refocus on the rocks. It took a few frustrating seconds, as he hadn't used the binoculars since his bird-watching phase two years ago, and it was hard to make out anything clearly through the rain.

Finally he found it. There it was, a faint shape that grew sharper the longer he stared. It was drawn in a kind of horrible rust red, all sharp angles and twisted lines. It took him one beat, two, to digest what he was seeing, and then he could feel the fine hairs on the back of his neck stand on end.

He knew exactly what it meant.

Sam jerked his bike upright and slung a leg over the seat, turning back for the house. He had to get home and start taking notes right away.

This was going to be historic.

Chapter Six

DAYNA

If Sage Widow was Dayna's second favorite place, the coven house was top of her list. The building itself was overly large, in a comfortable, sprawling kind of way. A farmhouse lived in so thoroughly that every corner had someone's personal mark. It was such a contrast with the reverend's cold, spacious home, which was filled with a mixture of sad thrift store furniture. A proverbial elephant graveyard of unloved sofas and and sagging armchairs.

Here, everything was mismatched, quilted together or slightly cracked, but every piece had a purpose. Everything had been sought out or built by hand. Reagan and her mother, Yemi, had filled their home with stacks of books, football trophies, patchwork quilts, and scattered pages of Reagan's spell work. Stashes of loose-leaf tea in silver tins sat on crooked shelves, and battered trunks and treasure chests nestled in nooks and crannies.

The house was full of her childhood, warm memories hidden in every corner. Memories of sleeping over in Reagan's squeaky-springed double bed, the two girls tucked under the bumpy quilt, filling the darkness with giggles. Memories of dancing in the kitchen, turning the radio up when Yemi went out for groceries. And best of all, the moment the three of them were camped out on the couch, bowls of popcorn on their laps, watching reruns of Yemi's favorite soaps. Reagan had grabbed a handful of popcorn, and casually, though Dayna could tell her friend was fairly bursting with excitement, told her she was a witch. And that Dayna could be one, too. Yemi could teach them both.

Dayna had been part of the coven from that moment on. They were her real family. Here, Dayna left everything that wasn't witchcraft behind. Here, Reagan Etomi was her best friend, and magic existed, and nobody quoted scripture at you.

The driveway was long and winding, and her hatchback stirred up clouds of dust as she whipped around the curves. Even on her way up the dirt lane she could feel the tension melting from her shoulders. She knew every dip, every turn, every pothole. She cracked the window and let the cool, pine-scented night air kiss her face.

This was home.

She parked crookedly next to Reagan. Her friend drove a blue mini-van covered with a combination of obscure band stickers, her Wexford Football club logo, and witchcraft jokes, and as Dayna passed the back she looked for a new one. Sure enough, there was a small square sticker on the left side of the bumper—*My other car is a stick*, with the silhouette of a witch on a broom.

Dayna grinned. The new sticker would send Bronagh into fits. She was always going on about how brazen young witches were these days. To talk about it so openly was asking to be drowned or stoned in her day.

This was of course, a terrible exaggeration, since Dayna was fairly certain Bronagh had not been alive in the fifteenth century.

She passed through the three gates leading up to the yard and through the wild garden, and the sensor lights kicked on as she walked through. It was exactly the sort of garden a witch was supposed to have, full of overgrown ivy and suspect-looking plants. Down the stone pathway, she pushed past the screen door, which shrieked her arrival to the entire house.

She found the coven assembled around the long wooden plank that served as the kitchen table.

Reagan bounced in her chair when she saw her, clapping her hands.

"Finally, for the love of all the gods, woman. She's got us waiting to open our blooming mouths."

If it were possible for Reagan to be any *less* like the people at school, she wasn't sure how. Today Reagan was wearing a patched dress, colorful against her dark brown skin, and her feet were bare. The dress looked as though someone had slain a patchwork quilt and made clothing from its hide. It would be hideous on anyone but her. With Reagan's beaded, blue-dyed locs and the black velvet choker she always wore, she managed to make it look like a high-fashion piece.

"Patience is a virtue, Reagan." Yemi was hovering over the table. She'd already poured black tea into five mismatched china cups, and now she looked up at Dayna, brows raised. "Come chop, Dayna. Biscuit? Jam tart? Pie?"

"Oh, uh. Tea would be nice." She raised a brow at Reagan as Yemi bustled over to the counter to collect another cup. "I brought Bronagh's tea. What's going on?"

Reagan leaned sideways in her chair, stuffing her hands into the pockets of her dress. Reagan refused to wear anything without pockets as a general principle. "She's been stress baking all day." Her dark eyes flicked between her mother and the other witches. "Apparently there's another coven coming to meet us, which I guess means we need an entire bakery's worth of desserts."

"Another coven? I didn't know there was one nearby." Dayna glanced over at Yemi, who was busy refilling the kettle on the stove, humming along with the transistor radio on top of the fridge. She knew Reagan's mother better than her own father, and as the woman came over and set her cup on the cluttered table it was obvious how preoccupied she was. The hint of an accent had returned, as it often did when she was stressed or excited, and she'd pulled her cloud of black hair into a tight knot at the base of her neck. She had the glassy-eyed look of someone who'd traded multiple hours of sleep for hovering over the stove.

When Dayna was anxious, she used cognitive behavior therapy. When Yemi was anxious, she made cookies, and her tendency to force tea on everyone increased. Dayna bit her lip, wondering what exactly it was about this other coven that was making Yemi so nervous.

"Thanks." She watched Yemi pour the tea, steam curling up from the surface. Tea would be good. It warmed the throat for what she knew was going to be a long, strange conversation. Of course, when you were surrounded by witches, most conversations were long and strange. . . .

Yemi gave her a sympathetic smile, pulling her into one of her warm hugs before pushing her gently back to study her face. "How are you dealing, my girl? I'm glad to see your face isn't scratched. Mercy, you should see that Morgan girl from your church. She's all slashed up."

Dayna blinked at her, startled. She'd been so preoccupied with thoughts of the other coven, she'd nearly forgot about the birds.

She set her backpack down, sliding into an empty chair. "I'm fine, Yemi. Honestly. But someone tell me about this coven. Why are they coming?"

"Don't ask *us*. They certainly weren't invited." Brenna, the fifty-something-year-old daughter of Bronagh, and the middle of the trio of Callighan women, sat at the opposite end of the table. She had her tarot deck spread over the tablecloth, and she flipped a card over and tapped one long red nail against it, her gaze distant. Now and again she'd tilt her head back to look at the dusty tapestry on the wall above the table, a colorful portrayal of the Celtic gods embroidered on green fabric.

"Their leader used to be part of our coven, back in the day." This from Faye, ex-surgeon and granddaughter to Bronagh, who'd inherited her grandmother's red hair and fair complexion but not her laugh. Her tea sat untouched.

Bronagh, the oldest Callighan, and their coven leader, winked at Dayna before plucking a scone off the plate in the center of the table. Bronagh's curly red hair was shot through with gray, and she had a shriveled-apple face and an easy laugh. She always wore outrageous floral patterns and knitted shawls, clunky costume brooches and pearls.

Personally Dayna suspected the grandma disguise might be a kind of ruse to lure her prey into relaxing.

"You've got the tea?" Bronagh inquired around a mouthful of scone, and nodded with satisfaction when Dayna slid the satchel across the table. She wasted no time ripping open the bag and dumping the contents into her mug.

Faye wrinkled her nose. "Don't talk with your mouth full, Grandmother."

Bronagh ignored her. "The other coven is on their way, invitation or not. I suspect it has something to do with those damn birds." She dipped her scone in her teacup, and Faye looked utterly horrified. "Oh, stop, girl. It doesn't affect the reading."

"Grandmother, haven't you had enough sweets?"

"Sod off." Bronagh moved on to her second scone, ignoring her granddaughter's disapproving scowl. "Reagan and Dayna, did you do your assignments for the week?"

"Oh yes." She'd nearly forgotten. Dayna leaned over to dig into her bag, bringing out the witch's ladder. She set the knotted strand of wool on the table, and Bronagh nodded approvingly. This spell had been more complicated than the last, but she'd still finished it the first night. "For luck."

"And how did it come off, love?" Brenna leaned over and took it from Bronagh before passing it to Yemi, who nodded her approval.

"Good, I thought"—she grimaced—"until the whole raven thing."

"Ah, but from what I hear, you're one of the few who came out of the incident without a scratch." Faye raised a brow at her. "Had your spell in your pocket, did you?"

Dayna nodded slowly, gaze drifting back to the yarn talisman. It was true, she *was* one of the only students who hadn't been scratched or battered by the charging ravens.

"We'll have to do something more complicated this week." Bronagh glanced over at Reagan's talisman, which had been artfully crafted out of leather cord. She'd even added a silver bead on the end. "For prosperity, I see. Very nice."

"Beautiful knot work, and how did the spell go?" Brenna said.

"Well, Auntie." Reagan beamed, turning out her pocket to show off a handful of coins. "Been picking them up off the sidewalk everywhere I go this week."

"Very nice."

Dayna eyed her friend's work, feeling envious. Not only did Reagan read voraciously in her free time, she'd been homeschooled, which meant learning the craft of magic as an elective to her coursework, and so she seemed to Dayna to be leaps and bounds ahead.

"Where are they coming from, the other coven?" Reagan tucked her witch's ladder back into the book she'd been working on for the last two weeks, a hefty text on astronomy. This was merely the top of the pile beside her left elbow, which was stacked with titles like *A Brief History of Time* and *The Fabric of the Cosmos*.

"Limerick," Bronagh said shortly, and then she murmured to Brenna beside her, "Perhaps our next lesson will be another round of protection talismans. It may be necessary."

"Speaking of homework, do you have any for the summer?" Faye gave Dayna a stern look. "Don't think we'll let you get away with only doing your spell work while you're here. It's just as important to get into a good university after graduation."

Bronagh made a *harrumph* noise at this, and Faye scowled. "Witchcraft doesn't pay the bills, Grandmother. You think she can walk into a grocery store and trade that luck talisman for food? We don't work on the barter system anymore."

"Land sakes, girl," Bronagh grumbled. "How old do you think I *am*?"

Reagan grinned. "Well, you *did* just say 'land sakes,' so . . ."

"Honestly, the sheer cheek."

Faye was still looking at her expectantly, and Dayna cleared her throat, pocketing her spell. "Uh, I don't have too much homework. Just some reading." She was dying with curiosity and here they were talking about homework. "Who's the one that used to be in your coven?" She noticed Reagan sat up a little straighter beside her. The Callighans had been very close-mouthed about their past. She knew they'd belonged to another coven when she and Reagan were little, but that was it.

Brenna and Bronagh exchanged a look, and then Bronagh sighed. "I daresay you've heard rumors of the King Witch."

"What?" Reagan leaned forward, nearly knocking her stack of books over. "The infamous King Witch, destroyer of worlds, devourer of man-parts? You can't be serious."

Dayna blinked around at the Callighans, who stared back at the two girls, straight-faced. They were joking, weren't they? The King Witch was practically a fairy tale, something Yemi had warned them about to scare them off black magic. A witch who had gone bad, whose magic had turned her cannibal. "Are you seriously saying she was in your coven?"

"Aye, and now she's coming back into town." Bronagh was still staring into her teacup. "I said no thank you, but she wouldn't be budged. Seems to think she has something important to do here."

"Why keep her here if you don't like her?" Reagan darted a look at her mother. "Have her stay at the hotel. She can buy her own jam tarts."

"If she's here, we can keep an eye on her," Faye said sternly.

Dayna tried to suppress a grin. "What if she gets snacky while she's here?" She nudged Reagan, who laughed. "I'm very attached to all my fingers and toes."

"Don't worry. I bet you don't even taste good." Reagan leaned side-ways in her chair, snapping her teeth.

There was a sharp *crack* from across the table, and Dayna and Reagan both jumped. Bronagh had slammed her cup down, and the table was dotted with drops of tea. "That's enough," she said, and her expression was dark. "There will be no joking about black magic in my coven. It is not a laughing matter."

Dayna exchanged a look with Reagan, brows raised. They'd asked about black magic before, but it was something that didn't get discussed at their lessons. Yemi had given them a very short explanation—*evil gods equal evil witch*—and left it at that.

Bronagh's reaction was . . . unnerving. Dayna shifted in her chair before standing up, using the excuse of getting more milk from the fridge. The situation suddenly didn't seem the slightest bit funny, and she felt she had to move, just to work off some of the nervous energy.

Yemi sank down into her seat. Her hands trembled as she picked up her teacup and then, apparently realizing it was too hot, set it back down with a rattling clank.

Dayna peered over the door of the refrigerator, her stomach twisting at the grim looks on the Callighans' faces. "What do they want from us?"

Brenna stood, toying with one of the feathers in her hair as she moved into the kitchen to rinse out her mug. "We'll know in about . . . five minutes."

"I have so many questions." Reagan's easy grin had returned almost immediately. She leaned back, propping her feet up on the chair beside her, ignoring a pointed look from her mother.

Brenna paused by the fridge, squeezing Dayna's shoulder gently. "All right, love?"

Dayna nodded quickly and slid the milk back on the shelf, following Brenna to the table.

"How many of them are there?" Reagan asked.

Brenna shrugged as she sat back down, her many bangles and bracelets jingling. "And how would I know?"

"You could use your magical inner eye, abi? Or, you know, you could have asked on the phone."

Brenna shook her head, clearly trying to repress a smile, before returning to her cards, muttering something about "cheek" under her breath, and Reagan grinned and rocked back in her chair, legs akimbo. She was wearing leggings under her many-layered skirt, so the position was not as indecent as it might have been. She folded her arms over her chest. "They're late. Can this King Witch person not keep track of time?"

Her voice was casual, and Dayna was grateful she was trying to defuse the tension. She didn't like how Bronagh kept glancing warily at the door, and the worried looks Brenna was shooting her tarot deck were almost as bad. The tension in the room was starting to make the air feel thick, harder to draw in and out of her lungs.

One breath in, long and shaky. Back out. Two, three, four.

Stop that.

Yemi sat back in her chair, cheeks still rosy from running about the kitchen. She fanned herself with one hand, shaking her head reprovingly. "Quit your sass and drink your tea."

"That's part of our charm, though. I'm the sass and you're the tea. Besides, I've had five cups and I'm ready to burst."

Yemi opened her mouth, and Reagan visibly braced herself for the lecture that was coming, a look of amused contrition on her face.

A sharp rap cut the conversation off and made Dayna jump. The knocking came a second time and then a third, and Bronagh sighed, dusting crumbs off the front of her shawl.

"They're here."

Chapter Seven

MEINER

The woman who welcomed them in filled the doorway, her colorful dress a cheerful contrast to the dark and drizzly weather. "Hello, hello!" She peered past them at the gray sky, waving them in. "It's wetter than a damp cat out there. Hurry in, the lot of you!"

Meiner forced a smile. "You must be Yemi. I'm Meiner and this is Cora." She took a breath, forcing herself to keep her hands at her sides instead of reaching into her pocket. She'd taken a pill that morning; she was fine. "This is my grandmother, Elizabeth King. You spoke on the phone."

"Pleased to meet you, Elizabeth..." Yemi faltered, focusing on Grandma King's face. Meiner cringed. The drive over had not gone well. Grandma King had unraveled bit by bit as they drew closer to the coven house. Now she was staring around the place—a vestibule with racks of boots on either side—with a confused and irritated look.

"Where the devil have you taken me, Stephanie?"

Meiner flinched. This was not the first time Gran had mistaken her for her mother, but it hurt every time the name came out of the old woman's mouth. She didn't remember Stephanie King, but it didn't mean she wanted to be reminded of her.

Yemi smiled, covering her surprise gracefully. "Why don't you all come in? I've the kettle on for some nice hot tea and we'll do introductions all round."

Meiner nodded, grateful, and they followed her into the kitchen. Even Gran went without protest, seemingly soothed by the promise of tea. They passed through a short hallway, the walls of which were covered in a variety of pictures. There were family photos, Yemi and a girl who was obviously her daughter, posing for their portraits, and several pictures of a group of Black girls in football jerseys on the field, arms around one another as they grinned at the photographer.

But the picture that really caught her eye was of a group of women sitting on a checkered blanket spread under an apple tree, faces turned up to the camera. Just behind them, clear in the photo, was a makeshift altar under the nearest apple tree, incense burning in the center.

Was that their coven? She tried to imagine a world where her coven picnicked on sunny days in apple orchards or took family portraits together, and completely failed. It was a ridiculous image.

They moved into the kitchen, and Cora stopped abruptly. Meiner, who had been glancing back at Grandma King to make sure the old woman didn't wander off outside, nearly walked into her. When she looked up her mouth dropped open. It was not the cluttered but homey kitchen or the giant, faded tapestry on the wall that caught her attention...

It was her.

Meiner couldn't look away. The wide blue eyes, the silver nose ring, the dusting of freckles across her pale cheeks...

The girl from Sage Widow sat at the kitchen table, blinking at Meiner in surprise. She seemed frozen, a teacup halfway to her lips, staring with wide eyes. Meiner opened her mouth and then shut it, unsure what to say.

Finally Cora said it. Loudly enough for them all to hear. "Whoa, it's Tea Girl. That's weird."

Tea Girl, for her part, blushed bright red and shifted in her chair. "Dayna," she said. "And you're Meiner, right?"

Yemi was already beaming at them. "Oh, you've met before?"

Dayna looked flustered. "Uh, at Sage Widow earlier today."

Oh no, she wasn't about to get away with it that easily. "Yeah, that's right, she practically stole the last satchel of tea out of my hand."

Dayna sputtered. "What? You *know* I had it first."

Meiner smirked, sinking down onto the seat across from Dayna. She couldn't seem to help herself. The other girl was so indignant, it made her want to keep going. "Aye, that's your official story, isn't it?"

Dayna flushed even darker. She looked fairly ready to burst, and then the girl beside her cleared her throat, flicking blue locs over one shoulder. "Not all of us know one another. Should we do introductions?"

The red-haired woman across the table clanked her teacup down. "Yes, let's get to know one another."

Meiner looked around the table. The teacup-smashing woman was pale, thin, and waspish. Her narrow glasses and tight bun at the top of her head gave her an angry librarian vibe. The woman sitting next to her looked related, though, judging by her warm smile, she was a good deal more cheerful. She also had an assortment of black feathers and silver beads in her hair, and parts of it were braided, apparently at random. An older sister or mother of the angry librarian, maybe. The woman on the other side had to be as old as Grandma King. She wore a blue knitted shawl with a clunky costume brooch pinned to the front. She was busy peering into her teacup, as if it were far more interesting than the other coven.

Then there was Yemi, their hostess. Judging by the warning look the older woman gave her, the Black girl with the blue hair and the stack of books was her daughter.

So, this was the other coven it was so vital they meet. She wasn't sure what to think.

Introductions began and ended, and Meiner tried to keep her eyes in the right places and not stare at Dayna, who she was very aware was still scowling at her.

"You've quite a bit of luggage with you, King." The old woman, Bronagh, placed a wrinkled hand on the table, spreading her fingers over the cloth. "Exactly how long are you planning on staying?"

Meiner's brows shot up, and she swiveled in her chair. If Gran was offended by the sharpness of the question, her face revealed nothing. For a moment, the old woman simply stared, and Meiner sighed, about to explain they might not get any sense out of her, that today had been one of her bad days.

Grandma King leaned forward, taking her teacup. Her hands were suddenly steady. "As long as it takes, Bronagh. We're going to need to pool our power. You don't have enough on your own, and there's nothing but hedge witches for miles."

Meiner blinked, feeling a bit of whiplash at how fast this version of her grandmother had returned. On top of that, it seemed she and Dayna weren't the only ones butting heads. No surprise that Grandma King had bad history with her old coven.

Grandma King leveled a pointed look at the other woman. "I think you know why we're here."

"I'm loath to admit it." Bronagh stared down at her teacup, a reluctant frown etching deep lines across her weathered face. "But yes . . . all my readings have been terribly dark lately, and none of them clear." Her eyes went narrow. "But that doesn't mean we needed you, King."

"You will," Grandma King said. "Something is waking."

"What is it?" Reagan asked. "What's waking?"

The blue-haired girl looked at Grandma King, her expression critical.

Instead of answering, the old woman began to turn, eyes fixed on the window. After a moment she spoke again, and her voice was a low mutter. "Where . . . where's the light?"

Meiner's stomach sank. "She's gone again, sorry. She . . . hasn't been herself lately."

For a moment they watched as Grandma King hobbled over to stare out the window. There was a beat of silence as the other coven exchanged looks with one another, and Meiner's nerves began chewing at her insides. Then everyone except Bronagh jumped as Brenna slammed one hand on the table in exasperation. She'd been shuffling through her cards for the entire conversation. "Again! It keeps coming up."

Faye, who'd been lifting her cup from her saucer, looked down at her plate, which was now full of tea. "What," she said sharply, "keeps coming up?"

Brenna jabbed her finger at the card in the center of her spread. "That."

The card Brenna pointed to was framed in smudgy black swirls. In the center, a crumbling brick building was bathed in flames, which were creeping up the base, licking at the windows. There was a black silhouette in the air halfway down, arms outstretched, legs splayed. Falling.

"The tower," she said. "No matter how many times I lay the cards out."

The tower. Change. Destruction.

Meiner bit the inside of her cheek, stomach twisting uneasily.

The others were silent, and then Brenna looked up from the cards, eyes round. "It'll be the death card next, mark my words."

"It's rarely in the literal sense," Faye pointed out, though she didn't look certain.

Meiner cleared her throat. "Uh, I'm afraid it might be this time. Gran had a premonition about a murder specifically. The murder of a witch. That's why we're here, because she thinks we need to stop it from happening again."

She saw Dayna's brows shoot up, and the Callighans exchanged a look between them. Slowly Faye said, "Again?"

Cora leaned forward at the table, expression eager. "We saw it on the way here, in—"

"The stone circles." Meiner shot her a dark look. She wasn't about to let Cora dominate the conversation the way she always did. Not here.

She told them about the body in the field, the tree of life on the woman's cheek.

Across from her Dayna had gone pale, her fists clenched on the tabletop.

"A murdered witch." Brenna tapped her nails on the table, lips pursed. Meiner noted she hadn't picked up another card.

"Gran seems to think there'll be more."

Another stretch of silence, broken only by Gran mumbling under her breath as she stared vacantly out the window.

Brenna turned to her mother. "What about the tea?"

"It's . . . murky," Bronagh muttered. The old woman tilted her cup this way and that on the saucer. "It suggests darkness, that something is coming. The rest is just . . . scone crumbs."

Faye snorted, leaning back to fold her arms over her chest. "Honestly, Grandmother."

Dayna cleared her throat, and everyone looked at her. She flushed. "Uh, I'm not sure if this is relevant, but on the way to Sage Widow, they were doing another protest at the church. They had signs with that verse on it, 'suffer a witch to live' . . ."

Faye folded her arms over her chest, her face twisted in a sneer. "Oh yes, everyone's favorite."

"You think one of those church lunatics would actually kill someone?" Reagan looked doubtful.

"They protested the liquor store last month," Brenna said, "but they didn't stab the clerk to death at any point."

"It's worth checking out." Bronagh looked at Dayna pointedly.

Dayna clearly wasn't happy, but she nodded. Meiner wasn't sure what the exchange meant. She didn't go to the church, did she?

"We go to the stone circle tomorrow." Everyone stared at Grandma King over by the window. She was still facing away from them.

Bronagh's lips twitched downward briefly before she smoothed her expression. "Oh, do we, now?"

"Our coven does. Come if you like."

"We're in this together, whatever the hell it is." Faye glanced over at her grandmother. "That's why they came, isn't it?"

"If we can find something the murderer touched, we could attempt a contact scry." Grandma King turned around, eyes glittering as she stared at Bronagh.

"Absolutely not," Bronagh snapped. "Don't be a reckless fool."

Grandma King only smiled and turned back to the window once more, and Bronagh pinched the bridge of her nose, squeezing her eyes shut in irritation.

There was a stretch of silence, followed by a soft *thud* as Brenna flipped another card over.

The back of Meiner's neck prickled. Heavy black lines against a white backdrop depicted a grinning, skull-faced man, the wicked lines of a scythe arcing above his head.

Death.

Chapter Eight

DUBH

This was how the cycle started, with the memories dropping back into place one by one.

The first: His brothers, not what they looked like, but the *feeling* of their presence. The tension among them. The anger when one of them hit him.

The second: the symbol, the strange sign with all its jutting angles and scribbled lines . . . He'd been tracing it for months now, on the bar at pubs, in the steam on the bathroom mirror, in the dirt with the tip of his boot. Now he knew it belonged to his family.

And the third. The certainty of what he needed to do, the parts he had to collect.

Dubh hooked a finger into the neck of his tie, tugging it away from his throat. It was coated in the thick stickiness of half-dried blood. He glanced over his shoulder at the blue cooler on the seat of his rental car.

For a moment he shut his eyes and remembered how he'd dragged her, screaming, into the center of the stone circle. How Witchkiller had its fill of blood.

Some force had driven him to wrench her mouth open. It hadn't been easy, but he wasn't satisfied until he had it.

Her tongue.

He was turning back to the road when the dizziness hit him. A surge of memory sent the world spinning, forcing him to jam his foot on the brake.

A woman's hand on his face, her nails sharp on his skin. Her voice murmuring in his ear.

Tongue and eye, hand and foot. Blood and bone, ash and soot.

He was still shaking with excitement when he drove into the parking lot. He pulled past the Irish National Heritage Park sign and into the first stall, ignoring the handicapped symbol.

The same force guided him now.

Pulling on his heavy jacket, he zipped it up over the blood-spattered suit and tilted the rearview mirror down. He growled under his breath at the spot of blood on the bottom of his collar and tugged his coat up.

Down the forest path to the center of the park, he passed two sets of tourists and a woman with a fluffy golden retriever in a service dog vest. The tourists didn't hold any interest for him, but he smiled at the woman. The kind of wide, charming grin that revealed all his teeth. He knew it was effective, and he wasn't the least bit surprised when she flushed and smiled back. The breeze pushed a few strands of hair off one shoulder, revealing a slender, pale throat. His hands would take up that entire space.

He didn't flinch when the dog abruptly growled and lunged forward. She gave a little shriek of surprise and hauled on the leash, struggling to pull him back.

"I'm so sorry. He never does this."

Dubh nodded and smiled and kept walking. They all did that.

The path led him past a length of circular fence that surrounded several thatched-roof houses, and Dubh was pulled up short by a memory: running barefoot in the dirt, chasing after his brothers, a woman's voice calling from the tiny, peaked-roof hut behind him.

The illusion crashed down around him as he moved closer. Surrounding the huts were groups of tourists in colorful clothing, all of them gawking and snapping pictures.

The village was a replica; he knew that. All the same it was dizzying to see it laid out like this.

He kept walking, making his way deeper into the forest. At last the path rounded the corner, and there it was: a flat, moss-green rock set atop two massive boulders. The stones were crooked, leaning, as if the earth beneath them had swelled.

A portal tomb.

There was a crackle in the underbrush, and Dubh moved forward slowly, the hair on the back of his neck prickling.

A man stood just beyond the tomb. He was taller than Dubh, but he had the same unnerving blue eyes, the same blond hair—though his was shorn close to his skull. In contrast to Dubh's blood-spattered suit, he wore only blue jeans and a faded white T-shirt.

"Olc," Dubh said. The rush of half-memories made his mouth taste bitter: Competition, anger, a fist in his face. Pain in his jaw. And all of that tied together by sullen loyalty. Blood was blood.

The man in the white T-shirt said nothing, but he swayed on his feet, blinking, shaking his head like a dog with water in its ears. A moment later he seemed to recover himself, and his expression went from confused to furious. He started forward, fists clenched, and Dubh stiffened. Another shuffle, and they both froze as a third man stepped from the trees.

Dubh felt a jolt of anger. He hadn't noticed him standing there. His instincts were better than that, but he'd been distracted.

The other man didn't share his brothers' blue eyes. His were dark, almost black. His hair was the same golden blond, tied back in a ponytail, and he wore a plaid jacket over a black V-neck.

Calma. The third, the oldest.

"I had to pay to get in." He sounded irritated.

Across from the tomb, Olc gave a derisive snort, looking over Calma's jacket. "Have you become a lumberjack?"

Calma didn't answer, only glanced from Olc to Dubh, his face calm. "Brothers," he finally said. Then he turned to face the stones, and Dubh and Olc did the same.

"I don't feel anything," Calma said.

There was distant laughter, and Calma and Dubh both looked around. There was a group of tourists heading down the path toward them.

"This is the right spot." Calma shook his head. "I remember it."

"This is *bullshit*." Olc slammed his fist into the one of the stones, hard enough that his knuckles cracked. He didn't flinch, just shook his hand out, dark brows drawn down. In the distance, the group of tourists paused to stare. When he glared in their direction, they turned and hurried the other way down the path.

"What now?" Calma said.

Dubh told his brothers about the woman, about the tongue in the cooler back in his car. About the words he'd remembered, *blood and bone, ash and soot*.

Calma looked thoughtful. Olc looked blankly at the stones in front of him. How did this already feel routine? Like a worn leather jacket he'd misplaced and rediscovered after a couple hundred years, which still fit perfectly. He wasn't sure what it meant. If it was a good thing.

Calma nodded, blond brows creased. "That seems right. The women—"

"Witches," Dubh corrected him, and again, Calma merely nodded.

"They never left. They're still guarding this place."

"Then it's hardly a hunt, is it?" Olc's voice was scornful. He'd always been the arrogant one. "That makes it too easy."

"There's a list." Calma blinked at Dubh. "But you've already started, haven't you?"

Dubh frowned. This was *his* mission; this cycle it was his turn.

"The judge was the first," he said sharply. Neither of them argued, because neither could prove him wrong.

"Do you remember the names?" Calma asked.

Dubh's expression went dark. "Only some."

"We need the list," Calma said. "We need to be sure."

"I'll wager she wasn't even on the list," Olc sneered. "Don't tell me you haven't killed before. That you didn't do it because you wanted to."

Dubh ignored him, reaching out a hand, brushing his fingertips along the tomb.

A wave of black crashed into him headfirst. He was on his back suddenly, staring at the tops of the trees as they whirled in dizzying arcs above his head.

A woman's face, smooth and pale, dark brows and plum lips. Her black hair long and straight. Not just a woman . . . his mother?

She pushed a book into his hands, insistent, urgent. The cover was stiff leather under his fingers, and the symbol etched into the surface burned like a brand. The graceful crossed pattern, the sharp lines stretching to the edges of the circle . . . the same symbol that followed him everywhere.

The woman's voice was warped and distant, someone speaking in a dream. He could see her lips move but couldn't make out the words.

Her face faded a second later, and the trees stopped spinning.

Dubh dug his fingers into the cool earth beneath him. He could smell pine and the faint scent of cigarettes from the collar of his jacket. Something stirred on the ground beside him, and he turned. Calma's face was pale. He brushed absently at the front of his jacket as he staggered to his feet. Even Olc looked slightly dazed, leaning against the stones. They'd seen it, too.

Dubh sat up, hands trembling. "The list. It's in the book."

Chapter Nine

SAMUEL

Saturday morning, the Bible study chat was exploding.

Sam's phone had been vibrating the entire bike ride to the station. At first he thought it was notifications from his true crime forums—he'd set up the Butcher thread to notify him when anyone posted—but each time he checked, it was another group chat notification.

He finally stopped halfway there and yanked it out of his pocket.

Morgan: *What's going on? Mam drove past the stone circle and it was taped off. Sam?*

Jillian: *No way it's a murder. Like anything interesting happens around here.*

Morgan: *Jill, that's seriously messed up.*

Morgan: @SamuelByrne?

She'd tagged him a few more times, which wasn't surprising. Morgan's face had been cut up during the attack, and she was refusing to go anywhere until the wounds healed, which left plenty of time to badger him. He sighed and slipped his phone back into his pocket. He wouldn't be allowed to update them even if he did learn something. His father would tear him a new one. Plus Sam wasn't going to be allowed anywhere near the case.

Ironic, since he seemed to be the only one in this town who had any idea what was actually going on. He'd been studying the Butcher for years, ever since he'd figured out the killer's pattern.

There were so many unanswered questions about the case. So many mysteries still unsolved. Sam's own theories had slowly developed over time, as his obsession with the case had grown. If there was a Butcher of Manchester expert, it was him.

And now the Butcher was here, right on his doorstep. It was as if Sam was somehow woven into this, destined to be involved in some way. It was fate, or the hand of God, maybe.

The thought made him shiver.

When he looked up, about to kick his foot back onto the pedal, the stretch of field to his left caught his eye. It looked . . . empty. Sam passed the field on the way to school almost every day, and it was usually full of livestock.

He frowned, moving closer, until his palms were pressed against the roughly hewn wooden fence surrounding the pasture. It wasn't that it was empty, he realized, but that the entire herd of black-and-white dairy cows were lying on the grass.

Cows, Samuel knew, generally did not lie this way, with their legs splayed in the air like broken fence posts. He stared, openmouthed, at the sight. It was bizarre, a sea of black and white stretching halfway across the field.

The field continued to be silent and still, and it hit him a second later.

"Oh *shit*." He jerked his bike back up out of the ditch and jumped on, pedaling until his thighs burned, heading straight for the station.

When he arrived, he was surprised to find only half the desks occupied. He'd expected his dad to call everyone in. Murder required a little overtime.

When he walked in, the sergeant was speaking to one of his men, arms crossed over his chest. "Send someone to clear out the stone circles. I don't want it roped off any more than it has to be. Hurts tourism if they're afraid to stumble over a dead body at any second. No need to create a panic."

"But, sir, we're going to have to call in—" The officer broke off when he spotted Sam, and his father turned, brows raised,

"Samuel. Why are you here?"

Sam forced a smile. "Ma got me to bring your lunch in. You left it in the fridge. Listen, Dad, the Kellys' farm—"

"We know." The sergeant waved him off. "We've already had three calls and I haven't even had my coffee yet. I'm sending someone over. You can put my lunch on my desk." He turned back to the officer, and Sam nodded and ducked by, making his way down the narrow hallway to the back.

He slipped into his father's office and crouched by the open door, setting his backpack on the floor.

"Look," his father was saying, "it's probably someone trying to throw us off the scent. Maybe they poisoned the cows, too, to make it seem like there's some kind of lunatic running around. The judge had enemies, right? She put loads of people away."

Sam froze momentarily, shocked. His father had to mean Judge O'Toole, the woman who sat in the back pew of the church every Sunday. She was a steely-faced woman and not particularly friendly.

But she'd been retired for years. Why wait this long to kill her?

"It had to be revenge," the sergeant continued. "He does a little internet search, finds the nearest serial killer, scratches that damned sign into something and, *wham*, you got everyone sniffing after a decade-old case."

"Wham," Sam muttered to himself, and pulled the first Tupperware container out of his bag. Leftover stew from last night. He'd gone back and grabbed it out of the fridge. His mother hadn't exactly asked him to bring it over, but he knew the sergeant was going to be busy today. He was just taking some initiative. And if he happened to overhear something while running the errand, well...

He walked over to the desk, footsteps light, and set it on the top. He could hear the officer protesting from next door.

"Sir, shouldn't we call it in? I mean, a murder—"

"Accident. We don't know it was a murder."

"Well, we don't know it was an accident either, sir. It wasn't like she fell onto her shearing scissors a half dozen times, now is it?"

"Watch your mouth."

Sam set the stew down and walked back to the bag. He was impressed the man was still arguing. His father had a way of plowing over any protests.

Next out of the bag was a ziplock baggie with a couple of dinner buns in it. His father was saying loudly, "There'll be questions, of course, all those rubberneckers on the way past. Have Bertie release a statement to the media." He cleared his throat. "No foul play."

His officer must have given him a look, because he sighed. "Just to avoid the panic. You'll see, it'll be someone who just got out of jail and had a few drinks to work up his courage. Then panicked and tried to make it look like a serial killer."

That, Sam thought, was still the very definition of *foul play*. Apparently the other man agreed with him, because there was only a bad-tempered grunt in reply and then the sound of footsteps in the hallway.

Sam placed the dinner buns on top of the container just as his father opened his door. He gave the sergeant a grin and held up a spoon. "Thought I'd lost this in my bag. Didn't think you'd appreciate eating with your hands."

His father gave him a long look as he set the spoon down on the desk, then Sam turned back to him, slinging his bag over his shoulder.

"Everything okay? Morgan says her mam drove past quite a scene in the stone circle."

"Of course, it's already spreading," his father grumbled, and stalked over to his desk. "It's nothing. Some addict, probably. We'll have it cleared up in a few days." He gave Sam a sharp look. "Don't you go reporting anything to your little friends. This is a godly town. This type of thing doesn't happen here, and I won't have you spreading rumors."

"Of course not." Normally Sam would have been annoyed by the casual scorn in his father's voice, but right now he was too eager to find out more. "Did they die in one of the circles or did someone dump them there?"

His father scowled. "That's none of your concern. You think it's right, to think about these things? You think God would approve?"

Sam bit back a retort that his father maybe *should* think a little harder about these things. Instead he replied, "I better get home. Lots of reading to do for Bible study." His father didn't answer, just cracked open his laptop and began typing furiously, so Samuel turned and made his way down the hallway, stealing a few jelly beans from Bertie's desk at the front. The older woman gave him a wave without looking up from her work, her round face pale.

The poor woman had probably never written up a press release like this one.

Sam rode home, his mouth full of jelly beans, already planning what he was going to post on the forums.

Chapter Ten

MEINER

The car ride over had tested the limits of Meiner's patience.

They'd carpooled, and of course Cora had claimed the passenger seat, keeping up a steady stream of chatter. She got in some subtle jabs at Meiner and managed to bring up the fact they'd dated briefly, darting a furtive look at Dayna in the rearview mirror.

Meiner's temper had surged so suddenly she'd sucked a breath in and held it, forcing herself to relax. *Of course she'd bring that up.*

Now they stood in the middle of a scrubby field surrounded by a cluster of slate-colored rocks. The stone circle amplified magic and allowed the practitioner a more direct line to power. The gods were only a whisper away, and any other time she would have been charged with excitement. It was a place of power, sacred, even.

But at the moment it just seemed . . . wet.

The sky overhead was gray, and there was a constant steady drizzle. It hardly seemed enough to warrant an umbrella, and yet the rain seeped through Meiner's thin jacket. It twisted her hair into damp locks, leaving her shivering.

Beside her, Cora shifted, reaching up to pull the hood of her raincoat over her face. Meiner silently hated her for being more prepared.

Reagan exchanged a grumpy look with Dayna and tugged her knit cap farther down over her brows. "What are we supposed to find here? A chalk outline? A flashing sign that says, *The murder was here?*"

"That would be helpful." Dayna kicked at the wet grass, crossing her arms over her chest. Droplets of water dotted her dark hair and ran down her face and neck.

When Dayna looked up and caught Meiner staring, she scowled, and Meiner smirked back, lifting an eyebrow. Sure enough, Dayna huffed and turned away.

Okay, she'd admit it, Dayna might be sort of cute.

But she was annoying as hell. *And* she seemed to overreact to pretty much everything. That was all Meiner needed, another version of Cora jumping down her throat all the time.

"What *are* we looking for? I mean, aside from a bunch of pointy rocks?" Cora demanded.

No one answered. Yemi, who clutched her metal tea thermos, looked around warily, as if she expected the murderer to pop out from behind one of the stones, and the Callighan women had drifted away from the group. Brenna and Faye were talking in low voices, heads bent together, and Bronagh was standing very still, face tilted to the sky.

Grandma King picked her way carefully around the standing stones, staring down at the flat gray rocks. She was turning a cigarette over in her hands, though she hadn't yet lit it.

Meiner frowned, trying to study her grandmother's face discreetly. How much of this was Gran's magic guiding her, and how much was the disease claiming her mind? Maybe they were chasing something that didn't exist.

It was all well and good to sit around and stare at the death card, or make dire predictions about coming doom, but what did they actually have to go on? Only that a witch had died. That meant nothing; it meant that witches had enemies. Sometimes lots of them. That was evident enough by the town's reaction to her grandmother. They'd stopped for brunch on the way over, and one of the women in the diner had gone sheet white at the mere sight of her, a fact Grandma King either didn't notice or pretended not to.

The rumors about her gran were ridiculous. Hyperbolic and hysterical, bedtime tales told to witchlings to scare them straight. If the witches in this town were stupid enough to believe them, it wasn't her coven's problem.

Of course, she wouldn't be that surprised if someone wanted to murder Gran next. It was clear she'd made enemies in this town, including her ex-coven.

She glanced over at Bronagh. Gran wouldn't tell her what had happened—likely she wouldn't remember, or would decide it was "none of her damn business"—but Meiner resolved to get Bronagh alone at some point, to ask her exactly why Gran left.

After all of this was over, that is, and they were finished standing around damp fields staring at rocks.

She grumbled under her breath, mood surging even lower. The tightness in her chest turned to a slow burn as she clenched and unclenched her fists, trying to wrestle her temper down, to keep her expression flat and unaffected.

Likely she was standing here in the pissing rain for nothing. She sighed and balled her fists in her pockets, wishing she was somewhere warm. Maybe somewhere with coffee.

Somehow it made her mood even worse to see Dayna and Reagan had inched closer, and Dayna had curled an arm around her friend, rubbing at Reagan's arms as they huddled together, stamping their feet and shivering.

"Hot tea, love?" Yemi raised her brows at Meiner, offering the thermos.

Normally she would have turned it down, but now she only hesitated a moment before accepting. She was freezing. Just wrapping her hands around the warm surface was a relief. A little self-consciously, she poured a bit of the steaming liquid into the cup Yemi handed her. Yemi smiled and patted her arm before turning away, and Meiner cleared her throat, temper fizzling out.

There was something about the woman that made a lump rise in her throat. Maybe the way she fussed over her daughter and Dayna, mothering both of them. Or the warmth of her personality. It wasn't possible to be any *less* like Meiner's grandmother.

"I'll take some, thanks," Dayna said, and when Meiner handed the thermos over, Dayna's fingers brushed hers. It was the lightest touch, but it was enough to send an electric current over Meiner's skin. When she took the thermos, Meiner turned away, annoyed.

Had Dayna done that deliberately?

There was a loud *ping*, followed by the sound of Dayna grumbling, and Reagan asked, "Sam again? Ask if he's still hanging out with that Bible study."

"He is."

Meiner shoved her hands deeper in her pockets, watching them as they bent their heads over Dayna's phone. "What a dick," Reagan said, still shivering and shifting from foot to foot.

Was Sam an ex, maybe? The way Dayna acted, something must have actually gone down. And what had Reagan meant by *Bible study*?

"You know, I can hex him for you if you like." Faye had wandered back over, pulling her hood lower over her eyes.

"Faye, *no*," Brenna scolded her. "We talked about this."

"Just a little hex"—Faye's smile was sharp, and Meiner wondered if the woman was actually joking—"to make his tongue shrivel in his mouth."

"You terrify me," Reagan said.

The distant sound of a car door slamming jerked her head up. When she turned back to the lot, there was a green minivan parked next to her car.

"Ah, that will be her now." Grandma King was staring at the van as well. She pulled herself up taller, shoulders square in her black sweater. She looked a little like she had before. Commanding, instead of lost and confused.

Meiner's stomach twisted. "Who?"

A family was spilling out of the van, a couple and two children. The driver emerged more slowly, a short, round woman with a bristly ponytail.

Grandma King didn't immediately answer as they watched the family approach. Finally, when they were less than ten feet away, she said in a low voice, "The one who found the body."

Meiner's eyes widened. Now that they were closer, she could see that the woman's red fleece vest had *Shamrock Tours* embroidered across the pocket. Underneath, the vest proclaimed her to be *Deborah*.

The kids ran forward, colorful rubber boots flashing pink and red against the damp grass. The parents followed, studying the stone circles with vague interest. The tour guide hung back, approaching almost timidly, eyes searching the field.

"Shamrock Tours, is it?" Gran smiled.

"Oh aye. We do tours of all the sights in this area." Deborah cleared her throat. Her gaze kept flickering to the nearest stone circle. "I better get to it. Feel free to listen in."

Gran turned to the others, eyes glittering. "Come on, then. Let's get the tour."

Dayna and Reagan shared an incredulous look, and Cora tugged her hood farther over her eyes, muttering bad-temperedly. Behind them, the Callighans whispered to one another, and Yemi placed the thermos back into her purse, brows furrowed.

Feeling her face start to burn, Meiner fell in behind her gran before the others came within earshot. She grasped her grandmother's sleeve. "We're here to get information, not a tour." Her voice was tight with controlled anger.

Grandma King jerked her arm out of Meiner's grip. "I'm not so far gone you need to treat me like an imbecile, girl. I'm not your mother."

The anger flared up abruptly, gnawing at her stomach, making her chest tight. Meiner stiffened and forced her expression into blankness, fists curled at her sides.

She was so fucking sick of this.

As Grandma King lapsed into her illness she did this more and more, going on about how foolish Meiner's mother was, how she should be grateful the woman didn't stay. How selfish Stephanie had been, cast out from the family manor, cut off from the King name forever. She'd grown up not knowing who she hated more, the woman who'd picked her boyfriend over her own family, or the one who'd forced her to make that decision Lately Grandma King was winning that particular contest.

"You're lucky she left. Now you'll get the coven."

Grandma King cackled and turned away. Cora was now glaring daggers at Meiner, who shrugged bad-temperedly. Cora overreacted every time the subject came up, and she didn't seem to clue in to the fact that Gran was very obviously trying to stir the pot.

Meiner had no intention of inheriting anything. She was gone as soon as she reached her full power. But she wasn't about to tell Cora that.

Gran was now following the tour guide over to where the family was standing. The husband looked them over briefly, shrugging, and the woman tugged the collar of her raincoat up under her chin, glaring at Grandma King.

Deborah launched into a history of the standing stones, raising her voice over the sound of the rain drumming on her umbrella. It would have been mildly interesting if Meiner's shoes hadn't been completely soaked.

The others looked unsure of this new development. Reagan pressed her lips together, brows furrowed, and Dayna shifted from foot to foot. Even Yemi looked impatient, glancing from Grandma King to the tour guide. Only the Callighans seemed unaffected. Brenna was even nodding along with some of the tour guide's "fun facts," a faint smile on her face, as if she found it all terribly interesting.

Somewhere near the end of the spiel both children ran into the field, and the parents followed after them. The tour guide trailed off, deflated. She tilted her umbrella back to look at Grandma King, and the rain sloughed off in miniature rivers.

"Nasty day out, isn't it?"

Grandma King smiled, and it wasn't a particularly nice smile. The tour guide didn't seem to notice. "Miserable."

There was silence then, and Meiner shifted impatiently. Her grandmother seemed to be waiting for something, like she was expecting the woman to just spit out a confession.

"Miserable," Grandma King repeated, and she smiled again.

Cora blew out another frustrated breath, and this time Meiner couldn't help but agree. She was opening her mouth to suggest they go, when the tour guide said:

"It's such a shame...." She paused, gaze drifting to the larger stone circle.

The other coven looked puzzled, but beside her Cora leaned forward eagerly.

There was her grandmother, standing unmoved by the rain and grinning like a hyena. *Shit, not again.*

The tour guide hesitated. "I'm sure you've seen it on the news. What happened to that woman."

Grandma King nodded, expression sorrowful. "Poor lass. They say she was found outside the stone circle. So strange."

"Inside." Deborah's voice was a dry whisper. Meiner barely heard it over the rain.

"What was that, dear?" Now her smile was downright grandmotherly, and Meiner felt a pang of disgust and horror.

"Oh, I was just... I was the one who found her. It was awful. She was inside the bigger circle." She pointed a shaking finger at the stones. "Just there."

"How horrible," Grandma King said with relish. She glided forward, taking the woman's arm. "You poor wee thing. It must have been traumatic."

"She was just *lying* there." The woman looked haunted, and Meiner noticed she was clutching a pendant on a chain around her neck, a silver replica of St. Brigid's cross. "She was... Her eyes."

"What about her eyes?" Grandma King was under the woman's umbrella now. Deborah's gaze was faraway and glassy, and she didn't seem to notice the old woman had weaseled her way into her personal space. Grandma King put a hand on her arm. "You tell us all about it."

Unease stirred Meiner's gut. She remembered the blank face of the garda as he rattled off the details of the crime scene. Deborah the tour guide had much the same look on her face now.

"They were still open, so wide." She gripped the handle of her umbrella with white fingers. "But that wasn't even the worst part. I . . . I shouldn't say."

Grandma King said nothing, only patted her arm. Beside her, Bronagh was watching, blue eyes narrowed. Meiner felt a pang of recognition. It wasn't just that Bronagh didn't *like* her gran, she didn't trust her.

"Her mouth was open, and . . . it was empty."

"Empty." Grandma King's voice was flat.

Deborah didn't look at her. She was trembling all over. "No teeth. No tongue. I can't close my eyes. I see it constantly. That and . . . the symbol."

"He left a symbol."

"It was on the rock in this awful rust color."

"Blood," Grandma King said softly, and Deborah nodded.

Laughter from the field made them glance up. The family was heading back, the littler child tucked under the father's arm, the wife looking thunderous as she dragged the older one by the hand.

Deborah's umbrella jerked in her hands. She blinked, expression bewildered. "Oh lord, I wasn't supposed to tell you that."

Grandma King patted her arm again. That hyena smile was back as she ducked out from under the umbrella and into the rain, making straight for the bigger stone circle.

Deborah wasted no time in bundling her customers back into the van, hurriedly waving good-bye to Grandma King. The old woman didn't notice. She was standing in the middle of the stone circle, a look of grim satisfaction on her face as she struck a match against one of the stones and used it to light a cigarette. The Callighans joined her there, passing their hands over one stone and then the next.

Meiner tried to remember exactly where the gardai had been standing when they'd driven up to the scene. She was fairly sure it had been in the center of one of the circles, where the grass was worn away, leaving shallow puddles in the shadows of the stones.

She hadn't seen a symbol, though.

Meiner wandered around the stone circles after the other witches, her shoes kicking up droplets on the wet grass. She wondered which stone had been marked. That tall one to the left, maybe, with the slanted top, or the flattest stone in the circle, almost tombstone-shaped. Someone could have written on that one pretty easily.

There was only silence now, save for the sound of the rain on the grass, and the witches' feverish mumbling. It was Brenna who found it. She moved a hand over the stone in the center, and something flickered under her palm.

A flash of rust red, and then slowly it seeped to the surface, a shape painted on the gray stone. It was strange, similar to a pentacle, but not one she'd seen before. There was no star inside, more like a complex pattern of crossed lines. It looked Celtic. And old.

Meiner couldn't hold back a shiver. It seemed sharp somehow, like the symbol itself might draw blood. It was vaguely familiar, too, though she couldn't place it. When she glanced over she was surprised to see Grandma King staring at the symbol with wide eyes. Her face had gone pale, and for a moment it looked like she was about to speak, but she merely shook her head.

Meiner frowned at her.

"Does anyone recognize it?" Reagan asked.

"It's familiar." Dayna looked frustrated. "Damn it, why do I feel like I should know this?"

"You're a little young." Bronagh's voice was heavy, and when they looked over at her she sighed. "It's a symbol I haven't seen in years, and one I'd hoped never to see again." She glanced sideways at Dayna. "That murder-obsessed ex-boyfriend of yours may have shown it to you."

Dayna's hand flew to her mouth. "Oh my god. It's a signature, isn't it?"

Cora looked annoyed. "A what?"

"A serial killer's mark," Bronagh explained. "Specifically the Butcher of Manchester's. He was all over the news years and years ago. They never caught him."

In the heavy silence that followed, Brenna let her hand drop, and the lines on the stone faded. Reagan nudged Dayna. "I'd say your ravens were definitely a bad omen."

"They're not *my* ravens," Dayna said, but her brow was creased with worry, her fingers tangled in the ends of her hair as she wrapped strands around them. Her obvious anxiety was unsettling to watch, and Meiner let her hand drift to her pocket, fingers closing over the reassuring shape of the pill bottle.

"Shit, Meiner, your gran."

Meiner turned at Cora's voice, realizing her grandmother was already halfway across the lawn toward the parking lot. Even from there they could hear her muttering angrily. "Those damn kids, trying to leave me behind."

It took Meiner a moment to realize where her grandmother was headed.

She sighed, glancing over at Cora, who looked exasperated. Then they both went after the old woman before she could climb into the van with the tourists.

Chapter Eleven

DAYNA

"Symbols in blood. How clichéd."

Reagan tapped her pencil on the flower-patterned teacup in front of her, frowning at her laptop—a battered hand-me-down with a chaotic assortment of rock-band stickers and NASA logos—where she'd pulled up a picture of the Butcher's calling card. This one was carved into a wall, but it was undeniably the same symbol. "You'd think someone offing witches would be more original."

"Why would a serial killer go after witches?" Cora demanded. "How does he even know who to target?"

Bronagh looked grim. "The only thing I know about him comes from the news, I'm afraid. I wasn't familiar with any of his victims."

Dayna stared at the picture on the screen, gut churning. The ravens had been disturbing enough, but this was far worse. Grandma King's warning about more witches dying had raised the hair on the back of her neck, and now it seemed chillingly accurate. The very term *serial* implied—no, *required*—more deaths. She kept glancing from Yemi and Reagan to the Callighans, trying not to picture losing any of them.

As far as she knew, there were few choices aside from her coven in town. A couple of hedge witches, maybe, a few people who dabbled in tarot in secret. But the real power in Carman was all here in this house. If someone was aiming to kill actual witches, the women in her coven might as well have giant targets on their backs.

"Okay, so, this serial killer." Cora glanced around at the others. "What do we actually know about him?"

There was a beat of silence as they stared at the screen, punctuated by the gentle clink of Brenna stirring sugar into her tea.

"We know he's got a Wikipedia page." Meiner held up her phone. "There's probably a dozen articles linked here."

"We know he's killing again, abi? And that he's able to tell who's a witch and who isn't." Reagan toyed with her choker, fingering the black stone in the front.

"Maybe he's a witch himself," Dayna said. Her thoughts were racing as she tried to imagine what that would mean. A killer who used magic was a terrifying thought, the twisted psyche of a serial killer mixed with the power of dark magic. She shuddered.

"Can't just be that." Reagan frowned. "First the ravens, and then this morning the news was going on about dead cows. Omens like that require serious juju, right?" She raised her brows at Bronagh, who nodded reluctantly.

"I'll get the scrying bowl." Yemi vanished into the living room.

"And I'll pray to the great oracle, Google." Reagan pulled the laptop back over.

Minutes later they'd assembled a makeshift research post at the long oak table, scattering notebooks and pencils between brass teapots and sugar tins, Reagan's computer set up on the metal tea tray to protect it from crumbs. The older witches were scrying and reading cards, save for Grandma King, who seemed to have lapsed into a kind of dazed silence, staring out the window above the sink. Meanwhile, Dayna, Cora, and Meiner watched over Reagan's shoulder as she pulled up article after article. Several times, Faye looked up from the shallow dish she was examining and muttered darkly about "witchlings these days."

After nearly an hour Reagan smacked her finger down on the exit button, her voice irritated. "There are so many articles, it's going to take hours to read through. And there's no hint of magic in any of these. He just seems like...a regular person."

"Oh sure. Killed people, diced them up, carved symbols all over the walls..." Cora said. "Totally regular behavior."

Reagan rolled her eyes. "You know what I mean. He's got no magic."

Dayna shifted, straightening up, her back protesting her hunched position. She was standing close enough that her arm brushed Meiner's, and the taller girl glanced at her, face unreadable. Dayna felt herself blush, which sent a flash of annoyance through her. "Um, do you mind backing up?"

"Well, excuse *me*, Your Majesty." Meiner took a step back, holding her hands out in front of her. "Didn't mean to offend your delicate sensibilities."

Dayna narrowed her eyes. "It's not my problem you don't have any sense of personal space."

"That's not it at all. It's just that you're so short I didn't notice you there." That annoying, cocky grin was back.

Yemi cleared her throat pointedly, and Dayna paused, feeling her face burn. The others were clearly pretending not to notice, save for Reagan, who looked as though she were trying to hold back laughter.

Meiner seemed to have a special way of pushing Dayna's buttons.

Thankfully Reagan came to her rescue. "Okay, let's think about the details of the murders. He takes a body part every time...maybe for some kind of ritual."

"Sure," Cora said, "but why witches specifically? And if Bronagh is right and the guy hasn't been active for years, why start now?"

"This isn't working." Faye shoved the bowl away bad-temperedly, and the water sloshed out over the tablecloth. This earned her a reproving look from Yemi. "None of this is going to work."

"We need hours and hours to assemble information, which we don't have." Brenna sighed. "We're running out of time."

"Or..." Reagan's eyes grew wide, and she looked sideways at Dayna.

"We need someone who has *already* devoted hours and hours to researching the Butcher."

It only took a second before it clicked, and Dayna groaned, shaking her head. "Are you really going to make me do this?"

Reagan shrugged apologetically. "You know I'd never suggest it unless it was literally a matter of life and death, but Faye's right. We don't know how much time we have."

"Let me guess." Meiner raised a brow. "The ex?"

Dayna ignored this, giving Reagan her most woeful look. "I hate you so much right now."

"You dumped him," Faye said pointedly. "It's not that bad."

"And it's painfully obvious he's still in love with you." Reagan grinned. "He'll probably hand over his life's work if you ask him."

Dayna waved a hand at them, face glowing hot. The very last thing she wanted was a discussion about her love life in front of Meiner King. "All right, okay," she said hastily. "I'll see what I can dig up."

Brenna was frowning, brows creased, and Dayna could guess what she was about to say. "It's okay," Dayna said. "Really. I got this."

"Of course she does." Faye jabbed one finger at Dayna. "You're strong. You're not going to put up with any of his church bullshit. Get in, get the information, get out."

Dayna cleared her throat, glancing at the floor. Meiner and Cora were both directing curious stares at her, and she had to force herself not to squirm in her chair. She *really* didn't want to have to explain anything to the new witches. Or talk about it at all, actually.

Brenna seemed to notice her discomfort, because she added hurriedly, "And in the meantime, what? If that doesn't pan out, what are we left with?"

"You know what I suggested before." Grandma King had turned from the window now, and she raised her thin eyebrows at Bronagh. "You know how effective it would be."

"And I can scarcely believe you have the balls to mention it to me again," Bronagh snapped. "We aren't doing a contact reading, King. If you know what's good for you, you won't let your witchlings do one either."

Grandma King scowled, tugging at the collar of her sweater. "I'll thank you not to tell me what to do with my own coven."

Dayna frowned at Reagan, puzzled, and Reagan shrugged. "What exactly is a contact reading?"

"Contact, as in, one of us must have come in contact with something the murderer touched, or the murderer himself." Bronagh gave them a sharp look. "And none of you are to ever attempt it."

Reagan gave a noncommittal shrug and kicked her boots up on the table. "I dunno, sounds like a solid plan to me."

Faye gave her a disapproving look and said, "Feet off the table, Reagan," at the same time Yemi cried, "Nawa o! Get your dirty boots off!"

Reagan rolled her eyes at Dayna. "This is why I never tell people about my two moms. They're so embarrassing."

Brenna ignored her. "Not a contact reading, then. A joint reading. With this many of us it should work."

There was a pause. The older witches glanced around the table at one another.

"We need at least seven for a joint reading, and there's only the five full witches," Yemi said. "That won't be enough power."

Bronagh was nodding thoughtfully. "But if they ascend, we could do one. It could work."

Yemi looked from the old woman to her daughter, frowning. "Their ascension isn't happening yet. They haven't picked their gods."

Brenna pressed her lips together, like she was fighting what she wanted to say. She gave Dayna and Reagan a meaningful look.

Dayna sat up straight. She'd picked her god years ago. Had known almost from the beginning she'd pledge to Danu. Reagan was the same way with the goddess Brigid, and when Dayna glanced over at her, her friend was leaning forward, hands on the table.

"Yes, we have, Ma. We've told you, we're ready."

"It's true. She's a great witch." When Reagan gave her a grateful look, she shrugged and grinned back. "What? You know it's true." Anyone could scry and read cards, but Reagan had dedicated herself to the craft her whole life, could recite every spell she'd ever learned.

"They're still young to have so much power." Yemi fidgeted with her teacup, turning it around on the saucer. "I don't know..."

Dayna pressed her lips shut, forcing herself not to comment, even though she felt ready to burst. She caught Meiner's eye almost accidentally and was startled at the look on her face. Meiner was staring at her grandmother with an expression Dayna couldn't pin down. Frustration? Longing?

Beside her, Cora shifted, her face eager. "*We're* ready—"

"Not you," Grandma King snapped, without looking at Cora or her granddaughter.

"But she just said they can't." She looked sullen, but Grandma King waved her off.

Brenna glanced nervously from her mother to Grandma King. "Er, well, best to do it on the first quarter moon. Tomorrow night, actually."

Faye nodded. "We'll have to pick one."

"We could do it together." It was Meiner who spoke now, and Dayna could see the look on her face had turned from frustration to hunger, probably more transparent than she realized. "Get it all done at once."

"Sorry, lass." Bronagh sounded apologetic. "You don't mix two covens' ascension days. It's too complicated to risk something going wrong."

"Reagan and Dayna are ready, Yemi. And we shouldn't wait," Brenna said gently. "Not with the way things are. With the way they may become."

Nobody had to ask what she meant.

"Aye, you're right. Tomorrow night," Grandma King said. "We'll do it then."

"It should be us," Meiner said, and Dayna sat up straight, anger pulsing through her.

"Hell no," Dayna said. "If anyone ascends it's Reagan and me." The scorching glare Meiner shot her now was nothing like the minor irritation and amusement from earlier. She scowled back, arms folded over her chest.

If Meiner wanted a fight, she was going to get one.

"It should be us," Meiner repeated, turning back to Grandma King. "Cora and I are both ready. And we're older."

"By, like, two years," Reagan protested.

"We've been practicing magic longer; it just makes sense," Cora said, and then scowled as Reagan cut her a sideways look and sucked her teeth.

Grandma King ignored Meiner. "Dayna's right. We're on your home turf, Bronagh, so we'll assist you with yours."

There was silence, and everyone looked at Yemi, who finally sighed heavily and said, "Oh, all right, then. I suppose it was going to be inevitable."

Dayna felt her chest swell with excitement. Beside her, Reagan burst up from her chair and hugged her, and Dayna laughed as she jumped up and down. Then she danced halfway around the table to hug her mother, and Yemi smiled reluctantly and patted her arm.

Dayna glanced over at Meiner. The older girl was staring at her grandmother with the kind of pure loathing that made a shiver drop down her back. A second later it was gone, and Meiner's face was completely composed again. Like a marble mask.

If she'd blinked, Dayna thought, she might have missed it.

But why should she feel bad? This was just as much their right. And she'd been waiting for ages. She hadn't counted on it coming so soon; she'd thought it would be at least another year. A witchling was supposed to be able to ascend as soon as she hit her sixteenth birthday, but Yemi had been so cautious. When they'd both turned seventeen, Reagan had joked despairingly that they would be Bronagh's age by the time they were allowed.

But now she might be a mere day from a direct connection to her goddess, to becoming a full witch.

She felt like she was vibrating in her chair; the excitement was really setting in. Soon she and Reagan would be full witches.

And the most important part: ascending meant having access to the type of power that could help protect her coven. They were stronger if she and Reagan ascended. Safer from whatever they might have to face.

There was a sudden *thud*, and Dayna jerked, startled. Cora had shot up, tipping her chair over. She scowled at Grandma King. For a moment it seemed she was about to say something, then she stomped out of the kitchen and vanished down the hall.

The witches looked at one another, all but Meiner, who stared straight ahead, her body rigid. Dayna could see a muscle in her jaw twitching. It looked like she was debating following Cora.

Dayna almost wished she would.

"Good." Bronagh nodded sharply, as if that settled it. Apparently it did, because Grandma King began to shuffle for the stairs.

"Very well. The quarter moon it is."

Chapter Twelve

DAYNA

When Dayna came downstairs on Sunday morning, she found her father at the kitchen table with an unfamiliar woman. She had long, pin-straight hair, the same brown as Dayna's. Her eyes were dark and set a little too deep, perhaps made more obvious by the bruise-like shadows underneath. The woman's eyebrows were very thick and black, and they knit together as she stared at Dayna.

A great deal of things hit her at once. Recognition first, swiftly followed by horror.

Your mother's coming home this weekend, her father had said. *She's doing well enough to be released.*

She'd completely pushed it out of her mind after everything that happened.

Dayna had seen pictures of Fiona before—there were portraits hanging in the guest room—but the woman at the table barely looked like that person anymore. It occurred to her exactly how little she knew about her.

When Dayna was younger, her father had explained that Fiona Walsh had gone away because she was very sick, and camp was full of fresh air. And she'd believed him for a while. Until little things began chipping away at this story. Dayna remembered the day she'd told Reagan, how her friend's reaction had made her realize other families didn't simply send people away.

A year later, she'd found flyers for Camp Blood of the Lamb in the church office and discovered people were sent there when they didn't fit in with the church. When they were unstable, or sinful. Or they were simply inconvenient.

After this realization, things had been different. Church members had commented to her father about what a quiet child she was. How well-behaved. Nobody knew it was because Dayna was petrified of being sent away. If she screamed too loud at a birthday party. If she cried when she fell down. If she didn't do her homework.

If she made her father angry, he might send her away.

Fiona's thirteen-year stay at camp seemed to have drained all color from her face and narrowed her down. She was incredibly skinny, collarbone showing above the sleeveless cardigan she wore. Her arms jutted out at her sides, pencil thin, and she held her teacup awkwardly, like she wasn't sure what to do with it. She sat very straight in her seat.

All Dayna could think in that moment was *What the hell did they do to this woman?*

The reverend spoke first. "Dayna, this is Fiona."

As if he were introducing her to a friend at brunch.

The woman at the table stood, unfolding long limbs. As she moved toward Dayna, it felt rather like being approached by a praying mantis. She lifted an arm, and Dayna flinched, almost expecting some sort of awkward embrace. Instead the woman's hand darted out, and she seized something between her finger and thumb. Her necklace, Dayna realized.

Fiona Walsh plucked at the cross pendant, examining it with a strangely intense interest. "This is an interesting piece."

"Saint Brigid's cross," Dayna said automatically, still staring at the woman's face.

"How lovely. I don't wear jewelry. It tends to—" She stopped abruptly, her face blank, still staring at the charm pinched between her fingers.

The reverend was there suddenly, looming over them. He took Fiona's arm and steered her back toward the table, his face grave. "Did you take your medication yet today?"

Fiona blinked rapidly. "Oh yes. I did, this morning before you picked me up."

Dayna watched this exchange, a bitter, ashy sort of taste growing in her mouth. He'd pulled her away so quickly, and the way he was looking at Fiona now . . . it was strange.

The entire thing was strange, actually. For years she'd snuck into the guest room and stared at the pictures on the wall, wondering what Fiona had been like before she'd grown sick and left. And now here she was in the flesh, and she was nothing like Dayna had imagined. She wasn't sure what she'd expected, but she didn't feel anything when she looked at her. Maybe a faint sense of trepidation.

Suddenly she was quite certain she didn't want to be here. Not with the reverend, and certainly not with this strange woman she didn't recognize.

She turned, stepping into the hallway. "I think I need a minute."

The reverend frowned. Stepping forward, he took her arm and bent close, dropping his voice low. "Listen, Dayna, she's here because she's better. We can finally be a family again."

She clamped her lips shut, even though she wanted to tell him she knew what he was trying to do, and that it wasn't going to work. It was too late. He couldn't absolve himself of guilt or make things better by trying to make them a family again. He had irreversibly screwed that up three months ago.

Besides, she already had a family, and he wasn't a part of it.

Dayna turned on her heel, blood thundering in her ears. "I'm sorry, I can't do this. I'm going back to Reagan's."

"I'd rather you didn't—"

There was a soft shuffle from the kitchen, and Fiona's voice drifted from the doorway. "Anthony?"

The reverend paused, clearly torn. Then he shook his head. "Be home by ten."

Dayna drove aimlessly. Down the highway and onto the back roads. She had no idea where she was going, but it felt good to be heading...away. Out of the village and into the green plains of the countryside. The wind blew her hair back and filled her lungs, and she breathed in, the turmoil of her emotions starting to dissolve bit by bit, her hands becoming steadier on the wheel. A bend in the road revealed the open skyline, and just above the rolling fields was the quarter moon.

Dayna frowned. Seeing the moon during the day wasn't that unusual, but it seemed so much larger than it should have been, as if it had moved closer to the earth in the last few hours. And it was red, a deep crimson that, Dayna noted uneasily, was precisely the color of blood.

She pulled up to a stop sign, letting the car idle.

She couldn't help remembering what Bronagh and Grandma King had both said: *Something dark is coming.*

She wanted to keep driving, to pretend it was nothing. It was campfires and smoke in the air, or a season thing...a blood moon. You could google it and pull up charts about when the moon waned and waxed, what was a wolf moon and what was a blood moon.

But she knew what a bad omen looked like. Ravens, dead cows, blood moons. *Serious juju*, wasn't that what Reagan called it?

Her concentration was broken a second later by movement in her rearview mirror, and Dayna jumped. There was a sleek black car behind her, waiting to turn at the stop sign. She'd been sitting there staring at the sky like an idiot. She jammed the gearshift, and the hatchback jerked forward with a wheezy cough.

Chapter Thirteen

DUBH

"**D**o you see this?" The car in front of him, a red hatchback with black doors, lurched forward. Dubh kept his gaze fixed on it, waiting while the car turned and began to head back into Carman. There was no way he was about to lose her gawking at the moon.

"Yeah." His brother's voice on the phone was a low growl. "We knew that was coming. Just get here already. Where are you?"

He tapped the gas, jetting through the stop sign before slowing. The witch seemed to be driving aimlessly, even recklessly. "This witch is on the list—"

"I *told* you," Calma said sternly. "The book first. We need to confirm she's one. We can't keep going on animal instinct, as much as that might appeal to you."

There was a distant cackle in the background, and a muscle in Dubh's jaw twitched as Olc said, "Tell him he's not the Butcher of Manchester, scourge of the countryside, any longer."

Anger flashed through him. He'd *told* them not to call him that. It conjured images of savagery, when he was in fact, precise. Not surgical exactly, but he was getting better.

"Don't call me that."

"Just get here," Calma said. "And, Dubh, don't touch her until I give you the go-ahead."

The call cut out, and Dubh ripped the phone away from his ear, slinging it onto the passenger side, where it cracked into the door.

How like his brothers to come into town and take over the whole operation. To take what was rightfully his. This was his mission, and his witch to kill. One of his brothers would inevitably try to take her away from him, like they always did. But this time he wasn't going to let it happen.

The girl in the beat-up car was something special, and he was going to have her.

His tongue slipped over his tooth, the jagged canine on the left side. *That* had been a good fight. He needed another one, soon. He could feel the need burning his insides, slowly creeping into his head. When it happened, his vision began to turn, a slight blur at first, crimson around the edges.

Again he glanced up at the skyline, at the low-hanging moon. This was not his vision. It was the cycle kicking into gear, as it always had. As it always would until his goal was accomplished.

The judge had been boring. Easy to lure in and overcome. There had been no joy in it, but it was a catalyst. Things were finally starting.

That afternoon, Dubh found himself standing in the center of a crumbling stone castle, watching the sun sink past the horizon. Pinpricks of orange light stabbed his eyes through the cracks in the stones.

"There's nothing." He glared around at the worn castle walls. "This is too open; she'd never leave the book here."

Calma, who'd been examining the moss-stained stones around them as if he expected the book to magically appear, gave Dubh a narrow look. "Have you remembered anything else?"

The question only enhanced his bad mood. Dubh's fingers curled into fists at his sides. "No," he hissed. "But I know we're wasting time."

"You're the one who said we should look at sacred sites." Calma lowered his voice as a group of tourists was led past by a round-faced tour guide in a bulky vest. "And now you've better things to do?"

He darted a sideways look at Olc, who appeared to be taking out his foul temper on the castle, chipping away at the wall with the blade of a rusted hunting knife. For a moment there was silence, punctuated by the patter of rain striking the stones. He looked down at the gaudy plastic flyer crumpled in his fist. Another crumbling castle full of tourists.

That's what this entire place was about, standing around staring at a great heap of bloody rocks.

He could be hunting right now.

Dubh longed for the days he did his work alone. When he'd hunted things that screamed and bled and pleaded with him. He'd hurtled through the underbrush, boughs breaking in his path, his hot breaths falling into rhythm to match his feet, Witchkiller clutched in his hand. He remembered long, wild hair in his fists and terrible screams, how they'd thrilled through his blood.

He'd always hunted the women. The witches.

For days he would be driven to track each of them, six at a time, always six. Sometimes one brother would be with him, sometimes both. But the best hunts were the ones he spent on his own.

Once it was done there was the period of rest, of blackness, of void. Of this he remembered nothing. And each time he awoke, the cycle would begin again.

This time, though, it was different. This time it was...complicated. The feeling that led him was strange, more urgent than ever before.

And still, all he wanted to do was *hunt*.

Instead, he was looking for a half-dreamed book in a crumbling tourist trap.

"Let's go." Olc jammed his knife back into his jacket, glancing up at the gray sky in disgust. "It's pissing down rain again. Even the damn humans have enough sense to clear out."

Dubh glanced around the ruins, surprised to see Olc was right. They were the only ones left. There was only the patter of rain and the distant sound of muffled voices as people made their way back to the parking lot.

"We sweep the place once more," Calma said.

The pure confidence in his voice—as if he expected, no, he *knew* he would be obeyed—grated on Dubh.

"We're wasting time. We should just go kill the witches," Dubh said.

"Why is murder always your answer to everything?" Olc sneered. Then he shrugged and turned to Calma. "But he's right. This is fucking useless. Let's go get food."

"You're thinking with your gut again," Calma grumbled. "We're staying."

"How about you blow me," Olc said, but he made no move to leave. This was the way it was. Olc was chaos. Calma was order. They fought constantly, but Calma put up with the insults as long as Olc did as he was told. And Dubh...Dubh was simply the youngest, always the bottom rung. Expected to go along with whatever his brothers said. To let his brothers take over his mission and make the decisions, to let them take the glory.

But not this time.

This was his time. His mission. And the freckle-faced witch was his.

Chapter Fourteen

CORA

"If we joined covens, we *could* do the ascension," Meiner said.

Cora glared at her. Meiner had been pacing the floor of Cora's guest bedroom for the past fifteen minutes.

Cora wanted to ascend, probably more than Meiner. Knowing the other witchlings would have a head start on them, that their power would shift from a trickle to a flood and they would leave her behind in the minor leagues, well, it rankled. She'd been practicing actual spells for years, preparing for when she'd have the power, leaving simple crap like scrying and tarot behind. Card tricks and staring into bowls of water no longer held her interest, and praying to the gods in hopes that one of them cared enough to lend a trickle of power was demeaning. But it didn't mean she wanted Reagan and Dayna in the coven.

"We're not joining," Cora snapped. "We don't need them." Especially not the stupid tea girl. This she didn't add, because she could already see the anger on Meiner's face as she swung around to stare at her.

"It's the only way we could do our ascension."

"Who exactly are you trying to convince? It's not like either of us is calling the shots here." She knew her voice sounded sullen; she couldn't help it. The coven should be hers when Grandma King died, not Meiner's.

For multiple reasons, number one being that it was her birthright. Her mother had been the leader when Cora was very young. She'd died suddenly, and without warning, and Grandma King had stepped into the role and never left. But that meant she, Cora, should be the next in line when the old woman was gone. It was only fair.

Besides, she knew Meiner better than she knew herself, and Meiner didn't actually want the coven. She dreaded the thought of following in her grandmother's footsteps. Cora could see the conflict on her face whenever the subject came up.

Meiner turned away, falling silent, and Cora picked at the flower-print bedspread. Meiner had been pissed off since the meeting. Cora was, too, of course, but a part of her was at least happy about Meiner's reaction to the whole thing. How she'd snapped at Dayna.

Now there was no way anything would happen between them.

Cora hated Meiner. But mostly, she hated the way Meiner made her feel. Full of spite and rage and hurt. But worst of all was the confusion. Cora was nearly always certain of what she wanted, except when it came to Meiner.

She wanted to be Meiner, or she wanted to be *with* Meiner. Or... It was too much to even think about. It made the rage in the pit of her stomach reignite all over again.

But as much as she hated to admit it, Dayna was exactly to Meiner's taste: the splash of freckles over her cheeks, the delicate hoop of her nose ring, the curve of her lips. When she'd come around the corner at Sage Widow and turned her full attention on Cora, it'd been almost startling. Something about her eyes was terribly haunted. Of course Meiner was fascinated by her; she was probably painting some contrived picture of sweeping in to rescue her from something.

Meiner could be annoyingly noble like that.

Cora huffed a sigh and collapsed onto the bed. They were holed up in her guest room until suppertime, since neither of them was comfortable hanging around the kitchen with Reagan and her mother. She could hear them out there now. Apparently Reagan had grown too enthusiastic while gesturing with a wooden spoon, and flicked the contents of her mixing bowl all over the tapestry on the wall—"That took Bronagh hours to make. Gods, girl, you've got butter all over Lugh!"—and Cora didn't feel like dealing with their annoyingly high levels of energy.

They were in Cora's room less out of choice and more out of habit. Cora was used to having the other girl around. They were cut from the same cloth, she and Meiner, ambitious and driven, burning with *want*.

There was a shuffle and thump from outside in the hall, and both girls stiffened as Grandma King's low muttering drifted past outside the door. Cora relaxed as the noise trailed off, and the thud of footfalls on the stairs followed.

She darted a look at Meiner, who had relaxed back against the window frame.

You had to be a special kind of fucked up to survive being raised by Harriet King.

Man-eater, the rumors called her.

The first time Meiner had told her was when Cora had just moved in. They'd been thirteen and fourteen, getting adjusted to staying in the same bedroom. She remembered how Meiner had looked leaning over the side of her bunk, her long white hair ghostly in the half darkness, telling horror stories about the old woman.

She ate men to fuel her magic. She'd pledged herself to the devil. She had a freezer full of body parts in the basement.

If asked straight out, both Cora and Meiner would tell you that, of course, they were just ridiculous rumors. But sometimes Cora would catch a certain look on the old woman's face, a kind of dark glitter in her eyes. And neither girl ever ventured out of their bedroom at night.

It was easier to brush things off that way. Like the shadows that lurked in the corners of the old house a little too long after sunrise, or the scrape and bump in the basement after everyone was in bed. If you didn't look or listen too hard, it didn't exist.

They'd survived together.

She kicked the side of the mattress with her heels, watching Meiner as she leaned forward to look out the window, white hair obscuring her face.

"We should be the ones ascending tonight. We'll be stronger than they will," Cora said. "They haven't had to struggle to survive. They're not like us."

Meiner glanced back over her shoulder, frowning. "There is no *us*. Don't try to pretend we're some kind of team."

Cora narrowed her eyes at Meiner. Being disagreeable was Meiner's way of dealing with her hurt, though she'd never admit it. She'd seen the look on her face when Grandma King had sided with the other witchlings. Cora wasn't sure why Meiner had expected the old woman to back them up; she wasn't that sort of person.

Their coven was not like the Carman coven. She'd seen the pictures on the wall and nearly pulled a muscle rolling her eyes. A gathering of witches did not automatically equal a family. You did not go on picnics and pose for portraits. It was completely ridiculous. But of course Meiner was reacting badly to seeing the way they were. Like it was something she was missing out on.

It shouldn't surprise her. Again and again, she'd seen some small part of Meiner that hadn't frozen over yet. Hadn't hardened.

That part made her weak. Would get her killed if she wasn't careful.

She closed the distance between them, leaning one shoulder against the window frame so Meiner was forced to look at her. "Don't try to pretend. There'll always be an *us*, whether you like it or not."

It hadn't been Dayna who'd been there for Meiner so many times after her grandmother had screamed at her, or put her through some ridiculous ordeal for "training." She distinctly remembered one incident before Gran had started turning senile. Cora hadn't been sure of the details, but she'd heard Gran screaming, and Meiner had retreated to their bedroom with a bloody gash down her cheek. She'd refused to talk about it, but Cora knew the mark was from the raven skull ring the old woman wore.

She still wasn't sure who'd initiated the kiss, if it had been her or Meiner, but she knew what followed. They'd gone from roommates to more.

Of course, that had ended as abruptly as it began once Gran poisoned

Meiner's mind, telling her Cora only wanted the coven. That she'd use anything to get power.

It wasn't a lie. Cora *would* do anything to get what she wanted. The fact that Meiner was incredibly hot was only a bonus.

But of course, Meiner had played the saint, acting disgusted, as if she hadn't been using Cora as much as Cora was trying to use her.

That had been almost a year ago, and Meiner liked to pretend it hadn't happened.

Meiner's face went dark. "If you're referring to us being together, that's never happening again."

Cora rolled her eyes and leaned closer. "Are you telling me you never think about it? Not once?"

"Back off, Cora." Meiner pushed herself away from the windowsill. Cora could see the tightness in her shoulders, the tic in her jaw, and the flush in her pale cheeks. She knew she shouldn't poke the bear, but Meiner made it so easy.

She stepped into Meiner's path. "You know it will end up happening again. You can only take so much of your gran before you do something a little reckless. And you've got to admit—"

Cora flinched when Meiner reached out and grasped her shoulders, expression full of unveiled fury. "You were a *mistake*, Cora. Get that into your head." Meiner's face was an inch away from hers, her voice a low, furious growl. "A moment of bad judgment and a personal low point for me. It's *never* happening again."

There was a beat of silence after that, and then Meiner released her and turned for the door. "We should make sure Gran is ready for supper."

Cora stayed frozen to the spot. Her face was burning, and her limbs felt strangely heavy. It was hard to swallow, her throat was so tight. *A personal low point . . .*

Meiner turned back to her, brows raised.

"You do it." Cora forced herself to speak, and her voice wobbled slightly. She hated herself for it. "She's your gran."

This wasn't strictly fair, since Grandma King had raised her after her useless aunt had kicked her out at thirteen. Still, it wasn't Cora that Gran was giving the coven to.

Meiner was still staring at her, solemn-faced, and Cora kept her expression blank. A fire had started in the pit of her stomach, and she wanted to scream.

Fuck you, Meiner King.

She looked away first, hating herself for it.

Meiner turned without saying anything and disappeared from the room.

In the kitchen, Yemi was chopping vegetables, and Reagan was tossing handfuls of carrots into a brass cauldron above the fireplace. Cora saw Meiner eye this setup with interest, and something about it raised her hackles. What if Meiner decided instead of combining the two covens, she'd just join the Carman coven herself? They wouldn't let her, would they? If you were an unattached witch it was almost impossible to find a coven. You had to be related, or old family friends, like her mother and Grandma King had been. Someone had to vouch for you. And there was certainly no jumping from one coven to another, as there was little if any contact between them. But Meiner had already met the others, so they might skip the vetting process. The thought made Cora's stomach twist.

Bad judgment. A mistake.

Meiner had made it clear she didn't belong with Cora. That, in spite of growing up together, in spite of being *together* in the way they had, she felt no loyalty.

Her fingers curled into fists at her sides, nails biting into her palms. Cora forced her expression into blankness.

Reagan flicked on the radio above the microwave. The news was saying something about crops dying, whole apple orchards and fields of strawberries. Meiner and Cora exchanged a glance, and Meiner's pale brows lifted.

More omens.

The dry shuffling of nylon compression socks on the tiles signaled Grandma King's entrance from the living room. She paused in the doorway and huffed a long sigh.

"Dinner will be ready in fifteen," Reagan said, then paused as her phone pinged, frowning down at the screen.

"Good." Grandma King turned to Cora. "Help me up to my room, witchling. I forgot to change out of these damn socks, and they're squeezing the life out of me feet."

Cora wanted to protest, but she was careful to keep her face straight while she waited for Grandma King to shuffle over. She put her elbow out, and Gran hooked one skinny arm into hers.

Resentment crashed through her, making her uncharacteristically silent as they made their way up. Why couldn't Meiner help her own grandmother up the steps?

Because, a nasty little voice in her head chimed in, *Meiner is the next High Witch and above things like this.*

She helped the old woman up yet another step, slowly, so slowly.

Grandma King seemed to run out of steam halfway. She stopped in the middle of the staircase, and Cora turned, sighing. She froze.

They were eye to eye, and something in the old woman's face had changed. There was an air of razor sharpness about her. The way her dark eyes glittered. The smile that curved her mouth.

"Gran—Mrs. King?"

Grandma King said nothing for a moment, just squeezed Cora's arm more tightly. "I have a proposition."

Cora blinked. She didn't seem to be able to get her tongue to work.

"My granddaughter is not prepared for what's coming." Grandma King's expression was stony, and Cora repressed a shudder. Here was the woman people talked about, the King Witch.

"I've tried to raise her to be ready to take on the mantle of leadership when the time came. When *this* time came. But it's grown clear she isn't strong enough. She lets emotion guide her. She is weak." The old woman spat this last sentence, and Cora forced herself not to flinch. She didn't like Meiner, exactly, but it was disturbing to hear her grandmother talk like this.

Still, what she was saying...?

Fire flared to life in the pit of her stomach. "What do you mean?"

"I'm saying you'll have to do, lass," Grandma King snapped. "You're vindictive and cunning and if you're trained properly, you'll be ready when the time comes. Meiner will never. That's why I stopped her training and she hasn't ascended."

"I *knew* it!" She should feel angry. Gran had been putting them off for ages. It would have been easy to chalk it up to her dementia, but Cora had had a sneaking suspicion she knew exactly what she was doing. She'd been right.

Her throat was tight with longing. All she'd ever wanted was this moment, though she'd imagined it with her mother. Even at thirteen, before her mother had become sick and handed over the mantle to Grandma King, she'd imagined what it would feel like. To have her mother hand over the title, the power that would fill her, the thrill of realizing she was in charge.

Still, she would take this, whatever the hell it was.

"If you train with me, it won't be easy. Not by half." Grandma King held a crooked finger up. "It will break you and put you back together. You'll go through a series of tests the likes of which you cannot dream."

It felt like the air had been stolen from her lungs. This was it, what she'd been waiting for. What she'd dreamed of for so long.

And yet, she knew it was a betrayal.

But Meiner's voice still rang in her ears.

A personal low point...

"I'll do it."

"You're sure?" Grandma King gave her a sharp look. "No hesitation?"

"I want this." She could hear the eagerness in her voice, and she wasn't ashamed. She wanted what she wanted. "I'll do anything."

"Anything." Grandma King's voice was flat, but her bright eyes combed over Cora's face, and she pulled the collar of her sweater a little closer around the left side of her throat. "You'll have to be fair certain of that. The kind of magic you'll need for what's coming isn't like anything you've experienced."

"I don't care." She was defiant now, stretched to her full height. "I'll do whatever it takes."

"Good." Gran fished in the wide pockets of her sweater, coming out with a thin glass tube. Cora watched as the old woman held it out, the dark rust-red liquid inside washing back and forth. "Take it."

Her hand shook slightly as she did so. The glass was cool beneath her fingers. "What is it?"

Gran ignored the question. "Drink it when you are alone, but only if you want this. There's no going back."

Cora nodded and thrust the tube into her pocket, throat tight.

"And, Cora, a word to the wise...I see how you prod at my granddaughter."

Cora opened her mouth to protest and then cut herself off when Grandma King raised a hand. "Don't underestimate Meiner's temper. She's not herself. Hasn't been for months." Grandma King turned away. Abruptly she was an old woman again, making her shuffling way down the stairs, gripping the railing. "Get me downstairs, lass. We're missing all the action."

Cora did as she was told, silent, triumphant. By the time they reached the bottom she'd composed herself, her face a mask of calm. But that fire had flared to life. It burned hot and strong in the pit of her stomach, and nothing could put it out.

Chapter Fifteen
SAMUEL

The basement was where he stored the charts.

At fourteen he'd begged his father to turn the drab, concrete square into a rec room. Over the years he'd scored a pair of overstuffed armchairs and a matching couch, as well as a huge old TV at various yard sales, and built a couple of shelves against the wall that he'd filled with paperback novels.

The focal point of the room was the bedsheet pinned to the wall, a print of a classic *Star Wars* poster. Sam had first hung it claiming he wanted to cover the cracks in the concrete.

Only he and Dayna knew what was actually behind it.

Dayna. He'd practically jumped out of his seat in the middle of the church service when she'd texted this morning. She wanted to talk, and considering that the town was buzzing with gossip and speculation, he had a pretty good idea why. Sure, that wasn't exactly why he'd been hoping she'd text, but he was picturing them poring over this thing, spending long evenings together, just the two of them.

Maybe she'd remember how good they were together. Maybe he could remind her.

He took the stairs two at a time, not bothering to lock the basement door behind him. Locked doors would be questioned, and besides, the stairs were so creaky it would give him ample warning if anyone were to make their way down.

Sam drew the sheet back slowly.

He kept the charts well hidden, since he knew what reaction they'd get. His father would flip out, and his mother would pray over him.

The sheer breadth of his obsession wasn't lost on him.

His "murder board," as he called it, had once held other unsolved cases, but the moment he'd realized the Butcher's pattern, he'd been hooked. It was a puzzle that needed solving.

The top portion of the charts was all timeline, stretching out from one side of the wall to the other.

1990—First kill?

First Use of Symbol: 2000, 6 in Manchester

2010, 5 on Isle of Man: Injured or killed?

Darting another look at the stairs, he unlocked his phone and checked in on the forums again. His post had only received a few hits from die-hard Butcher fans and amateur investigators who hadn't been able to let the case go.

He hadn't included much information, not wanting it to be traced back to him. Just that there was a murder and a rumor around town the Butcher's mark had been found at the scene.

He scrolled through the posts.

CrimeBuff69: If he resurfaces every ten years, then the timing is right.

TheCrunchyPuff: Bro, this would be in the news if this was true.

BananaSplit25: If OP is right, then this is a major cover-up.

JStofferton: Why choose in the middle of buttfuck nowhere to find new victims? Doesn't make sense.

CrimeBuff69: Unfinished business?

The last poster had shared a link to the same video Sam had seen floating around the internet over and over, with the title "The One That Got Away?" It was leaked security footage from years ago, of the barn where the last victim had been attacked. Sam had already seen it dozens of times, but he clicked on it anyway.

The main focus was the stalls—the owner had apparently installed the camera because of a neighbor's dog— but in the left-hand corner you could make out the broad red wall of the barn just beyond. There was a flash of movement as someone came running into view, a blur of gray and black. A taller figure pursued the first, and when the first one turned, long gray hair flying out behind her, the taller one lashed out, something in his fist glittering in the sunlight.

The first figure went down, out of sight of the camera lens, and a moment later the second walked casually out of view after her.

The first time he'd seen it he'd been chilled to his core, but now it just frustrated him. Who was the woman, and how did she get away after that? According to popular theory, the killer had slashed her with some kind of blade. It should have been a killing blow, but the gardai hadn't found her at the scene, and the killer never buried bodies or hid them—he left them out to be found—so it stood to reason she'd escaped. That she was alive and out there somewhere.

He replayed it again, watching as the figure turned, gray hair flying. The judge, she'd had long gray hair... hadn't she?

Sam chewed the inside of his cheek, hitting the replay button. *The one that got away.*

Was the last poster right? Was it possible the killer was picking up where he'd left off by going after Judge O'Toole? But why wait so long?

A faint chime came from somewhere overhead, and Sam hastily shoved his phone into his pocket, reaching up to pin the sheet back into place. He could hear his mother's footsteps as she went to get the door, and her muffled greeting. His pulse picked up when the basement door clicked open, and Dayna's voice floated down the staircase. "Sam?"

"Come on down." He kept the sheet in place, just in case his mother wandered down with her.

Dayna appeared around the corner. The sight of her was almost enough to knock him back a step. All the longing and guilt seemed to crash together in his stomach at once. It made him feel a little nauseous, actually. This was the first time in three months he'd seen her outside school.

He gave her what he hoped was an easy grin. "Ma let you in without giving you the third degree?"

Dayna shrugged, letting her bag drop to the ground beside one of the armchairs. "She didn't beg me to get back together with you, if that's what you mean."

He winced. His mother made no secret of the fact she thought he and Dayna should cut out "all their nonsense" and get back together. He was pretty sure she was already planning the wedding. Not because she loved Dayna, but because his mother was a devout disciple of the reverend.

As if his being with Dayna would get his mother bonus points with God or something.

He had to bite his tongue now, because he agreed with his mother about one thing—he and Dayna should be together. The gossip and rumors had been bad, yes. Everyone wanted to talk about the reverend's daughter "coming out" as gay. Or bisexual, as Dayna insisted.

Of course people had talked; it was a small town.

Though not even the town gossips seemed to know what had happened between Dayna and her father. He knew it was something that had turned the relationship from tense to completely sour. That she'd pulled away from anything to do with the church. Including Sam.

Once again, he tried to push the guilt down. It hadn't been his fault. He hadn't been the one to tell people at school. Besides, people were already moving on. With the attack of crazed birds and a murder on top of it, no one would even remember there'd been rumors.

"Yeah," he muttered, "sorry about her. Uh, how's Reagan? She still want to be an astronaut or whatever?"

"Astrophysicist."

Reagan Etomi and Sam had never got along; in fact, the first time he'd met Dayna's friend she'd called him a "total douchelord" right to his face. Whatever that meant. He couldn't remember what had provoked the insult. Something about his faith, no doubt. Or maybe his Bible study.

Reagan was aggressively atheist, a trait he'd found off-putting.

"She's fine. I'm sure she'll be thrilled to hear you asked. How's Morgan?" She pressed her lips together, and Sam thought she was probably trying to hold a grin back. "How's her face?"

Sam gave her a weak smile. "She's fine."

Dayna had caught Morgan flipping through one of her notebooks during a free period. It hadn't been more than a few days after the resulting blowup that the rumors had begun circulating. Dayna had made it obvious she thought Morgan was responsible.

"Um, how are you?" He frowned, looking at her a little more closely. She looked...stressed. "Are you okay?"

Dayna sighed. "Well, I'm sure you'll hear about it soon enough anyway. Dad brought Fiona home."

"Whoa, really? What happened at camp?" He regretted it as soon as the question came out of his mouth.

Dayna flinched as if he'd struck her and then tried to hide her discomfort a moment later, wiping her face clear of emotion. "Apparently she's cured. Anyway, part of the reason I texted you is because I need to be distracted. Honestly, I don't want to think about it right now. It's too weird."

Sam bit the inside of his cheek, fighting back all the questions he wanted to ask. Dayna reacted badly whenever anyone brought up the camp, or her mother, or her father, or the Bible study...anything to do with church, actually.

Sometimes a conversation with her felt like tiptoeing on a thin sheet of ice.

She'd already turned her attention to the wall, sinking down on the couch to stare up at it. "So, tell me...what's going on? I'm hearing it could be the Butcher."

"You are?" Sam frowned. As far as he knew, his father had his men keeping it quiet.

"Well, I may have a special source." Dayna tilted her head and raised her brows.

"Ah, gotcha." Of course, the reverend knew everything that went on in this town. Though...it was a little surprising he was sharing secrets with Dayna. He'd been under the impression they rarely spoke. "Yeah, all right. I'm pretty sure it's the Butcher."

"I figured. I guess your dad investigated the scene. I'm guessing he won't tell you anything?"

"No, but look at this." He propped his laptop on the edge of the couch and sat down beside her, very conscious of how close she was, her knee brushing his as she leaned forward to look at the screen.

"I'm the original poster." He darted a look at her as he pulled up his profile, AnonAmen. "I don't have an avatar or profile info, just in case." He gave her a serious look. "You can't tell *anyone*. My dad would kill me."

"Got it." Dayna leaned forward, peering at the screen. He could smell her perfume, vanilla and cinnamon. Her hair fell over one shoulder, and he wondered how soft it would feel right now, tried not to remember the sensation of running his fingers through it.

Dayna read the post under her breath. "Gardai released statement, no foul play. Sergeant determined to keep things under wraps." Her brows shot up, and she looked over at Sam, who felt his face burning.

"You don't sound impressed with your dad."

"I think he's going to bungle this really badly." It came out before he could stop it. But...it was true. He was a true-crime fanatic. He'd seen every serial-killer doc in existence, and his father was doing everything wrong.

"That makes me like you so much more." Dayna grinned, and her expression set something on fire inside him. He thought about reaching out, putting his hand on her leg. But she stood abruptly, turning toward the sheet on the wall.

"And this?"

Sam shut his laptop and got to his feet. When he followed Dayna to the far wall he reached up and pulled the pin out, letting the sheet drop back. Dayna's eyes went wide.

"We're broken up for three months and you go totally *Beautiful Mind* on me?"

He laughed. "It was like this before."

"You have *string*, Samuel," She reached out to touch one of the thin black cords crisscrossing the landscape of paper. Strings connecting events and victims, dates and times. She took a step back and looked up. "I knew you were interested in this guy, but . . . this is a lot."

He frowned. "Okay, but I'm not like one of those weirdos that buys John Wayne Gacy's artwork or anything. I'm not a *fan*. This case has just bugged me for ages."

Dayna held up her hands. "Whoa, I know that. That's not what I was saying."

Sam shook his head, already regretting his outburst. "Sorry, it's just, I know what some people would think." More specifically, he knew exactly what his parents would say. That his curiosity made him sick. Sinful, even. When Dayna only nodded he continued. "Um, once I knew he was in town I started on a few new theories. But look"—he hesitated, turning sober—"I'm serious. At first this seemed kind of exciting, you know, like living history. But . . . if it really is him, this is bad. *Really* bad. He's got five more victims to go."

Dayna looked back up at the wall, letting out a breath. "Yeah, I know."

Sam took a tentative step forward and touched her arm. "Hey, you okay?" When she turned, he took her other arm, feeling another surge of guilt. Her face was pale, and there were dark circles under her eyes.

"I'm fine." She didn't shake him off; in fact, his stomach swooped as she wrapped her fingers around his briefly before drawing away.

This was it; this was his chance. "I miss you, you know. A lot. I know you said you needed to think about it, but . . . it's been a little while . . ." He trailed off, heart sinking. Dayna was shaking her head.

"Please don't, Sam. I can't think about this right now. With Fiona and then this and . . . It's too much."

He forced himself to simply nod, to push down the disappointment.

Dayna turned back to the charts, clearing her throat. "Walk me through this. You've been obsessed with this guy forever. Tell me everything."

He brought her up to speed. On his theory that the Butcher was obsessed with the women he killed, stalking them for days beforehand. That each victim was special to him in some way. Even with the disappointment squeezing his chest, it was easy to talk about this; he knew the timeline inside and out, knew every theory. Every suspect.

This was his expertise.

"I'm just not sure how," he finished. "Most serial killers have a type. They're murdering for bloodlust, or sexual gratification, or the feeling of power. But the Butcher seems . . . random. But he's not—not with the way he stalks them. It's frustratingly elusive, his motive. Of course, these are only things I've pieced together from blogs and articles." He stood on his tiptoes, reaching up to touch one of the articles he'd pinned to the top. "But . . . I'm working on a theory. I've found other murders way back. As far back as the sixties." He searched Dayna's face, looking for some kind of sign she was taking this seriously. That she wasn't about to tell him he was a lunatic.

"The pattern matches. No discernible victim type except that they were women, and six murders each time, then a period of ten years between the next six."

Dayna was staring at him wide-eyed, and he continued hurriedly before she could interrupt.

"All in England, northern England to be precise. Closer and closer to the northern shore each time." He took a breath. "It's like . . . he kills in cycles."

The cycles. The pattern that had drawn him to this case more than any other. The reason he couldn't seem to let it go.

Dayna's brows were knitted together, but to his relief she looked thoughtful rather than incredulous. "Killing in cycles, and . . . you think his cycle in Manchester was when they started calling him the Butcher, and he started drawing the symbol."

"Right."

She looked back up at the charts again. "But there were only five victims on the Isle of Man."

Sam nodded, tracing a finger over the dates. "His last cycle. The sixth murder scene was in an old barn, where they found his symbol on the wall. There were also two different types of blood, and several long strands of gray hair. They couldn't find him or the victim, but they think she may have wounded or killed him, because he stopped after that."

"Until now," Dayna said grimly.

"Until now." Sam stepped back, examining the map just below the timeline. He'd marked each cycle with a red pin, which laid out the trail of death along England's northern shoreline, leading up to the Isle of Man between Ireland and England. Dayna followed his gaze, frowning.

"It's like..."

"Like he's been making his way here, to Ireland?"

"Yeah, but...why here?" Dayna said.

His chest swelled. The fact that she hadn't brushed his theory off, the fact she had seen it, too. He had to work to keep his voice even. "Exactly. Why Carman? This town is small enough that there's a chance of getting caught, and it doesn't have a good victim pool. It just doesn't make sense."

"Victim pool?" Dayna made a face at him.

"You know what I mean. He has to be here for something specific." *Like unfinished business.* Sam frowned up at the charts.

Dayna hesitated. "Um, when when do you think he'll kill next?"

"He'll have a cool-off period, they all do. There were three weeks between each murder last time."

"And this time?"

Sam folded his arms over his chest and blew out a heavy breath. "That's the question."

Chapter Sixteen

DAYNA

The witches were getting ready for the ascension when Dayna arrived. Yemi had put Cora and Meiner to work pouring great quantities of steaming tea into metal thermoses and shoved several bundles of bay leaves into Reagan's arms. "Brenna, if you'd get the basin, I'll bring the rest. I can't believe my baby witchlings are finally ascending!"

Cora grimaced horribly at this, chin in her hands as she slumped at the table, and Reagan shot her a narrow look and turned to Dayna. "Oya, set your bag there and help me with the bay leaves, will you?"

Dayna followed her out onto the back porch. In spite of the coolness of the night, Reagan had set up her workspace outside. She'd laid newspapers and mixing bowls out to shred the bay leaves into. This would later be mixed into a carrier oil and sprinkled around the ascension circle for protection.

"Okay, what's going on?" Reagan sat on the edge of the newspapers. Folding her legs, she leaned forward, elbows on her knees. "You have that look on your face. Was she there when you got home?"

Dayna sighed, sinking down across from her. She picked up a bundle of sage and began shredding it into the bowl, keeping her gaze on her hands as she worked. Reagan knew about Fiona coming home, but to be honest, Dayna had sort of hoped she had forgotten, because a part of her really didn't want to talk about it now that she was here.

She wanted to focus on something good. On the ascension. But when she glanced up at Reagan it was to see her waiting expectantly, her face grave. "I wasn't going to tell the others until after, but . . ." Dayna hesitated, then blurted out, "She's back. And she looks bad, like . . . really bad. I hate to think what camp was like."

She wasn't exaggerating; just thinking about camp made her stomach churn.

"God, I still can't believe he just sprang this on you." Reagan's eyes were wide. For a moment she watched Dayna shred leaves in silence. Then she said slowly, "How are you dealing with seeing her again? Emotionally, I mean."

Dayna shrugged, watching flecks of pale green dot the white insides of the bowl. She really didn't want to talk about that part. All right, yes, maybe she'd felt betrayed when she was younger, not understanding why her mother had abandoned her. Maybe she'd even felt bitter at being left with the reverend. But those feelings had dulled with age, and she had no desire to revisit them. It was the same with her OCD; if she could push the thoughts away, at least temporarily, then she didn't have to deal with them.

Again, it was quiet for a moment, and then Reagan leaned over, poking Dayna gently in the ribs. "Have you thought about looking into meds again lately? You're going through a lot; it's allowed, you know."

"Yeah, I've thought about it." She *had* thought about meds, many times, and the idea was terrifying. The thought of altering her brain chemistry, of potentially changing who she was. "I'm still not ready for that."

"Okay, but you know you can talk about it, right? It's all right to . . . I dunno, let it out."

"I know." Dayna forced a faint smile. That was the one problem with being so close to someone: Reagan read her a little *too* well. "But sometimes it's better not to. Tonight I just want to enjoy our ascension and not think about any of it." She could tell by the wry look she got that Reagan wanted to keep pushing the subject, but thankfully she didn't.

Instead she straightened up, clapping her hands. "Hey! We're ascending tonight, abi?"

Dayna grinned, her mood instantly lifted. "Hell yeah we are!"

And there was the flip side of having a best friend. They knew exactly when to change the subject.

When they went back inside, Yemi put Dayna to work at the kitchen counter while Reagan mixed the bay leaves into a shallow glass basin of grapeseed oil.

Cora, who'd just finished putting a series of waxy black candles onto a silver tray, flopped into a chair at the kitchen table and sighed heavily. Unsurprisingly, she seemed to be seeking every opportunity to avoid doing any work.

Dayna turned away to hide her grin. Nothing was going to kill her excitement right now, not Cora and Meiner's blatant jealousy, and not thoughts of Fiona. She was about to be a full witch and nothing else mattered.

Reagan paused on her way past, hands cupped around the basin of oil. She bumped her hip into Dayna's. "Hey, D, guess what?"

Dayna grinned, knowing full well what was coming. "What?"

"We're ascendiiiiing!" She stretched out the last syllable and danced out the sliding glass door, blue locs swinging behind her, and Dayna laughed.

Yemi watched her daughter go, clucking her tongue. Then she turned to hand Brenna a flat silver tin. "Here, Bren, you've got to try one. I used that wonderful tart recipe you found me last week, only I added a pinch of nutmeg. It turned out—"

Abruptly Grandma King thumped her cane on the floor. "Will someone get the damn *phone?*"

When the other witches simply stared, she grumbled and climbed slowly to her feet, hobbling toward the living room.

Meiner's face was flushed, and she paused in the middle of loading the picnic basket. "I'm hoping she'll be better by the time we do the ceremony. She's been in a mood all morning."

"One can hardly blame her," Brenna said. While the rest of the witches were preparing for the ceremony, she'd set her tarot cards in a neat fan on the kitchen table. Every time she didn't like the result, she'd reshuffle and lay them out again. The death and tower cards kept turning up, and she whacked a new card down with each word.

Can—*slam*—hardly—*slam*—blame her—*slam*.

Dayna flinched, wishing Brenna would take a break from her tarot. It was unnerving to see her so flustered.

She turned instead to watch Yemi as she went around decorating the doors and window frames with thick lines of salt. "What's that for?"

"Spirits. In case anything happens during the ceremony, they can't get in the house."

Dayna shifted from one foot to the other, feeling nerves flutter in her stomach for the first time. That was hardly reassuring. She knew powerful magic often sent up a kind of beacon to those who could see it, but she hadn't thought about what sort of signal the ascension might send up.

Bronagh, who'd been drifting around the kitchen, paused beside Dayna and draped an arm around her, pulling her into a hug. For a second Dayna felt the tension melt out of her as she inhaled the scent of rosemary and butterscotch. It was both strange and comforting, like being hugged by your grandmother, if your grandmother happened to be one of the most powerful witches in Ireland.

Bronagh patted her arm as she pulled away, and Dayna grinned down at the Werther's candy that was now in her hand. "There you go, love. It's all going to go well tonight."

Dayna smiled, retreating to the living room for another quilt. She pulled the purple-and-blue knitted blanket from the rocking chair by the fire and slung it over her shoulder, inhaling the scent of woodsmoke. When she turned, Faye was standing there, hands on her hips. "Do you need someone to take care of your mother?"

"Uh, what?" She blinked slowly at her, and then when Faye continued to stare pointedly, her mouth dropped open. "Wait, are you offering to—to *off* Fiona?"

Faye waved her off impatiently. "Of course not, don't be ridiculous.

But the right spell could send her straight back to camp. I could make sure she never comes back."

Dayna's brows shot up. "Sometimes you're a bit scary, you know that?"

"Is that a no?" Faye scowled, folding her arms across her chest.

"Do Brenna and Bronagh know you're offering this solution?" Dayna grinned at the affronted look Faye gave her. "Wouldn't they say you'd get it back threefold?"

Faye shrugged. "Don't say I didn't offer."

Dayna snorted and started to turn away, and Faye cleared her throat. "You'll have to take care of the white-haired giant, by the way."

"Excuse me?" She spun and stared at Faye.

"She keeps challenging you. You're going to have to put her in her place." Faye straightened her shoulders, as if she were the one squaring off against some invisible foe. When she smiled, it looked more like a snarl. "Unless you release the tension between you two in some other way, of course."

"Oh my *god*, Faye." Dayna whirled around, grasping the blanket to her chest, her face bright red as she fled the room.

Faye's laughter echoed off the bricks of the fireplace behind her.

Yemi flapped a hand at her as soon as she made her way back in. "Dayna, love, will you and Meiner load the rest of the tarts and cookies into the basket before you go out?"

Thankfully no one seemed to notice her face was glowing. "No problem."

She fetched an armful of Tupperware from the fridge, returning to the counter where Meiner was leaning, staring fixedly out the window. Dayna couldn't help wondering what she was thinking. Meiner rarely seemed to give away what was going on beneath the surface. She wasn't like Cora, whose strongest emotions were always written on her face for the world to see.

"Pass the basket, please."

Meiner started, looking at her for the first time, and then she glared down at the wicker picnic basket.

"Oh. Here." Her voice was curt as she shoved it across the counter.

Dayna rolled her eyes. Meiner was pouting just as much as Cora; she was just quieter about it. "Gee, thanks."

Meiner grabbed one of the containers and reached across her to shove it into the basket. Judging by her smirk, she was very deliberately in Dayna's personal space again.

She smelled like laundry soap and peppermint, and Dayna leaned back and smiled up at her.

Meiner paused, brows raised. "What are you grinning at?"

"I just didn't expect you to be so sulky."

Meiner's scowl was back in an instant. "I'm not *sulking*."

"Oh please, you absolutely are."

From the sliding glass door, Cora leaned in, snickering. "Yeah, that's definitely her sulking face."

"Shut up, Cora," Meiner snapped. She turned back to Dayna, shoving the tray of candles at her. "Bring this out, I've got the basket."

Meiner hooked an arm through the basket and moved out through the sliding door, toward the apple orchard. She elbowed past Cora, and the shorter girl staggered a step back before regaining her balance. Dayna caught her eye and Cora shrugged, turning to follow Meiner outside.

Dayna hurried after her, falling into stride. "Is she always like this?"

"Like what?" Cora didn't look at her, keeping her eyes fixed on Meiner's back.

"So bad-tempered."

Cora gave a short laugh. "You think that was bad? That was nothing. A little hissy fit, that's all."

Dayna's phone vibrated in the pocket of her sweater, but she ignored it, concentrating on balancing the tray of candles. It was probably the reverend, and she wasn't interested in talking to him.

She tried to push her irritation down while she followed Meiner into the apple orchard. She shouldn't let it get to her right now, not Meiner's little hissy fit, as Cora so succinctly put it, or her father's insistence on checking in. She wasn't even going to be annoyed at the memory of Sam asking her to take him back, or the surge of guilt and indecision she'd felt in response.

No, tonight was about the ascension. Nobody was going to ruin it.

Reagan was spreading a checkered blanket in the center of the orchard. The trees on either side were bent forward and gnarled, forming a crooked wooden archway framed in orange by the setting sun.

Dayna watched as Reagan handed Cora and Meiner bundles of sage and clematis to distribute in a wide circle around the blanket. She knew some of it. The circle was to keep out negative spirits and energy, and the candles were to light the way for the gods. She set down the tray and began to collect the wax pillars, placing them around the outside.

She wasn't sure about some of the others—the stone knife Brenna placed on the altar, or the withered branches Bronagh followed with. Seeing her staring, Grandma King—who was helping Cora distribute the herbs—spoke up. "Oak and ash," she croaked, "for luck and protection."

Dayna felt a flash of relief that the old woman was acting normal, and she glanced over at Meiner, who looked more at ease than she had a second ago.

"The stone knife for grounding," Grandma King continued, "for cutting away attachments to this earth. Candles to light the way." She waited while Faye came forward to place a silver hand mirror on the altar. "And the doorway, though they can use whatever entrance they well please." She gestured at the apple trees on either side. "We're at an entrance spot anyway. This works just as well."

Beside her, Bronagh gave her a sharp, sideways glance and cleared her throat loudly. "If you don't mind, King, I'll be running the ceremony."

Grandma King shrugged and said icily, "Only explaining what the witchlings didn't seem to know."

Bronagh set out the rest of the ceremony, scowling at Grandma King all the while. Reagan gave Dayna a wide-eyed look, mouthing, *Oh my god*, behind her hand, and Dayna bit the inside of her cheek, not sure whether to laugh or roll her eyes.

Thankfully Yemi joined them just then, and she placed the glass basin of oil at the center of the blanket.

"All in a circle, please." She waved at Reagan, who had stooped down to dig through the picnic basket for cookies. "Enough of that, my girl. Those are for after, when you need a sugar kick. Don't eat them all now." She shook her head and sucked her teeth. "Well, come on, then, we'll start as soon as the sun begins to set. Only a few minutes. Now, I know you girls have picked your goddesses." She looked pointedly at her daughter.

Reagan nodded, speaking around a mouthful of cookie. "Aye. I was thinking of Moritasgus. You know, the badger god? Just think how fast I could dig tunnels."

Dayna hid a smile behind her hand as Yemi blinked at her daughter in dismay. "Who?"

"I'm having you on, Ma. You know I'm pledging to Brigid. She's had her arse appropriated by the church, so I'm taking her back." Reagan laughed as Yemi shook her head.

"You give me wahala, girl. I'm going to have gray hairs. Dayna, what about you?"

"Danu."

The others nodded. Danu was powerful and benevolent, the mother god. A good choice. It was hard to tell, but she thought she had the goddess's approval. Sometimes when she performed simple spells she'd get a rush of power, or warmth flooding through her chest down to the tips of her toes, all signs your god favored you. Danu wouldn't turn her down... at least she hoped. Her stomach twisted at the thought, as she pictured reaching out and getting nothing back.

She told herself firmly that it was ridiculous. It wouldn't happen.

She was going to pledge to her goddess, and return home a full witch.

Home, where she could never ever let the reverend know what she'd just done. Where she'd have to be careful to hide her new power.

If he found out, they would have a reckoning far worse than the fight they'd had over Dayna being bisexual. Witchcraft was the ultimate sin. He would probably never speak to her again if he knew.

Dayna bit the inside of her cheek, feeling a little ill.

Yemi reached out, grasping Reagan's and Dayna's hands, surveying them both gravely. "Are you ready, girls? You will be full witches after this."

They both nodded, though Dayna swallowed hard, shifting from one foot to the other. Yemi gave her a reassuring smile.

"You have doubts and fears. Your old friends, maybe, and your father?"

Dayna nodded slowly, and Yemi clasped her hand more firmly. "I was the same way when I ascended. I was sure my mother was rolling in her grave back in Nigeria, she was so Christian. Juju was evil in my house. I never dreamed I'd become a witch when I set up my stand next to this strange old white woman at the market years ago." Yemi chuckled, tossing a teasing grin at Brenna.

"Aye, I bewitched her with my teas." Brenna grinned back, and Yemi shook her head, rolling her eyes, before returning her focus back to Dayna and Reagan.

"You have both felt the magic and you know the truth of it. You know it is good, abi?" When they both nodded, she smiled and waved a hand at them. "Oya, we get in the circle now."

They formed a circle, with Reagan and Dayna standing between Bronagh and Brenna, and Yemi across the basin from her daughter.

Bronagh clasped her hands and intoned, "We shall explain the ceremony. But before that, you'll need a Second." When they stared at her blankly she said, "Someone to stand behind you, to make sure you don't fall during the ceremony. The ascension can be surprisingly powerful."

Faye pointed a commanding finger at Meiner. "You'll do, tall one. Go ahead and stand behind her."

Meiner only glanced briefly at Dayna before obeying, her expression stony. Dayna was grateful the sun was beginning to sink behind the horizon, the shadows of the trees stretching over their circle. Hopefully no one would notice her burning face, or her horrified expression. She could feel how close Meiner was. And there was that laundry-soap-and-peppermint smell again as the older girl moved past her. Dayna told herself not to think about it. To pretend Meiner wasn't there.

Beside her, Yemi moved behind Reagan, and they all looked expectantly at Brenna to continue.

"You'll call the gods three times." Brenna nodded at Yemi, who reached into her canvas bag and brought out what looked like two shot glasses. "You'll drink the elixir."

The brown tealike substance in the basin, Dayna knew.

"Then we'll mark you as daughters of the gods," Faye said.

Yemi pulled the canvas bag onto her lap and out came two long crow feathers. "Feather for your right hand," she said, and then removed a pair of smooth black rocks. "Onyx for your left."

The rocks and feathers were passed down, and Reagan shot Dayna an amused look, accepting her feather and rock with a glib smile. "We really need this stuff?"

Faye gave her a sharp look from across the circle. "Magic is about meaning. The symbolism behind each object has power. Together they give words strength enough to reach the gods' ears."

Reagan looked sufficiently chastised, but her eyes still sparkled when she peered at Dayna from beneath her lashes.

Trying to hide her smile, Dayna accepted the rock and feather. Each of the women did the same, palms upturned, eyes shut.

That flutter in her stomach was back again, but this time it was a good feeling. Excitement rekindling. She could feel the low, expectant hum of magic in the circle already. It sent goose bumps crawling over her skin.

"Circle. Chloch. Cleite. Déanaimid gairmí ort."

It was Bronagh chanting. Beside her, Cora stared around the circle, expression strangely smug. Or perhaps that was just her usual expression. She seemed to wear it a lot.

The sun started to dip behind the tree line, and Faye lit the candle ring. Tongues of flames flickered and danced in the dimming light. Dayna shut her eyes again, trying to concentrate on the words, on the way they should roll off her tongue. She could only tell what some of them meant, something about stones and feathers and gods.

They repeated it three times, the names of their gods at the end. On the third repetition, something changed. The wind, which had been rustling the apple trees and blowing Dayna's hair back, suddenly died. With it, the sound of the birds chattering in the trees dropped off. It was eerily silent, save for the sound of Bronagh's voice.

Dayna shivered, feeling the electric hum of power in the circle grow with each word. Something was happening now, something that made her chest swell with excitement. Something good.

"Now," Bronagh said. "Drink."

The potion was bitter on her tongue and burned going down. When she had finished, Dayna dropped the cup on the grass, gagging. She'd tasted rum once. The burn was similar, though it tasted strongly of bergamot as well, like Earl Grey laced with strong liquor. She grimaced and then went still. Something had begun almost immediately. The fire trailed down her throat and into her belly, warming her entire body an inch at a time. Around her the orchard swayed, and the trees seemed impossibly tall.

The wind was back. At first, she heard the whisper of leaves, the sigh of the breeze rushing through the trees. She shut her eyes to listen, her hair caught by the wind, brushing her cheeks and throat. The distant sound of words came on the breeze, whispers in an ancient tongue.

She kept her eyes shut, feeling a heady rush of fear and exhilaration. Something told her not to look.

There'd been many times she'd brushed the edge of power. As a witchling she prayed to many gods and got a mere taste of the magic. Enough to do small spells here and there. Doing spells filled her with a kind of tingling electricity, but the results were subtle. A premonition here and there, a day that went especially well when you needed it to. But this . . . this was different. This was coming face-to-face with the source of her power.

As soon as the whispers started, the fire in her belly grew, extending tendrils of warmth through her arms and legs. Her limbs tingled, like she'd come in from the cold and sat down by the fire. It was the feeling she got doing magic, magnified several times over.

Bronagh had finished the chant, and now she said softly, "Hold still. Do not open your eyes."

Dayna squeezed them shut harder. There came the rustle of someone moving, then something brushed her cheek. A soft touch. The scent of bergamot and the jingle of bangles told her it was Brenna. A waft of some acidic smell hit her next, and she felt the cool touch of liquid on her face as Brenna painted lines and swirls on her cheek. The tree of life.

A moment later Brenna's touch receded.

"Thrice you will call on your gods."

She felt Reagan shift beside her. Dayna took a deep, shaky breath; the breeze was still whispering, and she wanted to be still and listen, but she forced herself to recite the beginning of the chant with Reagan.

Even as she chanted, she felt gooseflesh creep over her arms and legs. The wind was blowing harder now, dragging her hair over her face. She didn't lift a hand to brush it away. On the third verse the thing that had been stirring around her grew stronger, and the voices on the wind grew louder.

Now they were finished, and she could make out individual words. *Stone and feather*, the voices were saying. *Oak and ash. We see you, daughters.*

The burning inside Dayna's skin had increased, so hot it was almost uncomfortable. Despite this, she forced herself to stand perfectly still.

The wind rushed in her ears, and then it spoke. *I have seen the circle and I honor it. Will you accept me, daughter of oak?*

The goddess's voice was both strange and familiar. As though she'd heard it before, in a dream, maybe, or in the state between waking and sleep. Dayna's breath came out in a rush, and on it was the word *yes*.

Something hit her, a physical blow that passed through her body and vibrated her bones. She was knocked backward with a startled cry. Someone caught her. Meiner, she remembered a second later. She felt callused hands on her bare arms, though they gripped her gently enough, helping

her upright. She caught the scent of laundry soap again and knew some-
what distantly in the back of her mind that Meiner was the only thing
keeping her upright. Her bones were liquid, her blood fire.

You are remade, daughter.

Dayna could feel the magic now, surging beneath her breast. It was
an electric kind of energy, full of endless possibility. Bigger than anything
she'd felt until now. A sense of peace drifted over her like a woolen blanket, heavy and warm.

And then something shifted.

The wind was the first warning. It died abruptly, and Dayna's ears rang
in the silence. Then the scent hit her, overpowering Meiner's soap smell. It
was burning hair and rotting flesh. The sickly scent of overripe fruit and
the putrid skunk smell of still water.

The burning in her veins flared hotter in response, and Dayna shifted.
Beside her Reagan gasped.

Dayna opened her eyes.

Cora was directly across from her. She was on her knees, her face pale
and frightened.

In the split second before it happened, she met Dayna's gaze. Cora's
eyes, usually wide and light brown, had changed. Shadows crawled and
skittered behind them, like cockroaches running from the light.

Behind Cora, three of the pillar candles went out at once, leaving a gap
in the circle, a thin slice of darkness. Trickles of smoke twisted into the sky.

The sight sent a flash of cold panic through her.

Cora opened her mouth and *screamed*, a high, horrible sound. Her
entire body shook, and she snapped upright. Her body bent unnaturally,
horribly contorted, as if some invisible giant was twisting her back on
herself like a plastic doll. On either side the Callighan women stared in
shock, and for a moment it seemed someone had frozen the circle members.

Grandma King was the first to move, and she placed a withered hand
on Cora's shoulder. She opened her mouth, and then paused, expression
stricken.

Cora snapped upright, her mocking laughter echoing across the field.

Her arm swept out, and she batted the old woman aside. Grandma King fell back off the blanket and onto the grass, knocking her shoulder against the trunk of the apple tree with a startled cry.

Meiner's grip tightened on Dayna's arms as Cora paused in the middle of the blanket and stared around at them. Her gaze came to Dayna last and settled there. She smiled.

It was not Cora's usual smile. In fact, it did not seem like her face at all. It was as if something wore Cora like a poorly made mask. The sight raised the hairs on the back of Dayna's neck, as some primal instinct inside screamed at her to run, run, *run*.

"You. Suas ón luaithreach. Suas ón talamh."

She knew the words ashes and earth, but that was it. Dayna found herself clutching Meiner's hands on her shoulder tightly.

Cora launched herself forward, and Dayna shrieked as Cora's hands stretched toward her face, fingers crooked into claws. Then Meiner's arm shot out, and the heel of her hand crashed into Cora's face. There was a horrible-sounding *pop*, and blood gushed from her nose, down her chin and onto her neck, instantly soaking the collar of her shirt. She stumbled back, and then recovered almost instantly, smiling with blood-coated teeth.

Dayna stiffened, half crouched now and ready to run, adrenaline making her blood pump hot. But Bronagh was there, standing stern and tall beneath the apple tree. Her voice thundered through the orchard, impossibly loud, an electric buzz beneath her words.

"A bheith imithe as an gciorcal seo."

Cora jerked upright and then turned to the Callighans. Her grisly smile stayed in place, her movements eerie, puppetlike.

"You have no power over me." Her voice was the hum of a thousand voices. It made Dayna want to clap her hands over her ears.

"Leave this place." Bronagh drew herself up. In spite of the cardigan and the brooch, she was somehow imposing.

"Or we force your name from you . . ." Faye's expression was stony.

"And cast you into the underworld," Brenna finished.

Cora shrieked again, eyes wide as she stared at the three women. Then she was laughing, bloody mouth wide open. "After so long, sisters. This is how you treat me?"

Something crossed Bronagh's face, a flash of confusion—and perhaps, Dayna thought, fear. Then it was gone. She jabbed a finger at the thing that was not Cora. "Out. Out of the circle. Out of the orchard. You are not welcome here."

Not-Cora's smile only stretched wider. "Beidh mé ag ardú. I will see you soon, sister."

Cora's grin faltered, then disappeared, and her face went suddenly blank.

"Catch her," Bronagh barked, and Brenna stepped forward just as Cora crumpled, her body slumping forward into Brenna's arms.

Heavy silence followed. There was no wind to stir the trees, no birds chirping.

Reagan's face was pale, and Yemi, who was sitting on the blanket, looked completely shell-shocked. Grandma King was sitting up slowly beneath the apple tree, gingerly dabbing one finger at the bruise spreading near her eye.

Bronagh spoke at last, her voice full of exhaustion. "We should take her inside. She'll need something to get her blood sugar back up, and I believe her nose is broken."

They packed everything away, the silence among them heavy. Dayna looked over at Reagan, half startled to see the black symbol of the tree of life on her cheek. They had ascended, she'd almost forgot. She was officially a witch now, had more access to power than ever before.

But, as she looked at the bloody figure of Cora draped between Faye and Brenna, no amount of power seemed like enough.

Chapter Seventeen

MEINER

The effects of the potion seemed slow to wear off, and both girls staggered as they made their way to the house.

Since Meiner had been Dayna's Second, she caught her elbow and steered her straight ahead. Dayna started at her touch, then jerked away. "Hey. What are you doing?"

"You're going to fall on your face."

"I'm fine." Dayna waved her off, and Meiner raised a brow, watching the shorter girl take an experimental step forward. She swayed dangerously, then paused, face flushed, and mumbled something about feeling dizzy.

If the situation hadn't been so dire Meiner might have enjoyed this. She stepped forward and took her firmly by the arm, and this time Dayna didn't protest.

No one said much as they walked to the house. Their gazes were repeatedly drawn to the limp form of Cora hanging between Faye and Brenna. Meiner shuddered. She butted heads with Cora at least once a day, but never had she seen that ugly look on her face. That hadn't been Cora; it had been something that wore her like a Halloween costume. Something that puppeted her, moved her lips and her body and tore at Dayna's face with her nails.

She looked over at Dayna. Not-Cora had gone straight for her. And the look on her face when she'd spotted Dayna, as if she recognized her.

It should have been impossible. The candles and herbs scattered around the blanket meant protection, a circle that couldn't be broken. Yet something had. Something uninvited had crept in, slipped effortlessly into one of their bodies. Meiner had seen many disturbing things under Grandma King's tutelege, but this beat them all.

That *thing* had addressed the three women of the other coven—Meiner gave Bronagh an assessing look. It had not slipped past her that it addressed the older woman as *sister*.

More questions, and as long as her grandmother's behavior continued to swing wildly, there would be no answers. Not unless she went looking for them.

And on top of the crawling, uneasy feeling she got when she looked over at Cora, she felt a sense of horror at her own actions. She hadn't been afraid when she'd punched Cora, she'd been . . . excited. It felt *good*.

It was not the same with a punching bag. There was no give, no result upon impact. No reaction. She had *hurt* Cora, made her bleed. And something inside wanted more.

Sometimes she scared herself.

Beside her she felt Dayna stumble, and Meiner reached out instinctively, looping an arm around her waist as she would a drunk friend.

"God, you're absolutely sloshed. What the hell was in that tea?"

The other girl giggled, an abrupt and startling noise in the stillness. She looked immediately horrified, her hand flying over her mouth, and Meiner found herself amused despite everything.

Back in the house, she steered Dayna through the shoe room and sat her down at the kitchen table. At Yemi's instruction, Faye and Brenna took Cora into the living room.

"Lay her out on the couch." Yemi looked ashen but fierce, and she hurried over to the sink. "She'll be needing a cold compress for her head and sugar when she wakes. Meiner, love, will you bring over the cookie tin? I'll get the cloth."

Meiner nodded, snatching the pitcher in the middle of the table and depositing it in front of Dayna with one of the empty teacups on the table. "Drink water," she said, and then when Reagan swayed dangerously in the chair beside her, she added, "Both of you."

She made her way over to the counter, scooping up the tin. The Callighans were talking in low voices by the kitchen sink.

"Should be impossible," Brenna was saying. "The circle was complete."

"Nothing gets in unless it's invited," Faye said, and she cast a narrow glance in the direction of the living room. "This feels familiar. It isn't the first time we've had a circle broken."

Meiner stopped. Here was her chance to finally get answers. When Faye and Brenna paused and stared at her she dropped her voice to a whisper. "Tell me what she did. Why did she leave?"

Now it was Brenna's turn to dart a look toward the living room. Then she said in a low voice, "She was asked to leave. We didn't realize it, but she'd been practicing black magic."

Meiner braced a hand on the counter, taking a deep, shaky breath. She wasn't sure why she felt shocked. She shouldn't be.

"Very few beings are powerful enough to break a circle," Bronagh added. "But if the circle is already disrupted by dark energy from within, it becomes easier."

Meiner barely caught what she was saying. This was bringing back memories she usually tried to keep buried. Of Grandma King coming and going at all hours of the night, her eyes growing strange and wild. Hearing the rasping hiss of whispers late into the small hours of the morning, of tall, slender shadows sliding along the walls. Catching glimpses of movement reflected in mirrors and around corners, swirls of black mist pooling on the floor one minute and gone the next.

The question now became, was Gran *still* doing dark magic?

"You think she broke the circle again," Meiner said.

She saw Faye's expression turn to dismay, and Brenna flinch, a split second before a cool voice said behind her, "The first incident was years ago. I was just out of witchlinghood. If it had been me who broke the circle *now*, Bronagh, you would know. Most of you would be dead, and the rest half-mad and drooling in your tea."

The Callighans said nothing, only exchanged a look, and Bronagh gave a reluctant nod.

The anger flared in Meiner's chest. Gran hadn't even looked at Meiner, wasn't even going to address the fact that she'd lied to her all her life. That she'd raised her around black magic. That wasn't the type of shit you did around children. Things happened. People died.

Meiner's arm shot out before she could think about what she was doing, and she seized a fistful of the back of Grandma King's sweater. "How the hell could you—"

Something hit her full in the chest, cutting her words off. It felt like an invisible fist knocked her back a step, punching the air from her lungs. Meiner wheezed, hands pressed below her collarbones, eyes watering.

Grandma King turned, expression twisted with fury. "You think I owe you an explanation, girl?"

Meiner stepped back, pulse jackhammering in her ears as her grandmother moved toward her. Then she blinked, startled, as Yemi swept between them. The woman's good-natured smile was gone, replaced by cold fury.

"I don't know what kind of backward coven you run, Ms. King. Frankly I don't care. You are under *my* roof, and you will follow my rules. In this house we do not strike children, and we certainly do not use magic against them. If you cannot abide by these rules, you can take yourself off my property right now. Do I make myself clear?"

Meiner watched, astonished, as her gran slowly nodded. When her gaze shifted back to Meiner, she could see the anger buried there, but Gran said nothing. Instead she returned to the living room, Yemi following silently.

Meiner turned away from the counter to see Dayna and Reagan at the kitchen table, expressions slack with shock. She'd forgotten they were there.

Her cheeks burned. She couldn't stand the look Dayna was giving her. The surprise, turning swiftly to pity.

She had to get out. Had to clear her head.

Meiner stomped through the hallway and burst out the front door, into the cool fresh air of the garden. She made her way around the house and stopped just under the kitchen window, leaning against the wall, hands on her knees as she tried to collect herself. Her chest still ached, and the Callighans' words echoed in her ears over and over.

There was shuffling from the window above, and Meiner stiffened. "She'll be in there for a while," said a low voice.

"She'll not get away with *that* behavior again," someone replied. It sounded like Faye.

"Nay, she won't. I've never seen Yemi like that." Brenna's voice was amused. "Glad I wasn't on the end of it. I thought Grandma King and Ma would be at each other's throats; I didn't see that coming."

"Well," Faye muttered, "it's only a matter of time before that happens. The sooner this is done the better. That entire coven is a powder keg waiting to go off."

Brenna made a tsking noise but didn't argue. There was another shuffle and then silence. They'd moved back into the living room.

Meiner slumped against the side of the house.

It hurt because she knew it was true. Her coven was toxic, and she was no better, because more than hurt, more than betrayal, she felt *rage*. She pictured herself stalking back inside, through the kitchen and into the living room. Screaming at her grandmother that she was done, she was leaving. Storming out and never looking back.

She played it in her head over and over, letting her fingers drift over the thin, curved scar on her left cheek.

Gran might still be doing black magic.

If she was, Meiner was going to find out. And this time her gran wasn't going to get away with it.

She stayed outside, despite the cold night air biting at her through her jacket and the rain and mist that began to roll in through the garden. She stayed, hoping the cold drizzle would extinguish the burning in her chest.

Chapter Eighteen
DAYNA

The room was spinning. Dayna groaned, dropping her head onto her arms. The cup beside her rattled and nearly tipped over, and Reagan snorted.

"I feel absolutely plastered." Reagan's voice was slurred.

Dayna groaned again, this time in agreement. If she shut her eyes, her head spun, so she forced herself to sit up, trying to blink away the fog. Her mind felt like a bee's nest, full of frantic buzzing.

The ugly look on Cora's face when she'd spotted her. The way she'd spoken, threatening but familiar, like whatever had possessed her had *known* Dayna.

The hum of multiple voices and the way she'd called the others *sister*.

Meiner's hands on her shoulders, the smell of laundry soap. The way her arm shot out to fend off Cora.

Whatever the hell that had been just now with Grandma King...

For a split second she'd been afraid for Meiner. The look in Grandma King's eyes... Dayna repressed a shudder. If that was what she did to her own granddaughter in front of others, what did she do when they were alone?

On top of all of this, the power that had surged through her during the ceremony still burned in her breast. It kept bringing her back to the same thought.

She was a full witch now.

In spite of everything, it was still a big deal. Sluggishly she reached over and put a hand on Reagan's shoulder. "Reagan?"

Her friend was slumped forward, head on her arms. "Hmm?"

"We're witches now. For real."

"For real," Reagan mumbled. "Christ, my head hurts."

Dayna almost laughed, but she pressed a hand to her lips, knowing it would come out hysterical. She and Reagan were now part of an ancient tradition passed down through generations. Anyone could scry or read tarot, but *real* magic was only practiced once you ascended, could only be witnessed by your coven, or performed alone.

There was something both unnerving and exciting about being inducted to the most secret of inner circles. Tonight had been exhilarating and terrifying, and it felt like the start of everything.

"Dayna?"

"Yeah?" She tilted her head to look at Reagan and then had to fight another wave of dizziness.

Reagan's brow was creased. "I'm glad you're okay." She blinked, as if she were trying to clear her head. "When she attacked you I wanted—I wanted to use one of the protection spells I know. I've memorized a bunch, but . . . I've never used them, and I didn't know if they'd work."

"Reagan." Dayna struggled to sit up and then groaned, laying her head back on the table. "You *just* ascended. You're not even supposed to know that many spells yet." She reached across the table and grabbed Reagan's hand, whispering. "And . . . we're drunk."

Reagan giggled and squeezed her hand, swaying in her chair. "Very extremely."

Voices in the kitchen made Dayna sit up.

"The reverend's just called. She was supposed to be home by ten, so she'll need a ride." Yemi's voice.

"I'll take her."

The second voice, low and slightly husky, was Meiner. Dayna felt a jolt of surprise. Why would Meiner volunteer? She hated Dayna, didn't she? She tried not to think about having the other girl standing so close during the ceremony. Or her arm around Dayna's waist as she led her back to the house. It made her face feel hot.

There was a warm presence at her elbow. Yemi was hovering beside her. "Dayna, dear, I need you to focus, okay?"

Dayna released Reagan's hand, eyes fluttering open. She hadn't realized they'd shut. "Hmm?"

"Meiner will take you home, all right? She'll walk you to the door." Yemi frowned, hesitating. "Will you be okay . . . with your mother there and everything, I mean?"

Dayna nodded. By the time she got there the reverend would hopefully be in bed. He usually went to sleep at eight every night. She had no idea about her mother; maybe they stayed awake praying all night at camp. She grimaced, and Yemi looked puzzled.

"Dayna?"

She realized she hadn't said any of that out loud. "Oh yes. They'll be in bed. I'll be fine."

Yemi pursed her lips, but she only nodded. "All right." She frowned, shaking her head fretfully. "We were supposed to do this right. Sit down and make tea, talk through the next steps, but . . . that's hardly happening now." She gripped Dayna's arms, glancing over at Reagan. "Listen, the both of you. You'll have a power surge the next three days, and then you'll level off. You'll have to be careful not to eat too far into your regular stores of power in your enthusiasm." She gave them both a sharp look. "You'll set up your altar and pray to your goddess to renew your power at each new moon, but it takes a few days to recharge, so to speak, so don't go through it too fast. Understand?"

Reagan mumbled her assent from the table, forehead pressed to the tea cozy she'd pulled off the pot.

Dayna nodded and then winced, head spinning. "Got it."

Then Meiner appeared and helped pull Dayna to her feet. Dayna let

Meiner steer her through the house and out to the car, hyperaware of Meiner's hand on her arm as she steadied her.

Most of the ride was a blur. The burning in her chest kept surging, making her head swim. Several times she looked down at her fingers, almost positive she'd seen sparks coming from them. Like her entire body was a charged wire.

Now and again she caught Meiner looking at her. Her expression was hard to read.

When the silence had stretched between them long enough to be unbearable, Dayna cleared her throat. "I should say thanks, for saving me. I don't know what Cora... what she was planning to do. So, um, thanks for that."

Meiner glanced over, brows raised. When she shifted her gaze back to the road, Dayna thought she'd lost a bit of that stony countenance. "You're welcome."

A knot unraveled in her chest, and she slumped back in her seat. She might as well keep going. "And I'm sorry about being kinda standoffish when we first met... and... ever since." She bit the inside of her cheek.

"By standoffish, do you mean acting like a total brat pretty much all the time?"

Dayna sat up straight, indignant, and then caught sight of Meiner's grin and sat back. "Very funny. I think you enjoy setting me off."

"You may be right." Meiner slung one hand over the wheel. "It's very easy."

Dayna groaned, tipping her head back. "Could you please ask your car to stop spinning?"

Meiner snorted. "You'll have to text me tomorrow, tell me if you have a killer hangover. I'm curious if magic drunk has the same consequences as regular drunk."

Dayna wrinkled her nose. "Sure and I'll call you. Maybe I'll magic-drunk-dial you."

Meiner laughed, and Dayna bit her lip, falling silent. She had so many questions, but she was sure they'd wipe the smile off Meiner's face instantly.

After a second, Meiner sighed. "Spit it out."

"What?"

"You clearly have questions." Meiner tilted her head to look at Dayna, mouth quirking at the corner. "I'll give you three. And no, I have no idea what happened to Cora, or why she went straight for your throat."

Yes, that had been one of them. Dayna frowned. "Um, what happened with your gran..."

Sure enough, Meiner's expression went immediately stony, and for a second Dayna thought she'd shut the whole conversation down. But then she sighed, expression softening. "That was the *true* Harriet King. I haven't seen that side in months, but something about this place seems to have... I dunno, *woken* her temporarily." Meiner's lips twisted.

Dayna was startled by the surge of sympathy she felt, the impulse to reach out and touch Meiner's hand. "What was she like before?"

Again, she was almost sure Meiner was going to shut down, the way her entire body tensed up... but after a second the older girl said, "It's hard to explain. She's so different now. But she used to do the craziest shit when she was training us. Like... okay, I was having trouble learning a warmth charm once, and she locked me out for a full night. Middle of winter. She said it would teach me fast. I was *nine*."

"Holy shit." Dayna sat up straight, shocked. "That's horrible."

"I got the charm," Meiner said grimly. "Took me all night, though."

"Should have used it to burn the house down."

Meiner's brows shot up, and unexpectedly she broke into a grin. "Damn, that's dark. I like it." She turned back to the road, letting out a long breath. "Anyway, she did shit like that all the time. But now, it's like it never happened. She just... gets to forget it all."

"I'm sorry, that sucks," Dayna said.

Meiner only shrugged. "As soon as I ascend, I'm gone." A second later she blinked. "Uh, don't tell anyone I said that."

"I won't."

Meiner shifted in her seat, flicking her signal on. "Okay, you asked me all your questions, it's my turn. Starting with, how are you feeling?"

Okay, changing the subject.

"Still feeling *very* drunk, thanks for asking."

Meiner's grin was back. "Question two, are you making-bad-greasy-food-decisions-type drunk? Or dial-your-ex-at-three-in-the-morning-and-confess-your-undying-love-type drunk?"

"Like, might actually go through with drunk dialing *you* in the small hours of the morning, if you're not careful."

"And what would you say if you phoned me drunk?" Meiner shot her a sly look.

Her grin was slightly crooked, Dayna noticed. Her stomach fluttered, and she told herself it was the tea. "I'm not answering that!"

"You have to, it's my third question."

She tugged at her seat belt. "I dunno. Crazy stuff." She was fully aware she was approaching dangerous territory, only it felt like her head was wrapped in cotton, so what did it matter? "Like, girls are hot."

Christ. What was she doing? Reagan knew, of course, after many late-night sleepovers and crush confessions, but after her best friend, Samuel was only the second person she'd told.

"Girls are hot." Meiner pressed her lips together like she was trying to keep from laughing. "All the shit that happened tonight and you would tell me you think girls are hot?"

"Probably not, honestly." Dayna wriggled in her seat as another pulse of magic rushed through her. Her fingers tingled. "People at my school found out I liked girls *and* guys. It was a disaster."

Meiner's brows shot up. "Don't tell me. Did they try to pray at you?"

"Worse. The Bible study at my dad's church found out. A bunch of them go to my school. . . ."

"Oh hell." Meiner's grip tightened on the steering wheel. Her face had gone steely. "They told your dad."

"Yeah, and he didn't react well." Dayna caught herself twisting her hair between her fingers and forced herself to put her hands in her lap. Usually she tried to avoid talking about this, about what had come after.

It felt different with Meiner, though.

"I'm sorry." Meiner's voice was low and gruff. "People suck."

Dayna only nodded. She cleared her throat and forced her voice to sound light. "Okay, you got three questions. My turn. Um, what's up with you and Cora?"

Meiner sighed and rolled her eyes, as if she'd been expecting this. "Okay, but that's worth your entire turn, and you're not allowed to judge. We dated for, like, two weeks."

"Ah." It shouldn't have been surprising, but the thought of Meiner and Cora together was still strange. "Is that why she's like that?"

Meiner snorted. "There are so many reasons she's like that." She darted a sideways look at Dayna.

"Your turn."

There was a beat of silence, and then Meiner said, "Your coven, you're pretty close, huh?"

"I mean, yeah. We'd do anything for each other. Anything and every-thing." Her thoughts immediately went back to the cardboard sign—*You shall not suffer a witch to live*—and the grim certainty of more deaths. "I'd kill to protect them."

Meiner's eyes widened. A smile tugged at the corner of her mouth. "Well, I didn't expect that from you, Walsh. If you need help burying the bodies, you know where to find me."

Dayna grinned and dropped her eyes, fiddling with the seat belt at her waist. "Aw, thanks."

Meiner reached out and grasped her hand, drawing it away. "Hey, don't unbuckle that."

Dayna bit her lip as Meiner dropped her hand back into her lap. Her arm tingled.

She wanted to say something else, something clever, but then they were pulling into her driveway, and it was too late.

Meiner turned to face her. "Final question: What's your number?"

Dayna's grip tightened on the seat belt, and for a moment she only stared at Meiner. It felt like her insides were buzzing. "Uh..."

Meiner grinned at her expression. "So I can text you and make sure you get up to your room okay."

Meiner handed her phone over, and Dayna punched her number in, squinting at the blurry screen. "Done." She handed the phone back, feeling a little thrill run through her when her fingertips brushed the palm of Meiner's hand.

"Let me walk you up the steps, so you don't fall on your face. Yemi's orders."

Dayna was silent on the way up the driveway. She was glad for Meiner's help, because the driveway seemed to swell and tilt beneath her feet, but she felt suddenly self-conscious clinging to her arm. What did Meiner think of her? What if the other girl actually still hated her, and she'd just made a fool of herself with her drunken confessions and quasi-flirting? Maybe Meiner was going to go home and tell Cora and they'd both laugh at her. . . .

She was so deep in thought when they arrived at the front porch that she nearly missed the step and lurched forward.

"Whoa, steady." Meiner caught her other arm, facing her. Her fingers on Dayna's bare skin were ten warm points of contact, sending a new kind of electricity buzzing through her.

For one incredible, mad second, Dayna thought about going up on her tiptoes and pressing her lips to Meiner's. What would Meiner do? Push her off? Kiss her back?

She wanted desperately to find out.

A light kicked on, washing over them, flooding the driveway with brilliant yellow-white. Dayna jumped, guilty panic shooting through her. Meiner backed up quickly, turning for the door, as if she expected Dayna's father to come charging out.

"Well, the light is new." Dayna tried to keep the irritation out of her voice. No doubt this was one of her father's attempts to control his charge. They were going to have to have a serious talk, as much as she hated the idea. She wasn't about to let him turn the house into some kind of well-furnished Alcatraz. "I better go inside."

She looked up at Meiner, sure she saw a flicker of disappointment in her face. As Dayna dug into her shoulder bag for the keys, Meiner said, "Dayna?"

She turned, heart in her throat.

The white-haired girl was a tall, slender silhouette on the doorstep. "Just... don't forget to drink lots of water. Avoid the hangover, right?"

"I'll remember." Something fizzled slightly inside her. She wasn't sure what she'd been hoping for. "Good night to you, Meiner King."

Meiner hesitated, then turned back toward her car. "Good night."

Chapter Nineteen
CORA

In all the years Cora had been part of the coven, she would never have imagined herself sitting across from Meiner's grandmother in the middle of the night, in the center of the darkened forest.

"You're not paying attention." Grandma King's voice was waspish, and she reached out and smacked Cora's shoulder with an open palm.

Cora grimaced, pulling her sweater closer around her. Apparently it didn't matter that she felt ill. That she was still recovering from what happened earlier that night at the ceremony. That her face still throbbed after they'd reset her nose. She'd awoken in pain, an alarmingly wide gap in her memory. From the moment they'd closed the circle and begun the chant to the moment Grandma King had woken her—sweat-soaked, her entire body jerking in violent muscle spasms—she could recall nothing.

Maybe drinking the vial Gran had given her had been a terrible mistake.

Someone, or something, had taken the controls and moved her body like a puppet. A god, most likely, but one they hadn't invited into the circle.

What if it was still out there, waiting to jump back into her skin?

The thought made Cora feel ill, flashes of hot and cold buzzing over her skin. She glanced around the clearing. The forest was silent, stretched with long shadows.

"Pay attention, girl." Grandma King was scowling at her. "Your mind is still on the ceremony, isn't it? I warned you this would be dangerous. You drank the vial; you wanted this."

"What happened back there?" Cora glared at her. "And why can't I remember any of it?"

Grandma King ignored the question. "This is only the first part of your training, and here you are feeling sorry for yourself. Shall I pick up where I left off with Meiner?"

"No." The rush of anger made her words sharp. "I can handle it. I'm stronger than Meiner."

"Not yet." Grandma King glanced down at the basin between them, which was filled with the same rust-red liquid that had been in the glass vial. Frankly Cora still didn't want to know what it was, but she could guess.

"What happened to me?" Cora started, fists clenched. "Why won't you—"

Grandma King clapped her hands together sharply, startling Cora into silence. "Do you want power? More than the others, more than Meiner?"

"I— Yes." Cora squared her shoulders, her scowl furious. Of course that's what she wanted.

"Well, then. We'll speak no more of this." Grandma King smiled grimly and jabbed a crooked finger at the bowl. "Wicked deeds best done after dark. If you want this coven, you're going to have to do better."

Cora swallowed hard, forcing herself to change the subject. "What god will I pledge to? The . . . uh, the one you used to worship when Meiner and I were young?"

Grandma King cackled, slapping her knees. "Oh aye, witchling, I'd love to see you try. The god I worshipped would tear a little thing like you limb from limb."

That hardly answered her question. Cora frowned when Grandma

King reached into the bag, pulling out a flat metal tin. She dipped it into the liquid, filling the bottom.

Grandma King shut her eyes, her face expressionless. "Drink."

Cora stared at the tin, lip curled. The vial had been disgusting, like drinking salt and copper. "What is it?"

Grandma King's eyes snapped open. She smiled, a sharp, unpleasant expression. "Are you sure you want to know?"

Cora paused, pressed her lips together until they paled. She reached out to take the tin.

The liquid tasted the same, like pennies and rust, and she gagged and swallowed hard, eyes watering. The tin fell noiselessly to the grass, and Grandma King laughed.

"Now the grimoire."

It took her a moment to obey. She leaned forward on her hands and knees, stomach heaving. Nothing came up, though, and after a second she sat back and wiped her mouth with a groan. That taste was still on her tongue, and for the first time she wondered if she should have turned down the old woman's offer.

Then she thought about Meiner. The scornful way she looked at Cora. Brushing her off like she was unimportant.

She stiffened her back and reached for the leather bag. Pulling the heavy tome out, she slid it across the grass to Grandma King, letting go as quickly as possible. The grimoire was thick, and the binding was done in black leather. There was a sigil etched in silver on the front, one that Cora didn't recognize, and energy was rolling off it in waves, making the hair on her arms stand up. In all the years she'd been part of this coven, she'd never seen the book.

Grandma King rocked back on her heels, strangely agile for someone who had to be helped down the stairs.

"There you are, a ghra. It's been years." The old woman spoke not to Cora but to the book, smoothing a wrinkled hand over the pages as though she touched a lover.

Cora frowned. Was the woman having another lapse?

She rocked forward, hands clutching the grass, trying to see what was in the book. The pages were dry and yellowed, and they crackled as Gran turned them carefully. Cora could make out the upside-down words well enough to know they weren't English.

"Your rise to power will be different. Longer, full of trials," Grandma King said. "But you'll be far more powerful when it's complete. Pay attention to the words I teach you and how we set the altar."

"How many trials?" Cora sat up straight, a flush of excitement running through her. "How long will it take?"

Grandma King only stared at her in return, and Cora frowned, resisting the urge to reach out and shake her. She could see the glassy look had returned to the old woman's face. "Gran?"

"Hmmm?"

Cora felt like a coiled spring, the tension about to burst out of her in a scream of rage. "How many trials?" she repeated. "My rise to power, remember?"

Thankfully Grandma King seemed to shake herself out of it. "Oh yes. Trials. You will face more than your fellow witchlings, and none of them will be easy. You will have to work. To fight for your power tooth and nail. That is why they are asleep in their beds and you are here." She nodded gravely. "The others will ascend and go no further, but you . . . for you the ascension is only a gateway to more power. But"—she held up a finger—"you will have to be stronger than you've ever been."

Cora straightened her back and nodded. She wanted this. She was willing to do whatever it took.

The old woman fished in the bag once more, laying out several objects on the wooden altar between them. A piece of rock on a chain—*Flint*, Cora thought—dried sticks of kindling, a glass bottle filled halfway with water, a smooth oval stone, as black as ink. And lastly, a small glass box with gold trim that held a single strip of dried leather. These the old woman set out side by side. The kindling she placed in an empty glass basin, stained red on the bottom.

Grandma King bent over the basin, striking the flint against the black stone. Sparks showered onto the kindling, and the wood caught, glowing embers flaring to life.

"Shut your eyes," Grandma King said. "Repeat after me. No matter what happens, keep chanting."

Cora was about to ask exactly what might happen, but Grandma King had shut her eyes and was swaying on the spot.

Her voice was flat and cold, though the words that spilled out were strangely melodic. "Talamh, uisce, tine, fola. Teacht domsa, Caorthannach."

Cora's voice was halting and hesitant, and she stumbled over the words. She was pledging herself to someone. To something, she knew. It was reckless and stupid to not know exactly what, but right now she didn't care. She just *wanted*.

She almost broke off as something cold and damp touched her shoulder, crumbling down her arm. The scent of freshly turned earth broke around her, like dirt after the rain. She forced herself to keep chanting, to keep her voice strong even when cold water splashed over her face. She spat it out and continued, a mixture of excitement and dread building in her gut.

Something touched her right cheek. The smooth tip of the stone traced circles over her face, leaving warm liquid in a pattern on her cheek, trailing the smell of rust and pennies. Cora kept chanting, her lip curled in disgust.

Next came a sharp, hot pain on the exposed skin of her right shoulder. She gasped, trying not to flinch. And still she chanted, her voice high and strained. The heat retreated but her arm continued to burn, and tears prickled behind her eyelids.

Cora chanted the words until they felt seared in her mind. She didn't open her eyes when there was a horrible crash, and the wind picked up, howling through the trees, whipping her hair across her face. She raised her voice and continued.

Cool spots of rain began dotting her face, her neck, her arms. It washed away the film of dirt on her shoulders, the blood on her cheek, and the pain in her arm. She felt something then, an electric tingle that started in the soles of her feet and crept up slowly. The feeling swelled and grew until it took up the entirety of her insides, and she felt it would burst from her skin in a shower of sparks. Like the flint, she had the potential to ignite. To set the whole world on fire.

A hoarse voice cut through her reverie. "Caorthannach. Firespitter. Mother of the Flame, come to your disciple."

Cora's eyes snapped open. Grandma King was sitting in the middle of the picnic blanket, folded forward on her knees, a smoldering stick in one hand slowly going out in the rain. Her face was twisted in a biting smile and her eyes glittered. Cora would not have blinked if the old woman had shrunk in on herself and turned into a bat or a fox in that moment. Anything seemed possible.

Firespitter. Mother of the Flame.

Cora had heard those names before. Caorthannach. Mother of demons, and of the devil himself, if you believed the Christian version of events.

It should have scared her, but the feeling brewing in her stomach wasn't fear, not exactly. All she could think about was the kind of *power* this goddess must have.

The kind she might grant her followers...

"Now eat."

Cora looked down. The box with gold trim sat open between them. It was not leather inside, she realized, but dried meat. She reached out, hand hovering over the box. Her gaze flicked from the shriveled strip of meat to the unpleasant smile on Grandma King's face.

Cora fished in the box and took the meat, raising it to her lips. For a moment she considered casting it away. Going back to the safety of the house. Leaving all the questions unasked and unanswered.

The King Witch's smile grew, stretching across her face. A challenge. Cora squeezed her eyes shut.

She shoved the jerky past her lips. The taste of salt crashed onto her tongue. The meat was tough and sinewy between her teeth, and Cora nearly gagged at the sensation.

The patter of rain on the leaves slipped into the silence between them, and Grandma King's rictus smile stretched wider. "Now say it once more."

She did, stumbling on the words. Her mouth tasted of salt and copper, and she wanted to spit into the grass between them.

Then lightning struck, nearly knocking her backward. Something electric pulsed through her limbs, stiffened her muscles. Cora gasped as power coursed through her body. She was lit from the inside out. Her eyes rolled back, and she could see only white for a moment, and then into the nothingness someone spoke:

"I see you, witchling."

Chapter Twenty

DAYNA

The house was dark, and Dayna shuffled through the entryway and into the hallway, past the dining room, where the furniture loomed like dusty ghosts. As Dayna moved into the kitchen, there was a second, startling flood of light, and she jumped.

"Dad?"

"Dayna, I didn't hear you come in."

A woman's voice. Dayna paused, blinking. When she could see clearly enough, she made out the blurry form of Fiona Walsh in the doorway.

Dayna frowned, still squinting against the glare. "Were you waiting up for me?"

"I couldn't sleep." Fiona's voice was soft, and she rubbed at her arms, though Dayna didn't think it was particularly cold in the house. "The bed in the guest room is nice." She hesitated. "It's not what I'm used to, though."

The potion was still burning through her, making her brave enough to ask questions she probably shouldn't. "What was camp like? What did they do up there?"

Her breath seemed to stick in her throat as she waited for an answer, and she found herself pressing a hand to her chest.

Fiona blinked. It was hard to gauge her expression in the half-light, but Dayna thought she saw her smile drop, just for a second. "It was . . . fine. Lots of scripture readings, prayer meetings, that sort of thing."

She gripped the strap of her shoulder bag, knuckles white. "And that's it?"

Fiona hesitated. "I . . . I don't remember."

She was rubbing her arms faster now, and Dayna stepped farther into the kitchen, slightly alarmed. Her gaze dropped down to where Fiona's sleeve had ridden up slightly. There was a series of shadowy bruises on her pale skin.

Dayna frowned.

There was no way it was from the reverend, unless she bruised immediately, so most likely they were from camp. An ugly suspicion had been growing since she'd first met Fiona, and it was slowly turning into something worse. A hot, toxic anger eating at her insides.

"Hey, we don't have to talk about it. Let's get a cup of tea, okay?"

The rubbing slowed and then stopped, and Fiona's arms dropped to her sides. "Tea would be nice."

Dayna flipped the kitchen light on, darting a glance at her mother. Fiona Walsh's face was pale, and there were dark bruises under her eyes. She looked as though she hadn't slept in weeks.

Dayna felt slightly queasy. She knew what it was like not to sleep well. But this seemed like something more.

Dayna set the kettle on the stove and stretched up to pull a pair of clay mugs from the cupboard. "What's with the floodlight? Did Dad install it?"

"This afternoon, yes. And there's a camera at the front now. He said I shouldn't go outside without him, because of the murder." Fiona lowered herself delicately into the nearest chair, folding her arms in front of her. Her body language was timid, like someone expecting a blow at any moment.

There was abuse at camp. The thought was sickening, but she was utterly sure of it. Probably all in the name of their God and helping Fiona "get better." On top of that her father was continuing it, locking Fiona in, controlling her. Installing floodlights and cameras.

What the hell was that about? Was he expecting Fiona to try to escape or something?

Her insides were burning, anger making her chest tight. She wanted to storm down the hall and pound on her father's door. Wake him up just to yell at him. To ask who the hell he thought he was. He wasn't a shrink; he didn't know how to deal with mental health problems. He was just going to do more damage.

For a moment she stayed where she was, drawing in deep breaths, trying to calm herself. The way the magic buzzed through her right now, she worried she might tear the kitchen apart without lifting a finger.

"Listen, Fiona." Dayna paused as the kettle began to rumble, pulling it off the stove. "Are you going to be seeing Dr. Roth now that you're home?"

Fiona nodded, glancing down as Dayna slid a mug of tea across the table to her. "Yes, your father set up an appointment for the end of the week."

"That's what I figured." Dayna scowled, wrapping her hands around her mug. "Look, you've got to convince him to get you outside help. Dr. Roth isn't going to be better than camp; he's just another church lackey. Trust me, I've been to him before and he's useless. You need a secular counselor, one who asks questions other than *how high* when Dad tells him to jump."

There was a shuffle from the doorway, and Dayna turned to see her father standing there in his dressing gown, his brow furrowed with irritation. "Dayna, finally. I told you, I want you home by ten. There's a killer on the loose, and you're out running around with your friends until past midnight." His voice was getting louder. Dayna stood up, snatching her bag off the floor.

Of course he would ruin this, just when she was getting to speak to Fiona. "We were discussing the fact that you're saddling her with Dr. Roth. That's not good enough." Her anger leaked out, making her words sharp.

"Go to bed, Dayna. Tomorrow we'll discuss you ignoring your curfew." He glanced sharply at Fiona. "Both of you. You should be sleeping."

Dayna took a step toward him, suddenly furious. "She's an adult. Your *wife*, actually, and you're treating her like a child." Before he could reply she turned and marched into the hallway.

The reverend followed behind her. "Dayna, you can't just walk away whenever you don't like something."

She stopped just around the corner, turning on him, keeping her voice low. "Was there abuse at camp? Is that why you pulled her out?"

"What?" The reverend looked shocked. Dayna didn't think the expression was fake. "Why would you ask that?"

"She has bruises up her arm." Dayna frowned at him. "You really didn't notice?"

The reverend sighed, rubbing his eyes with a finger and thumb. "Oh, yes. Yes, I— Those are old. She fell during camp activities. Your mother bruises easily."

"Can you not call her that?" The word rattled in her ears; it didn't feel right. "It's . . . just Fiona. Fiona is fine."

"She *is* your mother." The reverend's expression hardened for a second, and then he just looked exhausted. "Look, she needed help, and that's why she went to camp. But she's okay now. Things can go back to normal."

Normal. As if bringing this stranger into their house was going to make things normal. The *lies* he told himself to ease his guilt . . .

Dayna narrowed her eyes, watching his face. He was avoiding her eyes, she realized.

"She'll be kept to a strict schedule here and won't be leaving the house. Eventually, when she feels up to it, I'll take her to church."

"Seriously? You're going to treat her like a prisoner? That's your solution?"

"She's doing so well. This is the best way to make sure she keeps up with her medication."

"The best way is to get professional help. Not Jesus camp, and not locking her up."

"She doesn't need outside help. She's fine now." The reverend was getting that look on his face again, like he was shutting down. It made the ever-present coals in the pit of her stomach flare to life, burning her insides.

"Are you sure about that? It looks like she's not sleeping."

"Dayna, that's enough." He stepped closer, clearly frustrated. "I know you insist on questioning me at every turn, but—" He paused, and then leaned forward so quickly that Dayna took a step back, startled. "Are you *drunk?*"

Shit. The tea. She probably smelled like booze.

"Dayna Walsh, how dare you sully this house with—"

She was already turning, halfway down the hall toward her bedroom. "Forget it. I can't talk to you. I'm going to bed."

There was a thump behind her, and her father's stern voice. "I wasn't finished. You're grounded for a month at least. *Don't walk away from me, Dayna.*"

She jerked to a halt in the doorway, feeling her heart stutter in her chest.

The memories flooded back without warning. The long arguments with her father, *she could be fixed, she could be helped.*

The men in dark suits at the door, there to convince her she could be cured by the church's camp program.

Talking turning to fighting. Dayna trying to leave the room. Her father yelling.

Don't walk away from me.

One of the men had blocked the door, and the other grabbed her. Fingers bruising her arms, faces full of righteous anger.

She'd screamed as they dragged her down the hallway, cried out for her father. The reverend had followed, watching them drag her away. His face had been pale and strange in those few, horrible seconds, his eyes glassy. She'd screamed a second time, trying to wrench out of the suited men's iron grasp, and her father jerked as if he'd been stung. Finally he'd called for them to stop. He'd sent them away and collapsed, trembling, into the chair at the kitchen table, hand over his mouth.

It was too late. She'd seen the blank look on his face. He'd been on the brink of turning her over. Letting them take her away.

Now for one second, two, she stood frozen in the doorway. There were so many things she wanted to say, so many terrible, angry things.

Instead she turned and kept going, letting the bang of the bedroom door do the talking.

On the other side she paused, breathing hard.

The rush of adrenaline made the magic flare momentarily, hot and bright. Dayna staggered forward, socks sliding on the wooden floor. She gaped down at her hands.

For the moment her father was entirely forgotten.

She'd seen the other witches make things float, pencils, erasers, coins. She'd watched jealously, wishing she could access the power to do actual spells. She'd memorized the spell in preparation for this, had always known it was the first thing she'd do. But pencils and coins seemed so small compared to the sheer amount of power rushing through her.

If this was only going to last three days, like Yemi had said, then she might as well use it.

She fixed her eyes on the heavy wooden dresser beside the door and cupped her hands together, fingers woven through one another as she'd seen Yemi do. Heart thumping, she whispered, "Bogadh," and inwardly *pushed*. The dresser tilted wildly on two legs and shot sideways, scraping across the hardwood floor. She grinned and then winced as it slammed into the door and wobbled onto its front legs with a *bang*. Everything on top crashed to the floor, spilling bottles of nail polish, aspirin, and a half dozen partially full bottles of nasal spray.

She flinched and went still, expecting footsteps on the stairs, or her father's voice through the door.

There was nothing.

Her sense of elation returned. That had hardly taken any power, and the dresser had to weigh a ton.

She hurried over to her bed, stooping down to pull the box from underneath. Her altar was technically a stool, wooden and small enough to fit inside the boot box, but it worked. She set it up as fast as she could, lighting the candles, sprinkling a few different herbs out before sinking cross-legged onto the carpet. There were a few items she'd collected over the years, things Bronagh had told her were good to practice with: a silver spoon, a bit of cork from a wine bottle, a few coins.

Dayna wove her fingers together again, letting the electric buzz pulse through her hands and arms. A whisper, and the objects shot into the air around her, so fast she had to clamp down on the power before the cork hit the ceiling. She couldn't help the grin that spread across her face.

She added more.

A book. A jar of skin cream. A stray flip-flop.

Dayna added another book, and another, until she had over twenty objects floating around her. It was exhilarating. She was full to the brim with magic. Powerful. Untouchable. The Butcher could try to come for her coven; she was ready for him.

Chapter Twenty-One

DUBH

Dubh stood at the edge of the lake facing the abbey, hands thrust into the pockets of his jeans. The water was flat and mirrorlike, reflecting the abbey and its green surroundings upside down beneath the surface.

His breath rose in the air around him. He smiled, attention fixed on the abbey, on people moving back and forth across the lawn, voices carrying faintly over the water, colorful insects swarming over the green grass.

Someone had spread a picnic blanket out, and a tour group had settled in the shade of an oak, snapping pictures and unpacking food. Laughter echoed, mingling with birdcalls in the trees above.

For one serene moment, time was suspended in that cool, still reflection in the lake.

Dubh waited. The only movement was the rise and fall of his chest, though he couldn't stop the smile that stretched over his face.

Any second now. The place was packed with tourists, it wouldn't take long.

One minute. Two.

A scream, high and panicked, echoing across the water.

Small figures ran back and forth over the lawn. Now there was shouting, crying, shrieking.

Dubh tipped his head back and smiled at the abbey.

The noonday sun now hung directly overhead, bathing the stone walls, glittering in the windowpanes of the abbey, reflecting back on the lake, making it look like the building was on fire.

Tiny figures crowded around a spot just under the oak tree. There was a figure on the grass in the middle of the activity, still and silent and stretched out on the lawn, as if she had fallen asleep on the grass in the shade. You wouldn't know the difference until you got closer. Until you saw the blood.

More people came running from all directions now, shouts and screams mingling, growing louder as the wind picked up and carried the noise.

Dubh's smile grew wider.

For a moment he allowed himself to watch their frenzy. To take in the noise. To imagine one of the tiny figures turning and spotting him there across the water, a dark silhouette. Like death himself.

Then he glanced back down at the cooler.

The last two witches he'd been sure about. But now ... now he wasn't sure. He needed the book, and the list inside, and he was sure he wasn't the only one looking by now. He had to find it before the witches did.

Dubh reached down to pick up the cooler at his feet. Turning, he walked back into the forest.

Chapter Twenty-Two

SAMUEL

It was always crowded in O'Neal's. The insides were done in dark cherrywood, with a marble-topped bar at the front that took up half the place. Mr. O'Neal, one of the church deacons, had bought the old pub years ago and turned it into a soda shop.

Sam slid into the corner booth, dropping his bag onto the table. Mrs. O'Neal waved to him from the bar, and Sam grinned. His Bible study met every Monday for breakfast during the summer, and hogged the booth for most of the morning, but the O'Neals didn't seem to mind.

He leaned back, glancing up at the TV on the wall. The news anchor was going through the weather report. He slid the lock off his cell screen. It was a futile gesture, since he would have had a notification if Dayna had texted him. He'd half hoped she would check in for new information about the case.

Not that he had any.

He'd hung around the house earlier that morning, hoping to overhear something as his father got ready for work. The sergeant had waited in the kitchen while Sam's mother had filled his travel mug, complaining about pushback from his force about something—how they were working the case, Sam would guess. Then his father had begun complaining about the Kellys' farm, and how people were calling in because the new paint on the barn was an eyesore from the road. "It's completely different colors in places, like they ran out halfway."

To his disappointment, his father had stomped out without saying more about the case.

Sam retreated to his bedroom, grumbling to himself.

A serial killer in town, and he's complaining about patchy barn paint. . . .

Sam had paused at the bedroom door, frowning. Why did that jog a memory? It wasn't as if he'd paid any attention to the paint when he'd spotted the dead cows. . . .

He'd realized a second later and frozen in the doorway. He hadn't been thinking of the Kellys' barn, or even one he'd seen in real life at all. It was the barn in the *video*.

He'd watched it over and over this week. Something about what his father had said made it click in his brain. There was a piece he'd been missing, he was suddenly sure of it.

Sam opened the link to the video again and rewatched it, flipping his phone over to enlarge the screen. He'd played it so many times that morning that his eyes started to glaze over right away, and he shook himself, squinting at the footage. Sure enough, there was something on the wall of the barn behind the blurry figures.

There was a small part of the wall that looked somehow *redder* than the rest. He hunched over his phone, squinting harder. It was probably just paint that had faded, or . . . the fuzziness of the camera. It was probably nothing.

Unless it was something.

Whatever it was, it had been enough to imprint on his subconscious after hours of watching the video. So maybe that made it something he should check out.

He blew out a breath and logged into his account, typing out a quick message.

Anyone see the red patches on the barn behind them?

The bell over the door jangled, and Sam jerked upright, shoving his phone into his pocket.

Morgan and her friend Amanda were the first inside, arms linked as they walked in, and Darius trailed behind them. Morgan paused just inside the door, long enough to announce, "The town is in an uproar, Samuel," before steering her friend toward the booth.

"She's so dramatic," Amanda said.

Morgan slid into the seat, flinging her blond braid over her shoulder. "It's not dramatic. There's a murderer in town. If anything I'm not being dramatic *enough*."

Sam sat up straight in the booth. "You— Who told you that?"

"People drove past the tape." Amanda leaned forward, eyes glittering. "The question is, who was it?"

"Mam is losing her mind." Morgan played with the end of her braid, wrapping it around her fingers. "She barely let me out of the house."

"My parents, too." Amanda frowned. "I had to tell them this was an emergency prayer meeting. Like, we're going to pray away the killer."

There was another jangle of the bell from the doorway, and a woman entered the soda shop. She had long brown hair in double braids and a round, cheerful face. She smiled and waved at Sam, bangles jingling.

"Morning, Samuel."

"Good morning to you, Miss Margery. How's the shop?"

"Oh, you know. Everyone drinking tea from bags these days, the heathens." She chuckled and patted him on the cheek as she walked past, and Sam grinned.

Margery Davis had been friends with his mother years back, though they had a falling-out when Margery had been asked to leave church. Still, she used to slip him chocolates whenever she saw him, and she seemed fond enough of him.

"You have a nice day, now."

Margery headed toward the back of the shop, where she began talking to Mrs. O'Neal. The second she was out of earshot, Amanda leaned over the table.

"That's the woman who wrote that article about Christian magic, isn't it?" She darted a look at Morgan, who arched her brows haughtily.

"I heard about that. She's probably a witch or something. You shouldn't be talking to her."

"Shut up," Sam said to Morgan, who only gave him an overly sweet smile.

Sam's phone buzzed, and he snatched it up, disappointed to see it was a message from his mother.

"Still waiting on Dayna, Romeo?" Darius grinned.

"You know, Samuel," Morgan said, "you should probably let that girl do her own thing. I heard her mam is back from camp. Did she mention that?"

Sam shrugged, suddenly irritated. "She didn't want to talk about it, and I didn't press her."

"I'll add her and Dayna to the prayer list. Hopefully the reverend brings her to church."

"Dayna doesn't want to go to church." Darius made a show of examining his nails. "Because Sam turned her gay."

Sam shot him a scowl, and Morgan said plaintively, "Darius, *don't*."

Before Sam could reply, Amanda nudged him and pointed at the TV. He glanced up, startled to see *Breaking News* in huge block letters.

Morgan was the one who asked Mrs. O'Neal to turn it up, since Sam was too busy staring at the box on the right-hand side of the screen, which showed a picture of a huge, castle-like building beside a lake, with the caption *Serial Killer Resurfaces?*

"...Katherine O'Brien, a professional poet and mother of two, was found outside popular tourist spot Kylemore Abbey. More startling still, the symbol at the scene is one associated with the killer that England once dubbed the Butcher of Manchester. This is the second murder in as many days, and according to our sources, the symbol has been found at both sites. The question all of us are asking is, is the Butcher back? And if so, why haven't we heard from the gardai on the matter?"

"Oh my god." Sam could feel the blood draining out of his face.

"Don't take the Lord's name in vain," Morgan said automatically, but she, too, was staring at the TV, eyes wide.

"Mrs. O'Brien." Caleb's voice trembled slightly. "My ma is friends with her. I mean . . . was."

"The Butcher." Amanda's face was pale. "Sam, is that true? Did they find that at the scene?"

Sam shrugged, feeling his stomach sink as his friends turned to look at him. "I have no idea. I didn't even know there was a second murder."

That, more than anything, was what filled him with dread. Not just that there was a second murder, but that it was *too soon*. It shouldn't have happened yet.

The Butcher had an MO. Sam knew it inside and out, and this wasn't right. There was supposed to be at least two weeks between each victim.

"I can't believe the Butcher is here in Nowheresville," Darius said. "Aren't there better places for his reign of terror?"

"Don't sound so casual about it, you freak," Jillian said.

"Easy for him." Amanda's gaze was fixed on the TV still, even though the reporter was now talking about crops dying. "The Butcher only kills women."

Sam glanced around the table, at his friends' pale faces and wide eyes. Nerves gnawed at his stomach. There was something off about this. Something that made cold dread ripple through his insides.

Why was the Butcher escalating?

Chapter Twenty-Three

MEINER

It had been one of those unnerving, feverish nights, where she wasn't certain if she'd slept or not. It brought back memories of other nights, her insides buzzing with that awful, pent-up energy. Meiner had taken her pill before bed, which always dulled the anxiety enough to sleep, so it wasn't that. It was simply her mind spinning in circles.

After she'd dropped Dayna off she'd ended up lying awake, her brain flicking from one image to the next. Cora's blank expression during the ritual. The Callighans, their heads bent together. The look in Grandma King's eye as she moved toward her.

Memories of the dark corners of her childhood home.

Her temper kept flaring. It felt like her blood was boiling in her veins, until she was literally sweating from the heat of it. Several times during the night she gave in, tearing off her sheets, pacing the length of the room. She wanted to destroy something. Snatch up the lamp from the bedside table and dash it to the floor, lash out at her reflection in the vanity mirror and watch it fracture under her fists.

But even with everything else, Dayna's freckled face kept popping up. The whole thing was confusing. Dayna had been so irritating, and the thought of her ascending still made her skin feel prickly, even now. But in spite of all that, she'd been dangerously close to kissing her last night.

What the hell had she been thinking?

Out in the kitchen, she dropped onto one of the chairs at the long table. The surface was crowded with empty bowls stained with batter and dirty wooden spoons. Reagan was at the stove, nodding along with the rock music blasting from the radio above the fridge. She looked up when Meiner came in.

"Bronagh brought charm necklaces for us this morning. Yours and Dayna's are there."

Meiner glanced down, surprised. Resting on the lid of the butter dish was a pair of bone charms on leather cords. She picked one up, running her fingers over the smooth surface of the shield knot etched onto the coin-sized disk. "Protection charm?"

"Aye, for the joint reading this afternoon." Reagan plucked hers from beneath her shirt collar, letting it dangle between her finger and thumb. "Doesn't exactly go with the rest of my accessories." She fingered the black stone in her choker and grinned when she noticed Meiner looking. "It's supposed to be from the Willamette meteorite, which would make it a couple billion years old. It's probably fake, but I thought it was pretty."

"It looks cool, even if it's not a billion years old." Meiner dropped the necklace beneath her shirt, feeling the cold surface of the charm settle onto her chest and slowly begin to warm.

On the counter, Reagan's phone chimed, and she scooped it up. "Cora and your gran are out getting supplies for the reading, and Dayna's heading over now."

She blinked, momentarily distracted at the mention of Dayna, as Reagan brandished a finger at the cupboard and muttered something under her breath. Two of the clay mugs floated down, wobbling slightly as they descended. As they reached eye level, she plucked them out of the air and set them on the table. "My magic's been overflowing since the ascension."

Meiner cleared her throat, trying not to let the jealousy show on her face. "Well, doesn't sound like a bad problem to have."

They both paused as Yemi drifted past the kitchen doorway, waving a thick bundle of smoldering sage, leaving trails of smoke and the sound of gentle humming in her wake.

Reagan's dark brows knit together. "She said cleansing is normal before a joint reading, but I swear she's been through the house, like, five times now."

"You can hardly blame her after what happened." Meiner picked up one of the knives from the counter and began toying with it, spreading her hand on the table and running the tip between the lines of her fingers.

"Abeg, have a care, Stabby Spice." Reagan thrust her wooden spoon at Meiner. "Just because you've an appetite for destruction doesn't mean I'll let you bleed to death all over the floor. Ma just cleaned it."

"Sorry." Meiner laid the knife down.

The front door slammed, and Reagan straightened up. "Perfect timing." As Dayna walked into the kitchen—wearing a very flattering gray sweater, Meiner noticed—Reagan slung one of her oven mitts at her. "You're on pancake duty."

Dayna caught the mitt, grinning. "Well, good morning to you, too, sunshine."

Reagan yanked her jacket off the hook by the door. "I've got to collect the eggs before the chickens go all cannibal on them. Make the rest of the batch since the Callighans are going to descend on us in the next hour." She added over her shoulder to Meiner, "Bronagh can eat her weight in pancakes."

Dayna turned to the stove, placing the oven mitt back on the counter as Reagan slammed the door behind her. "It's true. Last time she ate five, I counted." She spotted the teapot and reached for it. "Oh god, I need coffee, but this will have to do."

Meiner forced herself to smile. "How are you feeling?"

Dayna didn't look up as she poured the tea into a squat clay mug. "My head is pounding. Where's Cora and Grandma King?"

Meiner frowned, letting her hand drift to the knife again. "Out," she said shortly.

Narrowing her eyes, Dayna came to sit on the opposite side of the table, setting her mug down. "Out with it." When Meiner only stared, Dayna shook a finger at her. "Don't pretend I didn't tell you the most embarrassing shit *ever* last night. We're a little past shyness, aren't we?"

Meiner glanced in the direction of the hallway. They still weren't back yet; probably they'd be a while. Meiner grimaced.

"Something got in that circle, and that doesn't happen unless someone's opening a doorway. You heard the conversation after the ascension. She used to do black magic."

"And you're worried she still does." Dayna shuddered, wrapping her slender fingers around her mug.

"I'm pretty sure your Callighans are suspicious." Meiner shifted, a little uncomfortable. "But they haven't confronted her."

Dayna rolled her eyes. "The Callighans won't interfere with another coven, even if they suspect something's going on. They'll wait until shit hits the fan and then tell everyone they told them so. Classic Callighan move."

There was a moment of silence while Meiner digested this. Dayna got up to pour batter into the pan, and then turned to lean against the stove. "And what do *you* think your gran is up to?"

Meiner sighed. "If you're wondering if I know something, the answer is no. But I think she's hiding something."

The thought had kept her awake last night. She couldn't shake it. The easiest thing would be to go through Gran's room. Black magic left evidence, things Meiner didn't like to think about.

Dayna turned to place the pancakes in the oven, and Meiner shifted uneasily on the stool, wondering what she was thinking. When Dayna straightened, her face was serious. "If you think there's something going on that might put us in danger . . . it makes sense to figure out what it is, right?"

Meiner nodded. It felt weirdly gratifying to be on the same page as Dayna. "Um, your protection charm is here, by the way. Reagan said Bronagh made them for us."

Dayna scooped the charm off the butter dish and held it between two fingers, examining it carefully before looping the cord around her neck. When she attempted to move the bone charm to the front, she ended up tugging at the cord in irritation. "Shit, it's caught in my hair."

Meiner stood up. "Uh, want help?"

"Thanks, I have no idea what's going on back there."

Meiner bit her lip, carefully pushing Dayna's hair to one side, very aware of her fingertips grazing the back of Dayna's neck as she untangled the leather knot. Dayna's hair was smooth and clean under her hands, and she got a whiff of vanilla before she stepped back.

"Thanks." Dayna turned back to face her, and she nodded. For a moment neither of them said anything, and then the fractured sounds from the TV in the living room dropped into the silence between them.

"... another of the strange symbols found at the scene..."

Dayna frowned, moving into the next room to turn it up, with Meiner following right behind her.

"Katherine O'Brien, professional poet and mother of two, was found outside popular tourist spot Kylemore Abbey. Keep in mind, the details of this story may be disturbing to our listeners. More at ten."

"*Shit!*" Dayna sank down onto the couch. "This was why we *did* the ascension. We were supposed to find a way to stop this before he killed again."

Meiner was frowning at the TV. "That was fast. Don't most serial killers have...I dunno, time in between?"

"A cool-off period, that's what it's called. We were supposed to have *weeks*." She rubbed a hand over her face. "Samuel was wrong. This happened too soon."

Another murder. Another symbol at the scene, and, Meiner was willing to bet, another missing body part. Dayna exchanged a look with her, and she could tell they were both thinking the same thing.

They needed to do the group reading *now*—before another day passed, and another body was found.

Chapter Twenty-Four

DAYNA

Dayna was in the living room helping the Callighans set up when Grandma King walked in, trailed by Meiner carrying a stack of cardboard boxes. "The general store had enough lights to stock Santa's whole damn village," she said.

Reagan rubbed her hands together. "Good, let's do this up right. It will make a great Instagram picture."

Faye groaned, rolling her eyes to the ceiling. "This isn't a photo op, Reagan. This is serious."

"Auntie, you know my whole life is a photo op." Reagan flicked her hair over one shoulder and stuck a hip out.

Dayna grinned and mimed taking a photo. "Yes, so fierce. Now give me sultry."

Reagan stuck her hands under her chin and fluttered her lashes outrageously, and Faye clucked her tongue. "Honestly, you two are incorrigible."

"Reagan, did you hear that? We're incorrigible."

"That *does* sound like us."

"Oh, get that stick out of your bum, love." Brenna swatted at her daughter, who scowled back at her. "Hand me one of the crystals, would you, Dayna? We'll do a triangle setup, I think. That should work for all of us."

Dayna picked up the heavy crystal orb with its stand, moving over to where Brenna was arranging the table in the center of the room. She set it down carefully and watched Brenna fuss with the alignment. She could sense right away that Brenna had something to say, and sure enough after a moment she cleared her throat.

"Listen, love, have you been sleeping?"

Dayna blinked at her. Not for the first time she wondered if the Callighans could secretly read minds. "Not really." She shrugged. "I mean, I don't ever sleep well, but . . . yeah, it's been worse than usual."

"That's what I thought. I recognize the symptoms. Faye used to have a terrible time getting to sleep when she was in medical school." Brenna dipped into the pocket of her sweater and brought out a satchel with silver ties, which she pressed into Dayna's hands. "Sleep tea," she said. When Dayna looked at it cautiously, she laughed. "It's only herbs, no magic or drugs, I promise. I made the satchel up myself. It will help you fall asleep. Just drink one cup before bed and don't let it steep longer than three minutes or it will have some bite."

"Thanks." Dayna slipped it into her pocket.

It took the next hour to set everything up. Reagan and Dayna helped string the lights, with the occasional assistance from Meiner if they couldn't reach something. Reagan insisted on bringing the light-up model of the solar system from her bedroom to join the show.

To Dayna's delight, Reagan spent several minutes cross-legged on the fireplace hearth, making the tiny crystal planets spin through the air around them. Then Faye muttered about "show-offs" and Reagan made the planet Mars bump into the back of her left knee until she retreated to the kitchen.

Eventually Dayna found herself sitting cross-legged in front of the table, between Meiner and Reagan. The living room had been completely redecorated. Fairy lights hung from the ceiling like glittering ropes, and crisscrossed down the walls, and Faye had set up white pillar candles on every surface. The light danced and jumped on the crystals, sending shadows skittering this way and that, bright spheres flickering across the surface.

"No Cora?" Meiner directed this question at Grandma King, and the old woman shook her head.

"Said she feels ill. Doesn't matter anyway, you two are not ascended, so we technically don't need you to make this work."

Dayna could tell by the way Meiner stiffened beside her that she was close to jumping up and storming off, but after a moment she took a breath and stayed where she was, scowling at the crystals in the center.

Dayna could hardly blame Cora for wanting to sit this one out.

"Join hands," Bronagh instructed. They obeyed. Meiner's palm was cool and slightly callused, and her grip was firm. Dayna could feel the pressure of the rings she wore between her fingers, and the mere thought that she was sitting here holding Meiner's hand made her face burn. She prayed to Danu it wasn't obvious in the darkened room.

"Now, I would have liked a little more time to prepare, but as we all know, a second victim was found today." Bronagh looked around the circle, her face grim. "Which means we'll have to do this thing quicker than I would have liked." She glanced over at Brenna, who nodded, then continued.

"Scry with the crystal nearest to you only. With us connected, the crystals will be, too, so it doesn't matter which one you've got. And keep in mind our question—we need to know how the Butcher is choosing his victims. If we know who's next, we may be able to stop him."

Dayna let her gaze drift over the crystals. They were all roughly the same size, but the nearest one was clouded, and the one on the right side of the table had a faint pink tinge to it. The one Grandma King had brought was the clearest one, and it was set in an old-fashioned bronze base. She shifted her attention back to the clouded crystal, letting her gaze relax as Bronagh continued.

"Whatever happens, don't let go of the person next to you."

Dayna exchanged a glance with Reagan. Her palms felt suddenly sweaty, and she had to resist the urge to pull away.

Instead she focused on the crystal. She'd scried before, but not with so many people. It was distracting. Even the lights and candles made her want to look around the room. The candlelight reflected in the surface of the ball kept catching her eye, and finally her gaze relaxed. Spots of reflected lights danced across the crystal, bent and refracted by the curved surface.

With her mind clear, she immediately focused on her breath. On the oxygen leaving and entering her lungs.

Shit. She tried to clamp down on the panic before it started. To think of something, anything else. It seemed like the obsession was always just around the corner, waiting to pounce on any blank space in her thoughts.

The reading wasn't going to work if the panic kept invading.

She glared at the crystal, forcing herself to refocus. To zero in on the light dancing and bending on the surface. The flickers of candle flame that stretched and zigzagged in the crystal. The dancing shadows between, like smoke swirling across the surface—

No, not smoke, she realized—*fog.* Curling up and slowly clearing away like a strong wind was blowing. She stared, transfixed, as something came into view on the surface of the crystal—and then somehow she was *in* it.

She was standing in the woods—and yet, she marveled, she was also *not* standing in the woods, but sitting cross-legged on the living room floor—and there was an abandoned, crumbling stone house before her, covered in creeping ivy and moss. The roof was missing, and when she stepped closer, she could see strange symbols carved into the walls, swirling spirals and knots, intricate patterns that made it hard to focus.

She walked closer to the house, until she could peer into the window. In the center was an altar made from new, fresh stone. On the altar lay a book, bound in dark brown leather. The words inside blurred as she tried to read them, and Dayna squinted in frustration. This was something desperately important, something that would help her protect her coven. But in the vision, the words continued to squirm and reshape themselves.

She could only make out one thing on the page, a symbol. The one they'd found at the murder scene. There was something about the book that was strangely familiar. She could dredge up a faint memory of holding it, feeling the leather cover beneath her fingers. But it felt like the memory of a dream, or the elusive, ungraspable feeling of déjà vu. Already it was slipping through her fingers.

The crackle of underbrush brought Dayna upright, heart beating hard against her rib cage. She stared out the moss-framed window. Her breath stopped.

What stood in the clearing just outside the little stone house was not a beast, but it was not a woman either. She was tall, with black hair that rippled down her shoulders. Her eyes were wide and long-lashed, and her lips were the red of winter berries. She wore no clothes, and the surface of her skin was freckled and golden, like the speckles of a fawn. Massive antlers twisted from her head, six points that towered on each side.

When she saw Dayna in the window, she smiled. Her voice was low and musical, and she spoke so quietly that Dayna knew she shouldn't have been able to hear her at such a distance. "Hello, daughter of oak."

Too stunned to speak, Dayna only stared wide-eyed at this apparition, suddenly hit by the barest shadow of a memory. She'd stood here before, in the center of this forest, her back to the stone temple, asking the woman to guard . . . something. She couldn't remember what.

And here she was, all these years later.

Dayna blinked, surfacing from the memory as though she were waking from a dream. A dream of another life, another time. The sensation sent her mind reeling.

A memory within a vision couldn't be real, could it?

The woman stepped closer, and her face became grave. "We don't have much time."

Dayna gripped the mossy windowsill. She was pressed against the wall now, and she half wondered if she was going to stain her white sweater. The vision was so *real*; she could feel the rough stone beneath her palms, smell the scent of fir trees as the wind tangled cool fingers through her hair. "Who are you?"

"My names are many, but you may think of me as Cernunnos, if you wish." The not-woman stepped closer, and Dayna realized she was a giant.

The tips of her horns nearly brushed the bottom branches of the trees. "Daughter of oak, you must listen carefully. The world beyond yours is unbalanced. The deaths of our saints are unlocking her cell one by one. You must find the book. Find the list before he does."

Cernunnos. The god—goddess, clearly. Holy shit. Her words came out in a stammering rush. "Wh-what book? What do you mean *cell*? Who—"

There was a rustling in the underbrush behind the ruins, and Dayna jumped. The antlered woman's black-eyed gaze flicked away. She inhaled sharply, nostrils flaring.

"The black one is coming. You must go, daughter."

Another crack, the sound of a branch breaking, and the antlered woman began to fade back into the forest. "Watch for him."

Dayna leaned forward, trying to keep an eye on the woman, who seemed to be disappearing as she watched. The stone sill scraped her palms. "Wait!"

Cernunnos turned away, her voice floating behind her. "Wake up, daughter of oak. Wake up."

The woods were suddenly empty, leaving her staring at the spot where the woman had been. Another rustle, this time louder. When she turned to look out the other window, she saw only thick forest.

Another crack. Sharper, closer. The sound of heavy footfalls. It sent a sudden, cold pang of fear through her, and Dayna clutched the windowsill harder, clinging to the moss-slick stones as if they might anchor her. Something impossibly heavy was crashing its way through the forest toward her.

The antlered woman's warning echoed in her ears: *The black one is coming.*

Whatever that was, she didn't want to meet it.

She had to wake up.

The vision seemed impossibly real, though. Everything, the moss beneath her hands, the stones beneath her bare feet, the wind rustling the trees, and the dusky surroundings of the forest. At first it had seemed blurry and dreamlike. But now everything seemed incredibly vivid, like she'd sunk deeper into the vision without noticing.

But what did that mean? Did it mean she could be hurt here? Killed?

The thought sent a chill through her. She backed up into the center of the tiny stone house.

Another crash, a snap. Closer, closer. Dayna squeezed her eyes shut and concentrated on her heartbeat, frantic and birdlike, fluttering against her ribs. She dug her nails into the fabric of her sweater, fingers twisting and clenching as she commanded herself to wake up. Wake up. *Wake up.*

Wake up, daughter of oak. Wake up.

Footsteps pounding now, faster and faster. Barreling through the forest toward her. The stone structure beneath her shuddered and groaned.

Wake up. Wake up. Wake up.

"Wake up. Dayna, *wake up.*"

Reagan's voice.

Dayna's eyes flew open.

There was a perfect globe of light hovering in front of her, and at first she thought, *The moon looks strange.* Then her eyes focused, and she saw the crystal ball on the table in front of her. She blinked around at the circle. The witches stared at her.

"You were shaking." Reagan's eyes were wide and scared. Her grip on Dayna's hand was still tight, as if she were physically anchoring her to the present. "You were yelling at yourself to wake up."

Dayna slumped back against the side of the couch, releasing her grip on Meiner's and Reagan's hands. A second later she realized they were all still staring at her.

"Wha—" She sat up, and Reagan pointed, face grim.

"Dayna, look."

She looked down, heart pounding, at the dirt stain in the center of her white sweater and the flecks of green moss that had coated the walls of the dream house.

Chapter Twenty-Five

MEINER

They spent the evening at the kitchen table, researching the strange symbols they'd seen in the surface of the crystal ball. Yemi served them dinner—a dish she called jollof rice—as they pored over books and articles.

Meiner—like everyone else except Dayna, it seemed—had seen a series of pictures in the cloudy crystal. The ruins of a church, stained and covered in moss. The strange symbols that had looked so familiar.

Dayna's scream had jerked her from the trance. And the stain on her sweater... Meiner shuddered as she flipped through the book in her lap, trying not to think about how the stain had bloomed in the center of Dayna's torso like a gunshot wound. Leaching into the fabric out of nowhere.

Bronagh had explained that if your magic was especially strong and your state of mind a certain way—heightened emotions, maybe—you could get pulled completely into a joint vision. Apparently it didn't happen often, but Meiner thought once would be more than enough to put her off joint scrying for life.

It seemed the aftereffects of the ascension had opened Dayna up to it. What was less common, apparently, was for a god to insert itself directly *into* your vision. On top of that, none of them were pledged to Cernunnos. Bronagh didn't seem to have an answer for this, and even Grandma King just shrugged and said the gods did as they pleased.

Hardly an answer, in Meiner's opinion.

In her experience, the gods didn't show up unless things were especially dire. The thought made the back of her neck prickle.

"I think the symbols on the ruins may simply be older versions of what we know already." Bronagh was flipping through a very old, ratty-looking book with a yellow cover. "I swear I recognize the one with the knot work around the edges. I'm almost sure it's got something to do with spell work."

"We suspected the Butcher possessed some kind of magic," Brenna said. "Otherwise, he wouldn't be able to tell who's a witch and who isn't."

"The book tells him," Dayna said. "There's a list inside; that's how he knows. We have to find it."

"She said find it *before* he does," Meiner said slowly. "Which means he doesn't have it. How did he know to kill the first two?"

Dayna frowned. "Sam thinks he kills in cycles, which means...he keeps trying to repeat the list. Like...he remembers some of it, but... maybe just the first part?"

"Never mind all that. Does he have magic or not? Are we fighting another witch?"

They all turned to look at Cora, who'd just come down the stairs and was leaning in the kitchen doorway. She looked pale, and her blond hair was messy.

Brenna shook her head, staring down at her cards, which she'd laid over the entire end of the kitchen table. "Certainly not. Masculine energy all over this spread."

Grandma King snorted. "Of course there is."

Bronagh took a moment to catch Cora up on everything, and the others went back to silently studying their books.

After a long moment, Reagan passed her book to Dayna. "I wasn't sure about this, but...do you think it's similar?"

Dayna took the book gingerly and laid it flat on the table. The pages were very old, and they crackled beneath her fingertips. The symbol Reagan had pointed to in the center of the page was a small square with four other squares inside.

"Yeah, I saw this one on the wall."

"It symbolizes the god Lugh, associated with the law. The druids had their own courts, and they'd carve that symbol into the earth to invoke the god's wisdom."

The kitchen was utterly silent as the witches turned to look at the tapestry above the table. The god Lugh was depicted with what looked like a mini sun in one hand and a gavel in the other. Meiner could see the same realization dawning on all of them. "The woman who died," Dayna finally said, a little breathless. "She was a judge."

There was another deep silence, punctuated by the shuffling of Brenna's cards. Then Bronagh muttered faintly, "Someone's stained Lugh," and reached up to fuss at the oily stain near the god's left foot.

"So . . . what? Does this have something to do with the law? Someone with a grudge?"

"Dayna, what was it you said the dream-Cernunnos said to you?" Brenna paused in her shuffling.

"'The black one is coming.'" Dayna shuddered.

"The black one," Brenna mumbled. "Sure and that does ring a bell. Reagan, give me that."

Reagan looked surprised, but she handed the book over without question. Brenna flipped through page after page, licking her finger every now and again. Cora was looking gradually more irritated. Finally Brenna paused near the middle of the book.

"Found it."

The chapter featured a painting of a weathered stone temple, rounded, with pillars on both sides. Above the doorway hung a golden plaque. Meiner recognized the shape etched into the plate, the complex patterns of lines inside the circle. It was missing some of the sharper lines at the edges, but it was unmistakably the Butcher's symbol.

Dayna glanced over at Meiner, eyes wide, and Meiner knew she was thinking of the stone ruins in the vision. It was hard to tell from the drawing, but it might be about the same size.

"What does it say?" Cora's voice climbed with excitement. They'd all crowded in now, and her shoulder pressed against Meiner's. Meiner was about to lean away and shoot her a dark look when she caught sight of Dayna's irritated expression. She shouldn't feel a thrill at that, she knew, but it was a bit gratifying. She inched sideways, closer to Dayna.

There was a caption under the picture.

The temple of Carman, a witch who invaded Ireland with her three sons, Dubh (the black one), Olc (evil), and Calma (valiant).

There was silence for a moment as everyone took in the picture, and then Cora said, "Carman, as in, the village of Carman?"

Brenna continued reading.

"'She was locked away when she tried to take over Ireland, by the gods Lugh, Bé Chuille, the Dagda'"—she poked a finger at the tapestry each time, finding the corresponding gods—"'Crichinbel...' Hm, these last two aren't on the tapestry."

This time it was Dayna inching closer to Meiner, practically reading over Meiner's shoulder, which was just as distracting, but in an entirely different way. Half of her was concentrating on an illustration of Carman—a dark-haired woman clad in black, electric currents of power crackling around her—the other was distracted by the fact that Dayna's perfume was distinctly citrusy.

"'She died after being locked away, and they buried her,'" Faye was reading over her shoulder now, "'trapping her spirit in the grave.'"

"The bitch isn't even from here. She's from Athens." Cora folded her arms across her chest, frowning. "Is that all we're up against, then? A witch with a chip on her shoulder and a couple of dodgy blokes? Big deal."

Faye frowned. "Maybe. But look at the bottom. There seems to be some debate if she was goddess or mortal."

"If she's a god, her sons are, too." Meiner forced her attention back to the page, even though Dayna's hair was now tickling her bare shoulder as Dayna leaned over to peer at the book.

Faye shook her head. "It says Carman's dead, though. Buried in a tomb somewhere near Wexford. The brothers were banned by a spell, cut off from Ireland as long as there was water around it."

Bronagh sighed and sank down into the seat next to her daughter, picking up her teacup. "Perhaps the magic doesn't see it that way anymore."

They stared at her, waiting.

"That great bloody bridge they keep pouring thousands into, the Celtic Crossing or whatever they're so determined to call it," she grumbled. "Ireland isn't completely surrounded by water anymore, not really. It's connected to England."

Meiner's mouth dropped open. "Wait, the Butcher's victims started showing up—"

"As soon as the bridge went up. Then he could enter Ireland," Reagan said, and collapsed into the chair on the other side of her. "Damn."

Chapter Twenty-Six

CORA

"Again."

Slowly Cora opened her eyes.

The forest made the midday sky dark, the trees ominous, towering shapes above them. The glowing coals of the fire between them painted Grandma King's weathered face in orange and black. She looked like some kind of forest wraith, crouched beside the shallow glass basin of rust-red liquid.

Cora let out a heavy sigh. "We've already done it six times."

"And now you'll do it a seventh."

She stood across from Grandma King, in the center of the crude hexagram she'd constructed from fallen branches. Smoke rose from the pit between them, filling her throat and nostrils, making the headache pounding behind her brow a hundred times worse.

Her arms ached from the forest of tiny slashes she'd created with her dagger along the insides of her arms. She kept them on one small spot on both her wrists so they could be covered.

Blood trickled down her palms and onto her fingers. She'd protested this part of the practice initially. Why did a test run need real blood? But Gran had given her a scornful look that had shut her up fast.

Besides, she felt a surge of power every time she did the ceremony, even though she never said the final word, as Gran had instructed her. But it was like something pressed at the edges of her skin, something powerful inside her responded each time she chanted the spell. This power, and the promise of it, was the only thing keeping her on her feet, and even so, she swayed slightly, the trees blurring in and out around her.

She did the ritual again, wincing as she pressed the tip of the dagger to her skin, letting her blood drip to the ground inside the hexagram. When she finally came to the end of the chant, Gran gave her a wide, nasty smile and said, "Again."

At this moment, there was nobody in the world she hated more than the old woman. She shook her head slowly, cheeks flushed, hands trembling at her sides. "I'm exhausted. We've done this seven times now. I've got it."

"Have you?" The old woman narrowed her blue eyes at Cora. "Your mind wanders. Do you grow bored with this? Shall I hand things over to Meiner instead?"

"No." Cora scowled at her, the anger making her sit up taller. "I can do this."

Grandma King flipped her cigarette case closed, tapping a cigarette on the top. "We shall see." The old woman turned away, carefully taking a metal box from her bag, which she deposited onto the ground in front of Cora.

"What is it?" Cora leaned forward, wincing at the pain in her wrists.

She flicked the clasp back on the box and opened it slowly. It was lined with velvet, and in the center were two thick gold bands. Nestled just behind them was a long, wickedly sharp dagger. The handle was intricately done, gold snakes with ruby eyes wrapped up the silver handle.

Cora reached for the blade. She couldn't seem to help herself. The gold snakes were cool and smooth beneath her fingers.

"I've told you, your ascension will be different than the others." Grandma King watched as Cora picked up the dagger and turned it this way and that under the light. "You'll be tested. You must take your own sacrifice."

Cora stared at her. "Take . . . what?" Grandma King said nothing, and Cora shook her head.

"You mean . . ."

Grandma King nodded slowly. "Up until now I've provided it. But in order to trigger your ascension you must take your own, and it must be . . . significant."

Cora set the dagger down, her stomach turning. "What does that mean?"

"A central part of him." Grandma King's voice dropped lower. "A heart will do, or . . . the other thing men value so very much." Her thin brows were raised as she said this, and Cora's mouth dropped open.

"You're having me on."

"Don't go soft on me now, my girl." Grandma King climbed slowly to her feet with a groan. "We are not bound by common law or morals. We're witches, and we do what we must."

Cora blinked, trying to clear her vision. She didn't even want to think about it. She just wanted to go home and lie down. "What . . . what are the cuffs for?"

Grandma King turned away, collecting the grimoire off the grass. She didn't seem to have heard the last question. "Are you ready to go, witchling?"

"Yes." Thank god. Every muscle in her body ached, and her head throbbed in time with her heartbeat.

"Good." Grandma King slammed the grimoire shut. "Because here is your test. Find your way out."

"What?"

Grandma King scooped up the bags by the fire, including Cora's purse. Cora shot to her feet. "Hey, that's my—"

She paused, blinking. Her head was beginning to swim. Above her the treetops were silhouetted against the open sky, which tilted and swooped. She blinked again and jerked her gaze back down to the fire. "Wh-what did you put in the—"

There was no one there. Grandma King was gone.

"Fuck!" The word rang out into the empty forest. Cora stumbled forward, and the ground surged beneath her feet. Something rumbled overhead, and tiny, cold pinpricks of rain began dotting her skin. Cora cursed again.

That bitch had drugged her and left her in the middle of the forest. She didn't even know where they were, she'd just followed Gran's instructions blindly as she'd driven, too preoccupied to pay close attention. And now on top of everything, the heavens were about to open and empty themselves onto Cora's head.

Hadn't she done everything the old woman wanted?

She kept walking, teeth clenched against the rising panic. She was no innocent babe lost in the woods; she was a fucking witch. She would find her way back to the parking lot.

Swearing under her breath, Cora plunged onward, finding handholds on tree trunks as she passed. Without the light from the fire, everything was a dark blur, but somehow, she felt less dizzy.

They hadn't walked that long to get here, maybe five minutes? She shook her head, trying to rid herself of the fogginess. She wondered nervously if her vision was dimming or if the forest was simply becoming thicker and thicker as she walked on.

Another few minutes of groping through the steadily growing darkness, and then the rain began coming down harder, soaking Cora's thin sweatshirt. Shivering violently, she pressed on, too angry to stop to think.

She had to be going the right way. It was this way. She *remembered*.

The sun should be directly overhead at this time of day, and yet . . . the forest now seemed endlessly black. There was something unnatural about it. Even a forest at its thickest didn't block out this much light.

Cora sucked in a breath, ashamed that it was more of a sob. Branches broke beneath her feet. She didn't want to stop, because when she did . . . the sounds began. The crash of a tree branch too heavy to have fallen off by itself, the buzz of some creature she couldn't identify. The whistle of wind, and the rustle of branches, though she felt no breeze on her face.

Minutes went by; Cora didn't know how long. She should have been at the parking lot by now. Shaking, she pulled off the protection necklace Bronagh had given them this morning. Hanging it over one finger, she let it swing, whispering a guiding spell, invoking the name of Caorthannach. With the other hand she dug her lighter out.

The necklace swung back and forth, casting wild shadows over the trees around her. Then abruptly it went still. Cora felt it drag down on her finger, the cord cutting into her flesh.

"Shit!" She dropped it, backing away hastily.

Around her, the forest noises cut off all at once, and the silence closed in around her. She felt . . . watched.

Whatever it was didn't feel friendly.

Gasping, sobbing, she stumbled forward into the impenetrable darkness. She didn't dare question her decision. This was not a mistake; she would break through into the parking lot any minute now.

Something snagged her foot, and Cora went down, cracking her forehead on the thick trunk of the nearest tree. Twigs and stones cut into her face, and she squeezed her eyes shut, moaning.

Slowly she rolled over onto her back, a trickle of warmth spreading out over her forehead, trailing down her cheek. The treetops warped and spun above her, and resentment surged in her breast, overwhelming the pain.

"Where are you, Caorthannach? Why did you let that thing take me? If you're here," she growled at the treetops, "show yourself."

The second the command fell from her lips, Cora felt the ground shake beneath her. She stiffened.

Something struck her in the chest, hard, knocking her breath out of her body.

"You are mine, witchling."

Cora's head jerked up, her heart crowding into her throat. It was the same voice she'd heard in her head, but now the woman it belonged to loomed over her. She was tall, maybe the same height as Meiner, and she seemed to glow, as if the coals from the dying fire Cora had left behind were embedded beneath her skin.

Her hair fell in ringlets to her waist. On her head was a circle of orange-and-gold flowers, set with glass beads that glittered despite the darkness, a crown of flames against her black hair. The material of her dress was strange, gold-and-black scales that moved like liquid around her form. Cora wasn't sure if she was wearing it, or if it was part of her skin.

Her eyes were as inky black as her hair, the pupils impossibly wide. When she stepped forward, Cora scrambled back on her hands and knees. Terror flashed through her, leaving her breathless and gasping, hot and cold waves rushing over her skin. The woman was the most beautiful thing she'd ever seen, but there was something distinctly unearthly about her. The way she moved, the way her face turned this way and that as she examined Cora. As if she had not been born but formed herself out of nothing. The sight of her made Cora's skin crawl.

"You think to challenge me, to test me?" The woman's voice was a hiss, the rasp of silk on silk, and Cora blinked as the shoulders of her dress moved. A moment later she realized what she was seeing: not the dress, but a pair of *snakes*. Scales glittered black and gold as the slender bodies dropped from her shoulders, undulating, slinking down her arms.

"I never—" Cora hated how weak she sounded, how her voice trembled. "I wasn't—"

The woman moved so quickly Cora didn't have time to flinch, leaning down to catch her chin, tilting her face up so Cora was forced to look at her.

Cora's chest tightened. She'd been wrong about the color of the woman's eyes. They weren't just black; they burned with light at their centers, twin flames wreathed in inky darkness.

"You will continue to be tested. Your worthiness measured, your strength tried," Caorthannach whispered. Her mouth was close to Cora's ear, and the goddess's breath was like the kiss of a flame. "You will prove your dedication before I give you what you desire. Say you will prove yourself to me, Cora."

"Aye, I will," she gasped out.

Caorthannach reached down and seized both her wrists, hauling her to her feet with a single, violent tug. A moment later the skin beneath Caorthannach's slender bronze fingers began to burn.

"Please," Cora said through gritted teeth.

"You are mine." Caorthannach's voice was filled with hissing, with the crackle of flames. Her gaze was bottomless, drinking in Cora's face, paralyzing her. "Mine to do with as I will. Devote yourself to me and I will grant you unlimited power, the kind you'll need to face what's coming. Challenge me, and I will pull you apart piece by piece."

Cora could only nod. The skin beneath Caorthannach's fingers had become intensely painful, burning hotter and hotter. Her eyes streamed with tears.

Caorthannach bared her teeth in a shocking smile. Her teeth were rotten, cracked and chipped and crooked behind her full red lips. Cora flinched, and the woman's smile stretched wider. She opened her mouth, a snake about to swallow a mouse.

"Awake."

Something slammed into the side of Cora's face, knocked her backward, sending stars bursting across her vision. Then darkness crashed back into place and stayed.

Chapter Twenty-Seven

MEINER

Thursday morning the two covens were downstairs researching again, and it occurred to Meiner that right now might be a perfect time to snoop through Grandma King's room.

All she needed was a lookout.

Upstairs, she could hear the echo of voices in the bathroom; the door was slightly ajar. Evidently Reagan and Dayna were in there doing their makeup or something. Meiner started to turn and then paused as Reagan's muffled voice came through the door.

"I'm just concerned. You heard Bronagh. You got pulled in because of your emotional state."

"I'm fine, I swear. And she said it could be something *like* that, not that exactly."

There was a pause, and the thump of a drawer. "I just . . . feel like lately whenever we try to talk about anything serious, you push me away."

Oh god. Meiner grabbed the banister, half wanting to turn and flee down the stairs, half rooted to the spot. This was horrifying and fascinating and *completely* none of her business.

"That's not what I'm trying to do." Dayna's voice was tense. "It's just that I don't deal with this stuff well. It works better for me to just...not think about it."

"You mean push it down temporarily. You know, if you force it all into a tiny little box, it will eventually explode."

"Oh my god, that's so dramatic." Dayna laughed, and then the laughter cut off and she sighed. "Look, I'm sorry. That's just how I deal. Can we talk about this stuff later, when people stop showing up murdered? Once we've checked off 'catch serial killer' and 'stave off impending doom' from our to-do list, then I'll sign up for therapy or something."

Reagan sighed. "Abeg, I don't believe you."

A moment later the door swung open, and Reagan emerged from the bathroom. She stopped short upon seeing Meiner, who nodded and continued up the last step and into the hallway. Hopefully her face wasn't turning red. She could feel her cheeks burning.

For a second, she thought Reagan was going to accuse her of eavesdropping, but she only slipped past her and down the stairs without a word.

When Dayna emerged a moment later, she blinked at Meiner, who was now standing on the threshold of Grandma King's room. Meiner cleared her throat and said quickly, "Remember saying I should find out what Grandma King is up to? I'm going to search her room. Can you wait here?"

Dayna frowned, darting a look down the hallway. "I didn't say I'd stand guard. I don't know if I want to be a part of your coven's dirty business."

"Come on. Just for a minute? You said I should look, and everyone is downstairs. It's perfect." Meiner kept her voice to a whisper, pausing long enough that she and Dayna could hear the activities downstairs. Grandma King's voice was loud and cross as she snapped back at something Cora had said. "They'll be fighting for ages. Just stand there and make noise if you hear anyone on the stairs."

"What noise? You want me to caw like a crow or something?"

Meiner snorted. "No, just...rap on the wall or something."

"Brilliant, that will look super inconspicuous, me just standing here thumping away at the wall." Dayna was starting to cave, though; Meiner could tell by the way she uncrossed her arms and leaned a shoulder against the wall with a sigh. "Fine," she said at last. "But if you get caught, don't tell anyone I helped you. Your gran scares the shit out of me."

"Thanks." Meiner took a breath and crossed the threshold.

She started with the trunks in the corner where Grandma King kept her tools. If there were signs of black magic being used anywhere, it would be here. There were three ironbound chests, and though they were locked with combinations rather than old-fashioned lock and key, Meiner knew all of them.

She started with the far-left trunk. She lifted the lid and sat back on her haunches, blowing out a breath in disgust. It reeked like stale incense.

On top, there were thin silk scarves in various colors. These she knew were often used in protection spells. Gran would rip off a piece and bind the ingredients inside. Underneath she found bundles of herbs, dried berries, loose leaf tea, and a number of small animal skulls—mostly rodents, she'd guess. These she avoided touching.

There was also a small box in the corner, and Meiner lifted the lid, grimacing.

Bones.

These days, Gran used a combination of smooth river rocks and the bones of a chicken to divine the future. But these didn't look like chicken bones.

Pale and bleached with age, they sat on a bed of red velvet. As Meiner stared at them, a cold wave of recognition hit her. She made a disgusted noise in her throat and slammed the box shut. They brought back memories of lingering in the doorway, peering out while Gran crouched on the back porch, throwing the bones so they scattered with a hair-raising clatter over the wooden boards. Then low rhythmic chanting and an occasional rumble and shudder from the house, as if the very earth beneath was disturbed.

Meiner shivered. So, the old woman had kept the bones. That was . . . disturbing.

Not for the first time, Meiner wondered if it wasn't simply old age causing her grandmother's mind to go. It wasn't as if the doctors could diagnose a case of black magic.

Why had she kept these? And more concerning still... why bring them here?

Her sense of unease growing, Meiner quickly searched the other trunks. At first there was nothing damning, or even remotely interesting—only more spell ingredients, a pack of black-and-gold tarot cards that her grandmother rarely used anymore, and in one corner of the last chest, concealed in a velvet bag, a strange, squat little statue of a man with the head of a goat, which Meiner flipped upside down and examined carefully. The statue, while incredibly creepy, did not seem possessed of any black magic, and there didn't seem to be a hidden compartment anywhere. Still, she quickly snapped a picture of it on her phone before putting it back in the corner, disappointment settling in the pit of her stomach.

She made sure to close and lock all the trunks carefully and then wandered through the rest of the room.

She stopped short in front of the mirror. There was a single, hand-painted card stuck in the frame, just above the plastic-bagged toothbrush on the counter. Scarlet rope ran around the edges and ended in a noose in one corner. In the center a grinning skull peered out. Either by accident or very deliberately, Grandma King had set the standing hand mirror across from it; Meiner stared, transfixed, at the death's-head reflected again and again, an endless hallway filled with black ink skulls.

Then she shook herself, reaching out to snatch the card off the frame. Her gran could be so damn macabre sometimes. Her sense of humor had taken a strange, dark turn since the dementia.

Meiner stuffed the card in her pocket and turned, noticing one of the bottom dresser drawers was cracked open. She stepped forward, bending to dig through Gran's socks, wrinkling her nose at the scratchy wool.

Her hand hit something through the fabric—the bottom of the drawer, she thought at first. But no, she felt it give slightly under her fingertip.

Meiner shoved the socks out of the way, revealing a leather book. Her heart jumped, and she was reaching for it, just as she heard a hard thump on the wall. She froze, then hurried through the bedroom and back into the hall, only to find Dayna gone from her spot on the wall.

"What were *you* doing?"

She whirled around, finding herself face-to-face with Cora. Meiner frowned at her. She hadn't noticed it this morning, too occupied with Dayna and all the research they'd been doing, but Cora seemed different up close. She was paler than usual, and her face had a sharper quality to it. She looked tired and gaunt, though she'd tried to cover it up with lots of face powder and red lipstick. She was even wearing jewelry, which wasn't like her: a long necklace of rosary beads with a moon pendant, and a pair of thick golden cuffs that went halfway up her forearms.

Cora's eyes glittered as she stepped closer, peering past the doorway.

"Going through Grandma King's sock drawer, are we? You know she'll kill you if you touch her stuff, especially that."

"What I'm doing is none of your business." Meiner's temper flared instantly.

"I don't think Grandma King would approve of this, do you?" Cora glanced deliberately toward the stairs, brows raised.

Meiner shoved past her, knocking Cora into the door frame. "Hey!" Cora snapped at her. "What were you looking for?"

"Stay out of it." She marched down the hall, fully aware Cora was following. "It's family stuff."

"Family stuff, like you're trying to figure out what your gran hasn't told you?"

Meiner paused in the doorway. She'd been about to slam the door, but she could hear the smirk in Cora's voice. She turned and glared at her. "Get out of my face, Cora."

"You should be more careful." Cora's smile was sly. "After all, she obviously doesn't trust you enough to tell you everything. And now here you are, sneaking through her stuff like a—"

Meiner didn't let her get any further. A riptide current of anger crashed through her, sucking away all her calm. She lunged forward, fingers tangling in the fabric of Cora's sweater.

Cora's startled cry was cut off as Meiner slammed her back into the wall. "Shut. Your. Mouth. Cora."

Her temper was like something alive, pulsing in her chest. Calling for release. Oh, how she wanted to release it.

Instead she stayed where she was, frozen, fingers wrapped around Cora's collar, pressing her into the wall.

Cora's eyes were huge in her pale face, and Meiner almost released her. Almost backed up and apologized. A wave of horror hit her. She hadn't even tried to fight her temper this time, hadn't even realized she was about to explode.

"Think you're intimidating, don't you?" Cora hissed up at her. "You've no idea what you're dealing with, Meiner King."

Her regret was gone as abruptly as it had come, and Meiner shoved Cora into the wall a little harder. "I know well enough you want this coven. You think you should be inheriting it."

She was intensely aware of several things. First that Cora was trembling under her hands; second that Cora's eyes had dropped from Meiner's gaze to her lips and back several times now. Meiner knew Cora, knew how she thought, so it shouldn't have been a surprise when the other girl reached up and grabbed her shoulders, crushing her lips into Meiner's.

Meiner shook her off. "Are you *serious* right now?"

"Don't tell me you didn't enjoy it." Cora's expression was glittering, malicious. The rage surged again, making Meiner's limbs tremble, making her insides feel hot. She growled and drove her fist forward, knuckles crashing into the wall beside Cora's left ear.

"What the *fuck*, Meiner?"

Pain blazed through her hand and up her arm. There was a fist-sized dent in the wall beside Cora's head, and shame rushed in to replace the rage as fast as it had come.

This wasn't her house. She'd have to pay for that.

Cora's expression was defiant, but Meiner thought she saw a glimmer of hurt there. "You think you're better than your gran and me. But you're the same." She pushed away from the wall, back stiff. "No, you're worse, because you won't admit it."

Meiner watched her, speechless, as Cora flipped her blond hair over her shoulder and stalked away, slamming her bedroom door. For a moment she stayed there, seething.

The worst part was that Cora was right. These days she lost her temper at the drop of a hat, at the slightest provocation from Cora or Gran.

When she looked up, her stomach surged. Dayna was standing in the hallway, her face blank with shock.

"Why didn't you knock earlier?" Meiner hissed, her voice made savage by the anger burning through her.

Dayna's expression went dark. "I did. You didn't hear me the first time. You're welcome, by the way."

She disappeared back downstairs, and Meiner groaned. She slumped against the wall, hand throbbing, the edge of the death card poking her in the thigh like a grim admonition.

Chapter Twenty-Eight

DAYNA

Dayna stared out at the garden from her spot on the front steps, still fuming. Seeing Meiner's true temper had been shocking, and having a piece of it directed at her, however small, was not something she was going to put up with. She had half a mind to march back in there and demand an apology.

She wasn't sure exactly what happened, since she'd been around the corner. She'd heard some of the exchange—the louder parts, really—and the pause, and then Meiner's shout of disbelief, and the crash of a fist going through the wall.

Part of her was burning with curiosity, but honestly it didn't matter, did it? There was no excuse for the way Meiner had behaved toward Cora, and toward her, not to mention the property damage, and after Yemi and Reagan had invited them into their home. . . .

There was a thud from behind her, and Dayna jumped, turning to see Meiner in the doorway, her face flushed with anger. She marched past without a word, stalking across the driveway toward her car.

"Oh, I don't think so." Dayna sprang off the steps and followed her. She wasn't going to get away from this *that* easily. "Where are you going?"

"Away from here. Away from *her*."

"You can't just storm off after that. You punched a *hole in the wall*, Meiner. You think Yemi can pay for that?"

"I'll pay for it."

"You should go in there and apologize."

"Right now, if I go back in there, I'll punch a hole in her *face*." Meiner turned, marching across the driveway toward the cars, kicking up bits of gravel beneath her boots.

Dayna hurried after her, anger and disbelief making her sputter. "Y-you can't just leave . . . *Meiner!* What about the vision? What about the research? We still haven't even figured out where the ruins are, and we've researched every historical sight in Wexford." She skidded to a halt, shoes slipping on the gravel, as Meiner yanked open the door and slid into the driver seat.

Dayna huffed and climbed into the passenger seat.

"What are you doing?" Meiner flapped a hand at her. "Can we do this later? The ruins aren't going anywhere."

"Yeah, well, me neither." Dayna folded her arms over her chest, scowling at her. "How can you be this selfish?"

"Excuse me?"

"You heard me! Who do you think is next on the killer's list? Exactly how many witches do you think are in Carman? You may not care about your coven, but I do. I've been with those women since kindergarten. They're my family, and I won't let them—" Dayna cut herself off abruptly, annoyed to see Meiner didn't appear to be listening anymore. She was staring at Dayna, eyes glazed over, mouth hanging open.

"*What* are you looking at?"

"Kindergarten!" Meiner's face was flushed suddenly, her eyes glittering.

"What?" Dayna frowned as Meiner turned in her seat and started the engine without another word. "Wait, where are we going? What the hell was that about?"

"I just figured it out."

"Figured what out? The ruins? Meiner—" she protested as Meiner gunned the engine, sending up clouds of dust as they shot down the driveway.

Chapter Twenty-Nine
DAYNA

At the first stoplight, Meiner let the car idle, and Dayna turned to look at her. "You think you know where the ruins are, don't you?" She grimaced in the rearview mirror at the cloud of exhaust gathering behind them. Meiner's car seemed to be held together mainly by spells and duct tape.

At some point they would need to talk about what just happened, but right now she was happy enough to change the subject.

"I just realized... when I was in kindergarten my school went on a field trip to Raven Point. There were the ruins of this building in the woods beside it, and we got in trouble for playing in it. It's not a tourist spot, which is why I didn't think of it. It's just... there." Meiner's previous anger seemed forgotten; she looked excited, her face flushed.

"Ah," Dayna said. Silence settled between them again.

They rode for a moment without speaking, the rattling of the engine loud in the quiet. Dayna stared out the window at the green countryside whipping past, trying to concentrate on the thought of the ruins and not on the tense silence between them.

Finally Meiner darted a sideways look at her. "Look, I'm sorry. I was pissed off at Cora, not you."

"You still blew up at me." Dayna gave her an even stare. "And you *punched the fucking wall.*"

"I know, that was shitty and I'm sorry. It won't happen again." Meiner grimaced. "She just...makes me crazy."

Dayna tugged at a lock of hair, staring straight ahead. This wasn't over. Using Cora as an excuse simply wasn't going to cut it, not if Meiner and her coven were going to work with them for any extended period of time.

"Fine," she said shortly, and then added, "Tell me you at least found something when you were searching your grandmother's room."

Meiner shrugged, gaze still fixed on the road. "I dunno, nothing definitive. Old bones she used to do magic with, some book I didn't even get to look at before Cora burst in, and a seriously creepy statue...."

"What statue?" Dayna waited while Meiner pulled out her phone and handed it over. She squinted down at the picture, which showed a statue of a man sitting cross-legged, the head of a one-eyed goat on his shoulders. She grimaced. "What the hell is *that* thing?"

"No idea. I didn't stick around to google it."

"Maybe you should." Dayna pulled out her own phone, opened a search, and typed *half man, half goat with one eye.* Meiner made a disbelieving noise, but the first thing that came up was a Wikipedia page titled *List of one-eyed creatures in mythology and fiction.*

She showed it to Meiner. "See? Told you. Any idea what god your gran used to worship?"

Meiner shook her head, glancing quickly at the list before turning back to the road. "The second one...I've heard that name somewhere."

"Balor." Dayna bit her lip, reading through the information. "You better hope it's not him." She cleared her throat. "The deadly one. Balor of the evil eye. God of drought and blight."

"Well, that doesn't sound great."

"Maybe she used to worship him." Dayna frowned at the illustration of a fiery-eyed demon with goat horns. "We already know she did black magic, but that doesn't mean she's doing it now." She paused. "Though the fact she brought it doesn't exactly bode well."

"It could be something that was just in her trunks. She hasn't cleaned them out in years," Meiner said. "We don't have enough proof yet."

"Well, until we can *get* proof, we can't do anything." Dayna slipped her phone back into her pocket. "And finding the ruins is a bit more urgent." She glanced out the window. They were driving along the coast now.

"Maybe we should call the others. You know, let them know where we're going."

"Let's get there first." Meiner glanced in the rearview mirror, and Dayna could guess what she was thinking. She didn't want to face Yemi and Reagan right now, and probably didn't want to deal with Cora either.

Dayna focused on the road ahead of them and pressed her lips together tightly. She'd leave it up to Meiner to do the right thing and apologize when they got back.

When they pulled up in front of the low fence that hemmed in the forest, the parking lot was empty. "This is it."

Dayna slid out, banging the door shut behind her. A patchwork quilt of sunbeams filtered through the trees, painting them both in patterns of dappled light as Dayna followed Meiner down the uneven dirt trail. In the partial shade the morning air was biting, and she pulled her fingers into the sleeves of her sweater. Neither of the girls spoke as they walked, listening to the sounds of the birds in the trees above them. Dayna felt jumpy, her pulse picking up with every crackle of underbrush.

When the trail was wide enough, Meiner slowed, falling into step with her. "There's no one here. No cars, no footprints. Try to relax."

Dayna gave her a brief look and then glanced back down at the path, stepping over a thick root. Every part of the forest reminded her of the vision. Her nerves felt like bowstrings stretched tight, ready to break at every rustle in the bushes.

Just walking the path was bringing it all back. The distant, dreamlike memories that couldn't possibly be hers. The feeling of holding the book. The connection she'd felt to the horned woman, like she'd known her from somewhere.

All impossible.

"Wait, I remember this. It's just ahead." Meiner quickened her pace, and Dayna had to hurry to keep up with her long-legged stride.

"I don't see— Whoa."

When they came around the bend, it was not Cernunnos who waited for them.

There was nothing dreamlike about the forest anymore. Dayna was totally and completely in the here and now as they stepped into the small sunlit clearing in the woods.

Dayna breathed in deeply, suddenly hyperaware of the birdsong in the trees above them, the smell of pine, the wind rushing past her. It was all so *real*.

And so was the moss-covered tumble of stones set in the center of a cluster of oak trees.

The temple was here.

Chapter Thirty

MEINER

I t had been years since she'd been here. She'd forgotten the way the church seemed to hunker in the middle of the path, crumbled walls sticking up in points like a jagged stone crown. It was half swallowed by the hungry forest, wrapped in vines and covered in moss, as if it had emerged from the ground looking that way.

They moved closer, approaching the church as if it were a wild cat crouched in the center of the forest path. Meiner half expected to see something moving in the empty, green-framed windows, but it was still. The birdsong continued, and crows called to one another in the branches above them. It made her feel a little better. This was not the dead quiet that had fallen in the apple orchard before the candles snuffed out, before the horrible many-voiced entity spoke through Cora.

There was nothing here.

"This is it." Dayna clutched her arms as if she was cold, and Meiner could see her hands shaking. She thought about reaching out, touching her shoulder.

But shame kept surging through Meiner. She'd been so stupid.

Dayna moved into the entrance of the church and let out a shaky breath. "It's not here."

The walls cast the inside of the ruins partly into shadow, and Meiner moved slowly into the center, footsteps absorbed by the soft moss carpet.

Dayna traced a hand over the stone wall. She was staring at a group of symbols that had been carved there, strange, curling signs that Meiner remembered from the vision. They looked like things she knew—the shield knot and the triquetra—but they differed in subtle ways. Like someone had been trying to draw them from memory and got some of the lines wrong.

Dayna hunkered down to examine the base of the wall. "Here's the Butcher's mark. And this is the one that means Lugh. I don't know what the rest are."

"Let's get a picture." Meiner pulled her phone out and snapped a picture of the wall. Dayna stood from her crouched position, staggering slightly. Meiner caught her arm, more out of instinct than anything, and Dayna looked startled. A flush crept over her face.

Meiner let go quickly, but Dayna only mumbled, "Thanks," and brushed awkwardly at her sweater. Then she stopped and blurted out, "What was it Cora did that made you so mad?"

Meiner blinked, then scrubbed a hand across her face. Just remembering it made the anger flare to life again, but she tried to shove it back down and keep her voice even. "She . . . kissed me." It was almost gratifying to see Dayna's mouth drop open.

"Oh, I . . . Wow, I wasn't expecting that."

Meiner shrugged. "Neither was I. But that's probably what she wanted, to shock me."

When Dayna spoke again her voice was quiet. "I get why you were so mad. If you didn't want it, it's not okay."

"I didn't"—Meiner paused, face burning—"want it, I mean. But all the same, I shouldn't have lost my temper."

Dayna's mouth twitched upward, just for a second. "Yeah, or remodeled the wall."

Meiner grinned, and a beat of silence stretched between them, less awkward than before. After a second, though, Meiner realized the birds had stopped chirping.

From somewhere far away there came the crunch of underbrush. Dayna stiffened.

The back of Meiner's neck was beginning to prickle. "We should go."

She was moving for the door, when Dayna said, "Hold on a minute." Meiner turned to see her crouched near the spot in the floor she'd tripped over. One of the moss-covered stones seemed to have crumbled slightly, revealing a sliver of darkness. "I think it's hollow underneath."

Meiner watched, surprised, as Dayna started tugging at the rock. After a second Meiner shrugged and hunkered down beside her. With two of them shoving and pulling at the slippery stone, it finally gave way, and Dayna fell over onto her backside with a startled shout.

"Whoa, you all right?" Meiner offered a hand, trying not to grin, and Dayna rolled her eyes before allowing herself to be tugged to her feet. "Look at that."

There was a hole in the floor, a hollowed-out slot that had been dug beneath the ruins. Inside was a dirty burlap sack.

"Damn. Doesn't look like anything." Still, Meiner leaned forward and plucked at the cloth, and then blinked, startled at its weight. "Hold on, I think there might be something wrapped in this."

Gingerly she eased the bundle of cloth out of the dirt, setting it down on the stone floor between them. Dayna hovered eagerly as Meiner tugged at the edges, trying to discern where it could be opened without damaging whatever was inside.

When the fabric finally fell away, Meiner's heart stopped. Behind her Dayna let out a gasp. It was a book, bound in rich brown leather, closed at one side with a heavy golden clasp. There was a symbol etched on the front, the same spiky-edged rune that they'd seen over and over these last few weeks. The Butcher's mark.

Dayna reached a shaking hand toward the clasp.

Meiner's concentration was so centered on the book, her vision so laser-focused, that she didn't react in time. She didn't see the black shape hurtle itself through the entrance of the church, its mouth open in a silent snarl, until it was on top of them.

Chapter Thirty-One

DAYNA

There was a snarl, a blur in the air before her. Meiner shouted just as something crashed into Dayna's left shoulder, slamming her to the ground. Air left her lungs in a rush, and her shoulder *burned*. A snarling mouth full of broken, jagged teeth filled her vision.

The creature lunged for her throat, teeth snapping, and then pulled back with a growl, shaking its head. Blood splattered from its face, and Dayna saw the bone charm had pierced its muzzle.

The shaking dislodged the charm, and it skittered across the mossy floor. The black dog crouched low to the ground, its blue eyes narrowed.

Human eyes, she had time to think, and then it was springing toward her again, filling her entire vision. A scream ripped from her throat, and then Meiner was there, her white braid swinging behind her as she lashed out at the dog with a booted foot. There was a dull *thud* and a yelp as the boot connected, and the beast was thrown back, claws scraping the stone floor. It snarled again, hackles raised, its bright, savage eyes fixed on Dayna. Even though Meiner stood between them, it didn't even look at the white-haired witch.

When Dayna had scrambled back, she'd dropped the book in the doorway, and now the dog moved in front of it. Dayna braced herself, pulse drumming in her ears, breath coming in sharp gasps.

Meiner was mumbling furiously under her breath. Prayers for protection, it sounded like, arms held out before her. Dayna cast around, desperate for something to defend herself with. Her gaze fell on the broken stones of the church floor, and she snatched one up. Pain blazed in her shoulder, but she ignored it, hefting the stone—slate-gray and the size of her palm. The crackling energy of her magic pulsed in her fingers and the rock trembled with it.

When the dog moved again, she released it with a shouted, "Bogadh!" It was a wild, desperate bit of magic, absent of the cupped hands needed to direct it, completely lacking any finesse. It should have been miles off, but somehow the rock glanced off the beast's face, making it stumble and yelp.

Meiner's mumbled chanting grew louder, and the dog's ears went back. It flinched, and for a moment Dayna thought it would turn tail and run.

Instead it growled and slunk closer. She could see it pushing against something, as if Meiner's prayers were a physical barrier.

Dayna picked up another rock, panic washing over her. There was no way she'd get lucky with another throw like that. Desperately she tried to remember any of the spells she'd heard of, anything that might help them fight this thing. If only Reagan were here; she'd probably memorized a bunch for exactly this sort of situation.

Keeping her eyes fixed on the dog as it inched closer, she muttered a prayer to Danu. *Goddess, grant me light. Grant me protection. Grant me power, so mote it be.* The dog surged forward, and she reacted instinctively, arm snapping up, crying out the same spell a second time. She felt the power leave her in a rush, the sensation making her breath catch, and there was a sharp *crack* that echoed around the ruins as the dog was flung backward over the wall.

There was a distant yelp and a thrashing in the underbrush. Dayna stayed where she was, her chest heaving. All the hairs on her arms were on end, the residual power still prickling under her skin. It had felt like receiving an electric shock in reverse, the power flowing through her body, up from the pit of her stomach and out through the surface of her skin. No wonder Yemi had warned her about the post-ascension power surge.

Both she and Meiner were facing the woods now, on high alert.

From the forest came the crash of something moving, and then miles away, an indistinct voice yelling. Whoever it was sounded angry. The crashing sounds retreated.

"I think it's leaving," Meiner finally breathed, but Dayna could hardly hear her. All she could do was stare at the spot on the threshold of the ruins. The crumbling doorway, the moss-covered front step. Empty.

The book was gone.

"Where is it?" She took a step forward, stomach clenching. The forest around her seemed to swing wildly.

Meiner turned back to her, and her eyes went wide. "Dayna, your arm."

She already knew she was bleeding. She could feel warmth running down her arm, trailing into the crook of her elbow, accompanied by the dull throb of pain. None of that mattered, though. "The book is gone."

Dayna had felt something when she'd seen the cover of that book, an echo of the feeling in the vision. A sense of *rightness*. Like a puzzle piece clicking into place. If only she could have touched it, it would have told her things. Things that could save them.

"We have to get you out of here." Meiner's face was pale.

"But the book—" Dayna turned, and the world gave another nauseating twist, accompanied by a wave of knifelike pain. She sagged against the stone wall, head spinning. The blood coating her arm was thick and sticky, and the flow wasn't slowing. She felt faint, and hollowed out, and the edges of her vision blackened and blurred.

"Come on." Meiner stooped down to snatch up the protection charm, tucking it into her jeans pocket before hurrying over, yanking her sweatshirt off. Dayna winced as she pressed the fabric to the wound. "Hold that. Let's get you to the car."

Chapter Thirty-Two

MEINER

Meiner didn't relax until they were in the kitchen and she'd delivered Dayna straight into Yemi's and Reagan's arms. The walk back through the forest and the drive home had been terrifying. She'd been afraid Dayna was going to pass out, she'd looked so pale.

"She'll be needing stitches." Reagan's brow was creased, and she glanced over at her mother, who was rushing around the kitchen assembling hot water, towels, and the sewing kit. Meiner noticed Reagan kept her hand on Dayna's other shoulder, rubbing her back. "We'll have to call Faye." At Meiner's puzzled look she added, "She's a surgeon. Well, she was. This looks pretty bad. Do you know what animal it was?"

"Wild dog, it looked like." Meiner glanced at Dayna, who had her eyes squeezed shut. "It attacked us in the forest."

"Wild dog?" Reagan frowned. "What the feck? There aren't wild dogs in the area. Unless it's someone's pet gone off the deep end."

"There's no way it was someone's pet. I saw it up close and . . . it wasn't normal." Meiner crossed her arms over her chest, shaking her head.

"Its eyes . . ." Dayna shuddered and trailed off, and Reagan rubbed her back again, expression concerned. Meiner cleared her throat, stepping up behind Dayna.

"They were human."

Yemi and Reagan exchanged a look, and then Reagan took Dayna's arm gently and led her over to the kitchen sink, keeping her voice low. "Well, just in case, you'll need a rabies shot."

"Holy shit."

Both Meiner and Reagan jerked around.

Cora stood in the doorway, hands on her hips. "What the hell happened?"

Meiner took a deep, steadying breath before answering. "Dog bite."

Cora lifted a brow. "How did *that* happen?"

Still struggling to force her temper down, Meiner explained the ruins in the woods, the book, and the attack.

"You'll need stitches." Yemi paused by Dayna long enough to smooth a hand over her brow, frowning slightly. "I'll call the others."

"We'll disinfect this, too." Reagan bit her lip, glancing at Yemi. "We should take her to the hospital."

Dayna's eyes snapped open. "No hospital." When everyone stared at her she flushed. "They'll call my dad. I'm not supposed to be out of the house."

"I'm sure he'd understand, right?" Cora leaned forward and tugged the collar of Dayna's shirt aside to look at her shoulder. The move was bold yet casual, and Dayna didn't protest, just looked a little startled. Meiner clenched her fists at her sides. Reagan, too, noticed, jerked a hand toward Cora, and then went still, her dark eyes narrow.

"I'm supposed to be grounded," Dayna said. "Can't Faye do it?"

"Yes, Faye can do it, though Dayna *should* get checked for rabies."

They all jumped at the new voice, and Meiner turned to see the severe red-haired woman in the doorway, flanked by her mother and grandmother.

Yemi blinked and let the phone drop back into the receiver.

"What's happened?" Faye began taking her jacket off, listening to Meiner explain while Brenna and Bronagh bustled over. Bronagh examined the bite while Brenna brushed the back of her hand across Dayna's forehead, just as Yemi had.

Meiner bit her lip, trying to picture what her coven's reaction would have been if she'd been the one bitten. Nothing like this.

Faye rolled up her sleeves. "Move her T-shirt to one side. I'll start in a minute."

Meiner moved forward, and she and Reagan helped Dayna ease her shirt off one shoulder. Her gaze darted back up to Dayna's pale face, worry gnawing at her stomach.

"We had the book in our *hands*." Dayna was staring fixedly at the wall, brows furrowed. "We had it, and that's when it attacked. That's no coincidence."

"You had it and then lost it." Cora was by the fireplace, pacing back and forth. "You didn't see anything inside? What about the symbols on the walls? Tell me you at least got a picture."

Meiner glared at her. "We can talk after we've made sure she isn't going to bleed out."

"No. We need to talk now. Call Grandma King as well." Dayna's voice trembled. "We need everyone."

"I'll get her," Reagan said. "The woman's been tearing apart the damn house looking for who-knows-what all morning."

Meiner clenched her jaw shut, biting back a groan. That was all they needed on top of everything, for Gran to start losing it again.

Dayna was quiet for a moment, until Reagan had vanished upstairs. Then she turned back to the others. "He got to it before we did, which means there will be another victim soon. We should have called earlier, before we went. We shouldn't have gone by ourselves."

"You're right." Meiner grimaced. That one was on her.

"Yeah." Cora paused in the middle of her pacing, sounding distinctly annoyed. "I can't believe you lost the goddamn book."

Meiner shut her eyes against the hot surge of temper, scrubbing a hand over her face. She couldn't let Cora get to her again.

Grandma King appeared in the doorway, with Reagan just behind her. "What happened?"

They told her, or Meiner did at least. Dayna was watching, pale-faced, while Faye sterilized a needle in boiled water.

After she'd relayed the full story, Grandma King pulled Meiner into the living room, out of earshot of the others.

"Why didn't you call me before going to the ruins?"

The anger boiling beneath the surface was enough to make her reckless. "Because I don't know if I can trust you," Meiner hissed. "I never know."

Grandma King straightened up, anger written all over her wrinkled face. Her arm twitched, and Meiner glared at her.

"Go ahead, then, hit me. It's not like it's anything new."

For a moment, it seemed like she really would, and then the look of pure fury on her grandmother's face faded. Her brow wrinkled with confusion. "What was I saying, Stephanie?"

Meiner shook her head. Her chest felt hollow, breaths trembling and uneven.

"I think I like you better when you're losing your mind," she spat.

Gran said nothing in return, the lines of her face deepening as her brow creased. She wasn't even looking at Meiner anymore; her watery-blue eyes had gone vacant.

Meiner turned away. Taking a deep breath, she forced herself to wipe the emotion from her face before moving back into the kitchen.

At the table, Faye had the needle poised over Dayna's arm.

"All right," she said. "This is going to hurt."

Chapter Thirty-Three

DAYNA

I t hurt. A lot.

Having Faye sew up the wound in her shoulder felt like having someone slowly stitch a line of fire into her skin, but a half hour later the painkillers had kicked in, and Yemi had her drinking an awful-tasting healing tea full of ginger and garlic.

The other witches had moved into the living room, and Dayna found herself in the kitchen alone with Meiner. The silence stretched between them, and Meiner leaned one hip against the counter, staring down at her. They were close enough that Dayna could feel her cheeks start to burn. It felt like she could count the inches between them, calculate how many seconds it would take to close the distance.

Meiner frowned. "You're flushed. Do you feel sick?"

She blinked in surprise as Meiner reached out, pressing the back of her hand to her cheek. It was cool enough to feel good against her hot skin. Somehow, even overheated, she found she had goose bumps covering her arms. "Uh, I'm all right. Probably just too much excitement for one day."

"Oh, before I forget." Meiner dipped one hand into her jeans pocket, pulling the protection charm out. She pressed it into Dayna's hand, fingertips brushing her palm, making her pulse pick up.

On the counter beside them her phone pinged, and they both glanced over. The text display read, *Samuel*

Dayna groaned, feeling suddenly guilty. She'd used him for his knowledge of the Butcher, and then brushed him off the last few days. He was probably wondering what was going on.

"That's exactly what I need on top of everything."

"Is this the ex?"

"Yeah." Dayna rubbed one hand across her face. Her head was pounding. "Can you read it? My head is killing me."

Meiner asked for the code and then unlocked it, reading the text out slowly. "'I might have more information. Can we talk?'" She raised a brow when Dayna groaned again.

"I should say yes, in case he actually knows something, but it's just too much right now. Last time, he asked to get back together."

"And you told him no?"

Dayna hesitated. "He's persistent."

A grin tugged at the corner of Meiner's lips. "How about I text him back and tell him you're busy right now?"

Despite her headache, some small part of her was delighted by the expression on Meiner's face. She looked like she was considering tracking him down to tell him in person.

"What would you say?"

"I'll show you." While Meiner was busy with the phone, Dayna watched her as subtly as she could. Her smile was sharp, eyes glittering as she typed out the message. Dayna wanted to reach out and touch her, but she was a little afraid of what might happen.

"Here." Meiner held the phone up, and Dayna quickly looked away, and then down at the phone. Hopefully her face wasn't bright red.

Dayna can't come to the phone right now.

"Send it." It was probably a bad idea—it might only pique his curiosity—but she couldn't resist the grin on Meiner's face.

Meiner hit send. The response was almost immediate.

Who is this?

They exchanged a look, and Meiner edged a little closer so they could both get a clear view of the screen. Without saying anything, she typed out, *Her date.*

Dayna felt her face grow even hotter. Meiner merely lifted a brow at her, and slowly she nodded. Was the other girl writing that merely to put him off, or...?

She wanted to ask. She couldn't ask.

Meiner hit send, and for a moment they were both still, unmoving. Dayna realized they were incredibly close right now. That she was sitting on the stool leaning back against the counter, and Meiner was standing so close she was almost between her legs. They looked like a couple right now.

Meiner blinked, looking down at her. Her face was usually so composed, like marble. But now her expression flickered. Dayna wished desperately she could read her better.

"If he's too persistent," Meiner said slowly, "I can pretend to be your date in real life." Her eyes met Dayna's. They were so dark, still glittering with the same savage, beautiful light. Dayna clutched the sides of the stool with both hands, repressing a shiver.

It was a good shiver this time. Her headache had slowly begun to subside.

"Yeah," she said, and her voice came out a little uneven. "We might... we might have to do that."

There was a sudden shuffling from beside the fireplace, and Meiner sprang back, fast enough that Dayna felt a little dizzy.

Cora stood in the doorway, arms crossed over her chest. Dayna and Meiner both stared at the blond girl.

"We should be researching" was all Cora said.

Grandma King came back through the doorway at that moment, pulling her shawl around her shoulders. "The Callighans are leaving. We've agreed to another meeting tomorrow."

"Good." Dayna spoke before Cora could. "We need to figure out how to track him down before someone else dies."

Chapter Thirty-Four

DUBH

"**S**top touching it," Calma growled. "It's going to get infected."

Dubh dropped his hand to his side. He hadn't even realized he'd been probing the bloody cut on his cheek as he pored over the book.

"Who cares if it gets infected?" Olc was sprawled on the couch, his booted feet propped up on the coffee table, smearing mud on the hotel magazines. "It's not like it matters."

"You *know* we can't heal, idiot. If his face starts rotting off, it's going to be pretty obvious." Calma scowled at his younger brother. "Use your head for once, Olc."

"I'll stitch it later," Dubh said, mainly to shut the two of them up.

"We need to talk about procedure," Calma said. "It's getting too messy. Too public. Our handiwork is all over the news right now and I don't like it. If we could take them back to a room somewhere—"

"You know she'd hate that," Olc sneered. "Or are you going to find some kind of sacred warehouse?"

"We don't even know how many cycles we've been through," Calma snapped. "*This* is why we fail . . . every cycle up to this, every kill outside Carman . . . it's all been pointless."

Dubh shook his head. His brothers understood nothing. "None of those were failures. It was all leading up to this."

All the other women had been dress rehearsals, preparation for the real event.

It would be perfect this time. They had the book.

Now he understood why he'd been so driven to come here. To this country, to this town. The book had been calling him all along; every cycle it had been the one thing they were missing.

Dubh continued to page through it with shaking fingers. It had taken him longer than usual for the memory to come back, which was unnerving. But as soon as he'd seen it, it had all come flooding back. He'd known what it was. That it belonged to him.

He hadn't expected to attack her. Hadn't even remembered how to shift until he saw her hovering over the book, and then some instinct kicked in.

Just the thought was enough to send a thrill through him, and he tried to push it away, to force himself to concentrate.

The list was there, laid out page by page. He flicked through, a fire burning in the pit of his stomach. Yes, he'd been correct both times. And the third he'd suspected, though his memory had grown fainter as the list went on. She was next. The storyteller, the fool.

Crichinbel.

He traced a finger over the illustration, a pen-and-ink drawing of a woman with laughing brown eyes. He recognized her. He'd familiarized himself with anyone in town who had even the smallest touch of magic. She was an older woman, a dabbler.

He'd walked into her shop the first day he'd arrived here, like fate was guiding him.

The real question now was, what was he supposed to take?

Tongue and eye. Hand and foot. Blood and bone, ash and soot.

Dubh felt that force rise inside his chest, prompting him to pass a hand over the page. He hadn't realized he still had blood on his fingers. When he pulled back, there was a smear of red running across her eyes like a blindfold.

He smiled. Climbing to his feet, he tucked the book inside his jacket before turning to his brothers. "Let's go."

Chapter Thirty-Five

SAMUEL

The coffee at the station was completely disgusting, and Sam was on his third cup of the morning.

Since the family only had one car—a bone of contention he brought up at least weekly—he'd walked over to the station from Morgan's house, and his father had ordered him to sit in one of the empty offices and plan for next week's Bible study. When Sam arrived, his father had been on the phone, red-faced and yelling. The second murder seemed to have sent him over the edge completely.

Absently Sam ripped into another sugar packet and emptied it into his mug, listening to the dull thud of booted feet move past his door as he scrolled through the forum.

A few people had replied to his query.

UnknownPotato: They saw that ages ago. Nothing but uneven paint on the wall.

AlexaPanda: Maybe it's blood.

CrimeBuff69: I dug into this a bit and found . . . a lot. There's tons of wacko theories.

There was a link below, which led Sam to a website that had blown up the grainy footage and traced shaky lines over the red on the wall, creating a circle with a vague, squiggly blob in the center, and several white dots around the outside. Underneath was a long, rambling post about how the Butcher was supernatural, and he trapped his victims with black magic. Sam blew out a breath, shaking his head.

So . . . aside from insane theories and possibly imagined ghostly markings, he had a whole lot of nothing. The lack of clues should have frustrated him, discouraged him, even. Instead it just seemed to goad him onward, to fan the constant, low burn of his curiosity into full flame.

He needed to uncover what was really going on. Something in his soul demanded answers.

Sam sat up straight a second later when he heard his father's voice outside the door.

"Bertie, make sure desk three is clear. I can't stop NBCI coming, but they certainly won't be setting up shop wherever they please."

Sam listened intently. If they were calling in the National Bureau of Criminal Investigation, then maybe his father was finally taking this case seriously.

There was a high-pitched electronic beep from the front door, followed by Bertie's cheerful greeting. A moment later the office door creaked open, and Samuel's breath caught. Dayna stood in the doorway, hands in the pockets of her red sweater.

"Hey. What are you doing here?" He added hastily, "I mean, not that I mind."

"Your mother told me you were here," she said. "You mentioned earlier that you had some new info, so I thought I'd drop by." She jerked a thumb over her shoulder. "Looks like a lot of activity going on back there."

As she stepped closer it seemed there was something different about her. Maybe the way her skin seemed to glow, though that might have been a flush from the wind. And . . . did she seem taller? She was holding herself differently.

She hadn't answered his text from last night, and he was still thinking about who she might have been with; Carman was too small for a wide dating pool. Whoever it was, they were a traitor as far as he was concerned. Everyone knew he still liked Dayna, so who the hell was this guy to move in on her?

He pulled himself together a second later and dragged the chair out from beside him. Her timing couldn't have been better; he hadn't really had anything new when he had texted her, but maybe this was something new. "I'm eavesdropping. I'm pretty sure NBCI are on their way."

Dayna hurried across the room and settled in at the desk, shoving her bag onto the table. "Shit, really? Did your dad say that?"

"Yeah." He cleared his throat, determined to ask about her date last night. "Hey, so, when you texted—"

The beeper above the door went off again, and they both fell silent. Sam rose from the desk as quietly as possible and shoved the door open an inch. A second later he felt Dayna's presence at his elbow. She smelled like mangoes.

Through the open door he could see two men talking to Bertie at the front desk. After a moment his father joined them. To his frustration the men spoke in low voices, too low to overhear anything.

The strange men wore black suits and ties and seemed utterly serious. They couldn't have looked more like Men in Black if they'd tried.

He needed to know what they were saying, and he only had a minute at most before they shut themselves in his father's office. He turned to Dayna. "Quick, let me borrow your phone."

Dayna blinked at him, but she reached into her pocket and unlocked it. Sam pulled up FaceTime, pleased to see his contact was still at the top. He hit the button and waited for his phone to ring.

"What are you doing?" Dayna whispered. He hit the answer button and put Dayna's phone on mute.

"Stay here and tell me if my dad comes."

Surprisingly she didn't protest as he slipped out the door and down the hallway. The offices were mostly full, and a few officers even glanced up from their desks as he passed, but none of them stopped him. It wasn't a big deal for him to visit his father's office. He did it all the time to get extra paper, or to pillage the jar of candy his father kept in the drawer.

Still, his heart was beating hard by the time he snuck into the office. He glanced around quickly and set his phone facedown on the middle shelf in the bookcase behind the desk.

While he was there, he grabbed a handful of wrapped spearmints for Dayna—she'd always had a sweet tooth for them—and turned for the door. He stopped short, heart jumping. His father was in the doorway, flanked by the two men in suits, who were currently regarding him as if Sam himself might be the Butcher.

"Gentlemen, this is my son. Sam, this is Sean Smith and Dan Wesson, agents from NBCI." The sergeant's expression was unreadable, which usually happened when he was angry. Sam held up the handful of candy and gave his dad a wide grin. "Sorry, Dad, just raiding the candy jar."

He slid past one of the agents in the doorway, stomach churning. The man barely moved, and he gave Sam a long, piercing look.

A minute later, back in the empty office with Dayna, he let out a breath of relief. She was already leaning over the phone, her hair obscuring her face. The voices were slightly muffled, but they could make them out clearly enough.

". . . what you know so far," one of the men was saying.

"Information from previous cases." His father's voice was low, and Sam could hear the undercurrents of anger simmering there. "Look, I only called you because it's procedure, but . . . a serial killer in Carman . . . the idea is ridiculous."

There was an audible pause, and Sam winced. His father clearly wasn't bothering with politeness.

When the agent spoke again, his voice was quiet, but there was a definite edge to it. "You've had two murders so far. Not only should you be treating this like the Butcher may be back and already lining up his next four victims, you should be keeping all of this out of the press. Which is clearly not the case."

The sergeant grunted. "We have a leak. One of my men, no doubt. Some of them don't like the way I do things."

"Then I'd say they're a sight smarter than you are."

"What?" The sergeant sounded ready to explode.

"You have *completely* cocked up this investigation from the start." The second agent's voice was like the lash of a whip, and Sam's grip tightened on the edge of the table. Beside him, Dayna was staring at the phone, openmouthed. "You've done nearly everything wrong as far as I can see. You didn't tent the scene, and now it's completely ruined. You've a leak, so there's going to be loads of tourists tramping all over, and you can bet you're going to have press flying in from out of town. This is going to be a complete nightmare to work, and it's entirely your fault."

Another pause. Sam thought he would have given just about anything to see his father's face right now.

"You will be *very* lucky if you don't end up unemployed after this," the agent continued. "Possibly even facing charges for actively hindering the investigation."

"Unless," the other agent broke in, "you cooperate with us fully. We may be able to save you *some* of the utter humiliation you're bound to go through if headquarters gets wind of how badly you screwed this one up. You get it?"

Another pause, and then the sergeant said reluctantly. "So, the Butcher . . . Why come here?"

"We think he was injured during the last murder attempt, years ago," the same man said, and Sam sat up straighter. "Small town, small police force. Probably he figured it's easy pickings. The real question is when is he going to strike next? He seems to be escalating."

"Maybe he was shook up after the injury," the sergeant said. "He's . . . in a frenzy or something."

Sam pressed a hand to his mouth. He glanced up from the phone, watching Dayna's face as she listened. Her hair kept sliding over her shoulder and into her face, and she pushed it back impatiently.

The sergeant added, "Oh, and . . . I thought I'd ask. Does the phrase *widow incorporated* mean anything to you? You know, from the last Butcher case?"

A beat of silence, and then one of the men said, "No. Why do you ask?"

"We found a scrap of a paper at the first scene, on the judge."

There was a rustle of clothing and the *clomp* of footsteps, then: "We'll be going through the case file as soon as we set up. We'll bring our equipment in from the car."

Sam bit the inside of his cheek. It was annoying they hadn't touched more on the last victim from the previous cycle. The more he thought about it, the more it seemed likely to be the missing piece.

Everything he'd researched about the Butcher told him the killer was careful not to leave loose ends, the way he stalked victims beforehand, learning their routines, the lack of DNA at the scenes. Last time, his final victim had escaped before he'd finished his work. . . . That had to have bothered him. Especially if she'd inflicted a real injury on him—he would have had time to think about it, to stew over it for years.

There was a reason the Butcher was here of all places, in the middle of nowhere. *She* was here, the one that got away. The gardai didn't even seem to be considering that.

Another shuffle, and then a *thump* of the door closing, and Sam shot up from his seat. "They're heading this way."

Dayna jammed her finger into the button, hanging up the call. She straightened and slid her phone into her pocket just as the door opened and the sergeant poked his head in. His face was still a bit red, but he looked like he'd collected himself. Just behind him was Samuel's mother, who was tugging at the strap of her purse nervously, glancing back over her shoulder at the agents.

"Samuel, your mother is here to pick you up. Come help the agents with their equipment first though, will you?"

He vanished back down the hall, and Sam's mother walked into the office, smiling at Dayna, who grinned weakly back at her.

"Um, okay." He shifted in the doorway, reluctant to leave the two of them alone. His mother wasn't going to beg Dayna to get back together with him, was she?

"Dayna and I will wait here. Go on and help the gentlemen unload."

Sam turned to follow the agents out to their car. The taller agent smirked as he handed him a black case from the trunk, and Sam grunted.

"Too heavy for you, champ?"

Sam scowled at him, turning back to the station. "It's fine."

Once inside, he set the case down on the desk, his back muscles screaming. Dayna was just coming out of the spare office with Sam's mother behind her. She looked silently furious, her face pale, lips pinched together. His mother said, "Thanks for stopping by. I know it's hard to forgive, but I'm glad you did."

It felt like he'd swallowed a brick. He didn't say anything, only stared at his mother in dismay. He had a very good idea what she'd let slip.

This was going to be bad.

Dayna was already turning away, hurrying for the door without saying good-bye, and Sam followed her. Once they were out on the porch he reached out and caught her arm. "Dayna, wait—"

She whirled on him, and he took a step back. "*You* were the one who told your Bible study. You knew I thought Morgan was the one who had gone snooping in my notebooks, and you just let me believe that. You outed me to everyone, and then you *lied*."

He stared at her, panic rising in the pit of his stomach. "I—I would have told you, but I didn't know what to say. . . ."

"There's no excuse," she hissed, and then turned and stomped down the stairs, across the gravel lot. He trailed behind her. "There is nothing you can say to make it okay. They gossiped about it for *weeks*. My dad nearly had me sent away—" She broke off, eyes suddenly filled with tears. Sam felt like he might be physically sick.

So that's why she'd shut down. Her father had almost sent her to Camp Blood of the Lamb. Everything made a horrible kind of sense now, why she'd broken up with him, how withdrawn she'd become. She must have been petrified of being sent away like her mother. "I'm *so* sorry, I—I didn't know. It was just a prayer request—"

"So you were trying to pray the gay away, was that it?" She flung the door open. "Leave me alone.

"Dayna, please. I'm sorry. Dayna—" The car door slammed shut on the other side, and the old beater gave a roar as it shot backward in a cloud of exhaust. Then Dayna peeled out of the parking lot and around the corner.

Chapter Thirty-Six

CORA

It had been three days since she'd called on Caorthannach, and she had been able to feel the goddess in the back of her mind ever since. It was hard to describe the sensation; the closest she could come was the time she'd had her appendix out. She'd forever been bumping the stitches, forgetting they were there despite the dull throb in her side. Every time, she'd been shocked they were in her skin, stitching her together. That they were part of her body.

It was like that, if stiches were a millennium-old goddess with an insatiable appetite for blood.

Even now, she could hear the whispers. Hungry. Insistent. They were getting stronger every waking minute. Like a radio in the back of her mind, slowly tuning into a station she wasn't sure she wanted to listen to.

It scared her, and it excited her.

Cora leaned against the wall under the pub sign, foot kicked up against the bricks, a cigarette clutched between her fingers. It was full of light and noise here, a good distraction from what was going on in her head.

She couldn't stop thinking about the ascension, what that feeling of power—*her* power—would be like. And after that, the ritual Gran was teaching her, a gateway to even more power.

The words from the ritual kept running through her head. The chant seemed to be stuck on a loop, repeating over and over in her mind. And if that wasn't bad enough, she was still replaying the kiss in her head. Meiner's lips on hers had brought back memories, bittersweet and exciting.

Her fingers shook, and she gripped the cigarette tighter. She was sick of this. They shouldn't be fighting; they were the same. Both abandoned by relatives—Cora's aunt and Meiner's mother—both power-hungry and driven. It made sense they should be together, with Cora as the rightful leader of the coven.

This was her destiny. Once she had enough power she could prove that to Meiner.

She took a long drag of the cigarette, the orange tip flaring. The taste and smell of smoke was an assault on her senses, enough to fill her up and banish the ebb and flow of the whispers. The bell over the door jangled beside her. Cora looked up, releasing a thin stream through her nostrils.

A man and woman stumbled out of the pub, the woman wobbling precariously on a pair of thin stilettos.

The woman's companion looked past her slouched form, bloodshot eyes combing briefly down Cora's body before he smiled and turned away, saying something to the woman. Cora wasn't paying attention; as soon as the man had locked eyes with her, the whispers had surged.

She winced, cigarette falling to the pavement, sparks scattering over the sidewalk. The hum of voices all spoke at once. And then, just as abruptly, they dropped off. There was only one left. The soft, sibilant voice of the woman in the woods. Caorthannach.

You could have him. Take him.

Cora's head snapped up. She stared at the couple making their slow, shuffling way toward the parking lot.

The voice hissed over the rush of the blood in her ears, the pulse of her heart.

Do it, witchling.

What had the goddess said in the forest? She needed power to face what was coming. She could do this. *Had* to do it, for her coven.

Cora started forward, sweat breaking on her brow, slicking the palm of her hand as she dipped into her pocket and felt the slender shape of the dagger in its sheath. She hadn't been sure why she'd brought the knife that morning; it had been a split-second decision as she'd gone past the dresser. The light overhead had slid along the golden snakes on the handle, making the gems of their eyes glitter. She'd picked it up and pressed it into her palm. The weight felt right in her hand, so she'd slipped it into her bag.

Now, as she followed the couple into the parking lot, it still felt right. But the thought of it . . . of plunging the blade into a man's chest. It would not be like cutting paper, or watermelon, or even slicing into chicken at dinner. This was living flesh . . . a human being.

"I don't know if I can do this." She hadn't meant to mumble it out loud, and as soon as the words slipped past her lips she flinched. The goddess stirred in the back of her mind, and heat crashed through her, burning her insides. Cora clenched her teeth and squeezed her eyes shut against the pain.

You will. And then, *You must.*

There was a flash behind her eyes, and then she was seeing a second set of images. Cora started, drawing a sharp breath. Yes, she could still see the parking lot, half empty, surrounded by sad little shrubs. She could still see the man staggering down the center, heading toward a black pickup truck. But she could also see images laid over that. She could see the black truck careening down the road, veering wildly onto the sidewalk. The wide, white eyes of a woman in a tan jacket, grocery bags in both hands, as she turned, too slowly. Too late.

Cora didn't hear her scream, but she could see the woman's mouth open wide, a second before the truck was on top of her.

She shook her head, frantic, jerking herself out of the vision. She braced herself against the hood of the car in the space beside her, head spinning, breath ragged in her throat.

Cora had scried before. She'd even had her share of prophetic dreams, but this had been . . . something different.

Go, the voice in her head hissed, and she stumbled forward. Dazed, she reached into her pocket just as the man climbed into his truck. The man's companion was struggling to leverage herself onto the high step of the passenger side. She giggled and fell back.

Cora wrapped her hand around the hilt of the dagger, smoothed shaking fingers over the scales. She took a step forward.

The man snapped something at the woman.

Cora took another step forward, the knife burning against her fingers. It felt like a warning, or an admonishment.

She could do this, couldn't she? For the woman on the street. For the goddess. For herself.

The drunk woman laughed again and finally managed to mount the step. She'd barely shut the door when the man started the truck, slamming into reverse without bothering to look in his rearview mirror. Cora gasped, stumbling back as the truck came within a few feet of her, then peeled away, leaving a smoking rubber stain on the concrete.

She stayed frozen, gaping after the truck as it disappeared down the street.

Rage blazed through her a moment later, followed by furious heat, and Cora staggered forward, a scream of pain tearing from her lips. She swung wildly, fist crashing into the window of the nearest car, which broke under her knuckles, sending a spiderweb of cracks spreading out toward the edges.

She turned on her heel, stomping across the lot, ignoring the group of men who'd come out of the pub and were staring after her openmouthed.

She'd failed. Maybe it was the heat blazing through her, or the fact that the rage that drove her was not hers alone, but something told her the goddess would not have patience for long.

Chapter Thirty-Seven

DAYNA

Dayna didn't sleep that night.

She'd snuck in late, and Fiona hadn't been waiting up for her this time. Her father was in bed, too, thank god—she was still technically grounded, and he was probably furious with her.

She spent half the night running searches on her laptop, poring over the same articles on Carman again and again, going through lists of ancient Celtic symbols—she swore if she closed her eyes her vision would dance with them. Between this she ran searches on the phrase *widow incorporated* and found nothing helpful—which wasn't surprising, considering that the sergeant had likely done the same. When she did attempt to sleep she couldn't stop thinking about Sam, the guilt and panic in his expression. His stammered excuses. It felt like the bottom had dropped out of her stomach.

There was no excuse for what he'd done. And to think she'd felt guilty about brushing him off when he'd asked to get back together. Hell, she'd even considered it, however briefly.

What if she *had* taken him back and then found out? The mere thought made anger burn her insides.

Her wound seemed to throb with each heartbeat, and by the time she went to bed she was too keyed up to sleep. Her brain was more than happy to fall into the familiar patterns of feverish obsession. She was breathing just fine. Deep and even. So why did her chest feel tight? Was it hot in here? Were her breaths getting shallower? It was just the panic.

She tried all her usual tricks. Thinking of a favorite book or movie for each letter of the alphabet, mentally walking through the layout of the coven house, and even trying to remember every detail of her good memories from last summer. The lunch they'd had in the apple orchard for Reagan's birthday, or the time they'd all jammed into Reagan's mini-van to head to the farmers market and Bronagh had left all her Werther's wrappers on the floor. Faye had lectured her about it the entire way back, and somehow the wrappers had mysteriously ended up in her pockets.

But even the best of her memories didn't seem to be working tonight.

It was this kind of night that made her think twice about taking medication, that made her fears seem ridiculous compared to what she was putting herself through. She was so utterly sick of feeling this way. Of having nothing to fight this with. The counting game could only help until it couldn't.

One, the bars of light on her ceiling.

Two, her legs wouldn't stop shaking.

This was bullshit.

Chapter Thirty-Eight

SAMUEL

Sage Widow had changed.

As he entered the dimly lit interior of the shop he tried to remember the last time he'd been in. Vaguely he remembered shelves crammed with tins and boxes of tea, an aisle of coffee beans in glass jars, but now...

The aisles were narrow and crooked, and signs hung on chains from the ceiling, full of scribbled cursive that said things like *Potions A-Z* and *Spellcraft Ingredients*.

Sam gaped around for a moment before snapping his mouth shut. Apparently Margery had redecorated slightly since her expulsion from the church.

Honestly, it didn't bother him. He could appreciate the irony.

Shoving his hands into his pockets, he shuffled past the first few aisles. He wondered briefly—and blasphemously—if there was a potion he could make, some kind of magic spell, to ease the horrible guilt.

He hadn't slept much last night. Every time he closed his eyes Dayna's pale, freckled face appeared, her accusing look eating at his insides.

He took a breath and tried to shake the thoughts off, moving deeper into the store.

For the most part it was empty, though in the second-to-last aisle he nearly ran into a tall, skinny woman. Sam staggered to a halt, and then recovered himself quickly. "Oh, Mrs. O'Neal, hi "

The older woman paled and then abruptly shoved the bundle of herbs she'd been holding back onto the shelf. She gave him a strained smile and backed away. "I . . . I thought I'd come in for some tea—" She darted a look over her shoulder, still moving backward. "They don't have what I want. Uh, I'll see you later, Sam." She disappeared around the corner before Sam could say anything.

Sam stayed where he was for a moment, startled. What had that been about?

"Not many churchgoers caught dead here," a voice said behind him, "and now I get two in one day?"

He whirled around and then relaxed. Margery was leaning against the shelf at the end of the aisle, grinning at him. "To what do I owe the pleasure, Samuel?"

"I had a question I was hoping you could answer."

"Always happy to help out a friend." She gave him a wide smile, which made him feel a little guilty. He wouldn't have described her as a friend, exactly, not after his mother and everyone at church had basically abandoned her.

She seemed to interpret his hesitation as some kind of need for privacy, because she beckoned him into the back room. "Come on, I've got a nice little armchair set up back here for breaks and such."

They passed through the shop and by the front desk, and Sam tried to ignore the fact that the stand on the desk had a large selection of silver pentacles displayed on chains.

The back was stacked with boxes and crates, and there was a table in one corner piled high with jars of herbs. This was where Margery directed him, and Sam settled into one of the overstuffed green armchairs beside it.

"Tea?"

"Uh, no thank you. I shouldn't actually be too long. I just had a question about something . . . um." He winced. There was really no good way of asking this.

He wasn't proud of this line of questioning, but so far it was his only potential lead, as far-fetched as it was. Besides, he kept telling himself that even though *he* knew magic wasn't real, the Butcher might think it was. The symbol on the barn wall, if that's what it was, still might be a clue.

Margery raised her brows. "And what are we getting into, Samuel? Research for something, maybe? A new project?"

Margery knew about his true-crime fascination. She'd happened upon him reading one of his books in the coffee shop once and asked him about it. Sam had found she listened without judging, and he'd ended up telling her more than he'd meant to about his strange hobby.

He sighed. "You probably already guessed, but yeah, I'm looking into the Butcher. This is a long shot, but I thought you might be able to tell me what this was." He took his phone out and pulled the picture up.

Margery squinted down at it, frowning. He was watching her face as she stared at the picture, and so he was able to see a spark of recognition, followed by careful blankness as she turned back to him.

"What's this a picture of? What does it have to do with the Butcher?"

Sam gave her a long look. She'd definitely had some kind of reaction to the mark. "It's a shot of the side of a barn from ten years ago on the Isle of Man . . ." He trailed off, and then when Margery continued to stare at him, decided to take the plunge. ". . . where they think the Butcher tried and failed to kill a sixth victim."

Margery blew out a breath and glanced down at the phone again. Sam's gut began to churn. She *knew* something.

"What? What is it?"

"It's a mark that means banishing," she finally said. "It's magic."

There was silence for a moment as Sam tried to digest this. Again, he told himself that he didn't believe in magic, but other people did. And those people might be involved in this case. "You're sure?" he said. "It just looks like a bunch of scribbles to me." His stomach was churning again, only this time it was excitement. He might have made a break in a decade-old case. It seemed impossible. "That means the Butcher thinks he's doing magic."

Margery shook her head. "Not him," she said. "Whoever he is, this isn't his work. Not unless he's a very good forger. This is the work of a witch."

Sam frowned. "How can you tell?"

"Because I recognize it." Again, her expression was guarded.

"Does the witch . . ." He cleared his throat, feeling strange about calling someone that. "Does she have a scar on her face, or maybe her neck or shoulder? It would be a big scar, something that almost killed her."

Margery thrust the phone back into his hands and, to his dismay, began to walk back toward the front of her store, toward the door.

"I think you should leave, Samuel. You're asking after things you don't understand."

"No, please." Sam hurried after her. "Margery, come on. I've been studying the Butcher for *years* now. All of this fascinates me."

"I don't mean the murders"—Margery paused by the door—"I mean magic. There are more things in heaven and earth, Samuel, than are dreamed of in your philosophy." She looked at him a second time, more closely, and then sighed. "You're not going to let this alone, are you?"

"No," he said quietly. "I'm not. Honestly, I don't think I can."

"Her name is Harriet King," Margery said reluctantly. "It's her magic, I can tell just as well as if she'd signed her name. The way she draws the pentacle . . . And yes, she has a scar." She tapped the side of her neck. "A thick one, this side of her throat."

Sam's heart was beating hard in his ears now, so loudly he could hardly hear himself as he said, "How do you know all this? How do you know *her*?"

"She belonged to a local coven once, a long time ago." Margery handed the phone back to him, and he took it, just barely registering that she'd said "a local coven," meaning there were more witches in town. It seemed unbelievable, but that was hardly his main focus right now.

"Where is she right now? Where can I find her?"

Margery's dark brows furrowed. "You go looking for Harriet King, you go looking for trouble, Samuel."

"You don't get it." Sam held out both hands. "She's in danger. I need to find her."

Margery sighed. "I'd be more worried about your serial killer, boy." When Sam stared at her, she shook her head.

"Fine. If you want to find King, ask your ex-girlfriend. The last time they were in, she was with them all."

Sam's mouth dropped open as a wave of shock hit him, freezing him to the spot. Margery frowned at him and started to say, "Samuel—" but he was already moving, smashing the door open with one hand, his phone in the other. He dialed Dayna's number, getting her voice mail.

He hit the road running, still calling, still getting nothing, her voice echoing in his ears: *I'm not here right now . . . . leave a message. Not here right now. Not here right now.*

Shit.

Chapter Thirty-Nine

DAYNA

Dayna spent the morning locked away in her bedroom, listening to her father's heavy footfalls below. He clearly wanted to talk to her, otherwise he wouldn't spend so much time hanging around the kitchen.

She stayed where she was, sitting cross-legged in the center of her bed, hoping to wait him out. During the summer the reverend held court over the church youth program, and he was usually out of the house by early morning.

No such luck. When she crept down the stairs he was standing at the bottom, keys in his hand, shrugging into his jacket. "Obviously I wasn't clear enough, because you've been out repeatedly since we talked. As I said, you're *grounded*. I don't want you out of the house."

"I'm going to shower." She skirted around him at the bottom of the stairs and spotted Fiona through the kitchen doorway. In spite of the summer sun pouring through the windows, the woman was wearing a high-necked yellow sweater and a skirt that went all the way down to her ankles. She was staring at the wallpaper, her face slack, ignoring the cup of coffee in front of her. A second later Fiona turned toward her, and Dayna skidded to a halt, horror blooming in her chest.

Fiona's face was as pale and thin as ever, but what drew Dayna's attention was the mottled purple bruise around her left eye.

Her father was still in the hallway; Dayna could hear him stomping back and forth.

Had he done this?

The bruises on Fiona's arms, and now this. Dayna stared at her for a full moment, her mouth sour, then edged into the kitchen and smiled cautiously at her mother. "Good morning."

Fiona smiled wanly. Then the mug of coffee in front of her seemed to catch her eye, and she wrapped her hands around it. "Morning. Are you going somewhere?"

"Just to shower. Um, your eye looks painful. What happened?"

Fiona frowned, touching the corner of her eye with a fingertip. She winced. "I . . . don't know. I don't remember." Her eyes were starting to lose their focus again, and Dayna cleared her throat, alarmed. She had to get Fiona to talk to her, but she seemed to be fading in and out.

"Fiona, are you sure you don't know who it was—" She blinked as Fiona stood up abruptly. Her chair tipped over and crashed to the floor, and her eyes were wide and dark in her pale face.

"I don't *remember*. I don't remember who they are."

"Okay." Dayna held up a hand, alarmed. "Okay, that's fine."

"Where are you going? Are you going to see *them*?"

Dayna took a step backward. "What? Who?"

Fiona lunged, catching Dayna's sleeve in a tight grip, tugging her forward. "Tell me, please, you have to tell me who you're seeing. Where are the rest of them? I can't remember who they are."

Dayna's chest was tight with alarm, but she tried to stay very still, as if the woman were a wild animal she might scare off. She forced herself to keep her voice low and calm. "Fiona, I'm not going anywhere, okay? I'm staying right here, with you."

"Fiona."

Her father's voice made them both start. Fiona released her grip on

Dayna's sleeve, her expression confused. "I...Are we going to the church now, Nathaniel?"

"Yes." The reverend stopped beside her, slipping an arm around her waist. It was not an affectionate gesture, but rather a way of steering her toward the hall. Fiona's posture was stiff, and she was clutching her arms again as they started for the door.

"Your mother is right, Dayna. Don't forget you're staying in today. You're still grounded, and when I get back we're going to talk. We all need to start attending church again. As a family." The reverend looked back, but Dayna noticed he didn't make eye contact, staring somewhere over her left shoulder instead. "We'll see you when we get home."

She watched them go, stunned.

Her father was stern, it was true. And he'd maybe gripped her arm a little too tightly as a child, or pulled her after him a little too firmly when crossing the street, but...he wasn't physically abusive, was he? Could he have given Fiona that bruise?

And he kept insisting Fiona was fine now, but that outburst had been... strange. He could try to play it off as Fiona asking her not to go meet her friends, to stay home, but that didn't seem likely. The woman had looked panicked.

If she'd thought the reverend had been hiding something before, she was certain of it now.

After showering, Dayna retreated up the stairs to her room, still trying to figure out what the hell had just happened.

She collapsed onto the bed with a groan, her wet hair soaking into her pillow. Now she had a choice to make: either she snuck out and risked pissing off the reverend even more, or she called Reagan and told her she'd have to lie low for a while.

Still lying down, she fished in her open bag for her phone. Her fingers brushed over lip gloss, hair ties, her wallet...still no phone. She sat up so quickly her head spun, suddenly sure her father had come back in and taken it while she was in the shower.

He'd done it once before when she was grounded, and that had been another of their bigger fights. She growled under her breath, panic blooming in her chest. If he'd stolen her phone, she was going to make their last fight feel like a trip to the spa.

Dayna turned over her bag, dumping it on the bed in an explosion of tampons, gum wrappers, and receipts.

She sat back a second later, feeling foolish.

There was her phone, sitting on the very top of the pile, which meant it had been buried underneath all the crap in her bag. She snatched it up, relief making her slump back onto her pillow. Dayna checked her phone briefly, grimacing at several missed calls from Samuel, before she sat up again and began to sort through the garbage.

She really should try to be less of a total slob.

Dayna was placing the receipts in a pile in the center of the bed, when the block letters on one caught her eye and she stopped short, smoothing it out on her knee. Her breath caught.

Widow Inc.

This was it, what they'd been talking about at the station. Widow Incorporated.

The receipt was from the tea she'd got Bronagh from Sage Widow. She'd never really looked that closely at the receipts before, but the actual company name was Widow Incorporated. *That's* why there hadn't been any results when she googled it—Margery didn't have a store website.

This meant the killer had bought something at Sage Widow.

She snatched up her phone, heart beating wildly. She had to call Reagan.

Chapter Forty

DAYNA

F ive minutes later, Reagan parked at the end of the driveway. When Dayna slid into the passenger seat, Reagan tapped the dusty dashboard once, lightly, with the tip of her finger, mumbling something under her breath. The minivan coughed to life, filled with the sound of indie rock music and the smell of gasoline, sending up puffs of exhaust. Reagan was wearing a white NASA T shirt and a pair of cutoffs today. Her legs were long and toned against the ripped vinyl seat, and her gray running shoes were covered in mud.

"You're getting your van all dirty," Dayna pointed out.

"And good morning to you, too, sunshine." Reagan snorted. "I've just come straight from practice. Give me a break."

Dayna eyed her, amused. "Does Yemi know how you start the van now?"

"What she doesn't know..." Reagan raised an eyebrow. "Besides, this old bucket of bolts needs a little magical assistance, or it takes a full ten minutes to start. I got your text and drove like the wind." She waved her phone as Dayna buckled in. "Well, at least as much like the wind as this van goes. It was more like a tiny, very slow storm with lots of rattling and creaking." She peered at Dayna's face before shifting into reverse.

"How far? You look pale. Is it just the Sage Widow thing, or is there more going on?"

"You could say that." Dayna took a deep breath and told her about her mother's weird behavior that morning, and her father's reaction, which had been equally strange. After a moment she told her about Samuel, too. It felt strange to switch mindsets so drastically, from murders and witchcraft to her messed-up but thoroughly unmagical life.

Reagan whistled, a low, impressed sound. "Damn, woman. You have a lot going on."

"Yeah, maybe," Dayna grumbled, and smoothed out the receipt she'd been crumpling in her fist. "Anyway, let's ask Margery about this."

Reagan wrinkled her nose. "What exactly are we going to ask her? *Hey, Margery, served any serial killers lately?*"

"I don't know. Maybe we can ask her about weird customers, anyone that seemed off. You know, like had a weird energy. She is a witch, right? Maybe she picked up on some of that."

Reagan quirked an eyebrow. "I'm not one to look down on anyone, but she's a hedge witch at best. I'm not sure she'd be able to tell." She pulled into the nearest parking spot and shut the van off.

When she twisted in her seat to look at Dayna, her face was serious again. "You know you can crash with us, don't you? For as long as you need. Ma and I are worried. I know she doesn't want to pressure you, but she really wishes you'd come stay until this stuff with Fiona gets sorted."

"I know." Dayna followed her across the lot, mind still spinning, ignoring her phone vibrating in her pocket. She didn't want to speak to Sam, no matter how persistent he was being.

Reagan was right; she was already at the coven house every available opportunity, and she crashed in their spare bedroom all the time. It wasn't much of a stretch to imagine living there. She'd fantasized about that very thing multiple times. Growing up, she used to pretend Yemi had adopted her, that Reagan was legally her sister, and that she would never have to go back to the reverend. It had been a comforting idea, but now ... maybe it needed to be her new reality.

She didn't realize how tense she'd been until she relaxed slightly and felt the muscles in her shoulder scream in protest. Her dog bite was throbbing again.

"Thanks," she said. "I might have to take you up on that, at least for a while." She pressed her lips together, thinking hard as they entered Sage Widow, the bell over the door jangling. The mere threat of moving out might be enough to make her father realize things had gone too far. Maybe it would force him to get help for his wife.

They wandered down the first aisle, Reagan brushing her fingers over boxes and packages of dried herbs.

As she followed her down to the end of the aisle, Dayna found herself momentarily distracted. There was someone stalking across the porch outside Sage Widow; she could see him through the window, a cigarette trailing smoke from between his fingers. He was tall and thin, with startling blue eyes and curly hair that flopped in his face. It was the cigarette that stood out to her; this wasn't a place you were allowed to smoke, and he was quite brazen about it. But as he passed the window, it was the wound on his cheek that drew her eye. Fresh and jagged and sloppily stitched together with black thread. He turned his head and caught her looking, his mouth turning up into a wolfish smile.

Did she know him from somewhere?

She passed a wide display of beeswax candles, and when she came back into view of the window, it was empty. Dayna blinked.

When they got to the front there was no one at the desk, and Reagan hit the top of the silver bell on the counter, which let out a cheery *ding*, and stepped back.

"So, you and Meiner...?" Reagan trailed off, waggling her brows, and Dayna snorted.

"I have no idea what you mean."

"Come *on*. You two have been hate-flirting all week. Don't think I've forgotten the way you described her when you first met her. That she's super tall and weirdly intense." Reagan's grin was wicked. "I know what that means. You want to see how intense she'd be in bed."

"Ew, Reagan, don't be gross." Dayna slapped her friend's arm, and Reagan shrieked with laughter.

"You and Meiner sitting in a tree . . ."

Dayna's expression must have been somewhere between despair and amusement, because Reagan laughed again. "You know I'm giving you a hard time. But am I wrong? Look me in the eye and tell me she isn't fit."

Dayna bit her lip, hesitating, and now it was Reagan's turn to roll her eyes.

"I called that one."

Another moment went by, and Dayna began to shift from foot to foot. Her dog bite was still throbbing; in fact it seemed to be getting worse. "Should I ring the bell again?"

"Nah, just yell at her." Reagan grinned and leaned over the desk. The door behind it, which led to the back rooms, was ajar. "Auntie, you have customers!"

"Nice." Dayna paused, fishing in her bag. "Hold on, I'll phone the store, see if she's hiding in the back room."

She pulled out her cell and then nearly dropped it when it vibrated in her hands. The call display said *27 missed calls*.

Dayna's brows shot up. This was excessive, even for Sam. Maybe it was something other than his desperate attempts to apologize. "I think something might be wrong with Sam."

Reagan snorted, still leaning over the desk to try to peer into the back. "Understatement of the century."

"No, I mean, he's tried to call a million times—" She blinked down at the phone as it started to vibrate again. "He's calling now."

Reagan gave her a look, but Dayna answered anyway. "Sam? Is everything okay?"

There was a relieved sigh from the other end, and then Sam said quickly, "Where are you? Are you somewhere safe?"

Dayna frowned. "What? Of course I am. What's the matter?" He sounded completely out of breath.

"It's Harriet King," he said, and Dayna's mouth dropped open. He pressed on before she could say anything. "She was a victim in the last cycle. He's trying to get to her, finish what he started. She's not safe to be around, Dayna. You're not with her now, are you?"

He sounded panicked at the very thought. "No," she said hastily. "No, I'm just with Reagan. Sam, how did you know—"

"I need to meet with you. Like, right away."

Dayna hesitated, glancing over at Reagan, who had made her way around the desk and was frowning down at something on the floor behind it. "Uh, sure, want to meet at the Coffee Bean? I'm right— Reagan! You can't just go back there."

Sam was still talking, asking her something, but Dayna wasn't paying attention anymore. Reagan's eyes were wide, and she had one hand pressed to her mouth.

"Oh shit."

"What?" Dayna hurried around the side of the counter. Behind the desk were several piles of papers scattered on the back counter, and a garbage bin had been tipped over and its contents spread across the floor. Patches of blood were splattered across the rug where Margery usually stood.

"Nosebleed...maybe?" Reagan looked around, expression uneasy.

"Maybe," Dayna said, but the sight of the blood made her mouth dry. She let her gaze drift across the pattern of splotches on the floor, drops of blood leading from the back of the desk to the crack in the door.

"Dayna? What is it? What's going on? Are you at Reagan's place? I can come over—"

"I'll call you right back, okay?" Dayna hit the off button, cutting off Sam's protests.

"We should check on her." Reagan started for the door, and Dayna hurried to follow. The back was a spacious concrete room full to the rafters with cardboard boxes, and a wide wooden table with jars of herbs and twisted pillars of beeswax stacked across it. But no Margery.

"Should we call the gardai?"

"I don't know yet, just keep your phone handy." Reagan crept forward, footsteps light on the concrete floor.

"Hey, wait." A bar of light falling across the back end of the room had caught her eye. The back door was open. "I bet she's out for a smoke."

"If she is," Reagan said, and her voice was slightly uneven, "she needs a cloth, because she's still dripping blood."

She was right. When Dayna glanced down, she saw a scattering of coin-sized blood droplets leading to the back door. As she followed Reagan, she slid a hand into her pocket, pulling out her phone. A wave of cold panic spread through her.

The back door led to a porch that looked out on the woods, and when Dayna stepped outside she felt a surge of relief. There was an ashtray balanced on the railing, and Margery had propped her cigarette up on the side, where it was sending up gentle spirals of smoke. A red sweater hung on the post nearby.

"Margery?"

"What did she—" Reagan stopped. "Oh my god."

She saw it a second later. At first glance it looked like a pile of black fabric at the bottom of the stairs, or a garbage bag maybe, if she looked quickly out the corner of one eye.

But it was Margery. She was lying on her back, left arm stretched out, as if she'd been reaching for someone. Her black dress flared out around her body.

"Oh my god." Reagan's hand was over her mouth, half muffling her words. "Oh my god, Margery."

"Did she fall?" Dayna pushed past Reagan, her heart beating wildly against her rib cage. She hurried down the steps and then skidded to a stop at the bottom, seizing the railing as a scream tore from her throat. Close up she could see a series of bloody stains on the front of Margery's dress, and more horrible still...

The woman's eyes were nothing but two empty holes in her chalk-white face.

Dazed, she grasped the railing with shaking fingers. Reagan stayed where she was, still frozen, "Dayna, wha— You shouldn't—"

"Margery?" It was stupid. There was no way the woman was alive. She moved closer, off the last step and onto the small patch of grass along the edge of the backwoods. "Reagan, call the gardai."

"Oh Christ. Aye, I'm—I'm calling. You shouldn't go down there. What if whoever did this is still here?"

The tightness in Dayna's throat increased, and she felt a stab of cold panic as she turned back to Reagan. The bone necklace felt heavy against her chest. Would it protect her from a murderer? She searched her memory frantically for spells of protection, but the panic seemed to have wiped her mind clean. Her blood was suddenly thundering in her ears, and each breath burned in her chest.

Reagan had begun chanting under her breath—*so mote it be, so mote it be, so mote it be*—her voice trembling.

There was an awful, rattling gasp from behind them, and Dayna jumped. She turned, clutching the railing, pulse stuttering wildly.

Margery was blinking, slowly, very slowly. Dayna realized with a sense of dull horror that her eyelids were somehow still intact. She opened and shut them in a slow, horrible movement, her eyelids sagging inward each time. She let out another rattling breath, and Dayna scrambled forward. "Oh my god, she's still alive."

Margery's face was porcelain pale, and when she opened her lips the inside of her mouth was stained red. "First we were gods," she mumbled.

Dayna sank down beside her. Tears stung the backs of her eyes, and her voice trembled. "You're okay. Help is coming."

The woman's eyelids flicked open again, and Dayna shuddered at the gory emptiness of the sockets. Incredibly, Margery's lips twitched in a smile. "Gods and then saints"—she took a shuddering breath before continuing—"and then...witches, and now this..." Her hand flopped forward, and at first Dayna thought she was gesturing, but then Margery's eyes fluttered shut and her chest sank and didn't rise again.

Dayna's breath seemed to stop. She clenched her fists around handfuls of grass. "Margery? Help is coming—" She faltered. "Oh god."

"Is she . . ." Reagan's voice cracked. "Is she gone?"

Dayna stood up, breathing hard. Something along the edge of the forest caught her eye, a blur of movement just beyond the tree line. She jerked, muffling a gasp with one fist. Maybe it was just a bird or a racoon, or . . .

The trees. There was something wrong with them.

Without thinking, she stepped closer.

Each tree along the edge of the forest had been vandalized—harsh, circular slashes etched into the bark. The same symbol over and over. Dayna's hands flew to her mouth.

Behind her, Reagan was stammering into the phone. "We found her at the bottom of the stairs. Come fast. I think—I think she's dead. No, she's not moving. There's blood."

Dayna's gaze flicked back to Margery, sprawled on the grass. Thick trails of blood had seeped out and left patches on her sweater.

Her stomach flipped, and she stumbled back a step, toward the stairs. If she was going to be sick, she shouldn't do it here. The forest seemed to surge and warp, and Dayna clutched the railing, gasping for breath. She couldn't pass out; they had to get somewhere safe. Someone was out there. Someone who'd carved the same symbol into the trees with a kind of obsessive precision. Someone who'd stabbed Margery repeatedly.

"I'm staying on the phone. Aye, we're on the stairs at the back. Dayna, come on, she says to stay on the stairs."

The next six minutes seemed like an eternity. An eternity in which Margery did not move, save for the patches of blood widening slowly on her sweater.

Dayna and Reagan stayed together, clutching each other, the voice on the other end of the line like some fragile link to safety.

Dayna kept desperately grasping for something, anything, to guard them. A spell, an incantation, even a prayer that might ward off a potential attack. Instead, her mind kept circling back to the same thing.

Breathe in. Breathe out. Breathe in.

Her chest kept getting tighter, and she pressed a hand to her throat, fingers splayed, struggling to drag in another breath, and another.

Reagan had begun an incantation now, muttering a complicated spell under her breath, tracing one shaking hand in front of her. A faint shimmer appeared before them as Dayna gasped in another deep breath.

Whatever was in the trees shouldn't be able to get through Reagan's spell. Unless, of course . . . it was more powerful than them.

The wail of sirens in the distance made Dayna tense, and then the relief that shuddered through her came out in a sob. When the first officer began making his way down the steps, Reagan let out a strangled gasp and let her hand drop, and the spell flickered out.

"They're here. Oh, thank god, they're finally here."

Chapter Forty-One

SAMUEL

Sam checked his phone for the hundredth time.

It had been a full ten minutes since Dayna had hung up on him, and he kept trying to convince himself not to call her back. She was somewhere safe; she was with Reagan and not Harriet King.

But where was she right now? Why wasn't she calling him? She'd said to meet at the Coffee Bean, he was fairly sure of that. But he hadn't really been able make out what Reagan had said in the background. It had sounded like she'd cursed. Had she sounded angry or afraid?

Maybe Dayna wasn't as safe as she thought she was.

Sam glanced up and then back down at his phone, barely registering as someone sat down on one of the stools beside him. The Coffee Bean was usually quiet, but it was really packed today.

He'd give her another five minutes, and then he'd call again.

In an attempt to distract himself, he went to the counter to buy an iced latte, trying to ignore the barista's bemused expression. He was fully aware he had sweat stains on his T-shirt. When Dayna hadn't picked up the phone earlier, he'd begun frantically riding his bike across town to her house, hoping to catch her. Then he'd just as frantically ridden back as soon as she'd suggested the Coffee Bean.

He sat back down at the bar in front of the window and pulled up the message boards.

Sam had messaged a few of his forum mates less than five minutes ago, and CrimeBuff69 had somehow already managed to unearth old records for Harriet King—rent agreements, phone bills, old addresses. Sam didn't ask how.

He spent several long minutes trying to piece together the woman's history. Of course, it didn't help that his phone vibrated with a new notification every five seconds.

When he'd first logged into the forums, his mouth had dropped open. Since news of the murders had leaked, his inbox had been filling, but reporters seemed to have found the forums now, and his inbox was at maximum capacity. He had hundreds of messages, both from forum regulars demanding information, and reporters requesting interviews and asking if he had inside information.

The whir of the coffee grinder made him glance up from the screen, and he noticed the coffee shop was filling up faster than usual.

A blond woman in a pantsuit moved past him, smiling. At the counter, a man in black slacks and a checkered dress shirt was speaking quietly with a gray-haired gentleman wearing an earpiece.

None of them looked familiar.

He remembered what the agents had said to his father, that there would be press flying in. Apparently they'd all just arrived and were cramming into the same coffee shop.

He tried to ignore the pantsuited lady, who was talking loudly on her phone beside him. "Nothing, Reginald. I told you, the sergeant practically dragged me out by my hair." She paused. "No, the forum chap hasn't replied. Yes, I *know*. I'll keep looking, keep your knickers on."

He froze. Exactly how many reporters in this coffee shop currently had messages in his inbox? The thought was bizarre. They seemed to think he was going to be some kind of source for them, having been the first one to know the Butcher was back. As if he had some kind of inside knowledge of what the killer's next move was going to be.

He wished...

His inbox pinged again.

CrimeBuff69: I just found it. File is attached. Do you realize what this means?

Sam bit his lip, clicking on the file at the bottom of the message. It was a tenant agreement, drawn up ten years ago.

CrimeBuff69 had managed to dig up proof that Harriet King had been in Manchester when the Butcher first started carving his symbol. And here Sam was looking at a rental agreement on the Isle of Man.

If he'd learned anything from his obsession with true crime, it was that coincidences stopped being coincidental once they piled up like this.

Three places. Manchester, the Isle of Man, and now...the city of Carman.

Fingers trembling, he typed out, *He's following her.*

A second later the reply appeared in his inbox.

CrimeBuff69: Mate, if you think your gf is hanging out with her, you got to get to this lady NOW.

Sam stood up so fast his chair tipped back, crashing to the floor. He froze as everyone in the shop turned to stare at him. The reporter in the pantsuit blinked at him. Her brow creased, and she took a step toward him. "Are you—"

She was cut off a second later by the whoop of a siren from outside. The walls of the coffee shop were suddenly flickering blue and red.

Two police cars had rounded the corner, pulling into the lot so fast their tires kicked up plumes of dust. As Sam watched, a third pulled in behind, followed by an ambulance. The officers hit the ground running. The crowd inside the shop gravitated to the window.

The gardai and the paramedics vanished into the tiny shop next to the farmers market.

Margery.

A second later, the pantsuited lady shot out the front door, nearly spilling her coffee in the process, and several of the other reporters did the same. Sam scooped up his bag, his heart hammering, and he followed.

Across the road, a couple of uniformed officers had begun taping off the area. The reporters were already asking questions, and the pantsuited lady was holding a tape recorder. The nearest officer, a short, beefy man named Murphy, shook his head at her, annoyed.

Sam skidded to a halt in front of him. "Murphy, what's happened? Is Margery all right?"

Officer Murphy's expression softened. "Sorry, lad. You know I can't say nothing. You'll have to ask your old man."

Sam felt the reporters home in on him almost immediately and ignored their stares. The door at the front of the shop was opening. Someone leaned out to shout at one of the officers, but Sam barely heard them, shock rooting him to the spot.

Through the crack in the door he could make out a pair of uniformed officers, faces grim. And beside them, leaning against the wall with her arms crossed over her chest, her face pale and drawn, was Dayna.

Chapter Forty-two

DAYNA

It was both comforting and extremely annoying to realize that she knew every police officer on the scene.

Of course, she'd rather not have had Samuel's dad drive her home, since the whole thing was a bit awkward. Thankfully he'd merely lectured her about being careful and hadn't brought up anything to do with Sam.

The hall light was on, and she kicked her shoes off and hurried into the kitchen, expecting her father to be at the table waiting for her. Instead, Fiona was there, leaning against the stove as she watched the kettle steam. She glanced up when Dayna came in, her face concerned. "Someone called and left a message with me that you'd been in some trouble. Is everything okay?"

She pressed her lips together, searching Fiona's face. Yes, she was shaken. Dayna's insides felt like Jell-O, but Fiona seemed so delicate. Maybe sharing with her wasn't the best idea.

"Uh, everything is fine. I just . . . found something and had to call the gardai." She felt sick as soon as she said it. Margery wasn't *something*. She was a human being.

Well, she had been.

Instantly the image of those hollow red sockets came back to her, and she braced one hand against the doorway, feeling like she might be sick.

"You look like you've seen a ghost." Fiona crossed the room, reaching out for her arm, and Dayna let herself be steered to the table. "Sit, I can . . . How about I pour you some tea?"

This was so much like Yemi that Dayna found herself relaxing in spite of herself. "Thanks," she mumbled. "I think I need it."

"Will you tell me what happened? They say talking can help." Fiona gave her a hesitant smile, and for a moment Dayna wondered why she'd ever been wary of her mother. Yes, she had her odd moments. She was mentally ill, but so was Dayna.

And Dayna wasn't her father—she didn't shut people out or send them away because their brains didn't work the way they should. And here was Fiona acting like a real mother. Dayna would have given anything for those moments growing up.

It made her hate her father just a little more.

Fiona set the tea down in front of Dayna, hands shaking slightly, which made the cup wobble a little on the saucer before Dayna reached out to steady it. "What, um, what happened? I saw the cruiser out the window. Is it . . . you know?" Her eyes went wide when Dayna nodded.

Slowly she told her what had happened, going into the shop and finding Margery gone from behind the desk, following the blood trail out the back and down the stairs. And most horrifying of all, discovering Margery still half-alive at the bottom of the stairs and realizing her killer might still be in the forest.

Fiona's hands shook on the mug. "Her eyes were gone? He—the Butcher took them?"

Dayna nodded, swallowing her tea, which was still too hot and scalded her throat. She didn't care. "It was horrible."

Fiona's chair scraped across the tiles, and Dayna watched as Fiona got up and paced over to the stove, her back to the table. Dayna's stomach sank. She'd been right; Fiona wasn't ready to hear something this gruesome. She wasn't stable enough.

"I shouldn't have told you. I'm sorry."

"No."

When Fiona turned, her blue eyes were huge in her thin face, and Dayna blinked at her, feeling a trickle of alarm in her stomach. Fiona's eyes were too wide, too glassy. Her cheeks were flushed.

"No, it's good you told me. It's . . . good to know what's going on out there." She moved more quickly than Dayna had expected, and she leaned back in her chair as Fiona bent over her, patting one shoulder awkwardly. "Tell me more about it. How—um, how are you feeling?"

Dayna slouched in her chair, staring down at her tea. She tried to take stock of her body and then immediately wished she hadn't. Her chest was tight, which made her breaths feel shallow. "Okay, I guess. I think Reagan took it worse than me. I better call her tonight."

"What did the marks in the trees look like?"

Dayna looked up, startled. Fiona was staring at her. "Oh, um. Well, they were the Butcher's mark, I guess." She stood slowly, pushing her cup away, unease growing in her chest. "Are you okay? I'm not sure we should be talking about this—"

"Wait." Fiona's hand shot out, and this time her grip on Dayna's arm was tight, pinching her skin. "S-sit down—" she stammered. "We're talking like a family, that's all. Family doesn't have any secrets."

"Maybe you should lie down." Dayna took Fiona's wrist, gently prying her grip off. She kept a hand on her arm and tried to steer her into the hall. "Let's go lie down, okay? Do you need water or anything?"

Fiona seemed content to be steered down the hallway, but she was still staring eagerly at Dayna. "I want to know everything. Did you see the Butcher? Do you know what he looks like?"

"No, no one does. Come on, easy does it." She paused in front of the guest room door and eased it open, guiding Fiona inside. The room was done up as it usually was, in ugly pastel flower wallpaper. The reverend had placed a white porcelain water basin on the dresser and hung a dollar store blanket over the end of the bed. Dayna glanced around, startled to see Fiona hadn't made any changes to the room at all. Even her suitcase was still sitting on the top of the dresser, full of clothing.

"He didn't help you move in at all, huh?" She stopped at the end of the bed, gently steering Fiona until she sat.

"Were you scared?" Fiona's voice was a whisper, and her eyes seemed to glitter in the soft lamp light. Dayna repressed a shiver. "When you saw the body, did it scare you?"

"Yeah, it was scary." Dayna turned back to the dresser. "Fiona—Mam, do you want me to unpack your suitcase for you?"

Fiona didn't answer, and when Dayna turned to look at her, she was lying back on the bed staring up at the ceiling fan. When she spoke, her voice was distant and dreamy. "I didn't know you could be scared, since you're not a real person."

Dayna stopped short, hand hovering above the suitcase on the dresser. There was a pang in her chest, a sick feeling spreading down into her stomach.

Slowly she made herself move, unpacking the suitcase and tucking each piece of clothing away, mind racing.

It was becoming painfully obvious that Fiona was losing touch with reality, and Dayna's father was completely in denial that there was anything wrong.

If someone was abusing a child, you could call child services, but who did you call if the victim was an adult? There had to be someone she could contact who could help Fiona, someone outside Carman.

Tomorrow she'd look online and see if she could find a number to call.

By the time she was done folding the rest of the clothing and had tucked the suitcase into the closet, Fiona seemed to have fallen asleep, or at least she had her eyes shut and didn't stir when Dayna paused at the end of the bed.

She started to make her way out as quietly as possible, but something about the portraits on the wall caught her eye. There were three of them. The one in the center was of Dayna and her parents when she was small. In it, Fiona looked healthy and happy, and even the reverend was wearing one of his rare smiles.

What caught her eye, though, was that someone had drawn on the glass encasing the picture. Chaotic black scribbles now obscured both pictures of Dayna's face. Openmouthed, Dayna pressed a fingertip to the glass. Her hand came away black.

She glanced over her shoulder, and her heart seemed to stop in her chest.

Fiona was sitting bolt upright on the bed. Her eyes, wide and glittering in the dark, were fixed on Dayna's face. For one heartbeat, two, they only stared at each other, and then Fiona eased back down and turned to the wall, curling her knees up to her chest.

Dayna turned and hurried out the door. The sooner she could find someone to call, the better.

Chapter Forty-Three

DAYNA

The next morning, Reagan picked up Dayna as soon as the reverend was out the door and brought her back to the coven house. The Callighans had come over and set up camp. They only lived a half hour away, but Bronagh had declared it was too dangerous to be apart now, that it was safest in numbers. So it seemed every room in the old farmhouse would be occupied that night; even the pullout couch in the living room had been utilized.

Bronagh and Grandma King had both demanded to hear about the discovery of the body more than once. She answered what felt like hundreds of questions. Yes, Margery was a hedge witch who hadn't belonged to any coven. Yes, she had still been alive when they'd found her. No, they didn't get a look at whoever was in the woods.

Around lunchtime, Yemi put her foot down and insisted they all drink chamomile tea for their nerves while she and Brenna prepared sandwiches.

Dayna felt a surge of guilt. The reverend had already phoned the house three times this morning when he couldn't reach her on her cell. She knew Fiona must have told him what happened; he'd learned about the body. Plus she was supposed to be grounded. . . .

She didn't want to talk to him, or anyone, which was ironic, since her phone had been vibrating all evening. Sam had already sent her several frantic texts. Apparently he'd caught a glimpse of her at the crime scene and was freaking out. Dayna eventually caved and texted him back. Just a sentence: *I'm fine. Talk to you later.*

Reagan left the guest room without a word, and Dayna smiled weakly at Yemi before following her into the kitchen. Since Reagan merely collapsed into a chair, she wandered over to put the kettle on. Yemi had already cleansed the house, and the kitchen smelled vaguely smoky and herblike. There was a candle burning in the center of the table.

While she waited for the kettle to boil she flicked her fingers in and out of a candle flame on the counter and tried not to fixate on her breathing. Yemi had put Meiner to work at the kitchen table chopping vegetables for a stew, and Dayna caught her looking, brows raised.

"Trying to set yourself on fire?"

Dayna drew her hand away with a sigh before joining Reagan at the table, sliding the mugs across.

She wrapped her hands around her cup to stop them from shaking and stared down into the steaming surface of the tea, certain that Meiner was studying her face now. Hopefully she didn't look the way she felt.

"You think they'll call?" Reagan's voice was tight, like she was holding back tears.

She was talking about the gardai, Dayna knew. The officers who'd arrived on the scene yesterday had separated and questioned them briefly— *What time did you find her? When did you last see her?*—and when they were done, they said they'd call if they had any follow-up questions.

"I doubt there's much more they can get out of us. They wouldn't say anything about the other murders when I asked."

"Here, too." Reagan drummed her fingers on her teacup. "The guy might as well have said, *I'll ask the questions here.*" She lowered her voice deeper at the end of her impression, and Dayna snorted.

"I've been watching the news all morning and there's nothing." Meiner frowned. "Do they even have any leads?"

"I don't know."

Dayna felt her breath catch, which immediately sent her pulse racing. She hadn't slept last night, and the exhaustion combined with the residual shock was pushing her to the edge of obsession. She could feel it in the way her heart pounded in her ears, how she felt overheated and spacey. She needed sleep, but if she tried to nap right now, it would only tip her into a spiral that much faster.

She avoided Meiner's concerned stare and glanced over at Reagan instead. Her friend's face was blank, but she was clutching her mug a little desperately. When Dayna shifted in her chair, Reagan jumped. "I keep zoning out. And I can't stop thinking about her face."

Dayna could only swallow past the tightness in her throat and shake her head. She didn't want to talk about it. It was too overwhelming.

Before Reagan could say anything else, something vibrated on the surface of the table, making them jump. Dayna's cell phone was lit up and buzzing away. The screen displayed the word *Reverend* in bold black letters.

Dayna made an involuntary noise of distress, reaching out to slam her cell phone over. She didn't want to think about how furious he must be.

"Your dad?" Meiner asked, and shook her head when Dayna nodded. "Shit, you've got a lot going on. He won't show up here, will he?"

"He won't. He doesn't want any kind of drama his congregation might hear about." A problem that couldn't be packed up neatly and shipped off to some church camp simply didn't fit in with his plans.

"I can't stop seeing it...." Reagan didn't seem to have heard any of the conversation. "Her eyes."

Instantly it was all Dayna could think of. The chalky cast of Margery's skin, her eyelids opening and shutting like some gross parody, as if she were trying to clear her vision. The empty red sockets...

The room spun, stretching out and away. Suddenly there were vast amounts of space between her and the others. Yet the house felt small. It was too warm; too little oxygen was circulating, trickling into Dayna's lungs a gasp at a time. It felt like breathing through a straw.

"Dayna?" Meiner was on her feet now, reaching for her arm.

Dayna staggered upright, nearly knocking her chair over. "I can't talk about this."

"Maybe you need to." Reagan's voice came from a million miles away. "Maybe you need to learn how to process something instead of shoving it down for once. Keeping this in isn't good for either of us."

Dayna felt a surge of incredulity through the haze, which quickly turned to irritation. *Not all of us can emotionally process things in an instant,* she wanted to say. *Not all of us want to.*

But there was too little air left to waste it on this, and she wasn't sure the words would come out properly. Instead she turned and stumbled for the door. "I need air."

In the apple orchard the air was cooler, fresher. Maybe it was getting out of the confines of the house, or the cold air woke something in her lungs. Whatever it was, it always seemed to help. At least a little.

It was also freezing, and she'd been too flustered to throw a jacket over her tank top before coming out. Dayna shivered, rubbing her arms, trying to push the feelings of annoyance down.

Reagan knew better than most about the OCD, so she should know Dayna wouldn't handle this well. *She should know better.*

A moment later she felt guilt sink her stomach. Reagan had been just as affected by what they'd seen. It wasn't like she, Dayna, was the only one allowed to be traumatized here. It wasn't fair to be angry with Reagan.

She had to get herself under control. She hated arguing with Reagan, and it wasn't okay that Meiner had seen her like this. The other girl was always so coolly unimpressed with everything. She'd probably think Dayna was a lunatic.

She sat beneath one of the apple trees and shut her eyes, placing one hand on the rough bark, running her fingers over the knots in the tree.

One. Tree bark, nicks, and grooves, trails from insects under her fingertips.

Two. The wind. Her hair on her cheeks, across her neck.

Three. A face. Pale, tormented, twisted in anguish.

Dayna's eyes flew open, and she dug her fingers into the bark, ignoring the sharp pain as her nails bent back. How was she supposed to forget, when her mind only ever traveled in circles?

She shouldn't count her breaths. Shouldn't concentrate on how they entered and left her body, swelled and deflated her lungs. If they were deep enough, if they were long enough. The world was moving strangely, slowly. It felt like a dream.

"Dayna?"

She started. Her temple throbbed, and she realized she'd been tugging at the same strand of hair for the last few minutes. She let her hand drop into her lap, but she didn't turn around. *Meiner.*

How ridiculous did she look right now, sitting on the ground, one hand on the tree like she was afraid she might be swept away?

The crunch of footsteps sounded in the grass, and then someone sank down next to her. "You all right?"

Maybe if she stayed still long enough Meiner would go away.

Dayna caught a whiff of laundry soap as Meiner climbed to her feet. "Hold on a minute."

Now she was curious enough to crack an eye open, in spite of her spinning head. Meiner was on her tiptoes, reaching for one of the higher branches. She was wearing a formfitting black T-shirt and jeans today, and Dayna couldn't help noticing how the gesture stretched her torso out long and lean, a bare strip of white stomach showing the top of one hip bone.

She looked away quickly as Meiner grabbed one of the apples with a noise of triumph. "How long have you been having these attacks?"

Dayna hesitated, gaze searching Meiner's face. "Since I can remember. I—I was diagnosed with somatic OCD at fourteen. Stress triggers it." She paused and then snorted mirthlessly. "Well, everything triggers it lately."

"Here, stand up for one second. Hold the tree if you have to."

Meiner was standing over her now. In one hand she held the apple, green, pockmarked with brown. The other she offered to Dayna, who took it, letting Meiner haul her to her feet.

They stood toe to toe now, and it was very apparent that Meiner was a good deal taller. Dayna's heart was still beating hard. Her panic was there, but it was a distant pulse at the back of her mind, as if on layaway for later. She was grateful for the distraction.

Meiner slid her hand down, and Dayna felt the warmth of the other girl's fingers lock around her wrist. Meiner's face was serious as she pressed the apple into Dayna's palm.

"Tell me three things about this."

Her mouth dropped open. "How—"

"Don't question it." Her voice was stern, but one side of her mouth twitched the slightest bit. "Three things, Walsh. I'm not giving you your hand back until you tell me."

Feeling a little foolish, Dayna closed her fingers over the apple. Staring up at Meiner, she was struck suddenly by the change in her. Yes, the other girl still had a temper, but she was beginning to show a different side, someone who could be more open. When Grandma King and Cora weren't around, Meiner seemed like a totally different person.

She could feel her face flushing, and Meiner's grip on her wrist tightened.

"Um, it's round."

"That's a good start." Meiner's smile stretched wider. Dayna noticed her left canine was crooked.

"It's . . . rough." She moved her fingers over the surface of the apple. "It's a cooking apple."

"Good."

Meiner had moved closer, and Dayna's face felt hotter than ever. She had to tip her head back to look the taller girl in the eye. She was struggling to think about the apple and not the way Meiner's lips curved.

"It's—it's—" she stuttered, and then finished awkwardly, "it's an apple."

"Very astute." There was something sharp about Meiner's grin. She was somehow cynical even smiling. "You seem distracted."

Her eyes glittered as they met Dayna's. Meiner was impossibly close now, and she hadn't released her grip on Dayna's wrist.

Dayna bit her lip, forcing herself not to look away, even though her face felt like a supernova. "How did you know to do the three things trick?"

"It's how I used to deal."

Dayna blinked at her. She couldn't wrap her mind around the image of the tattooed and fiery-tempered Meiner panicking over anything. "Used to?"

"It never fully worked for me. Meds are more effective in my case." Meiner shrugged and took the apple from Dayna before releasing her wrist, turning the apple over in both hands. "But I use both now."

Dayna pursed her lips, stopping herself from saying, *Meds are scary.* Instead she said, "I froze, you know. When we found the—when we found Margery. I freaked out and Reagan had to do a protection spell, because I was too busy panicking."

"That's okay. It had to be horrifying."

"But it's *not* okay." She shook her head, tears stinging the backs of her eyes. "I'm supposed to be a full witch, but I was too panicked to even think straight. What if he'd really been out there? What if he'd come for Reagan, and I was too busy having a mental breakdown to help her? She's ascended, but her power is at a normal level now, and she's only one witch, and . . . and what if she'd *died*—"

"Hey, whoa. You can't think like that. You're both okay. You're both safe." Meiner frowned, eyes searching Dayna's face.

Dayna could feel her face burning as she blurted out, "I feel like I'm just . . . always afraid. And I'm too scared to even try medication. I just . . . What if I'm not myself? What if it changes who I am, or makes things worse?"

Meiner reached out, gently taking her hand again, pressing the apple back into her palm. "You know, I refused to take meds because I thought it made me seem weak. Like admitting I needed it meant I was broken. But that's bullshit. Reaching out for help is what saved me."

For a moment, Dayna just shut her eyes and let herself feel the warmth of Meiner's hand, the cool surface of the apple.

She was so tired of being anxious.

Finally she opened her eyes and offered Meiner the apple back. "McIntosh."

"What?"

"The third thing. It's a McIntosh."

Meiner grinned, and the expression lit something electric in Dayna's stomach. She felt like she had that night in Meiner's car. Impulsive, reckless.

Only this time it was the vacant apple orchard and the wind tangling through Meiner's white hair and the edge of her razor-sharp smile that made Dayna feel a little drunk.

Before she could second-guess herself, she reached out and seized the collar of Meiner's leather jacket, pulling her forward, pressing her lips to Meiner's.

A second later she pulled back, lips tingling, cheeks burning.

It was a nothing kiss. Barely a brush.

The apple dropped out of Meiner's hand, rolling on the ground at their feet.

For one beat, two, there was silence. She was still gripping the front of Meiner's jacket. "You know, that isn't usually how I do the three things trick," Dayna whispered.

"Sorry." There was nothing sorry about Meiner's smile as she stepped toward her. Again, their faces were only inches apart, and Dayna stepped back, stomach fluttering, fingers still gripping the leather jacket. Meiner followed, until Dayna's back touched the apple tree, the bark pressing into the bare skin of her shoulders.

Meiner smoothed one hand over Dayna's jaw, running her fingers under her chin, tilting her face up. Their lips met a second time. She felt Meiner's body along the length of hers. She was wrapped up in the scent of the other girl's clothes and hair and skin, and tasting nothing but her mouth, and she wasn't sorry either.

Chapter Forty-Four
CORA

The older witches wanted to try yet another reading, and when Cora protested, Bronagh suggested she find Meiner and Dayna and head to the library for research.

Cora didn't argue. The idea of getting out of the house was a good one.

Still, it was unnerving to see Bronagh taking over, making plans for them as Grandma King faded in and out. Back in the house, Cora had left the old woman shuffling around the living room, demanding to know why there was no record player. The King Witch had vanished once again, and Cora wasn't sure how to feel in her absence. A little relieved, certainly, but disturbed all the same. Her training wasn't going to happen if Gran didn't hold herself together.

She paused outside the door of the farmhouse, squinting in the direction of the orchard. It was only a stone's throw away, but the figures of Meiner and Dayna were standing beneath the farthest tree.

Cora frowned. They were awfully close. Were they...? Yes, they were. Her mouth tasted sour. There was something satisfying about calling in a cold, level voice, "If you two are about done, we're going to the library."

Meiner and Dayna sprang apart like she'd burned them, which only added to the satisfaction, though it faded as soon as she turned away.

Something tore at her chest as she headed for the car, leaving them to trail after her.

The sensation was painful enough to leave her momentarily breathless, and it had nothing to do with magic.

The city library was small, set in the center of everything. It had a tiny rose garden on the side, as if to make up for its lack of space, and a modest Ancient Mythology section. It was fairly empty on a Sunday morning, and she, Meiner, Dayna, and Reagan camped out in the window seat, spreading their bags and backpacks around them until they took up most of the available space.

Cora couldn't concentrate. Scooping her bag up, she mumbled something about going out for a smoke before hastily exiting. Outside, she leaned against the side of the building, near the benches in front of the flower garden. Her thoughts kept going back to the scene beneath the tree, seeing Meiner kiss Dayna. More distracting still, the ebb and flow of voices in her head seemed to have picked up. The hissing whispers seemed to increase with every moment. Her bag felt like it weighed a million pounds, heavy with the metal box, with the dagger inside.

Her hands shook as she lifted the cigarette to her lips. Every time she looked at someone she thought about her sacrifice. What about the guy at the vending machine? Or maybe that boy across the street waiting at the bus stop? She tried to picture plunging the dagger into his chest. What would it feel like? What would it sound like? It made her feel ill.

And each time she hesitated, each time her stomach turned at the mere thought, the hissing increased. The goddess's anger coursed through her. It was getting hotter every time, like her blood was slowly heating up the longer she put this off.

She had to get this done. She told herself it was to trigger her ascension, to become a full witch and help her coven, not because she was afraid of what the goddess might do if she refused.

Cora took a deep breath and tried to force herself to relax. In that moment she hated Grandma King and the goddess. She even hated herself, for her cowardice. She shouldn't be this afraid. She was a witch.

A shuffle in front of her jerked her head up, and she saw him—a boy about her age, maybe a little older. He was wearing torn jeans and a band T-shirt that said *Banshee Blood* in bold writing across the front. He came around the corner and settled onto the bench in front of the garden, head bent over his phone.

Something shifted in the back of her mind. It felt like something uncurling, slow and lazy, and then a voice said, *He will work, witchling.*

Cora sucked in a breath, closing her eyes.

She could hardly cut his heart out in the middle of the rose garden, could she?

Follow him, witchling. Do not back down this time.

Shit.

There was a definite note of warning in the goddess's voice. She was tired of waiting.

The boy stood up abruptly, phone to his ear. "Yeah?" He began moving for the sidewalk, still talking, and Cora frowned, straightening up. Maybe she could really do this. Maybe—

"Cora."

The sound of Meiner's voice brought her up short. She fumbled the cigarette, nearly dropping it.

"We're running out to get sandwiches. You want to come?" Meiner's voice was hesitant. The car ride over had been tense, and Cora had spent much of it fuming, but at the moment Meiner was a welcome distraction.

"Yeah. I'm starving." She turned away, forcing lightness into her voice. "I could eat the twelve apostles right now."

She was startled when Meiner actually grinned at her, and the expression seemed to ease some of that burning in her chest, just the slightest bit.

As Meiner turned to go back into the building, a flash of heat seared Cora's insides. She staggered to a halt, bracing herself against the wall, teeth clenched. The sensation stayed longer this time, rippling through her core, setting her insides on fire. She clamped her lips shut on a scream. A second later the burning cut off, and she forced herself to stumble after Meiner.

The hissing whispers had dropped sharply in volume now, though there was a new kind of malevolence to them, and Cora swallowed hard. The warning had been clear enough.

She was running out of time.

Chapter Forty-Five

MEINER

"Okay, so we get he's choosing the witches from a book. The question is *why*. Why kill witches specifically?"

Meiner sighed, stretching her legs out beneath the table, which earned her a sympathetic glance from Dayna. The other girl had been shifting in her seat, rubbing her arm just under the dog bite while she pored over her books, sandwich in hand.

She regretted not raiding the cupboards for pain meds before she left, for Dayna's arm, but also because her head was pounding. They'd been at the library for hours now, and hadn't made much progress.

Not that she was doing particularly well at concentrating. She kept glancing over at Dayna, at her profile, the fine lines of her features. At her eyelashes, which were ridiculously long, flickering slightly as she read, the freckles that dotted her cheeks. She could still remember the taste of Dayna's mouth. The way she felt pressed against her, the smell of her hair.

Shit. Meiner forced her attention back to the book in her lap.

A second later Dayna sighed. "We've got nothing. A couple symbols we don't know, one that might mean *judge*, and vague guesses who might be next." She trailed off.

"I swear it sounds like some kind of dark ritual, the way he's taking body parts." Reagan scowled at the laptop. She had the same article up and was scanning it over again. "But there's no hint at what it might be."

"This blog post talks about Carman making deals with humans and then screwing them over. Typical shady sorceress stuff," Cora said. "Tricky bitch. Still nothing helpful, though this article mentions her lover was banished, too. Apparently she was knocking boots with Angus Og, god of love. A good lay, I imagine." She wiggled her brows, and Meiner rolled her eyes to the ceiling.

It occurred to her suddenly that she hadn't actually wanted to murder Cora for most of the morning. It reminded her of when Cora had first moved in, when they'd been allies, not enemies, bonded by mutual hatred and angst. And then the training had started, and they'd become more than just hurt, angry teens—they'd been witchlings.

Until Gran had begun to lose herself, and the ever-present anger suddenly no longer had a clear direction. Their allyship had slowly twisted after that, into something new. Something ugly.

How long had it been since they'd been on their own, away from Gran for any extended period of time?

She hated to admit it, even to herself, but it was possible the anger she directed at Cora was . . . well, misdirected. The thought sent a flash of irritation through her. Had Gran known that was going to happen? Or worse, had she planned it that way?

Only the rustle of pages filled the silence now, and Meiner forced herself to push these thoughts away.

Another witch would be next, a fourth victim. The judge, the poet, and Margery . . .

Meiner sat up straighter on the bench. "What was it Margery said again? Something about witches and saints?"

Dayna grimaced, but Reagan answered for them. "'First we were gods . . . gods, and then saints, and then witches.'"

"Gods and saints." Meiner snapped her book closed. It felt like there were loose bits of a puzzle rattling around in her brain. All the pieces were there; they just had to figure out how they fit. "Hold on, who are the gods that put Carman away again?"

"The first is Aoi Mac Ollamain." Reagan leaned back against the window seat, then winced and rubbed her lower back. "God of poetry. None of us are pledged to him, so I don't know much about him."

"I'll look him up." Dayna was already typing the name into a search. "Whoa, check him out." She held up the phone, showing them the full-color illustration of a man with a mop of silver curls and a thick beard. He wore a golden crown at his brow and held a silver goblet.

"Isn't he fancy looking?" Cora raised a brow, and then frowned suddenly. "The second witch who died...wasn't she a poet? At least that's what the news said."

They could hear the rustle and hush of the library around them. Then Reagan said slowly, "And the symbol that means *judge*..."

"Holy shit." Meiner's stomach was churning now, and her voice was low and tense with excitement. She reached out and took her phone back, fingers brushing Dayna's.

Goose bumps ran down both her arms, though Meiner wasn't sure if it was the excitement of their discovery or the physical contact. She'd been distracted by the thought of kissing Dayna all morning. Even now, in the face of this discovery, it was hard to drag her mind away.

"The judge that was killed..." Reagan breathed. "A judge and a poet."

"'First we were gods'...Margery somehow knew, she was trying to tell you. They're killing the gods that locked Carman away." Meiner finally said it. "Or...at least witches that represent those gods." She frowned suddenly. "But why Margery? What's her connection?"

There was silence for a moment as they pored over the list of gods once again, and then Meiner cleared her throat.

"Your Margery didn't happen to be a writer, did she?"

Dayna's brows shot up. "Oh my god, yes. She used to write a column for the newspaper. It was a big thing a couple of years ago; she got kicked out of the church."

Meiner pointed to a line of text. "It says here that Crichinbel was a satirist. If she thought she was writing some kind of satirical commentary..."

There was a beat of silence, and then Reagan said softly, "What did Cernunnos say to you in the vision again? Each death is unlocking something?"

Dayna frowned, brows creased. "Uh, the death of your saints is unlocking her cell, something like that."

"Her cell," Cora said. "*Her* cell. She was talking about Carman."

"Holy *shit*." Meiner sat up straight, pressing a hand to her mouth. "They think they're resurrecting her."

Dayna was clutching the bite on her shoulder. Her face had gone pale, her eyes wide and distant.

"I don't think they *think* they're doing it"—her voice was barely a whisper—"I think they actually are."

Chapter Forty-Six

DUBH

*T*ongue and eye, hand and foot. Blood and bone, ash and soot.

Dubh didn't realize he was muttering it out loud until Olc's shoe crashed into the wall near his head.

"Bloody Christ, Dubh. Shut the fuck up." Olc leaned back on the mattress, tucking his hands behind his head. "We've got the book with all the instructions, so you can quit reciting that stupid rhyme."

Calma paused in the middle of tracing a warding sigil on the opposite wall. He'd already marked most of the room with charcoal, leaving swirling lines of smudgy black all across the walls. The shoe missile had smeared a line. He brushed his long hair back from his face and scowled over at Olc. "Do you *mind*? If we're going to stay here, we have to at least ward the damn place." He shot a sideways look at Dubh, who ignored him.

Shutting the cooler lid with a snap, Dubh pushed it to the end of the second bed.

This was the first place they'd stayed that wasn't a dump. It was a good location, small and out of the way. Hard to find if you didn't know where you were looking... As far as he was concerned, they were here until the whole thing was over.

Which wasn't long now.

Leaning over Calma, he took one of the charcoal sticks off the dresser and settled back on the bed, laying the book out flat.

Calma shot him an annoyed look but said nothing, returning to his scribbles. Olc gave a derisive laugh and threw one of the decorative pillows across the room. It bounced off Dubh's shoulder. "What are you drawing over there, Picasso?"

Dubh merely glowered at him and returned to the page. His fingers shook slightly, excitement curling in his stomach as he traced the figures in dark smudges on the page. The deepset eyes, the lines around their mouths. The shape of a face, and the slope of a neck, an arm, a wrist.

As the women slowly came to life on the page, the fire in his chest fanned to life.

He darted another look at the window. Calma insisted on keeping the floral curtains closed, but judging by the brightness of the light shining through the crack, it had to be almost noon.

Not long now.

Soon they would have all of the spell's ingredients. If it all went well tonight, they would have the rest.

Just a few more hours of waiting, and they would wake her.

Carman would rise.

Chapter Forty-Seven
DAYNA

"**I**f it's a resurrection spell they're doing, they'll need a powerful lunar event." The picture of Bronagh wobbled slightly on Meiner's phone before disappearing entirely. "How do you work this damn thing, Faye?"

Cora grimaced around at the half-empty library. "Oh my god, turn her down, Meiner."

Meiner jammed her thumb on the volume button, just as Faye shouted in exasperation from the other end, "For Christ's sake, you've got your thumb on the camera, Grandmother. Give it here!"

There was a brief and chaotic shuffling, and the screen pivoted wildly, flashing the ceiling, then Faye's scowling face next to Bronagh.

"That's better. All right, listen, they're running out of time with reporters swarming the town and the gardai investigating. I'll wager they use the full moon eclipse tonight. If they're doing a spell of this magnitude, that's what they'll be using."

Tonight. Dayna gripped the books she was holding to her chest, taking a deep, shaky breath. "That doesn't give us enough time. We're not ready to fight this."

"Aye, listen, just get back here, lunch is almost ready." Bronagh leaned forward, peering more closely at the screen. "Oh, is that *Celtic Myths and Legends*? Bring it with you."

"Grandmother, don't touch—"

The chat winked out, cutting off Faye's annoyed voice, and Cora snorted. "Good god, I need a smoke. Tell me when we're leaving." She stomped out, and Reagan sighed.

"I'm gonna go check out the books. Meet you back at the car." Reagan disappeared around the corner, and Meiner turned back to Dayna.

"I guess we should put some of these back— Hey, are you okay?"

"We're not ready for tonight, but we've got to stop them." The image of Margery's pale face swam before Dayna's eyes suddenly, and she blinked frantically, gaze blurred by tears. "We can't let anyone else die."

"We won't." Meiner stepped forward. Catching her arm, she tugged the books out of Dayna's grip. "Hey, it's going to be okay."

This was twice she'd lost her composure in front of Meiner now. And this time in public. She couldn't break down in the library.

"Hey, look at me."

Dayna blinked, startled, as Meiner slid a finger under her chin, tipping her face back, forcing her to meet her gaze. Meiner's face wasn't full of pity, as she'd feared. Instead her expression was glittering and hard. It sent a strange, delicious shiver through her.

"We'll stop them, and we'll make them pay."

For the second time that day she found herself desperately wanting to kiss Meiner King, but this time she waited for one second, two, and it was Meiner who dipped her head down to press her lips against hers, whose fingers tangled in her hair and tugged at the collar of her shirt, pulling her close for one electric moment.

Then there was a shuffle from somewhere behind them, and low voices as people passed by the shelves, and they broke away from each other. This time Dayna knew her face was definitely glowing.

Meiner cleared her throat. "I guess we should get back to the house.

I don't want to leave Gran with the others for too long. I don't trust her and Bronagh not to scrap."

Dayna paused. "Oh my god, I just remembered. Before . . . before we found Margery—" Her breath hitched, but she forced herself to continue. "Sam called me. He thinks your grandmother was the Butcher's last victim. The one who got away."

"What?" Meiner's brows creased. "How does he figure that?"

"When did your gran get that scar on her neck?"

Meiner frowned. "I-I don't remember, she's just always had it. It's not the kind of thing I'd ask her about."

"We should ask her—"

Coming around the corner of the bookshelf, Dayna pulled up short.

Fiona Walsh was standing between the romance and mythology bookshelves. She was dressed in a stuffy floral-patterned dress that went all the way from her chin to her feet, and she clutched her Bible to her chest, eyes wide.

Shit. Dayna started to turn away, alarmed. This couldn't happen; the reverend couldn't be here. Her coven and her home life were never supposed to meet. Each was too complicated, too volatile. An explosion was inevitable.

"Dayna," Fiona called out. "What are you doing here?"

Her heart sank, and she turned slowly. "Where's Dad?"

Fiona ignored the question, reaching out to grip Dayna's arm. "Your father wouldn't tell me where you were this morning. You have to come back with us. Stay *home*."

"Ouch, Fiona, let go." Dayna tried to tug her arm out of the woman's pincer-like grip and was alarmed when Fiona only grabbed her other arm and held on.

"No, Dayna—that killer is out there. Come back with us. You need to come home."

By now her voice had risen enough that other people in the library seemed to have noticed. There was what looked like a book club at the table, all staring at them, wide-eyed.

"Hey, get the hell off her." Meiner's voice was curt, and she took a step forward and started reaching for Fiona's arm.

"Get away." Fiona's voice echoed off the nearby shelves, and Dayna gasped as the woman suddenly threw her body back, still clutching both arms tightly. Dayna found herself being dragged away from Meiner, toward the exit. She tried to dig her heels into the carpet. Fiona was painfully skinny, but it was shocking how strong she was.

Fiona managed to drag her past two full bookshelves before there was the sudden loud thumping of footsteps, and Meiner appeared in front of them.

"Let her go."

In that moment while they were both frozen, Dayna looked down at Fiona's hands on her arm. She'd been clawing at her, trying to get her to release her grip, and had pushed up one of the woman's sleeves. "What is that?" At first glance she saw only a series of scratches, red and inflamed, but the pattern of scratches drew her gaze back.

There was something familiar about it, the shaky lines on the outside forming a circle, and the crisscrossed lines within. A wave of sick horror rolled over her.

It was familiar because she'd seen that mark over and over. At the stone circle at the first murder scene, carved into the trees behind Sage Widow, on the news constantly.

"That mark—"

Fiona released her abruptly and slammed Dayna back into the bookshelf, where she struck her shoulder just above the bite on her arm. She hissed at the pain and clutched the wound, blinking around at the bookshelves through tear-blurred eyes.

Fiona's eyes were impossibly wide and black. Almost all pupil. She launched herself forward, knocking Meiner out of the way, grabbing at Dayna's shirt, growling inches away from her face.

"I know it's you."

Dayna jerked back, and the book under Fiona's arm crashed to the ground at their feet. Papers scattered across the carpet. As Fiona bent to snatch at them frantically, Dayna reached out and grabbed the nearest one, shock rooting her to the spot. Red ink spiraled down into the middle of the page, the same word repeated over and over until it was sucked into the center.

Dayna, Dayna, Dayna . . . Her name. Just her name, a thousand times over.

Fiona made a strangled sound of protest, darting forward to grab it out of her hands. A second later she froze as a deep voice from the end of the bookshelves cried out, "Fiona, don't!"

The reverend was suddenly there, in his thick black jacket and white collar. He stood between two bookshelves at the end of the aisle, and Dayna wondered exactly how long he'd been there. How much he'd seen.

He looked furious. "Fiona! Don't touch her. Go sit in the car immediately." His gaze flicked from her to Dayna, and the anger drained out of his face. For a second he just looked exhausted, and then his expression hardened again, became stern. "Stay there while I get Fiona to the car. I need to speak with you privately."

Dayna only nodded, too shocked to protest. She folded her arms over her chest to stop her hands from shaking, watching as the reverend escorted Fiona outside.

Chapter Forty-Eight

DAYNA

They waited for a few minutes, Meiner staying close to her. Dayna kept glancing at the door, stomach twisting into knots.

Meiner kept her voice low. "Are you okay? Do you want me to stay?" Dayna swallowed and shook her head, watching as the reverend reentered through the glass doors and headed toward them.

"I'll meet you outside, okay?"

Meiner only nodded silently and turned for the door, giving the reverend a cool look as she passed him.

In the beat or two of silence that followed, her father slipped his hands into his pockets and Dayna took several deep, shaky breaths, trying to slow her racing heart. She kept trying to make sense of what she'd seen just now: the symbol carved into her mother's arm, the red spiral of her name snaking into the center of the page....

What the hell was going on?

The reverend's face was grim and white. "You should have told me you found that woman's body. I...I would have been there for you. I had to hear it from Samuel's father."

"I don't want to talk about that." Dayna's frustration surged. "I want to talk about Fiona. She just attacked me. You *saw* it."

For a long moment the reverend just stared at her, and then he sighed heavily. "I was hoping to avoid all of this, but...I think I have to tell you something about your mother, and I want you to listen without interrupting."

Startled, she nodded, unease stirring her stomach.

"After you were born, your mother was never the same." The reverend paused, brows furrowed. Then he squared his shoulders, as if he were steeling himself. "They called it postpartum psychosis, but...it never seemed to go away. For years, I tried everything, pills, doctors, psychologists. The mental health ward in the best hospitals. Sometimes she seemed to do better, but she'd always relapse, usually worse than before. The doctors... they seemed to think she wasn't a normal case." He frowned down at the bookshelves. "And at some point, when you were about four or five, her psychosis switched to a narrower focus..." He hesitated, eyes flicking up to Dayna's face. "You."

Dayna blinked at him. "What...what does that mean?"

"She became obsessed with you. Watching everything you did, talking about you constantly. Sometimes I'd catch her coming into your room in the middle of the night to just stand there and stare at you, for hours. She'd hurt herself sometimes, too, when the delusions got especially bad, run into door frames and things like that. She said it would make everything quiet again, at least for a while."

Her throat was too tight to swallow properly, and her voice was hoarse when she spoke. "Quiet?"

"The delusion, I suppose. It all seemed to be centered on her belief that you were...I don't know, not who you were supposed to be."

Dayna's mouth fell open. Suddenly the blacked-out pictures in the guest room made a terrible kind of sense. And what Fiona had said about Dayna not being real, and the symbol on her arm...

A strange, creeping horror was spreading over her skin.

"What else did she say about me?"

"Does it matter? She was delusional. It's one of the reasons I waited so long to bring her back here. I was afraid seeing you again would make her slip back into it."

She shook her head, not wanting to believe what he was saying. "You mean . . . it's me. I'm her trigger."

Her father nodded slowly, and the guilt on his face made her feel sick. "There's more."

"Tell me."

"The reason I sent her away . . ." He hesitated. "She— I came into your room and she was . . . um, she was standing over you with a pillow."

It felt like frost was creeping through her, freezing her core. "She was trying to smother me?"

"I don't know for sure, but I suspected it. That was when I sent her away."

She leaned back against the shelf, hand over her mouth. The room was spinning, and she dragged in a sharp breath, feeling suddenly light-headed.

Fiona had tried to kill her. The woman the reverend had brought back into her home had tried to murder her. And worse, the creeping suspicions were only getting stronger the more she thought about it.

The lines carved into Fiona's arm, the symbol of the Butcher . . . it reminded her of the way the root ink on her cheek had looked the night of her ascension, her pledge to the goddess.

Did that mean Fiona was on his side? That she was helping him in some way? Helping him hide, maybe, or . . . finding him victims?

It had come back to her suddenly, the strange way Fiona had looked at her, the way she'd grasped her arm and hissed, *Where are the rest of them?*

Dayna had thought she meant her friends, but . . . what if she'd meant the other gods?

She opened her mouth, hesitated, and then closed it again. She had to warn him about Fiona. But how did she tell the reverend his wife was somehow tied to a supernatural serial killer? Where did she even begin to explain?

"Y-you need to get her out of the house." It came out in a stammering rush, and as the reverend blinked at her she said desperately, "I can't explain how I know this, but . . . I think she's worse than either of us knew. So much worse. You need to send her away, to the hospital, or—or even back to camp."

To her frustration he was already shaking his head. "She needs time. I'll get her help. I'm going to see an out-of-town specialist tomorrow."

Just a few days ago that would have been a huge leap for him, but now . . . once again, he wasn't listening to her. "You don't understand, Dad, please. You have to listen. I think she's *really* dangerous—"

"I think you should continue to stay with Reagan."

Dayna froze, protests dying on her lips. The reverend's face was grim, and once again he wouldn't meet her eyes, shifting awkwardly with his hands in his pockets. "Just for now. Until I can get her sorted."

It felt like he'd knocked the wind out of her. She only stared at him, stunned, and the reverend cleared his throat. "I should get to the car. She has an appointment with Dr. Ross this afternoon."

So that was that. Fiona was going to stay, and Dayna was leaving.

It shouldn't be that shocking, not after the revelation about Fiona, but somehow it still felt like he'd sucked all the air out of the room.

She told herself this was exactly what she wanted. That living with Reagan was what she'd dreamed of as a kid.

So why did this feel so bad?

For a moment she just stood there, but the reverend had already walked around the corner and out of sight.

Chapter Forty-Nine

MEINER

They pulled up to the farmhouse, and Meiner paused, watching Dayna slide out and collect her book bag. Dayna had told her a bit of what happened, that her father had said it wasn't safe for her back at her house. Then she'd lapsed into silence. Meiner hadn't wanted to pry, but she couldn't seem to stop thinking about their run-in with Fiona Walsh.

There was something about the woman that disturbed her to her very core, and it wasn't just the overt aggression. The vacant expression maybe, or the hollowness in her eyes. Like a haunted house with no lights on. You couldn't be sure who—or what—was home.

Her mind kept flipping between that and what Dayna had said just before they'd run into Fiona. That Meiner's gran might have been one of the Butcher's victims . . .

It seemed impossible. Gran would have mentioned that, wouldn't she?

It didn't make sense.

They watched as Reagan pulled the van up, backing slowly into the spot between the Callighans' station wagon and Meiner's Datsun. Dayna had told the others what happened before they'd left the library and about the mark on her mother's arm. Reagan and Cora were talking about it as they climbed out.

"...how could she be involved if she's been up at the camp?" Reagan was saying.

"She probably just saw it on TV and copied it because she's a nutcase."

"Don't be a dickhead." Reagan flashed Dayna a quick sideways look, but thankfully Dayna seemed totally lost in thought.

Cora only shrugged, fishing in her pocket for her cigarettes, her hands shaking. Meiner frowned. She'd been too distracted to really notice, but Cora was unusually pale, and there were dark smudges under her eyes. And...had she lost weight?

When she looked up, Meiner caught her unguarded expression for a split second. Hungry, haunted, desperate.

She looks like an addict. She wouldn't be surprised if Cora had got herself hooked on something to enhance her magic.

Meiner watched her bring her cigarette up to her lips again, catching sight of the dark rust-colored stain under her thumbnail. Cora noticed her staring a second later and drew her hand back down, flicking her cigarette onto the ground.

The last time Cora had been stressed enough for nosebleeds, they'd still been sharing a room. She'd been fighting with her remaining family about something; Meiner had heard her hissing at them on the phone, and nearly every call had resulted in a bloody nose.

Meiner hesitated. They used to talk, a long time ago. She remembered lying in bed at night, staring at the ceiling as Cora's voice drifted up from the bunk below, both of them made a little braver by the cover of darkness. She knew things about the other girl no one else did.

Glancing back quickly, she saw Reagan and Dayna had moved over to the front gate, heads bent together. She turned back to Cora, keeping her voice low. "You okay? You look...pale."

Cora blinked at her, hesitating. Finally she shrugged, leaning against Meiner's car. "I'm just tired. You know how it is in a new place. I don't sleep a lot."

Meiner nodded slowly. For a moment she could have sworn Cora was about to say something else. She leaned back against the car next to her. "Yeah, I know. Me either."

Cora's smile was faint, but for once it wasn't her usual smirk. Then she turned away as Reagan and Dayna walked back over.

If Meiner thought Cora looked bad, Dayna was a close runner-up. Her normally glossy hair was tangled—she'd been working her fingers through it the entire ride over, and her skin was so pale her freckles stood out in stark contrast.

Meiner leaned closer, bumping Dayna's arm gently. "All right?" She tried to keep her voice casual, but she wanted to take her by the arms and look her in the face. To make sure she was okay.

"I just . . . I can't believe she carved it into her arm. It looked horrible." Dayna reached up, tugging at a strand of hair, and Meiner had to stop herself from taking her hand, from trying to distract her. But of course, she could hardly do that in front of everyone.

"Speculate all you want, but I think we have more immediate concerns, right?" Cora tipped her head back and blew smoke out through pursed lips. "As in, these guys are going to try to resurrect this bitch soon, right?"

Meiner exchanged a look with Dayna. *Tonight.* "Yeah." Meiner cleared her throat. "We're running out of time."

Dayna shook her head, like she was shaking off thoughts about her mother. "We have to stop them before they kill again."

From the corner of her eye Meiner saw Cora jerk suddenly, as if she'd been stung. Her eyes looked distant, and then she blinked, apparently noticing everyone staring.

"There's a way we can find them. But . . . the others won't like it." She cut the farmhouse a quick sideways look.

Meiner frowned. She wasn't at all comfortable with this sudden shift in Cora. "What are you talking about?"

"We might be able to access them—the brothers, I mean. Someone who's had contact is liable to be able to scry successfully. It could tell us where they are."

Meiner's mouth dropped open. "We've been over this. Contact scrying is *way* too dangerous."

"What else do you suggest?" Cora shot back. "We're running out of time, and this is the only way to guarantee results. Contact scrying is a direct link; it can find them no matter how warded they are."

"Bronagh shot this idea down already." Reagan shifted from foot to foot, clearly uneasy. "Oya, we should just go inside."

"That's right. It's incredibly foolish." Meiner scowled at Cora. "It's dangerous and completely stupid to attempt it."

Cora ignored this, gaze locked on Dayna's face. "Three victims to go. Just how many witches do you think are in this town? One of us is next, and you know it."

Meiner remembered the look on Dayna's face when she'd said she would do anything for her coven. Anything and everything.

"Absolutely not," Meiner said, at the same time as Dayna said, "I'll do it."

Chapter Fifty

DAYNA

Meiner seemed deeply unimpressed. She kept glaring at Cora, fists clenched at her sides, a muscle twitching in her jaw. She looked like she was barely holding herself back.

But Dayna couldn't help agreeing with Cora. The risk was worth it. It was worth it because of Margery, because the memory of her bloody eye sockets would be with Dayna for as long as she lived. Because she barely slept anymore, lying awake obsessing over each breath, feeling her legs twitch and shake.

But mostly it was because she was desperate for a way to protect them. To keep her coven safe.

They were the only real family she had left.

What her father said shouldn't have surprised her. She'd realized this on the car ride back to the house. He'd always been strange and secretive about her mother. It had taken him ages to even reveal she was mentally ill. And when he had, he'd skirted around the subject. Wouldn't tell her what it was, or what Fiona'd done. What her behavior had been like, or when she might be well enough to come home.

Maybe he'd thought he was protecting her. Or maybe he didn't want to risk Dayna telling anyone.

"I can pull you out if need be," Cora reassured them. "It's not hard." When Meiner gave her a suspicious look, Cora shrugged. "I've been researching. It seemed like a good plan in case we kept coming up against dead ends. Which... we have," she said pointedly. "It wouldn't have worked before because none of us have touched them, but since the dog bit her..."

Dayna shivered, reaching up, fingers grazing the bandage on her shoulder. The idea the wound gave her some kind of connection to the brothers was unsettling. It made her want to curl in on herself and hide. But it might be to her advantage, the perfect solution.

It didn't even matter that her burst of power from the ascension was so depleted, since scrying depended on the favor of your god and not your personal store.

Dayna took a deep breath, turning back to the others. "Okay, how do we start?"

Cora tapped the roof of the Datsun, where she'd balanced her "Resting Witchface" water bottle. "It's juice. Dark enough to use in a pinch. It will do in a pinch. We need a bowl, though."

Reagan looked doubtful. "There's a plastic bucket we collect eggs in."

Meiner shot her an irritated look. "Oh, so we've agreed to this now, have we?"

Reagan didn't reply, just moved to the side of the house, looking for the bucket. Dayna turned to Meiner, putting a hand on her arm. The other girl blinked and looked slightly subdued though still sullen.

"It's my choice," Dayna said quietly. "She's not forcing me into anything. You didn't see the— You didn't see Margery. I can't let that happen to anyone else. To any of us."

Instantly her thoughts flooded with horrible images. Reagan, sprawled on the grass, bloody and still. Or Bronagh, her face pale and drained of life. Brenna's crow feathers scattered in the dirt...

No. Dayna shuddered, telling herself to stop. She could drive herself mad thinking like that. And that was exactly why she had to do this.

Meiner still looked like she wanted to protest, but Dayna shook her head, jaw clenched. She wasn't going to risk losing anyone.

Meiner must have seen something in her face, because her brows shot up, and she took a step back.

Reagan returned with the bucket—she'd rinsed it out, but it still smelled faintly of chicken coop—and set it on the hood of the car. Cora leaned over, wrinkling her nose, before dumping the contents of her water bottle into the bucket.

"There now, we'll scry with this. Dayna, you'll be in the center. Scry like you normally would but try to picture the dog in your mind."

Dayna took her place in the semicircle. They stood close, close enough that her right shoulder was touching Meiner's and her left brushed Cora's. Scrying had never been her strong suit, and the dark liquid was harder to see into than the crystals had been, but she knew the logistics. Focus on the surface of whatever you were using—it could be anything, a bit of dark glass, a lake that reflected the moon, or apparently, an egg bucket filled with juice—and let your gaze go soft. *Go someplace else in your mind*, Yemi had once told her. *Be open to anything the surface is telling you.*

Dayna blew out a heavy breath and tried to soften her gaze. Tried to make her mind open.

The liquid was dark and smelled faintly of grapes. It was reflective enough that she could see their warped faces in the surface. Even with the curve of the bucket blurring their reflections, she could see the deep frown on Meiner's face.

Dayna straightened her shoulders, mentally shook herself. She couldn't think about Meiner right now. This was too important.

For a couple of minutes it seemed like nothing would happen. Dayna blinked slowly, almost sleepily. There was something mesmerizing about the purple-black liquid. Maybe the way the light rippled off, or the shapes of their warped reflections.

Something shifted subtly in the dark surface. One of the girls had moved, Dayna thought, faintly annoyed. But then, no, it was another shape. A face had appeared and then disappeared, not one of theirs.

Her shoulder throbbed now. A deep, pulsing pain, like a heartbeat. It sent a shiver down her back, but she stayed where she was.

A second passed, then two, and each one seemed to deepen the silence around them. There should have been noise, she realized. They were outside, on the farm. There should have been the distant sound of chickens clucking and scratching, the thump of hooves and breathy chuffing of horses in their paddocks. But there was nothing, only silence.

Her throat was suddenly tight, and every breath seemed labored, harder to drag into her lungs.

The liquid rippled, and Dayna wanted to refocus her eyes, to shake herself out of it. To stand up and gulp air back into her lungs. Meiner was right; this was a bad idea. This was dangerous.

Only... she didn't seem to be able to move.

Something was drawing her down, down into the liquid, into the black surface.

And now she was someplace else.

She was aware that she was at the coven house. That her body stood, muscles locked, in a semicircle with the other witchlings. That there was a bucket that smelled faintly of chicken crap and grapes within a few inches of her face. But... she was also in a hotel room. Or what looked like one.

Her panic dissolved the slightest bit. This was a vision, just like the last one, and Cora could pull her out if she needed to.

Dayna looked around at the room, at the dark cherrywood armoire, at the stone fireplace and the gold-framed oil paintings. It was dim inside, lit only with dull electric lights in lamps along the wall. Her gaze was drawn to a number of smudgy black sigils scrawled across the wallpaper, which was probably why she didn't see *him* right away.

There were two queen-sized beds with dusty velvet canopies in the center of the room, with a nightstand between them. An emerald-green washbasin and pitcher sat on top. On one side of it lay a thin silver box with a moon etched on the lid, and on the other, a leather guest book embossed with the name of the inn.

Beside the window in the far corner of the room was an overstuffed armchair, and in it was a man.

He sat barefoot and cross-legged, facing away from her at an angle, and he was surrounded by a scattering of white paper, pages spilled across the carpet, smudgy ink drawings she couldn't make out. In the dim light she could see his shape, his broad shoulders, and the way he sat stiffly upright.

She stepped closer, heart slamming at her rib cage. He was hunched over, resting an elbow on his knee, smoke curling up from the glowing ember of a cigarette between two fingers. With the other hand he was writing on the wall in jagged black letters.

There were names scratched into the pale wallpaper. Even in the dark she could read the first few, before the scrawling writing sloped off beneath his hand.

Crichinbel

Lugh Laebach

Bé Chuille

Morrigan

At the end of one of the beds sat a blue-and-white ice chest. It was nothing more than a plastic beer cooler, but something about it drew Dayna's eye.

The figure shifted, and Dayna's attention snapped back to him. The wound in her shoulder shot a sudden, hot lance of pain down her arm.

On the couch the figure stiffened, began to turn.

Something arrested her. Froze her bones in her skin. Or maybe it was Dayna doing this to herself, maybe she couldn't let herself move until she knew who it was, who was doing this.

She stood still, skin crawling, as the figure turned to face her. In the dim orange glow of the room, she met his eyes. They were light blue, an unnerving color, glittering in the half-light. His expression flickered, caught between shock and anger, and in that split second she had a flash of startling recognition. She knew him from somewhere.

And then the lights went out.

She'd been wary before but still aware she was in a dream. Her body was at the coven house, surrounded by her friends. She did not feel as though she could be touched.

Now that thin reassurance was extinguished, insubstantial as a guttering candle flame.

Fear crashed through her like a cold wave. It was a primal thing, instinct-driven and without direction, and she stumbled back blindly.

A rattling sound, scraping, like something metallic being dragged across the floor, and Dayna was suddenly breathing in desperate gasps. The air had turned cold, so cold each breath burned.

In front of her the darkness shifted, and she watched, the soles of her feet rooted to the floorboards, as shadow unfurled from shadow. The darkness took form, rising from the ground. Her mouth had gone completely dry, and so when the tendrils of inky blackness reached out, she could only let out a small, strangled gasp as something brushed her arm.

A rattle, a clank. *Chains*, she had time to think, before a voice spoke in the dark, and her mind was wiped clean by the terror.

Hello, little witch. Remember me?

Chapter Fifty-One

MEINER

Something had gone wrong.

Meiner had checked Dayna several times throughout the scrying session. Each time she'd been blank, not serene perhaps, but concentrating. She glanced over at Cora, irritated to see her smug expression.

The third time Meiner checked, Dayna's face had changed. Her eyes were wide and glassy. Not in a peaceful way, but with the kind of raw terror that sent a spike of adrenaline through Meiner's core. Before she could react, Dayna's body jerked violently. Once, twice. As if she were being shocked. Her arms were tight at her sides, like some invisible force held them there. Her eyes rolled back into her skull.

"Dayna." Meiner reached out, panicked, startled when Reagan caught her wrist with a cry of "Don't!"

There were two reasons for this, she realized. One was that you never woke a scrying witch, just as you never woke a sleepwalker. It could be jarring. Ripping their consciousness out of whatever place it was in and slamming it back into their body never went well. It had to return slowly. She'd forgotten.

The other reason was horrifyingly evident to all of them.

There were black marks appearing on Dayna's pale arms, first on the left side, just under her bite, then on the other. A moment later Meiner recognized them for what they were—handprints—and bile rose hot in her throat.

"Someone do something," she snapped, hands hovering over Dayna's shoulders. She wanted to grab her, to yank her out of the grasp of whatever had her. Dayna's face was pale, and her entire body shook and jerked in response to something Meiner could neither see nor hear.

"Get Bronagh." Reagan's voice was high and strained. "Get the Callighans, quick."

She was about to force herself to turn away, when Cora reached out and snatched the bucket from the hood of the car. Reagan screamed, just as Cora slammed the bucket to the ground, cracking the plastic, sending the black liquid gushing out into the dust of the driveway.

Dayna's eyes were wide and white, and her body spasmed once more, a final, violent jerk that snapped her head back. Then she went limp.

Meiner dove forward, arms outstretched, catching her under the armpits before she could collapse onto the driveway. She grunted, struggling with the other girl's still form.

"Let me see her." Reagan was there now, looping one arm around Dayna's waist, helping to keep her upright. She pressed her fingers against the side of Dayna's throat, and there was silence, only the sound of Meiner's own ragged breath in her ears. Then Reagan sighed, shoulders sagging.

"She's just passed out."

"We should get her to the Callighans'." Meiner looped her other arm under Dayna's knees and hefted her up against her chest, so that Dayna's head was lying on her shoulder. She could feel the pulse in Dayna's temple, her heart beating hard. Meiner's own heart felt like it might burst, and her whole body was trembling.

This was Cora's fault.

She could hear Cora hurrying behind them and forced herself to keep marching for the farmhouse. Making sure Dayna was okay was the first and foremost thing. There would be time to deal with Cora later.

They burst into the house, Reagan leading the way, talking breathlessly and so fast that Yemi—staring wide-eyed with alarm at the slumped figure of Dayna—had to tell her to slow down. The Callighans looked shocked when she explained, leaving out the part about Cora suggesting it. But Grandma King's eyes narrowed, and she shot Cora a suspicious look.

Cora flinched and looked away, and the anger boiled in Meiner's stomach again.

Instead of allowing it to spill out, she moved into the living room, followed by the rest of the witches, to lay Dayna gently on the couch.

Surprisingly it was Yemi who snapped at them. She stood with her hands on her hips, a bundle of smoldering sage still gripped in one hand. "How could you have done something so *completely* boneheaded? I expected better of all of you. I've been cleansing the house like mad, thinking it was the energy from the ceremony making the back of my neck tingle, when it's just you lot being *incredibly irresponsible*."

Meiner felt guilt surge in her stomach, and Reagan looked shamefaced. Cora was the only one who looked sullenly mutinous.

"Nothing else was getting results. We had to."

Yemi stepped forward, positively towering over Cora now, jabbing a finger in her face. "Listen well, girl. There's a *reason* we don't scry that way." Yemi snapped one hand out toward Dayna, making the three of them flinch. "This is the reason, you *foolish* girl." She turned her attention to her daughter. "Maybe I shouldn't have let you ascend. Maybe you weren't ready for the responsibility."

Meiner didn't know Yemi well, but from the shocked look on Reagan's face she guessed this type of temper was rare for the older woman. "I'm sorry, Ma—"

"Abeg o! I don't need your excuses." Yemi waved her away, and Reagan trailed off, dropping her gaze to the floor.

"Will she be all right?"

"She's fine," Cora muttered, "Just passed out."

Meiner curled her hands into fists at her sides, grinding her teeth. She wanted to seize Cora by her collar and *shake* her, but she couldn't let her temper get the better of her. Not when Dayna might need her.

The older witches ignored Cora, crowding around Dayna on the couch.

"Same treatment as last time," Bronagh sank down beside her, smoothing a hand over Dayna's brow. "Plenty of water and food when she wakes. She's all right. Though this has undoubtedly left its mark."

Brenna leaned down and pressed a finger to the black handprint on Dayna's arm. "In more ways than one, I'm afraid," she said grimly. "It's alarming that Carman has this kind of reach, trapped as she is. I hate to think of her resurrected and brought back to full power."

There was a moment of tense silence after this.

"She'll really wake up?" Meiner finally said. In the shocked whiplash of this chilling announcement, she was finding it difficult not to pace. She wanted to move, to *do something*, to wake Dayna up. To tell her that following Cora's mad plan had nearly got her killed.

Cora. Her insides lit up with rage all over again. This was her fault. Meiner had warned her not to. She'd told her. And Cora had ignored her and nearly killed Dayna.

"She'll be herself by tonight, I would expect," Faye said.

"Cora." Grandma King spoke for the first time. "Come outside with me a moment."

Meiner should have felt a sense of satisfaction. She knew what was coming, and it wouldn't be pleasant. Instead she found herself silently furious. *She* wanted to hit Cora, to scream, to rage at her.

Cora turned reluctantly, and Meiner moved to follow, fists clenched. Her insides were seething, restless with hot anger. She pictured herself seizing Cora's arm and wrenching her around, planting her fist in the blond girl's face.

As if sensing this, Grandma King turned, shaking her head. "Not you. You stay here."

"This is my business, too," Meiner snapped. "A member of *my* coven nearly got someone killed. If I'm supposed to be a leader someday—"

"A good leader wouldn't have let this happen in the first place." Grandma King tugged her sweater up higher around her throat and turned for the door, as if the conversation was finished. As if she hadn't just thrown a lit match onto Meiner's gasoline temper.

She wanted to take off after Gran, fury burning through her.

She wanted to scream at both of them, to drag Cora back inside and force her to look at the black marks on Dayna's arms.

And then Bronagh said, "She's waking," and Meiner's temper fizzled out as quickly as it had come.

On the couch, Dayna took a deep breath, eyes fluttering momentarily before opening. She blinked, looking around, bewildered. At the Callighans and Yemi, standing over her, and at Reagan, who hovered just behind them looking incredibly guilty. Her gaze drifted from them to Meiner, and some semblance of memory must have returned, because her eyes went wide, and she glanced down at her arms, wincing.

"Yemi, food," Bronagh snapped, and Yemi squeaked, flapping her hands in the air, her face alarmed.

"Oh aye. I nearly forgot. I've got her lunch in the fridge." She bustled away into the kitchen, and they heard the slam of the refrigerator door.

"Try to take deep slow breaths," Bronagh instructed. "And tell us what you remember."

Dayna blinked. For a second, she only stared at the roof. Then she looked straight at Meiner, who felt a chill drop down her back. Dayna's eyes were darker than before, it seemed. Or maybe it was an illusion caused by the shadows behind them, the weight of her gaze. As if she'd lived through years in three minutes of scrying. As if she knew things now she shouldn't.

Dayna turned back to Bronagh. "I know where they are."

Chapter Fifty-Two

MEINER

She and Dayna wanted to leave right away, as soon as Dayna remembered the name of the inn on the guest book. But Bronagh said they should wait, that they weren't rushing this because the next target had to be one of them, and they would take the proper precautions before waltzing straight into the lion's den. She'd given Dayna a sharp look as she said this, and that seemed to have quelled her. Meiner still felt restless and pent-up, pacing the living room as Yemi and the Callighans prepared a protection spell, until Faye snapped at her.

Grandma King and Cora had been gone too long, and there was no reason for them to leave her out of this. She was just as much a part of the coven.

But . . . they'd been acting this way for the past week now, hadn't they? Disappearing together, speaking in low voices, exchanging a look when they thought Meiner wouldn't notice. She'd written it off at first, thought maybe Cora was trying to suck up to her grandmother. But . . . that wasn't quite right, was it? Gran had never responded to anything Cora had tried in the past.

Now that she thought of it, the way Cora had reacted when she'd gone through Gran's things had been strange. She hadn't asked about anything

Meiner had found, and she'd known Gran had been doing black magic, too, that she might still be doing it. In fact... what was it she'd said?

She'll kill you if you touch her stuff, especially that.

How had Cora known about the book? Meiner had never seen it before. At least, she didn't recall it. And now she could only think about the smug look on Cora's face, the blood under her nails....

Gran used to use blood in her rituals. Or... still did.

They'd been outside for too long.

She left the Callighan sisters burning bay leaves over Dayna and stomped out onto the driveway, insides blazing. It was noon, and the sun was directly overhead now, the sky a clear blue color, the forest around the farm vibrant and green. It was a beautiful day, and Meiner was far too angry to appreciate it.

She'd been so stupid.

Maybe they'd been doing it together all this time.

The thought shook her, because it made a horrible kind of sense. Cora had been the one who'd been possessed in the circle. Maybe it hadn't been Gran who invited something in after all; maybe she'd simply been instructing Cora.

Meiner paused in the middle of the driveway, heart pounding hard against her rib cage.

The more she thought about it, the more furious it made her. They'd been doing it under her nose all this time. Cora had probably been laughing at her.

Her hand was still bruised from punching the wall days ago, but the rage was enough to drive out the pain. She was going to make both of them pay.

Except... where the hell were they?

She paused, looking around, blood thundering in her ears. The driveway was empty. She went quiet, breathing deeply, trying to calm her heartbeat enough to listen.

The air smelled like early summer bonfire smoke and pine, and she could hear the faint murmur of voices around the side of the house. She could make out Cora's voice, high and strained with irritation.

"We found out where they were hiding—"

A sharp crack interrupted this, and a grunt of pain. Meiner paused, her anger fizzling out momentarily. She'd been on the receiving end of this kind of conversation many times. She stayed where she was, still hidden around the corner.

"And the verses I taught you? The ritual? How is that coming? Or are you neglecting it to send your fellow witchlings on dangerous fool's errands?"

Cora's voice was sullen. "I've memorized the stupid thing. If you'd just tell me what it was for—"

"It will grant you the power you need when you need it. You'll know when the time comes."

"You keep saying that."

There was frustration in Cora's voice, and disappointment, and Meiner felt a surge of emotion strong enough that she had to brace herself on the wall of the house. *She'd* had this same talk with Grandma King, years ago. She'd had the words endlessly drilled into her, had been forced to set up the circle over and over, outside in the cold and rain until she'd completed it fifteen, sixteen, seventeen times. And through it all, she'd begged to know what the spell did, why it was so important, and she'd received no answer.

She'd always suspected it had something to do with taking over the coven, with being head witch. If it was the same ritual and Cora was learning it instead of her...

Meiner hadn't stumbled across evidence of black magic, but this was almost as bad.

She'd known something was going on, that Grandma King had stopped teaching her. That she probably wasn't going to ascend any time soon. But this...this was a new sort of betrayal. Grandma King hadn't forgotten anything; it was just that she was teaching Cora instead.

That explained the book. Gran had probably been teaching Cora all the things Meiner had never been taught. She'd never seen the black book because Gran hadn't felt the need to show her, not after she'd been replaced.

What did that mean for the future of the coven? Would Cora inherit it?

The thought of Cora in charge sent another wave of anger through her. She felt nauseous, sick with fury. When had Grandma King decided her own granddaughter wasn't good enough?

And on top of everything, well...it was *Cora*.

She was already insufferable; she'd nearly killed Dayna tonight and had set something loose that had permanently marked her. And Cora wasn't showing the least bit of remorse over it. She was reckless and overconfident. If she was in charge, there was no telling how she'd behave. Who else she would hurt.

"Don't make me regret my decision, girl."

"You can't hold the threat of Meiner over my head every time I do something you don't like. She doesn't even really want the coven. All she wants is to avoid becoming *you*."

This last bit was thrown at the old woman, and Cora's voice was loaded with toxic satisfaction. She must have got a reaction out of Grandma King, though Meiner couldn't think what.

"She doesn't want to be here," Cora said. "She didn't even believe you when we first got here. She thinks you're senile."

"And yet she stayed," Grandma King said evenly. "Because she does as she's told. She's grateful I took pity on her, saved her from her useless lump of a mother. As you should be. Instead you've shown nothing but disrespect since your aunt dumped you on my doorstep."

"This is horseshit." A thumping sound, like Cora had smacked something with her fist. "As soon as this is over, we're out of here. I'm getting us out of this backwater dump and away from these bitches. We don't need another coven."

"Don't get too confident." Grandma King's voice was dry, but Meiner was barely listening anymore. Her heart was pounding in her ears.

Cora had spoken about it so casually. *She* was getting them out of here. *She* had decided they didn't need the other coven. And Grandma

King hadn't protested. Was she handing over the coven soon, while she was still alive?

There was a low murmur as Grandma King said something, and Meiner frowned, straining to hear.

"She's right anyway." Cora's voice again. "She's just as bad as you are. You're both out of control."

"Which is why you fit in so well."

Gran's voice sounded amused, but Meiner placed a hand on the wall, anger boiling through her. A moment later there was a shuffle from around the side of the house, the crunch of footsteps on the gravel. She pushed off the wall, moving farther into the middle of the driveway so it didn't look as if she'd been eavesdropping.

When Gran came around the side, Meiner glowered at her, and the old woman simply looked at her blankly and passed by. Meiner's nails cut into the palms of her hands. Her whole body was rigid as she watched her grandmother reenter the farmhouse.

A second later Cora came around the corner. She stopped short when she saw Meiner, and her expression went from sullen to suspicious.

"What, were you spying on us?"

"Wondering if I heard you plotting, you mean?" Meiner kept her voice cool, folding her arms across her chest. "Yeah, I did. And as far as I'm concerned, Gran is out of her fucking mind. Dayna is okay, by the way. If you even care."

Cora's smile was vicious. "I don't, actually. None of them matter." She started to move around Meiner, toward the door.

A growl ripped loose from Meiner's throat, and she shot a hand out, catching Cora's arm and jerking her back. "What the hell does *that* mean?"

Cora pulled out of her grip, face flushed with anger, eyes glittering. "It *means* we're leaving as soon as this is over. I know you want to stay here and *join* them or something, don't think I haven't guessed. You want to leave our coven. To get away from Gran and me. Well, you're not. We're leaving."

"You can leave," Meiner snapped back at her. "Good riddance. You two can leave and run your own coven together and you can be in charge all you like. Then she'll die and you'll be on your own."

Unshed tears were glittering in Cora's eyes now, and her face was twisted in fury. "You are so *stupid*, Meiner King," she hissed.

"What is that supposed to mean?" Meiner took a step toward her, fists clenched, but Cora didn't move.

"Once I'm gone, how long do you think it will take for you to start taking out your temper on your little girlfriend? You *need* me. All that pent-up aggression has to go somewhere. And believe me, she can't handle you." Cora whirled around, marching for the door, turning to say over her shoulder, "We're damaged, Meiner, which is why we work together. If you stay here, you'll spread that damage to her."

All the words Meiner wanted to scream after her seemed to have turned to ash in her mouth, and she stayed frozen in place as Cora vanished into the house, slamming the door shut behind her.

Chapter Fifty-Three

DAYNA

They left the house in a convoy, Dayna riding in Meiner's rust bucket Datsun, and the rest of the witches piled into Reagan's minivan. Grandma King stayed behind with Cora, who Dayna suspected was in for a long lecture.

The road they found themselves on was a winding, dead-end affair, with cherry blossom trees along both sides. It was not so much a road as a forest trail pretending to be one.

In spite of the late afternoon sunshine, Dayna was plagued by a persistent chill. The dark shape that had seized her in the vision had been unspeakably terrifying, filling her stomach with sick dread. She had felt hands on her arms, ice-cold fingers biting into her skin.

Whatever it was had gripped her so fiercely she'd felt it was about to break through her skin. In her panic, she'd reached into her own core and drawn out all the magic she could, tearing herself from the creature's grasp.

It felt like she'd used up all her power at once, and yet she'd barely pulled herself free.

Dayna darted a sideways look at Meiner, who'd been sullen and silent for the entire car ride. She kept drumming her fingers on the steering wheel and glancing in the rearview mirror, brow furrowed.

The silence made Dayna antsy, and she wracked her brain for something to talk about, anything at all. She didn't want to think about the fact that her arms burned in five perfect fingerprints on both sides. She'd rolled her sleeves up to look earlier and it had made her stomach roil, her skin prickling hot and cold with dread.

Her insides felt strangely hollow, as if she'd used the last of the extra magic from the ascension. She felt... drained.

After several more moments of sullen silence from Meiner, she finally worked up the courage to ask, "Did something else happen while I was... well, you know. Something you're not telling me?"

Meiner blinked, narrowed her eyes at the rearview mirror, and answered without looking at her. "When what? When Cora nearly got you killed with the stupid, reckless idea you went right along with?"

Dayna sat up straight, bristling. "Excuse me?"

Now Meiner did look at her, and her face was dark. "You could have died. Cora doesn't care about your safety; she cares about results, power. What those things can get her. If you listen to her, you could very well end up dead."

"I'm an adult." Dayna could feel her temper surging. This had been her choice; she'd known what she was getting into and she'd made a conscious decision that the benefits outweighed the risk. And now Meiner was lecturing her like... like she was a child or something, "And I'm a damn good witch, Meiner King."

"Not good enough, though. You could have died." Meiner cast a pointed look at the marks on her arms, and Dayna's mouth dropped open.

Anger made her chest tight. She drew a breath and spat, "I'm ascended, which makes me a full witch. I handled it."

At the word *ascended* Meiner's mouth twitched down. Her fingers tightened on the wheel. "You don't get it. Cora will get you killed. And when she does, she won't feel any kind of guilt. She's a monster."

Dayna took a deep breath and tried to keep her voice even. Meiner wasn't mad at her, not really. She was mad she hadn't listened to her warning, maybe. She was mad at Cora. "I can handle myself."

"Well, it doesn't matter anyway," Meiner muttered. "Because apparently as soon as this is over, we're gone."

Dayna stared at her in disbelief. "You're seriously leaving just like that?" It shouldn't have been an issue; people had long-distance relationships all the time. But they weren't actually together, and the way Meiner was talking...Her throat felt tight, and she didn't know how to ask the question she wanted to.

"There," Meiner said, her voice flat. "There's the address."

The car hunkered under one of the trees, engine idling bad-temperedly. Meiner's hands were nervous on the wheel, fingers tapping an uneven rhythm. Dayna sat on her own hands to keep from fidgeting. She didn't want to sit here; she wanted to argue, to seize Meiner by the collar and make her *look* at her. They needed to talk about this, to fight about it instead of sitting there in angry silence. But the inn beside them was probably where the murderers were deciding on their next target, and now was simply not the time.

The inn itself was unspectacular. Somehow rustic without being quaint, like someone had slapped a B and B sign on the family cabin. The shutters were green, and someone had planted begonias in the window boxes.

There came the familiar squeal of a fan belt, and Reagan's patchwork van pulled up behind them, her mother in the passenger seat. The witches spilled out of the van one by one, with Bronagh the last to climb ponderously out of the sliding door.

"Callighans in front," Bronagh said. "If the brothers aren't there, we go through their room, see what we can find. If they are there, well"—she lifted her brow, expression dark—"they won't be happy we're dropping in on them like this."

Faye followed close on her grandmother's heels. She rotated her wrists and cracked her knuckles. "I *do* hope they're in." She tilted her face to the windows of the inn and showed all her teeth in an approximation of a smile.

The driveway leading to the inn was a narrow dirt lane with a red mailbox at the end, and the name of the place—the Willow Moon Inn—was stamped on it in the same gold letters that had been on the leather binder.

The front door was unlocked, and the foyer, which was done in rich red and burnished gold wallpaper, was empty when they walked in. The small, cluttered desk at the front was unmanned, and there was a bell sitting in the center of the papers and files. The grubby index card beside it read, *Ring for service.* Reagan reached for it, and Brenna tapped her shoulder, shaking her head.

"We don't want to tip them off if they're here." The Callighans moved behind the desk, and Bronagh began prying open one of the cupboards on the wall. Rifling through the folders inside, she pulled one out with a noise of triumph.

"Guest log." Bronagh set the book on the desk. "Look for three people, same room. The place isn't big."

They crowded around the desk, and Brenna flipped through the book, which consisted of rows of orderly handwriting logging each room number and the amount of guests, their check-in and -out time and the date. She skimmed until her finger had reached today's date, her long nails a splash of red against the faded pages. There was only one entry of three, and it was a check-in with no check-out.

"That's them." Dayna took the book from Brenna, and when she rolled a fingertip over the black lines of the words *party of three,* a shiver seemed to trail down her back. The man from her vision might be there. When she walked in, would she feel the same way she had in the vision? Would she find herself frozen on the threshold, arms stiff at her sides, chest tight as she struggled to drag in breath?

She clenched her fists, trying to force her thoughts away from their usual course, from fixating on her breath. "This is them."

Nobody asked how she knew. Not only because there were only two other guests staying the week, both parties of two, but because all of them were staring down at the paper like they'd felt the same chill.

It was them. The witch hunters. Here in this inn, somewhere over their heads.

"Well," Bronagh said, "let's go see who we're dealing with."

Chapter Fifty-Four

DAYNA

I t was the room from her vision.

The main difference was, of course, that the beds and the chair were empty. The sheets on the beds were thrown back in a careless tangle, and the room was filled with drifts of laundry and papers scattered across every available surface. Dayna wandered in before she really thought about what she was doing, and Bronagh hissed at her. Something about checking for traps.

She hung back and looked around while the Callighans moved past her, muttering spells under their breath, hands in the air. The hotel room didn't make her feel the way she'd thought it would. Now that she was here in person it didn't seem all that threatening.

"All right, come in, it should be fine now." Brenna waved at them, and Dayna glanced over at Bronagh, who was still muttering and tracing a finger in the air as if she were admonishing any dark magic that might be hiding in the corners and then up at the black marks and swirls on the walls. They were done in a smudgy, shaky hand, as if whoever had traced them had been in a hurry.

"It's fine," Faye said waspishly. "Hardly expert-level work."

Dayna wandered in, staring down at the papers strewn on the desk. She picked one up, and then dropped it as if it burned her hand. The symbol on the paper was not well drawn, the lines shaky and heavy-handed, but she recognized it as the Butcher's symbol.

There were no names on the wallpaper, though. That had simply been a part of... what? Whatever was going on in the man's head?

The room seemed to have passed inspection, for Bronagh had finally paused in front of a cupboard in the wall, head cocked to one side. As she stared, the cupboard door drifted open a bit at a time, as if entirely of its own volition. Faulty hinges or a warped door, perhaps, though Dayna thought it probably had more to do with Bronagh's stern gaze. You tended to do what you were supposed to when the oldest Callighan looked at you that way, even if you *were* only a cupboard door.

Behind the door was a heavy iron safe. Bronagh sank to her knees with a grunt. She did not touch it, just let her hands glide over the door, as if she were warming her palms on some sort of heat radiating from the surface.

"Spelled," she muttered. "Nasty, too."

Yemi shifted uneasily, placing herself in front of Dayna and Reagan.

"Ugly stuff," Bronagh said, and she waved Faye and Brenna over. "We'll need to concentrate. Reagan, watch the hallway."

Reagan didn't argue. She seemed almost relieved to shuffle out of the room and plant herself as sentry at the door, and Yemi followed, the two of them speaking in low whispers.

While the three older women broke into the safe, Dayna drifted around the rest of the room. The symbol that had appeared at the crime scenes repeated itself on many of the papers. Like one of the brothers had drawn it over and over in the heat of obsession.

She bit her lip, suddenly uneasy. It reminded her a little too closely of her mother's chaotic scribbles on the page at the library.

When she glanced at Meiner, she was frowning thoughtfully at the twisted sheets on the bed. Then she turned, stooping to pick through the nearest pile of clothing.

"Have these people never used a dresser drawer?" Dayna wrinkled her nose. "Uh, why are you touching their manky clothes?"

Meiner didn't look up. "Ticket stubs, parking slips, anything to give us a clue where they've gone."

It was smart, and as much as Dayna's skin crawled, she forced herself to join Meiner in pawing through the dirty laundry. She found nothing in the pockets of a sweater, and a pair of grass-stained jeans proved empty.

She saw Meiner pick up what looked like a silver snuff box on the nightstand by the bed, flinch, and then put it back in place, face twisted in disgust.

Fishing in a pair of torn corduroys earned her a slip of white paper. She unfolded it, finding a receipt for gas from an area she recognized. It seemed the witch hunters had visited the Cliffs of Moher. Dayna frowned, puzzled. Why visit a tourist spot in their hunt for witches? Maybe they'd been following someone?

Meiner made a noise of triumph, straightening up with a white slip in her hand. "They went to Glendalough."

Dayna waved her own receipt. "Moher."

Meiner shook her head, brows creased. "What the hell?"

Another slip revealed a pamphlet about the tombs at Newgrange and a receipt from somewhere in Cork. "I don't get it." Dayna let the receipt flutter to the floor. "They went sightseeing between murders?"

"Sacred sights," Brenna said from her crouched position by the safe, and then went quiet as Bronagh snapped at her to concentrate, unless she wished to lose a hand. Dayna took a step away from the safe.

Brenna was right though; the tickets and receipts were from locations that all had some link to the gods.

From the safe cupboard there came a sharp click, and Bronagh made a noise of disgust. "Nasty magic, but it fades fast. Give it a moment."

There was a second of loaded silence while they all stood in front of the safe, and Dayna tried to peer past the Callighans. There was something flat on the floor of the safe. Her stomach fluttered.

It was the right shape for a book.

Let it be the book.

Finally Bronagh reached in and pulled out a heavy brown leather journal. Etched into the cover was Carman's symbol.

For a moment Bronagh only stood there staring down at the book. Her face looked stricken. Then she shook herself, tapping the cover with one finger. "There's powerful magic in this."

Dayna couldn't seem to stop herself from reaching for it. Something about it drew her almost helplessly, a magnetic pull she felt deep in her guts. This time there was no wild dog to stop her. She *needed* to touch it.

Her hands shook as she wrapped her fingers around the spine. Bronagh blinked, but she didn't protest when Dayna drew the book away. In fact, Dayna could feel the older woman studying her with interest while she cradled the book in her arms. She didn't care; all she could do was stare at it.

It was so strangely familiar that an ache had started in her chest. It was like something in her had been missing, a memory, a stretch of time she had not known was gone. She badly wanted to sit down and pore over the pages, to rediscover what she'd forgotten.

Dayna smoothed one hand over the cover, and as she did she was hit by the unshakable certainty that she'd done this before. This cover, the symbol on it, smooth and flat under the tips of her fingers, was familiar. She'd held it before.

Just as fast as it had come, the feeling was gone, and Dayna stared wide-eyed at the book, feeling a little dizzy. The book was magic, obviously. It was some kind of spell. Simply another of those strange déjà vu surges.

She'd never held this book before. Had never even seen it before the joint reading.

"Let's go." Bronagh straightened up, her lined features filled with satisfaction. "I think we've some reading to do, but they'll be back in..." She checked her wrist, or maybe the back of her hand, Dayna wasn't sure. There was no watch. "They'll be back soon." She frowned then, suddenly uncertain, eyes searching the room. "Yes, they've gone to do something." She squinted at the doorway and then blinked when Reagan appeared suddenly, Yemi hovering behind her, face anxious.

"There's someone downstairs, a woman, I think. We'd best be on our way."

Chapter Fifty-Five
CORA

Cora stared around the empty parking lot. In the distance she could see the sloping concrete walls of the skate park across the lawn, through the thinning forest.

She knew the reason she'd been banished here, why she hadn't been allowed to go with Dayna and Meiner to find the brothers. Because she'd disobeyed Grandma King; she hadn't followed her instructions like a good little witchling.

And the other reason. Because she was supposed to be hunting her sacrifice. She still hadn't picked someone, and the goddess was stirring within her, restless. This was the last step before her ascension, and she was running out of time.

The thought made her throat tighten, and she swallowed hard and stalked across the concrete lot. She'd picked this spot because it was an older skate park. No one came here anymore, and she needed to be alone to work up her nerve.

She crossed the lawn, the strap of her duffel bag heavy on one shoulder, the silence of her surroundings filling her head. The sun had dimmed now, and fog was beginning to roll in as she passed through the forested area, but there were lights above the park. Enough light to set up an altar.

The ritual would calm her, she told herself, help her find her center. Prepare her for what she had to do. It was almost out of habit that she started to set up the ceremony, drawing the six-sided star with chalk from her bag, dragging the knife across her wrists one more time, feeling the blood drip between her fingers. Once again, as she got to the last few words in the chant, she felt the surge of power and stumbled to a halt. For a minute she considered spitting out the last word, just . . . finishing the spell. Gran wouldn't tell her what it would do, but she was sure it was the next level after her ascension. A way to get more power than the others would have. So maybe she could just skip straight to it. . . .

But Gran kept saying she would know when the time came. That she had to be patient. Cora drew in a deep breath and let it out, frustrated. She opened her eyes, letting the last word wither on her lips.

The place was eerie in the evening, its concrete ramps casting long shadows into the center, her every move echoing off the grafittied walls.

She finished the next ritual faster than usual, less carefully. Probably the crimson liquid had stained her teeth in her hurry. She didn't care.

Her hands were shaking.

Give me the strength to do this, she begged.

There was no answer, and Cora curled her fingers in the fabric of her dress, resisting the urge to smash the glass basin on the concrete. Why was the goddess always showing up at the least opportune times, but when she wanted her, she was nowhere to be found?

A few minutes of silence and then she shot to her feet, snatching up the candles. *I can't do this.*

She'd just thrown the contents of her altar back into the bag when the heat blazed through her, making her double over, palms on her thighs. Cora gasped, blinking back tears. It felt like molten lava had been pumped through her veins, and she staggered forward, knees striking the pavement hard.

It took longer to fade this time, and Cora was finally left on the pavement on her hands and knees, shaking and gasping for air. The anger that surged through her was almost as bad, and she ground her teeth, letting out a low growl.

She had to do this soon.

The echo of voices across the open space jerked Cora upright, and she blinked around at the cracked concrete walls. The nearest one had been emblazoned with *Tiocfaidh ár lá. Our day will come.*

She remained completely still. In the silence, the sound came again, laughter and the clamor of deep voices. She scrambled to her feet and snatched up her bag, and then relaxed as a group emerged from the trees. Kids, nothing more. Barely out of high school.

There were four of them, three boys and a girl. The boys were one and the same, sloppy replicas in matching wide-brimmed hats and torn jeans, passing a cigarillo back and forth as they moved across the grass, smoke leaking from lips and nostrils. The girl was in the midst of them, a sheep among wolves, tall and fine-boned in a low-cut powder-blue sundress. The boys ringed her as they walked, subconscious body language all turned in on her, honed like hunting dogs scenting blood. It made Cora's skin crawl.

The group was halfway across the lawn before they spotted her, and the tall girl in their midst was forgotten as their gazes refocused on Cora. She kept her expression blank, feeling their eyes trail across her body, hungry and unapologetic. Together they were brave.

Cora hitched her bag higher on her shoulder. She kept walking, meeting the tallest one's gaze. His smile was sharp-edged and a little horrible if you looked past the boyish features and down to the truth of him.

Cora did not correct course. She did not look away. The magic pulsed inside her, and she could turn him to ashes if she pleased.

They passed one another, and the conversation died. The tall girl glared at Cora as they moved by. She did not like her dogs baying after another fox, Cora thought. Her mouth tasted sour.

The tallest boy paused, still smiling that smile. Smoke trailed from his nostrils as he flicked the stump of the cigarillo into the grass between them. "Smile, beautiful. Your face is too perfect to scowl at a bloke like that."

Cora's mouth was still filled with the copper-and-rust taste of blood. Her teeth felt coated in it, as if the gore had stuck in the cracks.

She smiled.

The boy's smirk faltered. His skateboard hit the grass soundlessly at his feet and he froze on the spot. His friends didn't seem to notice the way he was staring; maybe the dim light hid his expression. They barked with laughter and elbowed one another.

"Pete, you dog."

"Get her number, yeah?"

She could do this, couldn't she? The final step to ascension.

The others kept walking, leaving their friend frozen, blinking in shock, his eyes wide and white in the dim light. His gaze was locked on Cora's face. He looked somehow paralyzed. His fingers twitched at his sides, as if he were desperately trying to move his body. Cora frowned at him.

For one beat, two, she didn't understand.

And then the voice in her head came, like the rasp of scales against silk. *Give him to me. He is perfect.*

Chapter Fifty-Six

DUBH

It had been too long since he'd last killed a witch.

The urge was back, and as they sat outside the house of threes, he almost trembled with anticipation. He had a score to settle with this one.

"I want the final blow," he said. Again, his tongue went back to his chipped tooth, probing the sharp, uneven edges. He wasn't particularly happy the other two were coming with him. He did his best work alone, and this was personal, but they'd insisted.

"If you can even get close enough." Olc twisted in his seat to sneer at him. "I'll wager she breaks your jaw and sends you squealing again."

That wasn't what happened. He remembered it all too well, the farm on the Isle of Man, the red barn. The burning pain as she'd turned and lashed out at him.

Dubh sat back, stretching his legs the length of the seat, running his fingers along the raised symbols along Witchkiller's sheath.

Olc may have been a brutish oaf, but he was right about one thing: This witch wouldn't go down easily.

"I'm done waiting." Olc pushed the driver-side door open, boots hitting the gravel. "The others are gone. It's clear."

"The blond one," Calma said. "I didn't see her leave."

"She's gone." Dubh shoved the door open with one foot and slid across the seat, balancing Witchkiller's sheath over his shoulder. The weight was comfortingly familiar. "I can feel it. It's just her." Greedily he eyed the house, the narrow, peaked windows that ran along the top of the second floor. She was in there; he could feel the stench of power. She was old now. Slower. But still deadly.

"Let's go."

Calma grunted bad-temperedly, but he said nothing, only followed Dubh up the winding driveway. The evening had turned to fog and drizzle, and the second half of the driveway wound up and vanished into the mist, obscuring the gates at the top.

For once, Dubh welcomed the rain. It felt right. Like the night itself was preparing for what was to come.

Halfway up Dubh felt the witch's power move. She'd been sedentary until now, and for some reason it made him nervous. Her magic felt suddenly restless.

"I think she knows we're coming."

"Let her know. It makes no difference," Olc said.

They paused at the first gate. Oak trees rose above it, ringing the house, and Dubh breathed in deeply, feeling the fire flicker and brighten in his veins as he neared. They always fed him, the oak trees.

They passed through the second gate, and Dubh's skin burned unpleasantly as some spell of protection skimmed over him, kept off by the barrier he'd cast around himself that morning, though just barely. Walking beside him, both his brothers made noises of distaste deep in their throats, twin growls as they pushed forward.

Witchkiller felt heavy in his hands, as if it could sense her, and pins and needles rushed over his arms, raising the hairs on the back of his neck, making him shudder. Again, the magic did not touch them, and they passed through the second sanctuary unharmed.

The third gate nearly threw them, because it was not all there.

The high, arched rails of the gate flickered in and out, and the gap in the hedge vanished and reappeared. If the magic hadn't broken on the brothers' skin and spilled around them, they wouldn't have seen the true location of the third gate at all.

But if they squinted just right, it stayed put as they passed through, Dubh's skin tickled and stung fiercely, as if every exposed inch was being brushed all over by nettles.

They moved through the third gate, through the last enchantment and into the inner sanctuary, and Dubh's blood sang to him, to his sword, to the need burning in his chest.

In the garden beyond the last gate, between the wind-rustled lilac bushes and the ivy-covered trestles of the archway leading to the house, stood the King Witch. Waiting.

Chapter Fifty-Seven

SAMUEL

It took him nearly thirty minutes to bike across town to the Etomi farm, even pedaling as fast as he could. He wobbled the last few feet up the driveway, completely winded. But he forced himself to keep going. Dayna wouldn't pick up her phone, and he didn't have anyone else's number. He was sure the Butcher was coming for Harriet King next.

Margery is dead.

Margery, whom he'd talked to only hours before the attack.

He leaned his bike against one of the oak trees overhanging the driveway. He noted with some relief that the drive was empty—Dayna wasn't there—and turned for the house.

Sam stopped, breath freezing in his throat.

There was someone there already. Three someones, actually, standing at the entrance to the garden. The middle figure was shorter than the others and dressed in a collared shirt and jacket. In his right hand, glittering in the light of the evening sun, was a sword.

Sam was rooted to the spot beneath the tree, terror paralyzing his muscles and bones.

He'd pictured himself charging in, triumphant, warning Harriet King before the killer arrived, maybe getting her to admit she was the final victim from the Isle of Man before whisking her away to the station. Maybe telling the others about it or Bible study tomorrow. Sam the serial killer catcher. Sam the hero.

He'd never dreamed of arriving *after* the killers.

Killers. Plural. The Butcher was a triad, a team.

He'd thought he'd solved this thing, that he knew all about the Butcher, but he'd been so wrong.

His entire body twitched as he tried to convince himself to move.

Finally, just as his hand was beginning to drift to his pocket, to his phone, there was movement from the farmhouse. He hadn't noticed the fourth figure in the center of the garden, she'd been standing so still.

It was an old woman. She had wild, iron-gray hair, and her face, though lined with age, was like steel. There was something about her that made a chill drop down his spine, and he suddenly remembered what Margery had said: *You go looking for Harriet King, you go looking for trouble.*

The old woman raised a hand, palm facing the men, as if she were telling them to stop. Then she twisted her wrist, moving her fingers in the air, and the front of the house seemed to . . . ripple. It was the only way Sam could think to describe it. Something passed through the air directly in front of the door and traveled up and out. Suddenly there were strange markings all across the front, traced over windowpanes and doors. Swirls and pentacles and complicated knot work, all done in what looked like a thick rust-red liquid.

A moment later the lines faded, and Samuel blinked rapidly, shaking his head. He told himself he'd imagined it. The shock of the situation was making him see things. Or . . . it had been a trick of the light.

The men moved forward, and the one at the front spoke, his voice a guttural snarl that echoed across the open space. "King Witch."

Samuel shuddered, but to his surprise the old woman put her hands on her hips and faced the first man straight on. "About damn time."

Sam crept forward, clutching the side of the nearest car. What the hell was she doing? Why wasn't she running for the house?

The man lifted his sword, pointing the blade at the woman. "The moment I came here, I knew you'd follow. I've let this game carry on long enough."

I knew you'd follow?

That couldn't be right. Sam's head was spinning now, and he took a staggering step backward before freezing in place. Here he'd thought the Butcher had been following Harriet King from town to town, trying to get to her. To finish what he'd started on the Isle of Man all those years ago. But . . . she was the one following him?

Why?

Without warning, the old woman's arm snapped out. The first man was picked up and hurled abruptly back, landing with a crash on the fence, chunks of wood scattering around him.

Sam yelped and then clapped a hand over his mouth. The old woman hadn't touched him. Hadn't even gone *near* him.

The paint on the front of the house had flared bright again, glowing with sick red light. It looked almost radioactive.

What the *hell*?

This wasn't possible. It didn't make sense.

His pulse was galloping, and he felt slightly faint, but even through his shock, he realized the sigils on the house looked familiar. In fact, some of them looked *exactly* like the one from the photo of the barn.

It all seemed impossible. And yet . . . it made a horrible kind of sense. It was one of the only explanations that fit. . . .

There was a reason the Butcher hadn't been able to kill the woman all those years ago. A reason she'd survived the horrible wound.

Harriet King was a witch.

Witchcraft was real. *Magic* was real.

There was another crash from the garden, and a blast of the same sickly red light, but Sam was already scrambling backward, heart in his throat, searching blindly for his bike handlebars in panic.

He managed to get onto the seat and get his feet on the pedals, nearly tipping over twice before he kicked off, starting down the driveway, sending up clouds of dust as he pedaled frantically away.

Chapter Fifty-Eight

DAYNA

The Callighans stayed to talk to the hotel owner, and Bronagh sent the rest of them home.

Dayna rode back with Reagan and Yemi. She said it was because she needed to talk to them, but judging by the look Meiner gave her, she knew it was a lie. Their argument was on the back burner, but that didn't mean it was resolved.

Reagan seemed to pick up on it after several seconds of driving in silence. She pursed her lips and gave Dayna a look in the rearview mirror. "Out with it, woman. What's going on with you and Meiner?"

Dayna hesitated, then shrugged. "Meiner is acting weird, like... standoffish. She won't say why. I think it's something to do with Cora."

Reagan's brows shot up. "What, you think there's... like, something there?"

"Not like that. At least I don't think so." She told them about the argument, how Meiner had acted when she'd said they were leaving.

"Wow," Reagan said. "Sounds like some shit went down with her coven."

Yemi sucked her teeth. "Mmm-hmm, what did I tell you? That coven is trouble."

"You said no such thing," Reagan retorted. "You were all, *Invite them in for tea, I'm sure they're lovely.*"

Dayna grinned, and then her phone buzzed in her jacket pocket. She fished it out and read the text out loud.

Reverend: *Come get the rest of your things. Your mother is going through them.*

"Shit." She fumbled her phone and nearly dropped it, the sudden rush of anger making her hands shake. "Oh my god, why is he letting her do that?" She squeaked in surprise as the van took a sudden turn, tires squealing. "Whoa, what are you doing?"

Reagan looked grim. "We're going to your house, obviously."

"Slow down, Reagan," Yemi said, but she didn't contradict her daughter. "I've half a mind to come in and have a word with your father, Dayna."

Normally she would have protested. She didn't want her coven involved, and the thought of dealing with her parents right now was exhausting. All she wanted to do was go to Reagan's house and pore over the book in her bag. She hadn't even got a chance to open it yet, with everything going on.

And maybe if they just went back to the coven house, she could talk to Meiner, see if she could get her to confess what was wrong.

But the memory of the symbol scratched into Fiona's arm was still fresh, and if she was involved in this somehow . . . Dayna's fists were clenched, nails biting into her palms. What would happen if she discovered the box under the bed, discovered her altar?

Reagan drove like the devil was after them, and they pulled into Dayna's driveway five minutes later. She took a breath, steeling herself. This wasn't going to be pleasant.

"Wait here, will you?" Dayna said, and when both women looked like they were going to protest, she said sternly, "I'll be right back, I swear. But please, stay until I text. I'm going to talk to my dad, and this is going to be messy."

Reagan sighed. "All right, but if you don't text in twenty minutes, we're coming in, spells blazing."

Dayna grinned in spite of her churning stomach. "I believe you."

Chapter Fifty-Nine

CORA

It was getting dark now. The last rays of light from the sinking sun painted the boy's face in alternating patterns of shadow and light. He was so utterly still. Cora had closed the distance between them before she realized what she was doing, driven by curiosity.

She moved around him, cautious at first, and then as he stayed rooted to the spot, she grew more confident. Trailing a hand over his shoulder, a finger along his chest. His body shuddered under her touch.

"You really can't move, can you?"

Despite the fear that churned her stomach, a cold thrill ran through her. Finally her goddess was showing her power.

Again came that liquid sensation in the back of her mind, the presence of Caorthannach's shifting, sliding scales. *I give him to you, witchling. I grant you my power. Are you not pleased?*

"Aye," she whispered. "I'm pleased. I'll..." She faltered, reluctant to say it.

There can be no power without sacrifice. You cannot win this war without me.

That was it. She wasn't doing this for herself, or for Grandma King. She was doing this for her fellow witches, for a greater cause.

Cora dipped into her purse, drawing the dagger out. The box hit the grass at her feet with a soft thud, and there was a hiss from the boy. In the dusky light his eyes were frantic. His mouth twitched, as if he were trying to move his lips.

Cora clenched the dagger in one hand and reached out with the other, seizing the bottom of his T-shirt. She meant to yank it up, to expose his bare chest. Instead she curled her fingers into the fabric, snarling softly to herself. Why couldn't she do it?

There would be more deaths if she didn't do this. Without this, who would be strong enough to fight? What was one life in exchange for many?

Cora curled her fingers tighter, hating them for shaking. Hating herself for her cowardice.

She had to do this. Take the heart. Say the words.

This was her ascension. She'd been waiting for so long now.

If it makes it easier, the goddess hissed, and then without warning Cora was hit with a barrage of images, flashes in the back of her mind, an old-fashioned moving picture in her head.

The boy at a house party, head thrown back, laughing, a beer bottle clutched in his hand. A girl passed out in a bedroom upstairs, a single bottle on the floor, amber liquid leaching out into the carpet. The boy in the doorway. His sharp smile, the light in his eyes as he glanced over his shoulder.

The boy in the bed. On top of the girl.

And then later, beside his locker, surrounded by his friends. The laughter, a slap on the back, a punch to the shoulder.

The scene yanked Cora out of this reality and plunged her into her own past, a particular house party as a teen, a boy who'd reacted badly to the news she wasn't interested, who'd followed her around the party until she was six beers in and swaying on her feet.

And Meiner, there suddenly out of nowhere, full of rage and vodka. Cora hadn't been sure what happened after that; everything was fuzzy. But there'd been rumors the boy had peed blood the next day.

And if Meiner hadn't been there?

There was the girl in the bed again, only now the hair spread across the pillow was blond, and Cora was looking straight into her own face, eyes shut, lashes flickering against her cheeks. Across the room the bedroom door clicked shut.

The images cut out, and Cora reeled back, shaking her head. She felt plunged from darkness to light too suddenly, dazzled. And angry. Filled with the kind of rage that stuck in her throat and choked her.

That made it justice, she realized. In fact . . . that made it easy.

And it was. Sliding the blade between his ribs was surprisingly easy.

The dagger was impossibly sharp, and her arms were strong. The only surprising thing was the noise the boy made when the dagger slipped in, a startled grunt. Cora jumped back as he slumped sideways, sagging to the ground as if someone had cut invisible bonds. He fell to the grass, and Cora took a shaky breath and rolled him over with the toe of her boot.

Her entire body was trembling, and the sky above her surged. But as she knelt beside him, wrapping her shaking hands around the golden snakes of the handle, her voice was surprisingly steady.

"I'm not sorry."

Chapter Sixty

SAMUEL

Sam stood in the middle of the half-empty parking lot, clutching his Bible to his chest. His hand kept drifting to his pocket, to his phone, and then away again. He knew if he called the gardai, it would be the sergeant responding. The sergeant who, for all his grumbling and growling, was still his da. And there was no way his da was prepared to go up against something like that. He'd be killed.

The sun was starting to sink behind the line of shops, silhouetting the peaks and edges in orange and black. Gravel crunched beneath his shoes as he stepped slowly forward. Through the window of O'Neal's he could see his Bible study in the corner booth.

Amanda and Jillian seemed to be watching Darius argue with Morgan. Darius shoveled fries into his mouth, rolling his eyes at her. Morgan was in the middle of saying something, her face earnest as she jabbed a finger at the Bible on the table in front of her. No doubt emphasizing the importance of the "emergency Bible study" she'd just called—the news had broke about Margery and the group was eager to discuss it in detail.

Sam stepped onto the walkway in front of the shop, clutching the railing with one hand. There was a pang in his chest as he glanced over at Sage Widow. The yellow tape was gone, and the lights were back on in the windows. There was a tall, thin woman moving around inside the shop, someone he didn't recognize, and he remembered Margery's words about the coven in town.

Witches were real. They were here in Carman. And Dayna had known all along, he was suddenly sure of it. All her questions about the Butcher made sense now.

Was everything he'd believed a lie? Or merely just an incomplete picture? He wasn't sure how he was meant to go back to normal now. If normal was even achievable after witnessing what he had.

Sam glanced back at O'Neal's, at his Bible study, at the brightly lit insides of the shop. Mr. O'Neal was sliding a tray of milk shakes onto the table, and he could hear muffled laughter even from here.

Through the windows of Sage Widow he could see the tall woman in front of the shelves, rearranging a display of salt lamps which glowed in the dusky insides of the store.

All his life he'd believed one thing. He'd thought that belief had been solid.

But mystery had always called to him, hadn't it? Poking around in the dark was terrifying and thrilling, chasing the unknown was his calling.

There were always new things to discover.

Sam had covered his walls in unsolved cases, drawn in by the patterns, by the secrets. It had driven him into darker corners than he could possibly imagine, uncovered things he'd never dreamed of, but he knew now that he'd only touched the tip of the iceberg.

He wanted to know.

He took a deep breath and gently placed the Bible down on the railing. Then he turned to walk across the sidewalk and into the orange-lit glow of Sage Widow.

Chapter Sixty-One

MEINER

The drive back to the farmhouse was lonely.

It had made her chest feel strangely tight when Dayna decided to ride back with Reagan, but she shouldn't have been surprised. She hated herself for snapping like that. Someday, she'd succeed in driving everyone away, and there would be no one left at all.

Her temper was getting worse, and more disturbingly, she didn't seem to be able to keep a lid on it anymore. And in the heat of the moment she didn't *want* to. It was like itching a bite; it felt so good to give in.

She would apologize to Dayna later. She'd make it right somehow.

Right now though, she had more pressing problems. For a moment she only sat there in the driveway, the car ticking as the engine cooled. Then she reached into the bag on the passenger seat and pulled out the silver box she'd slipped into her pocket while the other witches had been intent on opening the safe.

Meiner bit the inside of her cheek, stroking a thumb over the crescent moon etched into the surface of the lid. The sight of it in the hotel room had made her chest tighten, a pang of shock passing through her.

Meiner could hardly count the number of times she'd told her grand-mother to put it away, that she couldn't smoke in restaurants and shops and people's houses. It was rarely missing from her gran's hand or pocket, so how did the brothers come to have it?

She cracked the box open, wrinkling her nose as the scent of tobacco hit her. The box was empty. She tried to remember when she'd seen Gran carrying this last. Days ago? A week?

The back of her neck prickled, and she pressed the lid closed firmly.

Her thoughts were spinning madly. Grandma King had been in the room, so what did that mean? That she'd somehow known where the men were and searched the room? But why leave the safe unopened? And why keep it a secret from both covens?

It didn't make sense, which left the more obvious and horrible conclusion: she'd gone to see the brothers. . . .

A deep breath, and Meiner pushed the driver-side door open. She was going to confront her, demand answers.

She climbed out and blinked around, surprised no one else was back. It was nearly full dark now, and the driveway was still empty. Grandma King and Cora must be home, of course, but neither Dayna and Reagan nor the Callighans had returned yet. Meiner went the rest of the way up the driveway, stopping at the first gate. She frowned.

The gate was splintered on its hinges, as if something had knocked it inward. *What the hell?*

There was a distant crash from the house, and Meiner jumped. A second later, white light blasted through the windows, and her heart dropped.

She could sense it now; the distinct prickle of strong magic being used. There was something off about it, too, something dark. And . . . there was something strange about the front of the house. Were those sigils . . . ?

Another crash. A muffled yell from the house.

Gran.

Meiner lunged forward, running full tilt, pulse pounding in her ears. She was through the first gate, the second, the third, chanting a protection prayer as soon as her feet hit the tile in the hallway. The vestibule was in a shambles, boots and shoes strewn over the floor, and one side of the wall was blackened. There was a scream from the kitchen, and Meiner barreled

in, skidding to a halt at the entrance. She stared in shock, barely registering the dull *thunk* as the silver box hit the floor at her feet.

Every inch of the kitchen walls was covered in bloodred symbols,
scrawled in a shaky hand.

Worse still, there were three men facing off with Gran. Grandma King
was backed into a corner by the sink, and when Meiner burst in, the men
looked up, surprise clear on their faces. In the beat of silence that followed,
Grandma King threw her hands up and let loose a vicious curse, her voice
snapping out like the crack of a whip. The nearest brother was thrown
back against the cupboards, his sword skittering across the tiles.

The old woman surged forward, throwing hexes, pressing the other
two brothers against the wall, sending dishes and cutlery crashing out of
their cupboards and drawers. Teacups and saucers shattered on the tiles,
and the shards skittered across the floor, whipping up to hang ominously
in the air for one beat, two, the sun glittering off the white surfaces, jagged tips pointed at the intruders. Then Grandma King flung her arms out,
words cutting the air just before the shards missiled forward, embedding
themselves into the walls with sharp little *chunk, chunk, chunk*s and goug-
ing bloody tracks across every inch of the brothers' skin.

The man with the sword scrambled to his feet, using his blade to
guard his eyes from the flying shards. He struck out toward Gran again,
and Meiner began another prayer under her breath, wishing desperately
she knew more. She was still a damn witchling. How was she supposed
to fight this?

She snatched a heavy bowl from the counter and whipped it at him,
and he grunted as it glanced off his temple, staggering backward.

"Kill that bitch, Dubh." The brother with the buzz cut snarled at her.
"Finish her—" He didn't get anything else out, because Grandma King
sent another nasty hex his way, snapping his head back.

"Meiner"—Grandma King did not take her eyes off the men—"run,
witchling. Go get the others." She threw up her hands as the long-haired
brother came at her, spitting out another hex as she warded off something
Meiner couldn't see.

"I won't leave you." Meiner turned toward the counter, looking for something, anything to throw, and felt herself slammed backward. Her shoes slid, and she screamed, striking her shoulders and back painfully on the cupboards.

"Go, you fool." Grandma King stepped in front of her. "You won't last."

"I would if you'd *trained* me," she gasped out. It was a ridiculous time to bring it up, but she couldn't seem to help it. One of the drawers came shooting out beside her, and she flinched, before reaching out to snatch up a steak knife. From her position on the floor she couldn't help looking up at the walls, at the symbols dripping down the white wallpaper. They didn't look like anything she'd seen before, and she felt a sick squirming in her stomach if she looked at them for too long. "But you're making *Cora* head witch."

Grandma King grunted, hand up to block another spell.

One of the men cried out as Grandma King's magic pressed him against the far wall of the kitchen, scraping his back against the towel hooks as he was dragged up toward the ceiling. Meiner watched, eyes wide.

"You aren't like me, child. You won't do what needs to be done."

"What the hell are you talking about?"

"You'll see. Tarraing forsa!" Grandma King jerked an arm up, like she was conducting an orchestra, and suddenly the shaved-headed brother was struggling to walk toward her. The air around him shimmered, turned thick.

"Cora won't be any better." Meiner climbed to her feet, brandishing the knife, gaze flicking from one brother to the next. Both Dubh and the shaved-headed brother were approaching again, more warily than before. Again, she glanced at the symbols on the wall, the smears of red against white. "These runes . . ."

"I do what needs to be done," Grandma King repeated, and then she snapped, "Balor, glacaim mé ort!" and clapped her weathered hands together.

A metallic rasp seemed to coincide with her motion, a blade drawn from a scabbard played in stereo, and an awful, heavy weight filled the room. Meiner darted a frantic glance at her grandmother, struggled to draw a breath into her lungs, feeling gooseflesh erupt over both arms.

There was something there in the kitchen with them, something far more terrifying than the brothers. She could feel its presence, and it was strangely, horribly familiar. It reminded her of childhood, of nights spent barricaded behind the bedroom door, she and Cora barely breathing under their sheets, the darkness quiet and heavy around them.

A strangled cry jerked Meiner's head up, just in time to see it happen.

Something rippled in front of the brothers, a shimmer in the space before them, and then a slash of light split the air. The three men staggered back. Two of them clutched at their necks, faces pale, blood inexplicably gushing between their fingers. The one in the center pivoted slightly, and the same invisible force missed his throat, slashing his shoulder open. He screamed, face twisted in pain and rage as his brothers crumpled on either side of him.

The old woman lifted her hands again as the one with the sword charged forward. Grandma King threw another blast of light, but this time he ducked, driving his blade up.

Meiner only half saw it happen. She saw her grandmother's body stiffen, blood running down the groove in the blade, dark and smooth. Across the room there was a thud and a groan as one of the men turned over, blood still pulsing from his neck. The man with the sword stood back, panting.

"No!" Meiner pitched forward as her grandmother slumped to the ground. When she tried to catch her the old woman pushed her off. "Run."

She looked up, heart in her throat, as the brother with the sword approached. He was smiling, an awful expression. He seemed unaffected by the huge bloody gash running down the left side of his face. "That was easier than I thought."

The rage hit Meiner then, molten hot and as bright as any magic. It drove her forward, sent her crashing into him. The knife clutched in her hand met resistance and then slid past, piercing the man's chest. He screamed, his sword hitting the floor with a metallic clang, and she felt the warmth of his blood rush over her hands. Something flared to life in her chest, smoldering embers that filled her with heat to the tips of her fingers. The rage wanted *more, more, more.*

She reared back, about to plunge the knife in again.

"Dubh!"

One of the brothers was calling his name, and Meiner was yanked off roughly, thrown against the cupboards for the second time, striking her temple. She blinked, dazed, her head throbbing.

No, it couldn't be either brother. They'd both been on the floor, their throats slashed by Gran's spell. She struggled to sit up, head spinning.

Olc, the one with the shaved head, was still on the floor, blood spilling out onto the slick tiles. He clutched his chest, gasping and wheezing. How was he still alive?

More staggering still was the sight of the long-haired man standing up, clutching his throat, the blood still flowing between his fingers and down his neck, saturating his T-shirt. He was leaning over his brother, brow furrowed, but Dubh was already struggling to his feet, ignoring the gaping wound in his chest and shoulder.

Beside Meiner her grandmother stirred slightly, wheezing, and Meiner looked up just as the old woman seized her wrist in a cold, iron grip. She jerked in surprise as Grandma King slammed her hand down onto the kitchen floor, pushing Meiner's palm into the pool of blood spreading across the tiles. "Use it," she rasped, nodding at the rune repeating on the far wall. "Trace that . . . Say your pledge to Balor . . ." She paused, eyelids flicking open and shut, struggling to speak. "Save them all."

Shocked, Meiner jerked her hand out of the blood. She stared at Grandma King's pale face, twisted in pain, and remembered the dark shadows that skittered across the walls of their house, the faint whispers in the hallways, the heavy presence of *something* that seemed to suck all the air out of the room.

Balor. The goat-headed god. The god of drought and blight.

Grandma King wanted her to pledge herself to *that.*

"Are you insane?"

The old woman's voice was like steel rasping on concrete. "You have *no choice.*"

There was a shuffling sound from across the kitchen. The third brother had climbed to his feet, and now he stooped down to pick up his sword, blood splattering the tiles. Her grandmother's blood, mingling with the brothers' on the kitchen floor.

His eyes were fixed on her. Meiner couldn't breathe.

They should be dead.

The god her grandmother had pledged her soul to had slashed their throats, and yet . . . it still wasn't enough.

Her grandmother's words came back to her now. *You aren't like me, child. You won't do what needs to be done.*

Was this what was needed to be done? Pledging herself to one monster to stop another?

The brother with the sword took a step forward, a smile curling the corner of his mouth. "We're going to wipe your town off the map, witch. First you and your coven, then all of Carman." He smiled, crooked and horrifying. "And then the whole damn country. Ireland will burn for what it's done to her."

Meiner glanced around, frantic. Her gaze fell on the symbol on the wall, which seemed to be illuminated by the rays of the setting sun creeping through the window. Her hand was still wet with Gran's blood. It would be easy to press her fingers into the tiles, to trace the simple, clean lines of the rune.

She glanced over at her grandmother, half expecting to see her glaring up at her, only to find her slumped on the ground, unmoving.

Die alone, or pledge herself to a dark god. *Save them all.*

Lose her soul.

Become her grandmother.

No.

There was nothing but a fork within reach, and Meiner snatched it up, head spinning. Dubh paused and looked at the fork, brows raised.

He was about to move again, and Meiner braced herself—fork or no fork she was going to fight him—and then there came a distant thud from outside, the sound of a door slamming. The brothers jerked in surprise, and Dubh tilted his head, eyes wide. Then he looked back at the one with the long hair. "Too much magic," he muttered. "Let's go."

The long-haired brother looked like he was going to protest, and then he jerked suddenly, fishing into his pocket to pull out his phone. Whatever was on the screen made him smile, wide and horrible, the sight made even more macabre by the blood gushing down his front. "Fine. We've got to get to Newgrange before sunset anyway, and I want to make a stopover first."

Meiner stared at them, unable to look away from the ghastly spectacle they made. Dead men walking. She felt hollow with shock as they moved for the sliding door at the back of the kitchen. They were walking away, leaving a wide trail of glistening blood in their wake.

The one with the sword, Dubh, stooped down to pick up the silver box, cradling it in his palm with a nasty smile. "I told you I'd be back to get this when you took it from me all those years ago." His grin stretched wider, into a snarl, and he shoved the box into his pocket. "I win, witch."

The door banged shut and then the brothers were gone.

Chapter Sixty-Two

DAYNA

The moment she walked through the door, she knew things weren't going to go well. Fiona was waiting for her in the hallway, arms crossed over her chest. The woman had on a bathrobe and her hair looked tangled, as though she hadn't washed or brushed it in days. The back of her neck was already prickling as she stepped in and eyed Fiona warily.

"Where is he?"

"There you are." Fiona's dark eyes were wider than they should have been, her pupils dilated, like she'd ingested large amounts of caffeine. Dayna took a step back toward the door, clutching her bag beneath her arm. The edge of the leather book dug into the top of her rib cage. She regretted saying she'd hold on to it.

"Where's Dad?" She edged around Fiona and moved down the hall into the kitchen. Empty. "He sent me a text."

"I'm afraid he didn't." Fiona's voice from behind her was a hiss, and alarm sparked along the surface of Dayna's skin, raising the fine hairs on her arms. The woman's cheeks were flushed, eyes wide and feverish.

A split-second decision was all it took. Her father wasn't here, he hadn't texted her, and she wasn't going to stay here. Fiona wasn't safe right now.

She was turning for the door when Fiona lunged.

Dayna gasped, scrambling back into the cupboards. Her mother's hands were claws, wildly grouping for her hair and clothes, scratching her face.

"Stop! What the hell are you doing?" Dayna's arms shot out, the heels of her hands connecting with her mother's shoulders, sending the woman stumbling.

"I know you've got it!" With a savage scream Fiona regained her balance and barreled forward. Dayna felt her book bag wrestled from under her arm and Fiona shrieked, hands swiping through the air as she grabbed for it.

"You stole it. You're monsters, all of you!"

Dayna watched in horror as Fiona pulled the leather book from the bag, holding it out triumphantly. "Give me that!" Dayna lunged for the book, and Fiona jumped back, eyes glittering. One of Dayna's hands closed over the cover, and Fiona yanked it away. There was a tearing sound as the book was wrenched open, and several pages floated to the ground.

Fiona gathered the book in her arms, cradling it against her chest. "I know what you are."

Dayna was no longer paying attention. She had gone still, frozen.

One of the papers had landed faceup on the floor, revealing a colorful illustration. The top was inscribed with *The Morrigan*, and underneath were three women in black robes.

The one on the right was stooped with age, her face lined, her eyes glittering black. She held a delicate, twisting hourglass made of crystal. To her left stood a dark-haired woman, laugh lines at her eyes, a smile on her lips. There was a large, hook-beaked bird on her shoulder, a raven. Standing on her other side was the youngest woman. Her gaze was faraway, fixed on something in the distance, crimson lips set in a firm line. In her hands she held a long, slender sword, the point tipped toward the earth.

The picture was striking, but it was not the artwork that made Dayna stare in shock. Ignoring her mother's frenzied muttering, she stooped to pick the paper up.

She knew the picture, or at least, what it represented. The mother, the maiden, and the crone. But what made her heart stop in her chest were their faces, so finely detailed, so artfully painted. So *familiar*.

It felt like a bolt of lightning had pierced her core, had lit her up from the inside out and crystallized her bones like sand. This wasn't possible.

The mother, the maiden, and the crone. Her mentors. Her coven members. Her *family*, staring up at her from the page.

The Callighans.

She remembered the way the black scrawled writing had looked against the wallpaper. The name that had been next. Morrigan. *The* Morrigan.

The Callighans were next on the list.

Chapter Sixty-Three

DAYNA

She had to tell them. Had to let them know they were in danger.

Reagan was still waiting for her in the driveway, Dayna thought. She would run out and they'd drive straight to the coven house. Dayna turned on her heel, blood pounding in her ears, and then stopped, shocked.

There was a man in the doorway. He was short, slender but muscular, dressed in a gray cotton T-shirt splattered with blood. Wavy blond hair framed his face, where a thin red scar ran down his cheek.

"You." The sight of him sent a shock of cold through her, and she was too stunned to move. She realized suddenly that she'd seen him before, twice now, at Sage Widow. He'd bumped into her in the doorway the first time, and then she'd seen him on the porch weeks later, before finding Margery. Finding the body must have wiped it completely from her mind; she hadn't remembered that until now.

She recognized the boyish face and blue eyes. The blond curls and the charming grin.

Fiona edged toward him, her smile wide, eyes glittering with that mad light.

She'd been lured here.

"Do you have any idea what you've done? These men—" She broke off, frozen. Her mother's face was changing again, but this time it was accompanied by a strange, low chuckle, a laugh that seemed to build and get louder, that made all the hairs on the backs of her arms stand up. Dayna flinched, panic cutting through her anger. What the hell was this?

When the woman spoke, it sounded nothing like her. Her voice was a low, raspy growl. "Idiot child. I saw through you, but you never saw me. You and your father are fools."

Dayna stared at her, mouth open, panic crawling slowly through her. "Who are you? *What* are you?" Her voice was shaky.

"I've waited so long," the thing that was not Fiona whispered, and the woman stroked one pale, spidery hand over the cover of the book. She flicked her wide-eyed gaze to Dubh. "I did well, didn't I? I knew who the Butcher truly was. I followed your pattern and knew I had to return when you came to Carman." She darted a sideways look at Dayna, her smile crooked and too wide. "I knew it was her, look." She tucked one hand into her pocket and came out with a tattered scrap of paper. It was covered in Fiona's wild handwriting, the same thing repeated over and over.

Dayna, Dayna, Dayna.

And at the bottom, where her not-mother was indicating:

Dayna, Dayna, Dayna, Daya, Daya, Daga, Dagda, Dagda. The Dagda.

The Dagda. One of the gods who'd locked Carman away.

This was insane. They couldn't possibly believe this.

"I'm not a god, I'm a witch." Dayna turned back to the blue-eyed man. "And my coven knows where I am. They're just outside—"

Her words ended with a scream as he struck her across the face, sending her staggering back. Her cell phone cracked onto the tiles and skittered underneath the kitchen table, where the light on the screen flickered weakly.

She braced herself on the kitchen counter, head spinning. For a few seconds she could only blink frantically, trying to clear her vision, her ears ringing. She'd never been struck before. It was shocking, but the adrenaline was enough to drive her back up, fingers curled into fists. The man was moving toward her again, only this time he took slow, leisurely steps. He was still smiling, face lit with ugly enjoyment.

To her horror there were others in the kitchen now. A taller man whose face was a mask of blood, his blond hair long and tangled, held a dish towel across his throat, and another man with a short, bristling buzz cut and heavy black brows. The man with the buzz cut had a thick scarlet line across his neck that was gushing blood all down his already soaked T-shirt. While she watched, he snatched a tea towel off the kitchen counter, knotting it around his throat like a handkerchief.

Three brothers, she had time to think, and then the shortest man was nearly on top of her. She turned for the drawer, throwing her hands up, gasping the spell out. There was one beat, two, when nothing happened, and she felt the emptiness in her stomach twist and thought she might be sick.

Yemi's warning rang in her head, about not burning through the magic too fast. But she'd used it all to fight the shadow.

She had no magic left.

A second later the scar-faced brother crashed into her, shoving her back into the edge of the counter. The wind left her lungs in a rush, and Dayna wheezed.

She turned, just as fingers tangled in her hair and her head was wrenched painfully back. Her mouth opened in a silent scream, but it was all she could do to draw breath. The sound of her not-mother's feverish mutterings filled the kitchen, as one of the brothers tried to get the book from her.

"I'm holding it for her," Fiona protested. "She'll want to see me."

The brother with the shaved head laughed unkindly. "Angus Og, you sad bastard. Still running around after her like a kicked puppy centuries later." He snorted. "God of love, my pockmarked left ass-cheek."

"Our mother entertained herself with you." The brother with the bloody face curled his lip at Fiona. "You were a plaything, nothing more. Now give us the book."

"It's mine. You said I could come. I want to see Carman again—"

"Olc," the man holding Dayna's hair growled from somewhere above her head. "Do us all a favor and shut that bitch up."

There was a sharp crack, followed by the sound of a body crashing to the floor. Dayna jumped, then tried to twist around in the man's grasp, but the motion sent pain blazing through her scalp. He caught her arm and pulled it behind her back, and she gasped. Her skin crawled as his breath tickled her neck.

Her left hand was still free, and she reached out blindly for the open drawer, but he dragged her backward. "No knives, no iron," he rasped, and then sharply, "Leave her, Olc. There's no time. Get the book and wait in the car. And find something to bandage your damn face."

The one with the bloody face grunted, a noise of disappointment.

"Get that thing around her neck."

The brother with the bloody face, Calma, came forward. He scowled at Dayna, who flinched back as he reached for her throat. His face looked murderous, but his fingers only closed around the leather cord around her neck. He jerked it hard enough that she gasped in pain as the leather broke, and then threw the bone pendant to the ground, face twisted with disgust.

Dayna's mind was racing, and horror sent a sick chill through her. Her body was completely drained, so she had no way to protect herself.

What good was a witch without magic?

There weren't many spells she could do without raw power, but there were oaths, prayers of protection. As soon as Calma turned away she began mumbling under her breath, all the invocations she knew: for protection, for revenge on her enemies, for strength. She got through the third one as the scarred brother dragged her down the hall toward the door, and then he jerked her against his chest, releasing her hair, and a hand pressed over her mouth. Her nose filled with the overpowering scent of smoke, and a wave of repulsion and terror washed through her.

Can't breathe. Can't breathe. Can't breathe.

Panic rippled over her skin, constant, unending. There was no logic, only animal terror.

"No spells from you, witchling." He sounded almost amused, and unexpectedly a trickle of anger mixed with the fear pulsing through her, burning in her chest like a brand. It grew hotter the more she focused on it, until it blazed through her. Rage.

She wasn't a witchling. She was a full-fledged witch.

Dayna dragged air in through her nose. *Fuck this.* She was going to survive. She was going to stop them. She was going to call the cops on her weird, possessed mother and get on medication once she got out of this.

The one with the bloody face met them in the kitchen doorway. "Her friends are waiting in the driveway. We go out the back." He glanced down at Dayna. "Don't we just need a piece of her for the ceremony? Why don't we just cut off a bit and go?" He grinned at the horrified look on Dayna's face. Apparently he'd found bandages somewhere and had done a sloppy job of binding his wound, winding them around his face and neck so that he looked like a half-wrapped mummy. When his brother snorted at the sight of him he scowled.

"Shut up."

"We're not cutting off any bits yet," the one called Dubh said. "We need her alive to bait the last ones on the list. Now get her in the car."

The Callighans. She wasn't the only one in danger.

Dayna stopped struggling, allowing herself to be dragged out the back door, toward a shiny black car parked on the narrow backstreet. Her mind was racing again, fear making her pulse flutter frantically in her throat.

Reagan and Yemi would only wait so long before bursting in. They would see Fiona Walsh on the floor, the open drawer, the spilled knives. They would know something had happened.

And it didn't matter that they wouldn't know where the men were taking her. Witches had ways of finding out. With Grandma King and the Callighans, there had to be a way to trace her.

Her coven would find her. They would tear these men apart to get to her.

She held on to this thought as the man shoved her into the car, forcing her to sit between him and the shaved-headed Olc, who told her in no uncertain terms what would happen if she tried to reach for the door. Dayna didn't reply. She shut her eyes and breathed in deeply. In and out. Long and even.

She could wait.

Chapter Sixty-Four

MEINER

Meiner's phone rang again and she ignored it.

It was an easy thing to do, since the sound seemed to be distant and echoing. Nothing felt real. This was all some fucked-up dream.

She glanced down and realized she had blood splashed across her front, up her arm and shoulder. And her hand was still covered, a gore-encased glove. A wave of nausea ran over her. Grandma King had thought her too weak to lead the coven, and in the end maybe she was. She hadn't been able to pledge herself to her grandmother's god. Hadn't been able to save her.

Cora had returned minutes later to find her sitting in the middle of the kitchen in a pool of blood, too shell-shocked to pick herself up off the floor. Once Meiner had told her what happened, the blond girl seemed to recover herself surprisingly fast. She'd lifted Grandma King onto the couch in the living room.

Seeing the still figure took Meiner's breath away all over again, and she hunched forward, gasping, hand braced against the brick fireplace.

Grandma King was dead. It seemed impossible.

Cora disappeared into the hallway for a moment, leaving Meiner with the body, and in spite of the bile rising in her throat, she edged closer, frowning. One of her grandmother's arms was up on her chest, and her loose blouse had been torn away at the shoulder. The edge was stained with blood, and there was a deep cut on her arm, not a jagged slash, but even and deliberate. She remembered suddenly, through the haze, seeing one of the brothers stoop over her gran briefly, before they left. She'd assumed they were checking to see if she was dead, but...

Had they taken blood?

Suddenly furious, she stalked forward, reaching out to pull up the old woman's sleeve. Then she paused, startled. There was a mark above the cut, a black ink pattern etched into her grandmother's weathered skin. It looked like a strange cross between a pentacle and a spiderweb, and Meiner squinted down at it, puzzled.

She didn't remember her gran having any tattoos. But then, there was so much that her grandmother obviously hadn't told her.

The silver box, for a start. Dayna had been right: her gran and the Butcher had met before. She was willing to bet he'd given her that scar.

"I guess we have to clean up the kitchen."

Meiner jumped. Cora was in the doorway, looking pale and hollowed out with shock.

Meiner only nodded and turned back to Grandma King. "Did you know she had—" She cut herself off abruptly. The skin on her grandmother's shoulder was bare. There was nothing but traces of blood showing through her tattered blouse now.

Meiner blinked.

Cora didn't seem to be paying attention. She was staring at Gran, her eyes glittering. "We should go after those motherfuckers. Where did they go?"

"Newgrange." Meiner couldn't seem to take her eyes off the tear in her grandmother's blouse. She knew *something* had been there.

It wasn't like she was driven mad by grief. She hadn't loved her grandmother. She hadn't even *liked* her. Of course, the woman had raised her. Had been a constant presence in her life, as unwelcome as that may have been through the years. Mostly she didn't know what to feel, so she just felt numb.

But she'd definitely seen something, and now it was gone. Another of her gran's secrets.

Cora's face was set in stubborn lines. "They're going to keep trying to pick us off like this. We need to find them, and we need to kill them. It won't be easy, but we can do it. *I* can do it." Her eyes flicked over Meiner's face, her voice holding an unspoken challenge. "She was going to pass the coven on to me, so it's my call. I say we track them down."

Any other time Meiner would have balked at this, but she felt too numb to argue. Cora was taking charge in an emergency, the perfect time to step in and take on the mantle of leadership.

Everything seemed so far away from reality that it hardly mattered.

"Sure," she said, her voice hollow. "You do that."

Cora's brows knit together. She scowled at Meiner. "You can't sit around and feel sorry for yourself, Meiner King. You think your grandmother would have done that? You think she would have wanted that?" Her face twisted, like she was about to say something else and then thought better of it.

Now it was Meiner's turn to look at Cora, narrowing her eyes. "She never actually said she left you the cov—" Meiner started, and then jerked to a stop when there was the rattle and groan that signified the Callighans were coming up the driveway in the station wagon.

When Meiner and Cora went to the front door, the Callighans were in the garden staring up at the sigils on the front of the house, and Bronagh swept them over with a steely gaze. "What's happened? It stinks of dark magic."

Meiner only stared at her. Cora was the one to explain, while she retreated to the front room and sat down in front of the shoe racks, feeling like there was a physical weight on her chest.

She kept thinking about her grandmother's last spell.

Balor, glacaim mé ort.

She had repledged herself, Meiner was sure of it, which meant she hadn't been practicing black magic until the very end.

Not that it made anything better. . . .

"You don't want to know what the kitchen looks like," Cora was saying.

"I can hazard a guess," Bronagh grunted. Then she sighed. "Still calling on the same god who got her kicked out of Carman so many decades ago. The coven dissolved after that. Some of us quit after witnessing true dark magic for the first time."

"She said she would do what she had to," Meiner mumbled.

"And she did." Bronagh wove her fingers together and tipped her head forward, like she was saying a little prayer or a spell in the direction of the kitchen. "They're wounded, and gods or no, wounded animals are reckless when they're backed into a corner." She waited for Faye and Brenna to follow Cora into the kitchen, and then sank down beside Meiner, skirts pooling at her feet.

"Humor me a minute, lass."

Meiner flinched as Bronagh reached out and grasped her hand, turned it over to look at her palm. She had cleaned herself up as best she could in the bathroom, and the blood was mostly gone, but Bronagh still narrowed her eyes at her hand as if she could see it somehow. "Did you do it?" she said softly, and when Meiner shook her head Bronagh's face softened with relief. "Good lass. You made the right choice, though I know it must have been hard."

"Bronagh, Gran . . . she had a tattoo on her—at least, it looked like one. It vanished when she died."

"What did it look like?"

Meiner hesitated. "Like . . . a weird spiderweb, mixed with a pentacle maybe. And sort of . . . spiky looking."

The older witch frowned. "It sounds like a spirit trap, something to draw in spirits and bind them. But you draw it on the ground, never on yourself, unless you're asking for possession."

Meiner swallowed hard and nodded, not wanting to hear any more. What exactly had her grandmother been planning?

The two of them started, and Meiner jumped to her feet, as the front door thumped open.

It was Reagan, standing on the doorstep, breathing hard. Her dark eyes were wide. "Dayna. When I dropped her off...We think— We're pretty sure they have her."

Meiner gaped at her, dumbstruck. The news seemed to penetrate the wall of numbness surrounding her. "What?"

Reagan opened her mouth to say something else, and then there was the roar of an engine as Yemi turned the minivan around in the driveway, which brought Faye, Brenna, and Cora back into the front room.

Reagan didn't bother to explain again. "All of you, get in."

Chapter Sixty-Five

DAYNA

They were going to kill her.

She knew this with a kind of distant, horrified certainty, because when they led her from the car, across an open stretch of green field, they didn't bother to blindfold her. And when they reached the massive green mound in the center, the tomb had been set up for a ritual.

She recognized the area, the bleached stones at the front, the huge, fenced-off entrance covered in swirling runes. The last time she'd been to the Newgrange tomb had been a class field trip years ago. It had been busy, full of tourists and sunshine. Now the mound loomed over them in the dim light, the dirt lanes around both sides still and empty.

Dubh clutched her arm tightly, shoving her down into the center of a sprawling hexagram. She'd initially thought it was made of white branches, some of them burned or charred. But from the ground, her cheek pressed into the grass, she could see the hexagram was made of bones. Some of them old, cracked and splintered and bleached by the sun, and some disturbingly fresh, stained red in patches.

She swallowed the bile rising in her throat, and watched as they hacked at the grass, turning up the earth inside four points of the hexagram.

Dubh created a shallow hole, into which he dropped a shriveled bit of red meat. A tongue, Dayna realized, horror crawling up her spine. She looked away while he repeated this process with other body parts, muttering under his breath. When the impatient one, Olc, tried to grab something out of the cooler at his feet, Dubh slapped his hand away.

"No. This time it needs to be in order. Go watch for the others."

Olc grumbled under his breath at this, but both brothers went, moving around either side of the tomb.

Beside the rocky wall of the mound they'd set out a scattering of black stones, and a goblet full of what looked suspiciously like blood. Carved into the stones around the entrance was Carman's symbol. Dayna stared at it, eyes watering. The carvings filled her with a kind of creeping horror. They meant something was about to happen. Something horrible.

They still had two points of the star to fill, which meant they had taken a fourth victim recently. Dayna swallowed hard. She would be the next point, and then the Callighans.

Dubh released her, stepping outside the circle. Dayna's muscles were coiled, her body flooded with adrenaline, and for a second she thought about scrambling to her feet and making a break across the field. She was practically on the balls of her feet when she noticed Dubh watching. He seemed to be able to guess what she was thinking, because a cruel smile curved his lips.

"Go ahead," he said. "I like it when they run." He gestured across the field. "I'd be able to see you for miles, and you don't have any magic left. I can feel it."

She watched, feeling sick, as he hunkered down beside her, balancing a thin silver cigarette case on his knees. He seemed so casual as he took one out and lit it up, like he was a tourist pausing for a smoke, instead of someone about to sacrifice a stranger in the center of a hexagram.

Dubh saw her watching and grinned, tapping the top of the silver case. "Broke into your friend's car earlier and took this right out of the old woman's bag. Knew it would fuck with her when she realized I was coming for her. Did she go batshit when she saw it was missing?"

He thought she'd been looking at the silver case, she realized, though it had hardly been the first thing on her mind. "No," Dayna said. "Didn't seem to notice it was gone."

That wasn't true. She remembered now; Grandma King had torn apart the house looking for something, and they'd dismissed it as more of her dementia showing.

Dubh shrugged, but his smile had vanished, and Dayna felt a little spark of satisfaction at the lie.

"They're not here yet." The man with the shaved head reappeared, walking across the grass to stand at the edge of the hexagram. He had the leather book tucked under one arm, and he tipped his head back to survey the sky. "Our window is closing. We should kill her now and take what we need."

"You don't kill the bait, idiot," Dubh growled at him. "Have a little patience for once."

"Are you sure this is it? We only have one chance." He frowned down at the hexagram.

"It's exactly as it says in the book."

Every muscle in her body was still screaming for her to run, but Dayna forced herself to stay very still. The tomb and the hulking rocks surrounding it cast long shadows as the sun crept inch by inch toward the hilltops. The coming darkness was somehow both threatening and comforting. Under cover of the shadows, she reached out slowly, while Dubh was still glaring at his brother, her fingers closing around a long, sharp bone on the inside edge of the hexagram.

She shifted, covering it with her arm. It was about the right length, and she shuddered at how perfectly it hid beneath her forearm. An arm bone, probably, splintered at the end where the wrist should have been. She pressed her arm against the makeshift dagger and forced herself not to flinch when Dubh turned back to her, smiling, and said in a low voice, "Bone."

"What?" Her stomach plummeted, and she braced herself, sure he'd seen the makeshift dagger she'd stolen.

"In case you were wondering what we'll be taking from you." His eyes glittered. "Blood and bone, ash and soot. Your friends are on their way."

She tried not to let the relief show on her face. He hadn't noticed the subtle gap in his hexagram.

Slowly, she pressed her thumb against the tip of the bone, pricking the skin until she felt a drop of blood bead on the tip. Sometimes, blood magic was stronger. Yemi didn't approve, saying it could lead to darker things, but she had little choice. She waited until he'd turned back to the field and then whispered a quick spell of protection.

"Sciath dom. Cosain dom. Please, Danu, hear me."

Nothing. No familiar rush of power, not even a spark. Her stomach sank.

Her friends were coming, and they were about to walk into a trap. Dubh was right about one thing: the brothers would be able to see them coming. Dayna dragged in a shaky breath and clutched hard at the grass beneath her fingers. When she got the chance, she would have to use the bone dagger. But could she?

She tried to imagine the bone in her hand, throwing herself forward, plunging the jagged point into living skin.

Dubh paced toward the point of the star, and she saw him finger the hilt of his sword. "Try not to look so worried, witch. You won't be the only one to die tonight, just the first of thousands. After she rises she'll purge the land of the descendants of the Tuatha de dannan. All who wronged her will die in agony. The rest of your coven, for example. Maybe we'll even save the white-haired witch for last," he said, and he bared his teeth. "Not because she needs to die, but just for fun."

Dayna's fingers wrapped around the bone dagger, and she narrowed her eyes at Dubh's back when he turned away. She remembered her words from the car ride—it seemed like an age ago—what she'd confessed to Meiner. Now she knew it was true.

She would kill for her coven. And he would be first.

Chapter Sixty-Six

MEINER

A fire had replaced the numbness. A burning in her chest that ached and pulsed, and Meiner slammed her foot down on the gas pedal, the car growling and rattling as it shot down the back roads. The wood-paneled station wagon in her rearview mirror did not fall behind; Bronagh was going just as fast.

When she found the brothers, she would make them pay for what they'd done. For killing her grandmother, for taking Dayna.

Dayna. The name repeated in her head with each beat of her pulse. *Dayna, Dayna, Dayna.*

They had her, were probably planning on sacrificing her. What had she said to Dayna last? She couldn't remember her words, just the emotion behind them, the anger. Hot and irrational and misdirected. She hadn't been mad at Dayna, and yet they'd fought. She'd seen the wounded look on the other girl's face and she hadn't apologized. Too stubborn. Too stupid.

"They know we're coming." Reagan's face was ashen, and she kept fiddling with her seat belt. She looked how Meiner felt.

In the passenger seat, Cora gripped the door handle, knuckles white. "Of course they do. They've killed one of us, taken another. They know we'll come after them."

Gravel popped under the tires as Meiner pulled into the lot. They met in the center of the lot just as the sun slipped below the fields stretching out around them. The three Callighans' faces might have been stone masks, save for the flicking of their dark gazes as they looked at one another. Cora was white-faced and tight-lipped, her fists clenched at her sides. Reagan looked grim and determined, and her lips were moving constantly, as if she were silently reciting spells back to herself, or saying protection prayers. Yemi kept running her fingers over the charm necklace at her throat.

Meiner shifted from one foot to the other. Her entire body felt charged with that familiar, buzzing energy. The anger pulsed through her in waves, clenching and unclenching her muscles, sucking the breath from her body. Meiner was done fighting it. She was going to release it, let it burn and rage out of control.

The tomb was a huge, ominous mountain in the distance. Dayna was there somewhere.

"Wait a moment, girl." Bronagh caught her sleeve as she turned. "Protection first."

"That will take too long." It came out in a snarl, and Meiner cut herself off, surprised, when Bronagh's grip tightened, and the old woman yanked her back.

"Protection," the old woman snapped, and Brenna added, "You'll need it."

"We'll all need it," Faye said.

Meiner forced herself to stay where she was while the Callighans began a protection spell, chanting, low and steady, in fluid Irish. She felt that familiar prickle of energy over her skin, raising the hairs on her arms. As eager as she was to get to Dayna, the magic felt good. It made her stronger.

Cora, too, seemed to feel the same thing, for she tipped her head back and shut her eyes, lips moving. Meiner wasn't sure if she was chanting along or mumbling her own spell.

It seemed to take forever, as Meiner felt layer after layer of protective magic drift over her skin. She shut her eyes and ground her teeth. Dayna was in the hands of the same men who'd spilled her grandmother's blood all over the kitchen floor.

Magic was too distant for this. Too impersonal.

She wanted to get her bare hands on them. At her sides, her fingers flexed involuntarily. She could almost feel them around their throats, closing around their thick necks, choking the life out of them.

She knew she would try to kill one of them. All of them. She'd become more like her gran than ever before. She didn't care.

The knowledge gave her a rush of adrenaline, and she glanced toward the tomb, hands twitching and tingling. The rage needed release.

At last Bronagh stepped back. Her lined face was slack, her eyes shut as she raised her hands. "The gods' blessings and protection on you, sisters." Then her eyes snapped open, and her face went hard. "We should go."

Yemi tilted her head back, staring up at the dark sky. "Oya, we don't have much time."

Meiner set off at a run, plunging into the darkness. Blood rushed in her ears, blocking out her ragged breaths. She ignored Cora, who cried out behind her, "Meiner, wait! We go together."

Bronagh's voice was already growing distant as Meiner's long stride took her deeper into the darkness. "Don't waste your breath, girl. The devil himself couldn't stop her."

The clouds overhead were so thick that only the barest slivers of moonlight slid through. She shouldn't have been able to see, and yet she could. Something else the Callighan women had obviously thought of. Grudgingly she admitted to herself that the magic had been necessary. Still, it had eaten up precious minutes, and Meiner put on another burst of speed.

Nearing the tomb, she could make out the shape of it more clearly. They were approaching the back. She could see movement at the base, someone walking around the stone wall. One of the brothers had seen her.

She slowed as she neared the edge, and it was probably what saved her. A second later she ran head-on into something solid where there'd been nothing before. The force snapped Meiner's head back, and she heard something crack. Pain spiked through the center of her face, and warmth gushed from her nose and down her chin. She staggered and went down hard on her knees.

It wasn't just her face. She could feel the first layer of her protection gone, shredded through by the dark, vicious energy that lined the space before her. When she looked up, eyes watering, she could make out the distortion in the air. Anger surged through her. If she'd paid more attention, she'd have seen that, but she'd been too eager to push forward, to get to Dayna. This was why emotions were dangerous. They made you reckless.

The thought was distant, a faint echo in the storm of rage. It didn't matter. Broken noses didn't matter, pain didn't matter. All that mattered was Dayna.

She'd been such an idiot this morning. She wasn't leaving town when this was over. Dayna was the only thing that made any of this bullshit worth it. She was the one good thing Meiner had, the only thing she hadn't fucked up. Until this morning, until she'd almost broken that, too.

Cora's voice came from behind her, exasperated. "Meiner, you complete muppet."

Meiner said nothing, just stayed there in the center of the field, still reeling. Something was digging into her left knee, a rock, probably, but it was only a footnote to the pain in her face. She started as something brushed her cheek. Cora's hands were cool, her slender fingers smoothing over Meiner's brow, onto the bridge of her nose. She flinched, about to pull away, and then the pain began to recede, slowly at first, dulling a bit at a time. Then it was entirely gone, and her shoulders slumped in relief.

"It's not fixed, but at least you won't feel it for a few hours."

Meiner stared up at her. She knew what sort of picture they made, her on her knees, her face a mask of blood. Cora standing over her, expression calm, determined. The clear leader.

How long had Cora been wishing for this?

She should have been grateful. The pain in her face was gone. In fact, she felt stronger, better than before. But with it came a slow, creeping feeling across her skin. Cora should not have been able to do that with a simple touch. Magic was rituals and chants and the slow, steady buildup of energy. What Cora had done was a small thing on the surface, but it shouldn't have been possible. Not for her. She wasn't even ascended yet.

Even as Meiner thought it, she realized it was wrong. Somehow she knew, just looking at Cora. At the shadows on her face, at the hungry light burning in her eyes. She had seen that look before, on Dayna's face after the ceremony. It had both fascinated and disturbed her.

"You did it, didn't you?" Meiner whispered, and she was surprised to hear her own voice break, to hear the hurt buried there. "You ascended."

Cora didn't speak, only continued to stare down at Meiner. She did not deny it.

When Meiner took a deep breath, it felt like her lungs were full of shattered glass.

The others had caught up, and still Cora said nothing, only offered Meiner a hand, which she took reluctantly. The other girl tugged her to her feet, lips pressed shut. The silence was as good as an admission. Cora did not look apologetic or ashamed, but she did flick Meiner a wary gaze, as if she were expecting her to say something.

Yes, it hurt. But it didn't matter now. None of her previous worries mattered, about the coven, about becoming her grandmother. Grandma King was gone, and Dayna was still there, and Meiner would kill all three brothers to get to her. And if they'd done something to her, anything at all, she'd kill them for that, too.

Dayna was still alive. She had to be. Gods, let her be alive.

Brenna arrived, stretching out a hand, bracelets jangling faintly in the silence. "It's down," she said curtly.

Bronagh kept her voice low. "They know we're coming. We spread out, half around one side, half around the other. We want them in our circle. Does everyone know the shield knot protection spell?"

It was the most basic of spells. Everyone nodded.

Faye turned a stern scowl on them. "Let us do the heavy lifting, just keep to the circle and send your protection over us."

Nobody argued, though Meiner thought bitterly that she hated feeling so helpless, forced to stand back and let someone else save Dayna. She wanted to charge in and start swinging.

"We have no element of surprise," Bronagh said. "But just keep walking, keep talking. We'll surround them. Let's go." She started forward, and the way she moved was regal, as if she were making an entrance at a party, rather than walking over a dark field toward a massive stone tomb.

They followed, and Meiner pressed eagerly forward. She'd be the first one after the Callighans, she was determined, though Cora was matching her pace, apparently just as eager to get there. Meiner glanced sideways. The blond girl's expression was hard and glittering. There was a smile playing on the edge of her lips. Meiner's stomach turned. Cora wasn't scared or worried: she was *excited*. She was anticipating this.

They split up, and Yemi, Reagan, and Faye disappeared around the side of the tomb.

Finally, after what seemed like forever, they rounded the side and the entrance came into sight. The brothers had set up their ritual to the left of the tomb.

The six-pointed hexagram, glistening and bone white in the silvery light, the bundles of oak leaves, the stone basin, the goblet of blood—it was not a ritual that Meiner had seen before, and yet, it was familiar somehow. The sight of it felt like lead weighing on her chest.

Two figures stood looking toward the center of the star, and one was turning to face them, but all Meiner could see was the figure crouched in the center of the hexagram. Dayna, her face bruised and dirt-smudged, her gray sweater falling off one shoulder. When she spotted them, her eyes went wide with alarm, and Meiner felt rage crash through her, molten hot. It mingled with the buzz in her system, with the magic lying dormant there, and she lifted her hands. She wasn't sure what she was going to do, maybe lunge forward and strangle the nearest man. Maybe throw a burst of uncontrolled magic.

Before she could do anything, Cora broke the line and hurtled forward.

Chapter Sixty-Seven

CORA

It was the magic that drove her forward. As soon as the first figure, dark and broad-shouldered, his eyes glittering in their mask of blood, turned around and smiled, something deep in the pit of her stomach roared to life. The magic surged through her body, sending raw energy crashing through her. It begged to be released. *Demanded.*

The sensation drove all rational thought from her head, and she charged forward before they could stop her. Throwing up her hands, she let the power burst up and out. She heard the chaotic laughter of the goddess in her ears, and a rictus grin stretched her lips, an echo of Caorthannach's mirth.

The bloody-faced man screamed as he was thrown, brought up short as his back met the nearest tree, folding his body into a U-shape with an ugly *snap*. He crumpled at the base of the trunk and did not get up.

Now that she was near enough, she could make out the hexagram— made of bones, she realized with a cold and terrible thrill—and Dayna within it. The objects on the points of the star, too: goblet, stone bowl, oak branches...

Grandma King's words echoed in her ears: *You'll know the time when it comes.*

Cora's blood sang with recognition. She could already hear the chant in her head. The power battered against the insides of her skin. Everything was as it should be.

Now. This was it.

Her moment to put things right. Kill the brothers and trap Carman forever.

She realized a second too late that she'd been distracted by the hexagram, just as one of the brothers turned from the crumpled figure beside the tree. He smiled, sharp and savage as his hand snapped up. An invisible force slammed into Cora's side, snapping her head to the left, smashing her body against the earth. Her face pressed into the cool grass, and the sky tilted and blurred overhead.

Someone was yelling. No, chanting. Several someones, from either side of her. The fluid syllables of Old Irish washed over her as she squeezed her eyes shut, struggling to pull air into her lungs.

Chapter Sixty-Eight

MEINER

At first all Meiner could see was Dayna, lying in the center of the hexagram, her face pale. Then Cora charged and everything went to shit. In the flash of stunned silence between Cora throwing the first brother into the tree and the second brother retaliating, Meiner managed to collect herself enough to figure it out.

The hexagram, the tomb, the objects laid out before it...it was all familiar. Incredibly, she recognized it. This was what Grandma King had been teaching her, or, at least, what she'd started teaching her. What she'd been preparing her for. Of course, all of that had ended abruptly. Whatever Meiner was supposed to do, she didn't know the full ceremony.

Frustration surged through her, but it was short-lived, because Cora hit the ground hard beside her. Reagan and Yemi continued chanting, but the three Callighan women moved inward, toward the hexagram, joining hands. The wind caught Meiner's hair and dragged it across her face, and through the curtain of white it looked as though Bronagh's pupils had dilated completely, filling her eyes so that only darkness stared out of the old woman's face.

Three voices spoke in perfect unison over the sound of the chanting, mingled with the howl of the wind. Or . . . became the howl of the wind. She wasn't sure.

The remaining brothers braced themselves. The nearest one struggled to pull his sword from the sheath at his waist, fighting some invisible force inch by inch, expression twisted with pain. When the blade at last rang free Faye faltered in her recitation. It was enough that the man took a step forward against the press of their magic, an ugly smile crawling across his battered face. Moonlight glittered along the length of his blade.

The shaved-headed brother turned toward Dayna, pulling a hunting knife from inside his jacket.

Reagan and Yemi were still chanting, voices ringing out more loudly still, and Reagan pressed forward, tugging out of her mother's grasp. She searched the ground for something as she recited her prayer, coming up with a fist-sized rock. She threw it, hard, and the rock hit him with enough force to knock him off his feet, knife flying out of his hand.

Meiner checked Cora quickly—she was struggling to her feet—and then turned on her heel. Half crouched, she started toward Dayna, and then froze. Incredibly, the man at the base of the tree had come to life, crawling toward the hexagram on his hands and knees. His long hair was matted with blood, and his back was unmistakably broken. His progress was a grotesque parody of human movement, a jerky puppet show. He looked up at Meiner, at her shock and disgust, and his bloody smile was like a wound in the center of his face. In his hand was his brother's hunting knife.

No.

Meiner launched herself forward, and for the second time that night, she felt something smash into the length of her body, sending her staggering back with a burst of pain.

Along the edge of the tomb Reagan broke off her chant and brought a hand up, calling out, "Ar ais as!" A deft twist of her wrist, and the man was flung backward several feet. Dubh had begun moving toward them, sword raised menacingly, and Reagan threw her hands up, resuming the protection chant.

Impossibly the bloody-faced brother was still moving. His body seemed even more twisted now, more broken. And yet somehow, he was inching his way across the ground.

Meiner barely felt any pain, barely paid attention as the blood trickled down her face, too intent on the crawling man. He was heading toward the hexagram. Toward Dayna.

No. "Dayna, behind you!"

Chapter Sixty-Nine

DAYNA

Dayna watched everything from a distance, shock hollowing her insides.

She was rooted to the spot. An invisible hand was squeezing her lungs, and she felt each panicked gasp in the closing of her own throat. Horror seized her bones and muscles, freezing her to the spot.

Meiner's cry woke her, but it was too late.

She shot to her feet, turned, and the bloody-faced brother barreled into her. The bone dagger in her hand went up, and she slashed at his face just as she saw the knife in his hand, a moment before it plunged past her skin and filled her shoulder with fire. The bloody-faced brother stumbled back with a sharp cry, clutching his face, but Dayna wasn't paying attention to him anymore. The bone dagger tumbled to the grass as white-hot pain drove up into the side of her chest. Then she was on the ground, in the center of the six-pointed star, and she could only see the endless night sky.

It was getting darker, and at first, she thought it was the edges of her vision fading, that she was sliding into unconsciousness. A moment later, she realized that a dark shadow was slowly moving across the full moon, blocking out its light.

No moon, no stars, she thought. Only darkness. And then, so much blood.

There was. It gushed from her shoulder, staining the grass, soaking into the thirsty soil. It felt like her body had an endless supply to offer, and it was giving it all. When she glanced over, her stomach surged, and she turned her head quickly, sure she was going to be sick. Through the bloody wound she'd seen a flash of white.

The bone in her shoulder.

Shouldn't she feel it more? Shouldn't the pain be worse?

The witch hunter loomed over her suddenly, his back hunched and crooked. He lashed out with a boot, kicking over the goblet of blood, splattering its contents across the nearest point of the star. He limped forward, and Dayna shrieked as he seized her wounded shoulder. Blackness surged at the corners of her vision as he flipped her over onto her stomach, pressing her shoulder hard into the dirt at the sixth point of the hexagram.

The earth trembled beneath her in response, and there was a cry of triumph from the witch hunter.

This was followed by an answering scream of outrage from across the hexagram. She thought it was Meiner, and then she couldn't remember why Meiner would be screaming in the first place.

The air was restless, stirring. The wind whipped the witches' hair around their faces and screamed past the standing rocks, but nothing touched her in the center of the hexagram. Nothing could reach her here, not while she was busy with the business of dying.

Something in the earth beneath Dayna shifted once again, and she shut her eyes, head spinning. The spell was almost complete. Carman was waking.

Chapter Seventy

MEINER

Meiner pulled herself to her feet in time to see the witch hunter with the broken back plunge his knife into Dayna's shoulder.

"Dayna!" The protest was ripped from her throat, her cry mingling with the other witches'. With Reagan's scream.

Meiner was moving, running for the hexagram. Her only thought was to get Dayna out of it before the witch hunter went back. Dayna wasn't dead. She couldn't be.

But there was so much blood. It spilled out onto the grass and stained the fabric of Dayna's shirt, spreading alarmingly fast. The witch hunter stooped down to grab Dayna, and Meiner put on another burst of desperate speed.

The ground surged beneath her, bucking and heaving under her feet as a low rumble started up, growing louder. The shadow was almost completely across the moon now. The night was so black it was hard to make out more than shapes in the darkness.

Meiner cried out, gritting her teeth, stumbling toward Dayna on shaky legs as the earth surged up to meet her, knocking her off balance. Everyone else seemed equally thrown off; even the brothers weren't moving, though the one with the sword attempted to stumble toward the Callighans.

After a moment the earth stilled, the roar breaking off. Meiner dove forward, throwing herself on the brother with the broken back. She jerked him up and off Dayna, a savage scream ripping from her throat as she threw him down outside the hexagram and put her fist into his face.

The skin on her knuckles bruised after three punches, broke after five. She hardly felt it.

She was roaring, throat raw, blood rushing in her ears, hitting him again and again. His face was a bloody mess, but she didn't stop.

The buzz coursed through her, lighting every inch of her skin. She was *alive, alive, alive*. It felt so good to give in, to let the rage take over. She hit him again and again, teeth bared in a savage snarl.

When she broke away, rearing back, her fist raised to strike again, she heard it. The wheezing gasp from the hexagram.

The ground seemed to drop out from under her.

Dayna.

She turned and stumbled forward, snatching at Dayna's arm. Her hand slipped over the girl's skin, slick with warm blood, and she tightened her grip on Dayna's wrist. With a grunt she pulled her up and out of the bone hexagram, depositing her limp body on the grass. She straightened, whirling around with her hands up, the buzz of magic surging as a deep voice said from behind, "It's too late."

The brother with the sword was smiling up at the tomb above them, his expression exultant. "Can't you feel her?"

As if triggered by his words, the roar began again.

A sharp, terrible crack followed, echoing around the clearing over the sound of the wind. Horror churned in Meiner's stomach. A deep split appeared along the surface of the grassy tomb, continuing down to break open the stone wall, which began to crumble in on itself. On the ground Dayna rolled over, limbs flopping bonelessly as she blinked up at the tomb. She looked dazed.

A low, angry buzz was coming from the mound, like someone had disturbed a nest of wasps.

Something was coming to life; something was waking.

The three brothers turned to face the tomb, faces tilted up to the mound. When they turned, Meiner saw black smoke leaking from their mouths, from their eyes. Their mouths moved in unison.

"D'éist me do ghlaoch. I listened to your call."

As one, their gazes flicked across the hexagram, fixing on the Callighans. Carman had begun to wake, and now the pentacle needed one last piece. Bronagh moved before they could, more swiftly than the old woman should have been able to, her daughter and granddaughter behind her. The witches were emanating a strange silvery light, as if they'd pulled the moonlight down for themselves.

They crashed together, witches and hunters, screams and cries drowning out Yemi's chanting, light eating away at the darkness. Meiner tensed, watching as Brenna flung one of the brothers across the clearing, at the same time Faye was sent crashing against the trunk of the nearest sapling, her expression twisted with pain and dismay as black smoke wreathed her.

As they were separated, the light from the three witches dimmed, and Meiner felt her chest tighten with dread. Something had happened to the witch hunters; the cracked tomb had bestowed new strength on them.

The shortest one, Dubh, charged forward. He swung his sword in a wide arc, and Bronagh caught it in clasped hands, her face like steel. They stayed locked there for a moment, Dubh's face filled with an ugly, eager light. Meiner realized with a horrible start that the smoke pouring off him seemed to be actively seeking the woman's face. It curled upward like it was alive, probing at Bronagh's skin. She turned her head away, but it persisted, twisting sooty tendrils up toward her eyes.

Dubh jerked his sword out of her hands, and Bronagh cried out, a thin arc of blood trailing through the air, splattering her gown. The witch hunter thrust the blade forward, his smile wide and ugly.

"No!" Meiner stumbled to her feet as the steel struck home, vanishing into the black dress, plunging into Bronagh's middle. The witch's face drained of blood, her mouth opened slightly.

She fell. It was a slow, gentle movement, as if she sank down onto the grass of her own accord, skirts billowing around her.

Above them, the barest sliver of silver moon had returned.

There was a terrible scream from Faye, echoed by her mother, and the two women were at Bronagh's side the next instant, so fast that Meiner had not seen them move. Brenna's scream was half animal, the shriek of a wild bird, and she crooked one clawed hand at Dubh, sending him backward, crashing into his brother.

This time the ground shook so powerfully that Meiner pitched forward, falling hard onto her hands and knees. When she looked up, the black smoke was billowing out around Bronagh, consuming the air around it, engulfing the three women.

Dubh turned from the Callighan women, his face triumphant. His sword was still gripped in his right hand, still stained with Bronagh's blood. His eyes were all pupil, tear ducts leaking black smoke. His gaze raked across the hexagram, came to rest on Dayna. Meiner stiffened.

Reagan hurtled forward as the witch hunter limped toward Dayna. She placed herself in front of the bone hexagram, hands raised, her voice low and furious as she chanted under her breath. The shimmer in the air slowed Dubh, and his face twisted with the effort. His body moved as if he waded through sludge. Still he moved forward, and Reagan's arms shook as she held them aloft. He was fighting the magic.

Meiner could think of only one thing to do. Even though it was reckless. Even though she had no clue what it might do, and every instinct was screaming to go to Dayna. They had run out of options, and now all she had was the mad hope that Gran had been on their side all along. That she had known all of this was going to happen.

She ground her teeth and forced herself to step past Dayna on the grass, past the line of bones, and into the hexagram.

Chapter Seventy-One

CORA

She should have been worried about what was happening to the Callighans, about the black smoke consuming them. But all Cora could do was stare at the hexagram in horror. Blood had been spilled there. And not the right way. This wasn't how it was supposed to go.

Meiner had dragged Dayna out of the pentacle and deposited her into Reagan's arms, and now she stood in the center like *she* would do the ritual. Like this was *her* moment.

Cora stepped past the bloody-faced witch hunter, who was on his back on the ground, his rattling gasps loud even above the wind.

Meiner's arms were spread wide, her head tilted back. Her lips were already moving in the familiar shapes of the words Cora knew so well. This was *her* spell.

Cora didn't care about anything. Not about Dayna, or the Callighans or the witch hunters. It might as well have been Cora and Meiner facing off across the bones.

She should have known it would come to this. It was always meant to be this way.

The ground began to shake again, and the wind picked up, stinging her cheeks, whipping her hair across her face. Cora pushed forward, against the wind, against the bucking earth. Step by halting step, her eyes fixed on Meiner's face, on her lips, which never stopped moving.

Cora threw herself into the circle, anger propelling her. She would not let Meiner take this from her, too.

Her hands connected with Meiner's chest, and the white-haired witch stumbled out of the hexagram, eyes wide with shock.

Cora pulled out her dagger. The golden snakes were warm beneath her fingers, as if they were ready. Her lips were already moving, her voice loud above the howling wind. Pain blazed across her skin as she dragged the blade down the inside of her elbow, followed by the liquid warmth of blood trickling down her arm. She repeated the process on her other arm and let the knife drop, holding her hands out, letting the blood run off the tips of her fingers. She tilted her head back, and the wind ripped at her hair and clothing as she screamed the last few lines into the storm.

Beneath her feet the ground went abruptly still. The wind dropped off, leaving a dull, distant ringing in her ears. Outside the hexagram her fellow witches were nothing but statues, still and pale. The silence was stifling and dark, like a pair of heavy velvet curtains had swept down over the show, putting an end to everything. Had seconds or minutes passed? Cora couldn't tell; she could only feel the steady pulse of blood leaking from her veins.

She felt the magic shift around her and knew the spell was working. The familiar, euphoric rush of energy crashed through her. This time it did not cut off, but crested higher, stiffening her muscles, sending goose bumps over her skin.

Cora became distantly aware she was laughing, face tilted to the light of the full moon above. A high, wild sound carried away by the wind. Her fingers curled and flexed at her sides.

This power could tear down skyscrapers, drain oceans, level mountains. She was alive with it, electric. She—

Something crashed into her chest, buzzing, alive. This was a new energy, one she'd never felt before. It surged within her, demanding and aggressive, running down the length of her arms. There was a terrible tearing sensation on the surface of her skin, and pain knifed through her. Cora choked on her laughter, jerked her head down in shock.

The wounds on her arms had grown deeper, the slashes widening and elongating. The blood no longer trickled in thin tracks—it streamed down her pale skin, soaking the grass.

"No. Stop—"

She screamed as another wave of pain rocked her. Something dragged on her wounds. The same furious energy attached itself to her arms, drawing the blood out faster than should have been possible. It pooled at her feet, thick, scarlet, spreading far too fast for the earth to consume. Fear crowded in Cora's breast. She felt the blood drain from her face so quickly her head spun.

"Cora!"

The shout from outside the circle was muffled, and when she looked up, swaying on her feet, Meiner was on the outside, pushed back by a thin haze that had risen around the hexagram. She was battering at it with her fists, as if the haze were a solid wall. Something was keeping her from stepping over the circle. From interrupting the spell.

The pull on Cora's blood was a physical sensation. She could feel her magic draining, her life force slipping away. Above her the gray sky warped and stretched, spinning in slow, lazy circles. This time when she closed her eyes it was because her eyelids were so heavy. She was so tired.

The voice of her goddess brushed her mind like silk, slithering over her thoughts until Caorthannach was all she could hear.

Tá áthas orainn. I accept your sacrifice, witch.

Cora felt her knees give way. She felt nothing as she crumpled; the pain was gone. There was only the softness of the grass against her face, as the heavy, velvet darkness descended.

Chapter Seventy-Two
DAYNA

S everal things happened the moment Cora dropped in the center of the bone hexagram. The earth stopped shaking, and there was a strange, distant cry that sounded remarkably like a raven. The black smoke vanished, leaving Faye and Brenna on the ground, fingers clutching at the grass, and Brenna gave another animal howl in the stillness.

Bronagh was gone. In her place was only a strange, elongated streak of black. Like soot staining the grass.

Meiner appeared beside Dayna—and Reagan followed a second later—sliding her arms around Dayna's waist and under her knees, gathering her against her chest. Meiner stayed still, and Reagan pressed her hands against Dayna's shoulder, against her wound, and a groan tore from her throat. The pain made darkness creep into the edges of her vision, and tears blurred her eyes.

"Stay still," Meiner muttered, low in her ear. "Let her bind it. You're bleeding all over." At last Reagan succeeded in wrapping her sweater around Dayna's shoulder, and Dayna blinked tears back as she tied it firmly.

She blinked the haze out of her eyes and looked around the clearing. The moon hung full in the sky once again, lighting the field and the tomb, painting everything below it in silver.

Miraculously the tomb's face was whole and smooth, and Dayna wondered momentarily if she'd only dreamed it had cracked, if she'd been delirious from the wound in her shoulder.

There was still a faint haze of black smoke lingering; it wrapped around the base of the rocks and drifted over Cora's still form, blanketing the ground. The brothers were gone.

"Bronagh." Yemi's voice from behind them sounded tremulous with shock, and Dayna turned, wincing at the pain that shot through her.

Brenna and Faye were both sitting up now, staring at the empty spot where she'd been. Dayna swallowed past the tightness in her throat. The black smoke had consumed Bronagh completely.

Impossible. Their coven leader couldn't be gone, not really.

Her attention was pulled away as Meiner set her down gently, moving toward the crumpled form in the center of the hexagram. Dayna saw with a sickening lurch in her stomach that Cora wasn't moving.

Meiner seemed hesitant to approach, her face stricken. Yemi followed cautiously, kneeling on the grass beside her, and Reagan looped her arm around Dayna's waist, helping her limp slowly after them.

Blood decorated the grass in a glossy dark pool at the center of the hexagram. The symbol itself had been broken, the bones scattered across the ground.

She tried not to look at the figure in the circle. "What did she do?"

Meiner's expression was so complicated, so full of hurt and horror, that Dayna wanted to slip her arm around her shoulders, to steady her.

"It was the ritual." Meiner's voice was low and hoarse. "The one my grandmother started to teach me when I was younger. I memorized part of it, and then she just . . . stopped." Meiner scrubbed her hand over her face. There were unshed tears glistening in her eyes. "She taught Cora instead. I thought— I didn't know . . ."

"That she was setting you up to be a sacrifice?" Dayna whispered. The idea was unspeakably horrifying, but it was the only explanation. And then at some point she must have changed her mind. "How did she know"—she waved a hand at the tomb—"everything?"

Meiner let out a shaky sigh. "She had visions all the time. She was famous for them. But this . . . She must have seen this years ago."

"We should take her body back," Yemi said softly.

Dayna nodded, glancing back at the flattened spot on the grass where Bronagh had lain only moments before. At least they could take Cora's body home.

"Come on." She reached out, tugging gently on Meiner's sleeve, and then let her hand slip down the length of her arm, weaving her fingers through Meiner's. Meiner started, and then allowed Dayna to entwine her fingers with hers. "Let's get the hell out of here."

Chapter Seventy-Three

DAYNA

The funeral for Cora was in Limerick, the Sunday after. It was dark and misty, though it did not turn to full rain, which was both a blessing, and in Dayna's opinion a curse. She'd half wanted it to rain; it would have suited the somber mood.

They'd lost so much in the space of a week. No one knew what had happened to Bronagh's body, and this more than anything seemed to haunt Brenna and Faye. The women clung together under the oak tree, and Dayna couldn't help thinking they looked wrong without Bronagh. Uneven somehow.

The witch hunters, too, were a mystery. They'd vanished the moment the tomb sealed shut. There was no closure to it, though, and Dayna scanned the graveyard uneasily as they stood beneath wide black umbrellas, listening to the preacher talk about death.

There were still so many unanswered questions. The thought of Fiona's strange scribblings kept coming back to her. The jagged handwriting, the same word repeated endlessly.

The Dagda.

She wanted to dismiss it as ridiculous, as nothing more than the ramblings of a madwoman, but...Fiona wasn't exactly mad, was she? And what was it Dayna had felt when she'd touched the book? And that strange sense of déjà vu, and the distant memory of the horned woman in the woods?

All mysteries that would need to be solved. Secrets to be uncovered.

But for now, she wasn't going to look. She needed time to grieve. They all did.

That reminded her—she still hadn't returned her father's calls. Fiona was there with him, and she had no desire to find out if the woman was still possessed or not.

She turned her attention back to the service.

Having a preacher preside over any of the witches' funerals was ridiculous, doubly so with Cora. But her family had arrived in town—out of nowhere, as far as Dayna could tell—and demanded her body. Cora's father was a tall blond man who seemed to be followed around by a great entourage of people taking notes at all times. A politician, maybe. She noticed he didn't cry, staying smooth-faced through most of the ceremony. There was a tight-lipped strawberry-blond woman next to him in a collar of pearls and a tweed dress. Cora's aunt, Meiner had explained, and the sour look on her face didn't speak well of the woman.

Dayna looked away from them, back to the preacher, who was talking about the shortness of their time here on earth.

For all the talk of death, she kept thinking about the spot on the grass where their leader had disappeared.

She said as much when the ceremony wrapped up, and the coffin, cold and dark, had been lowered into the earth. She waited to say it until they were heading back through the graveyard, toward the parking lot.

"She might not be gone." Dayna's voice sounded croaky from disuse; she hadn't said anything for most of the morning. She glanced back at Faye and Brenna, who were trailing a ways behind them, arms around one another. Faye was standing tall, supporting her mother as they walked, her face grim. "Not permanently."

Yemi shook her head. She'd exchanged her usual colorful, flowing clothing for a somber black dress. "Oh, love, we may never know if she's gone or not. That's the way with magic. Especially dark magic."

No one said anything further, but most of them glanced back in the direction of the dispersing funeral crowd and Cora's fresh grave. Dayna's fists were clenched at her sides, and that familiar fire blazed to life in her chest, a surge of magic as sadness and anger warred inside her. She couldn't, *wouldn't*, accept that a piece of her family was gone.

As they passed beneath one of the tall oak trees at the edge of the iron wrought gate, she felt Meiner move closer, linking her fingers through Dayna's. Both girls held on tightly, almost desperately, as if they might anchor each other.

Dayna felt her stomach flutter, a strange mixture of exhilaration and fear.

Meiner's grip on her hand was both thrilling and strange. It felt like a promise without spoken words, a thing of unknown potential.

There was so much of the unknown laid out before them, enough that scrying would only illuminate the smallest piece of their future, a flickering candle in a stadium of inky darkness.

As they passed under the stretching branches of the oak, there came a peculiar croaking from overhead, and Dayna tilted her head back to peer into the branches. There was a single glossy-feathered raven perched on a branch halfway up. It tilted its head, black eye following the group as they proceeded to the parking lot.

Dayna said nothing, but she kept glancing back as they walked, keeping an eye on the raven all the while it kept its eye on her.

Chapter Seventy-Four

MEINER

In the weeks that followed, Meiner found herself able to enter the farmhouse's kitchen again. At first she couldn't walk in without noticing the empty chair where Bronagh should have sat and the spot on the floor where Gran had died. She'd kept picturing it the way it had been. The cupboards thrown open, cutlery and shards of plates and bowls scattered across the tiles.

And Gran's body, broken on the floor, blood collecting beneath her.

It was the memory of what came before that really haunted her. Of following Gran and Cora around the side of the house. Of the anger she'd felt overhearing them. The betrayal.

Funny that Cora had insisted they leave after everything was over. That she was going to drag Meiner away from this place.

And now here she was to stay. There was a bitter kind of irony in it.

Meiner stood on the porch just beyond the sliding glass door in the kitchen, watching the sun sink down behind the apple orchard, the trees throwing up tall, scraggly silhouettes against the orange light. The summer heat had faded over the last few days, and her breath wreathed her head in a silvery crown of fog.

She stood still, shivering, hands in her pockets, and she tried not to think. Not to remember.

Because of course, Meiner was not the one her grandmother had betrayed.

Neither she nor Cora could have known what that spell did. Maybe if they'd bothered to look it up. If they'd known where to look. Maybe if they'd mentioned any part of it to the other coven, to one of the Callighans, this could have been prevented.

Cora would still be alive.

Cora, who'd been just as much of a fool as Meiner had been, fooled by the old woman even as she'd thought they were fooling Meiner.

It had occurred to Meiner many times over in the following weeks that for all her years of living with the old woman, she'd never really known her. She couldn't even think about the fact that, like Dayna, her grandmother's blood had been used in the hexagram, couldn't bear to dwell on what that might mean.

Meiner had refused to go back to the house in Limerick, but she'd hired workers to pack up her grandmother's things and ship them to Carman. She'd uncovered a great deal of damning evidence. Pages and pages of notes in tiny, cramped handwriting, all detailing bargains with spirits, especially the bargains Carman had struck with mortals.

The notes went back years, right up until her grandmother had begun to show the first signs of losing herself. She had tracked the brothers' whereabouts. Searching for Carman in order to make a deal. So it seemed her gran's run-in with Dubh on the Isle of Man had not been a coincidence. It was hard to tell from just the writings, but Meiner thought Grandma King had probably been following him. Maybe he'd caught her in the act and attacked. Or maybe he'd just seen her as a potential victim, when she was, in fact, the hunter.

From the notes, a disturbing story had emerged. As far as Meiner could piece together, the spirit trap Grandma King had tattooed on her arm was meant to draw a piece of Carman in, and the spell she'd taught Cora to seal the rest of her back in before the goddess could take full possession of Cora. A bargain would be struck with Carman, as far as Meiner could tell. The old woman had intended to help raise Carman if she'd promised to restore her to her full power.

So . . . that's what she'd betrayed everyone for. To get her mind back.

Harriet King had not been able to handle fading away a bit at a time, and so she had been prepared to throw everything else away to get it back.

Of course, things hadn't gone that way. Gran hadn't been there when Cora did the spell, and so she had simply sealed the goddess away for good.

Cora, the accidental hero at the end of all this. The thought was unsettling.

If Cora hadn't done what she had, Carman would have risen. If that had happened, Meiner would certainly not be here, standing in the center of the porch watching a trio of ravens peck bread crumbs from the rail.

She watched as Dayna placed another chunk of bread crust on the rail. It was hard to take her eyes off her. Off the outline of her shoulders, the tops flushed slightly from the sun, the stray freckles that dotted the expanse of tanned skin above her tank top—she was just starting to wear tank tops now that the wound beneath her shoulder was healing.

On the railing beside Dayna's left elbow sat the book—she rarely went anywhere without it these days, and Meiner often caught her staring at it, expression faintly puzzled—and on the rail beside it sat a small white pill container and a mug of tea, which was sending a steady ribbon of steam twisting up into the cool morning air.

It was easier to forget her scabbed-over knuckles when she looked at Dayna, to forget the way the blood had looked speckled across her skin. The way she'd lost herself to the red-tinged rage of her temper. It was still there beneath the surface, dormant for now. Soothed by the illusion of peace.

The rage was like her magic, never far out of reach. When she thought about it, the back of her neck prickled. The anger had been so much stronger than it ever had been. It had felt . . . different. Alive. Impossible to control.

Not that she'd even tried.

She didn't want to think about it, so she watched Dayna instead, and she tried to forget.

"If you keep on with the bread crusts, they're going to get fat," Meiner said.

Dayna pulled back, and the ravens stared at her. The one in the center, and the biggest of the three, ruffled its feathers indignantly, as if it heard and disapproved. She wouldn't have been surprised to learn that was the case.

All three birds watched them intently, heads swiveling this way and that, sharp beaks moving back and forth. Three sets of beady black eyes tracked Dayna's movement as she stepped back from the railing, and then Meiner's as she came to stand beside her.

Dayna grinned up at her, leaning sideways to bump her shoulder. "I thought you didn't like birds."

Meiner stared, first at her, then at the ravens. The ravens stared back. "These ones are all right."

The middle bird cocked its head, made a conversational *chock-chock*, and then took off in a flurry of black feathers, nearly knocking its brethren off the sill. After a moment the other two followed suit, and Meiner and Dayna stood watching them, a silent, temporary good-bye. They watched until the birds were tiny, distant M-shapes in the sky, until they were specks. Until they'd vanished into nothing.

And then Meiner looked down, pleasantly startled as Dayna hooked an arm around hers.

Before allowing herself to be dragged back into the candlelit warmth of the kitchen, into the gentle chaos of Yemi's pie baking and Reagan's indie rock music and the scent of peppermint tea, she took one last look over her shoulder. The sky was serenely blue. Cloudless, filled with the scent of pine and woodsmoke. Summer was fading, and the horizon was empty of ravens, but something told her they'd be back.

Chapter Seventy-Five

DUBH

They waited until the graveyard was empty, until the last of the mourners had filed out in a somber, black-clothed line, until the sun had sunk below rows of gray tombstones. The three brothers were slow to approach the gravesite, both because they were wary, and because their bodies had been damaged nearly beyond repair.

The black smoke had dropped them five miles across the field, away from the witches, but it had literally *dropped* them, and from a fair height.

One of Dubh's lungs had collapsed. He'd been strangely used to the slow inflation and deflation, and now there was only stillness in the left side of his chest. He trudged forward, glancing over at his brothers. Calma was limping, dragging one foot behind him, his face fixed in a scowl. His back was still broken in several places, but that morning Olc and Dubh had wrestled him flat on the bed and straightened him out as much as they could, and now he wore a back brace to keep his spine in place. He wasn't happy about it. Olc was in the best shape, though one of his arms hung limp by his side. He'd told Dubh he'd felt it snap when he hit the ground.

They would need new bodies soon.

Finally, after their slow, shambling approach, they gathered to stare down at her grave. It was a temporary marker, somber gray, with the barest of inscriptions carved into the surface.

Cora Whelan

Daughter and Friend

Sad, to have one's life reduced to two lines scraped into the surface of this bare rock. Dubh glanced down at the duffel bag at his feet. Slowly he unzipped the pocket of his windbreaker and pulled out his cigarettes, tapping the end of one on the crescent moon on the top of the silver case, before flipping his lighter open. His brothers watched silently as he played the flame over the paper. He waited for the tip to flare orange before taking a deep drag, filling his remaining lung. He tipped his head back to blow smoke up into the sky, and then stooped down to unzip the duffel, throwing a shovel to Olc, who caught it with his good hand, and to Calma, who began digging almost immediately, stomping on the edge of the shovel to break the earth.

Dubh stood back and watched, smoke leaking from his nostrils.

Neither of his brothers said anything as they dug, both of them sullen and silent. When the black smoke had wreathed him she had spoken to him, and only him.

It took a half hour to reach the lid of the coffin, and Calma and Olc dug around the edges, widening the hole enough for Dubh to drop down into it. He was reaching the end of another cigarette, and he took one last drag at the filter and then dropped it into the dirt, grinding the sparks out under his boot.

"Lift it."

The lid scraped noisily as Calma and Olc leaned into the grave to pull it back, both brothers grunting and red-faced. Gradually, inch by inch, the corpse of the blond witch was revealed.

Cora's hair was spread artfully across the pillow. Her hands were folded neatly at her breast. She wore a light blue summer dress, and her face was made up to look as lifelike as possible.

Even with all of this, she did not look peacefully asleep, as corpses were meant to. Her brown eyes were wide open, as if she'd been staring at the roof of her coffin.

Dubh stared down at her. He had not been sure until now. He'd seen the black smoke wreathe her, and he'd guessed. Now he was certain.

Still, he waited.

Behind him, his brothers shifted, but neither of them spoke.

The witch's eyes fluttered shut, and then open again. She blinked slowly, several times.

Her mouth twitched, jaw flexing, as if she were figuring out the movement. At last her gaze slid to Dubh's face, and her red lips curved into a smile.

"Finally."

Acknowledgments

I have to say a huge thank-you to everyone who made this book happen. For starters, to the people who beta-read, Fallon, PJ Sheridan, Meghan, Emma, and Kellie, thank you for reading this book when it was in its earliest, most awkward stages and helping me make it less terrible.

And to Rebecca Sky and Jordan Stratford, who both read and said lovely, blurby things and encouraged me during the torment that is the submissions process.

To the wattpad4, thank you for letting me shout at you girls when I'm stressed, and send you random, weird questions at odd hours of the day, and for the constant support and all you do to lift me up as a writer and a person; you girls mean so much to me and I love you all.

To the WordNerds, Sunday has become my favorite day of the week because of you guys. Thank you for alternately listening to me rant, and celebrating with me, and sometimes both. Also, for the many long chats brainstorming and bouncing ideas off one another (a special thank-you to Megan and Emma, who allowed me to frantically Google-chat you at one point when I was stuck on something). Love you, Nerds.

To my family. It's weird to thank my mom, because this book will horrify her, but thank you anyway. For homeschooling me and letting me read all day.

And to my sister, who *may* read this? Maybe not. Either way, I'm dragging you to Ireland with me.

And most of all, to Karen, Rick, and Shaun. This book would, without question, not exist without them. Thank you for the massive amount of support you've always shown me—it means the world.

To Silvia Molteni, who is the true meaning of "rock-star agent," and who believed in this project even in its earliest stages. Thank you for working so hard to take it to that next level and make it a better book.

And to Hannah Allaman, who was just as excited about Dayna and Meiner's story as I was from the very first day. Thank you for believing in me and my witches and for flailing with me over all the things. You made this process so much fun, and the book so much better.

To the entire team at Freeform, you're all fantastic, and I'm so proud to be able to say I've worked with you.

And a huge thank-you to the British Columbia Arts Council, for giving a new author the support they desperately needed in order to tackle a big project like this head-on.

And lastly, to the witches. Tiffany, Kayla, Rebecca . . .

This entire book is dedicated to you. I mean, honestly, what else do you want from me?

Photo © Becky Forsayeth

E. LATIMER

lives on Vancouver Island with her husband; one small, destructive child; and a cat named Muse. She can usually be found camped out in a coffee shop or the local library. When she's not writing, talking about writing, or daydreaming about writing, she makes vlogs with the WordNerds, drinks too much tea, and reads excessively. Her first novel was *The Strange and Deadly Portraits of Bryony Gray*.